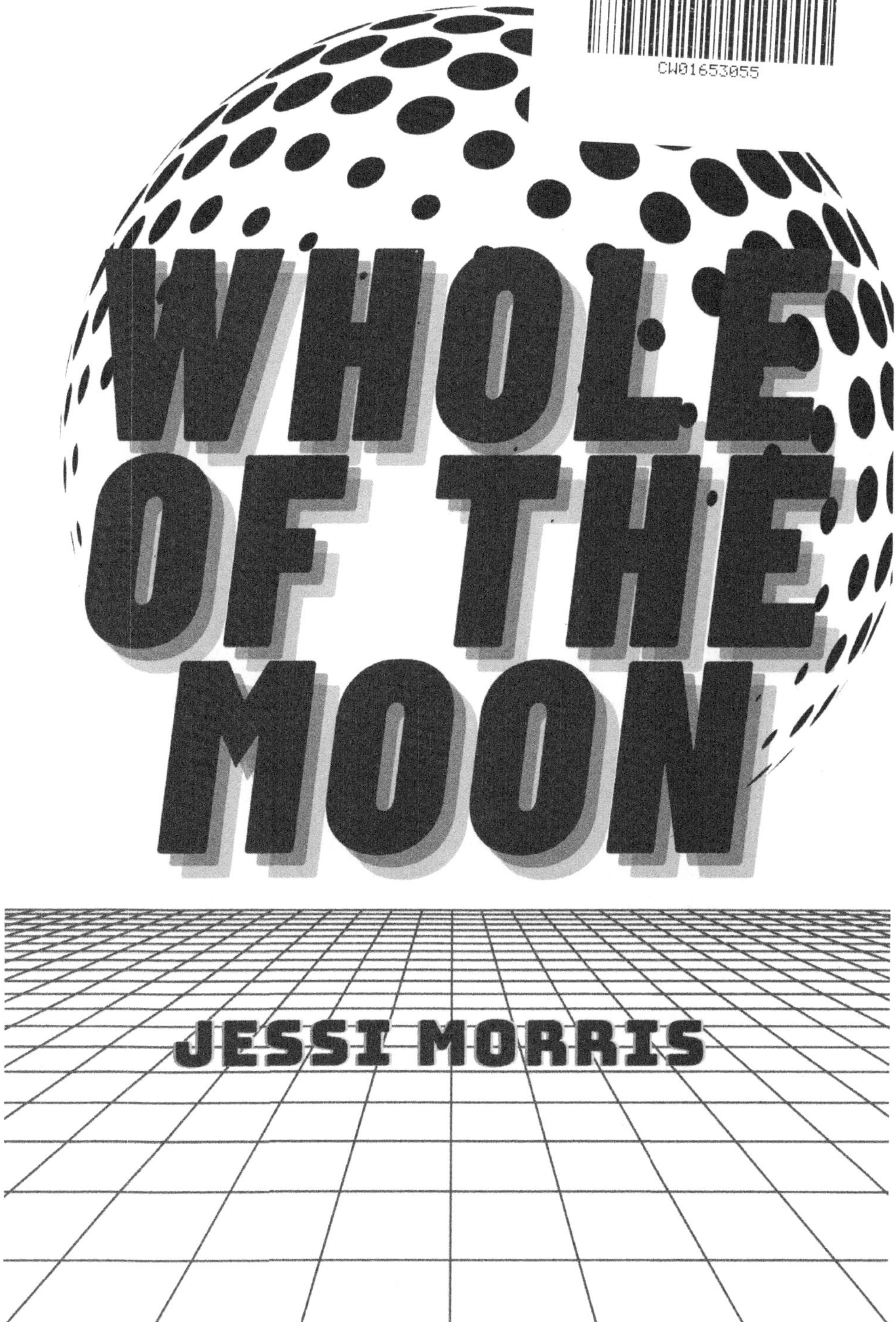

WHOLE OF THE MOON

JESSI MORRIS

Book Cover by Gail Weiner

Illustrations by Gail Weiner

First UK Edition, 2024

Published by Simpatico Publishing United Kingdom

ISBN: 978-1-0687848-2-8

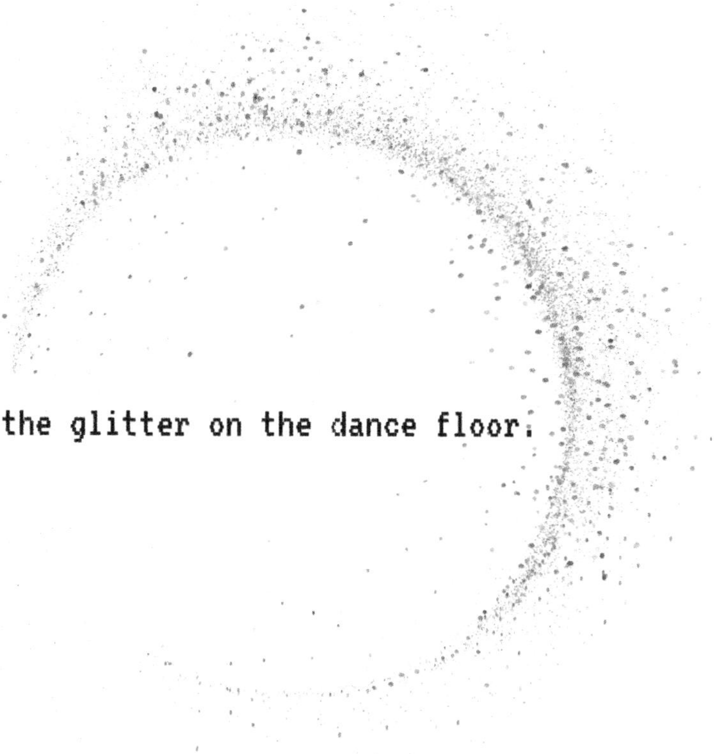

I am the glitter on the dance floor.

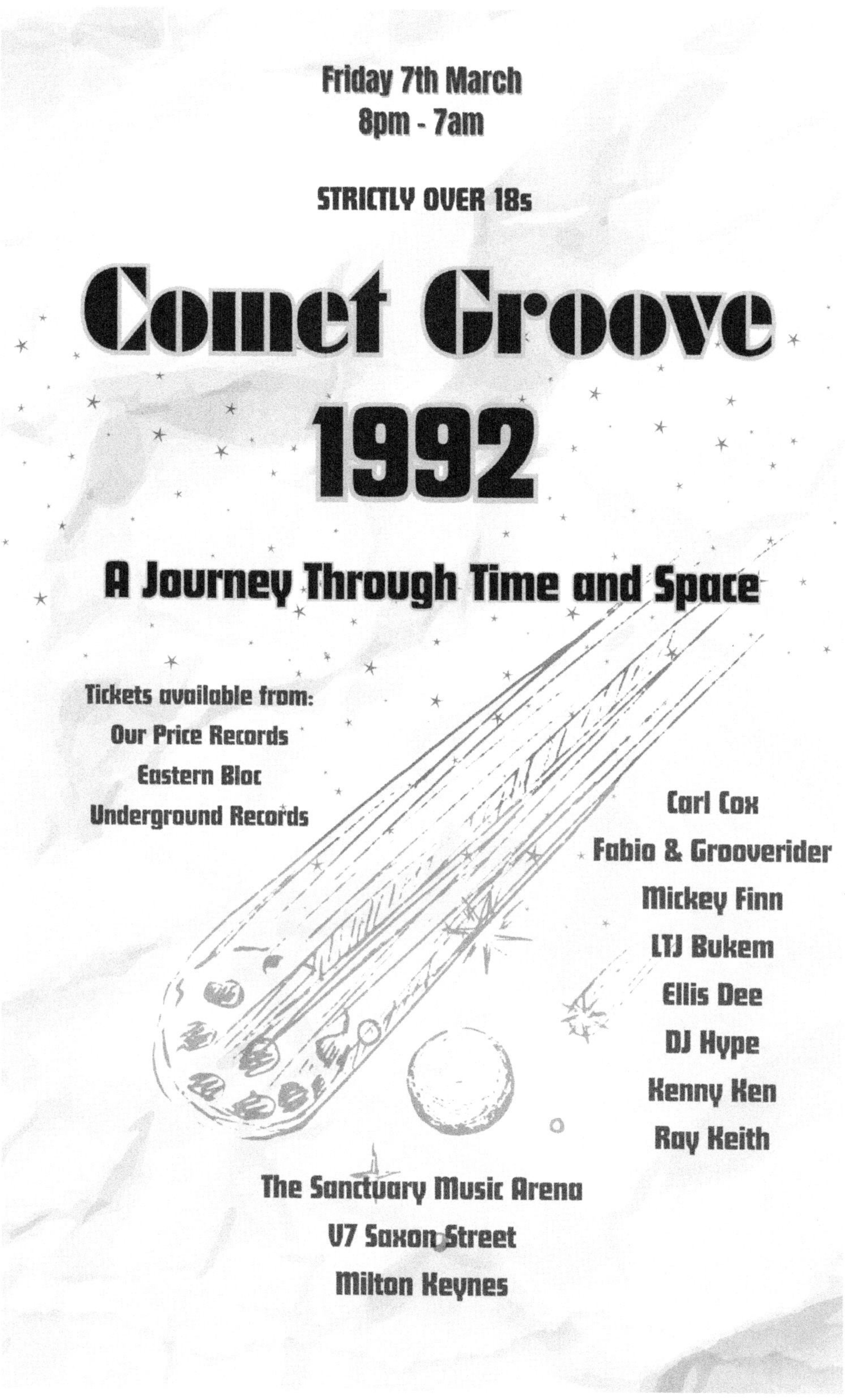
Friday 7th March
8pm - 7am
STRICTLY OVER 18s
Comet Groove
1992
A Journey Through Time and Space
Tickets available from:
Our Price Records
Eastern Bloc
Underground Records
Carl Cox
Fabio & Grooverider
Mickey Finn
LTJ Bukem
Ellis Dee
DJ Hype
Kenny Ken
Ray Keith
The Sanctuary Music Arena
V7 Saxon Street
Milton Keynes

Playboy

Pure heaven, this moment. I'm off my nut in some warehouse in Hackney, three pills deep and riding that peak where everything just makes sense. The strobes catch all them bodies moving like one massive creature, and I swear I can see the music making patterns in the air. Bass so heavy it's rattling my back teeth, sweat running down the walls, and I wouldn't have it any other way.

It's all hitting at once - the scratch of sequins against my skin, heat of bodies pressed close, air thick with smoke and Vicks and cheap body spray. Colours bleeding into each other while the music surges through my veins like liquid electricity. Some geezer slips an ice cube in my mouth and the shock of cold sends shivers down my spine. This is what being alive feels like - pure, unfiltered feeling. No rules, no holding back. Just me and the music, going absolutely mental.

That's when I spot him through the lasers - this fit as bloke throwing shapes near the speakers. Dreads flying as he moves, muscles straining against his vest, skin gleaming under the strobes. Way he's dancing, all fluid grace, has my heart going mental.

Gemma catches me staring, her mad curls flying everywhere as she follows my gaze. 'Go on then!' she shouts in my ear with a knowing grin. 'I'm off to make shapes!' Then she's gone, swallowed up by the heaving masses.

I follow him to the chill-out room, where he's settled in a corner, expertly rolling a spliff. Up close he's even fitter - all high cheekbones and full lips, those dreads tied back now. He catches me looking and smiles, this dangerous grin that goes right through me.

Next thing I know, he's pushing off the wall, cutting through the scattered bodies like he owns the place. Slides onto the cushions next to me, pulling out some Tiger Balm. I'm tilting my head back eager as anything, his fingers on my skin send shivers down my spine as he rumbles in my ear, 'Name's Alex.'

'Steve,' I manage, flicking my lighter. The flame catches his face just right, and bloody hell - that third pill's hitting now. Swear I can feel my skull glowing from the inside.

His fingertips trail down my back as he leans in close. 'Got something better for you to suck on,' he purrs, lips ghosting the corner of my mouth.

I'm rushing off my tits, but then I spot Chris going mental on the dance floor, and my stomach drops like a stone. Best mate since school, knows everything about me except this bit. But then Alex's hand slides up my thigh, sending electricity through every inch of me, and I think, fuck it. Crash my mouth to his and the warehouse, the music, Chris, all of it just... turns to smoke in the lasers.

We're going at it proper filthy, his hands everywhere, when Gem appears in a cloud of glitter, waving another pill. 'Last one!' she squeals. 'Let's blow the roof off this place!'

Next thing I know she's dragging me off, the pill already dissolving on my tongue. Catch one last look at Alex before he disappears like smoke in the lasers. Gutted, but that's how it goes sometimes, innit?

Rest of the night's pure magic. Just riding that last pill, hands up reaching for them strobes, sweat flying off my hair as I stamp about like a nutter. Can't feel my feet anymore, can't feel nothing except the music pulsing through every cell. Broken glass crunching under my trainers, but I couldn't give a toss. Got Gemma next to me, both of us screaming along to some tune, grinning like we've lost the plot.

The sunrise hits us like a slap when we finally stumble out. London's got this weird beauty at dawn - all quiet streets and morning mist, like the whole city's coming down with us. The sky's gone this mental shade of pink, making everything look soft round the edges. Air's proper sharp after that sweaty warehouse, has us pulling our jackets tight and huddling together like penguins.

Night bus is rammed with ravers, everyone got that thousand-yard stare. Streetlights leaving gold trails through the windows while Laila's still going at it with her glowsticks. My jaw's aching something chronic, and them tiles on the bus floor are starting to breathe.

By the time we make it back to mine and Chris's flat, the comedown's creeping in like a bastard. Laila's bouncing about like she's made of rubber, her blonde pigtails flying everywhere, still full of beans. Chris is trailing after her like some lovesick puppy as they disappear into his room.

Me and Gem end up sprawled on the sofa, my body feeling like it's made of concrete.

'Roll us a spliff then,' she demands, nodding at the baccy tin. I grumble but my fingers are already moving. Tell her about Alex while I'm at it, the fit bloke I was snogging.

'Bloody hell, Steve!' she laughs. 'Falling arse over tit for anything with a pulse!'

I just shrug, going red. 'What can I say? Twenty-two, free and single. Just playing the field, figuring out what I like.' Give her a cheeky wink. 'Equal opportunities, that's me.'

She just smirks, nicking the spliff. 'Lucky Chris didn't catch you though. Can you imagine? He'd have a proper mare!'

We crack up at that, them manic comedown giggles. That's what I love about Gem - she just gets it. Gets me.

MTV's on in background, and I'm getting well lost in that Losing My Religion video. Laila's high-pitched giggling filters through the wall while me and Gem pass the joint back and forth, her hair tickling my face, still smelling of vanilla even after all that sweating. The weed's doing its job, mellowing out that comedown edge when Gem breaks the silence.

'Gutted I can't come to Portugal,' she sighs. 'Would've been mental.'

'Could've caused all sorts of trouble,' I agree, trying not to show how much I wish she was coming. Three weeks in the Algarve without my Gem. 'You in that tiny bikini...'

She shoves me, grinning. 'You'll have a right laugh without me. Probably pull some fit Portuguese bird... or bloke.'

'Maybe,' I say soft, tucking her hair behind her ear. 'But they won't be you, will they?'

Something shifts in her eyes then, something that could change everything. But I ain't ready for that. Not yet.

So I just lean in, kissing her gentle. We get lost in it for a bit, while Michael Stipe does his tortured artist thing in the background. Maybe Portugal's exactly what I need - sort my head out, figure out what I want. Who I want.

But that's tomorrow's problem. Right now, I'm happy just being here with her, coming down easy while the sun comes up outside.

Yellow Sunshine

Stepping into Hugo's is like falling through the looking glass. Dark wood, cosy booths, and British accents - place is rammed with sunburnt expats trying to make it feel like home here in the Algarve.

The buzz is already mental when this three-piece band struts on-stage. They launch straight in, and fuck me - I can't take my eyes off the tall drink of water up front. Proper fit in his knackered Ramones tee and cowboy boots, and this voice that's got me sitting up straight like I've been shocked.

Nearly chuck my snakebite down my front when he catches my eye mid-song, giving it this proper smouldering look that cuts right through all the screaming birds down front. Christ! Reckon I'll have scorch marks on my jeans after that.

He's bloody mesmerising. His fingers dancing over the guitar strings, hips swaying to the beat. Then the cocky bastard launches into 'The Whole of the Moon' like he's leading an army into battle. Pointing and winking, working the crowd - some of the girls look ready to pass out.

Proper gutted when it's over. But he shoots me this sly nod and wink as he hops off stage, cutting through his fan club like it's nothing. And I'm just standing there, heart going mental through my shirt, trying to get one last look at that leather jacket before he vanishes. Chris and Laila are on about leaving, but I can't move. Not yet.

Last orders is done, and Chris is off his face, inviting every bugger and their mother back to his uncle's. I spot him by the bar - our rock star from earlier - chatting with the barman. His shirt rides up as he grabs the tequila bottle, flashing tanned skin that makes my throat go dry.

Next thing I know, he's sauntered over to fall in step with me and Chris, flashing this killer grin. The sort that's probably left a trail of swooning girls across continents.

'Jack,' he says, cool as you like. I just about manage to stutter out my name before he's turned those baby blues on the fit little brunette dangling off his arm. 'And what might your name be, love?'

'Mandy!' She's practically gagging for it. But he's already off, winking like a right charmer. 'Sarah, was it?' She's giggling, insisting that it's Mandy, honestly! But she couldn't give two shits what he calls her, long as he keeps laying on that accent.

'And which rainy corner of dear old Blighty do you hail from, darlin'?' Mandy's just getting into her whole life story, when this gaggle of shrieking birds comes tumbling out a side street, nearly taking us all out. One of them waving her heels about, going on how they'd thought Mandy was lost for good.

'We were about to call the flying squad, Mands!'

Jack shoots me a 'get a load of this' look, leaning in close to mutter, 'Reckon these might be the rest of the Cardiff hen party, eh?' But he keeps one big paw resting proper possessive on Mandy's lower back, steadying her on her wobbling pins. Smooth bastard.

We come crashing through the door of the flat like a proper tidal wave, Chris already bounding over to get some rave tunes shaking the foundations. Jack makes straight for the kitchen, banging down shots like they're going out of fashion. I get stuck chopping lemons while this lot go absolutely spare. It's way past 2am and the noise level's creeping up to 'police intervention' territory. Jack's loving it, course - holding court in the middle of the chaos, soaking up all that dazzled female attention. He's got his tongue halfway down Mandy's top, making a right show of the salt before he downs another shot, and the girls are just losing their minds over it.

I'm gagging for a smoke, desperate for a breather from the madness inside.

Jack perks up like a meerkat, grinning. 'I'll come with you, mate! Could murder a ciggie myself. There's a shop by the all-night petrol station.' He plants this messy kiss on Mandy's flushed cheek. 'Keep my seat warm, Mands!'

Can still hear the girls cackling as we stumble out into the warm night. Door slams behind us and thank fuck for that - my ears are ringing something chronic. Just us now, walking down the cobbles under the orange glow of the streetlights.

I'm sneaking little looks at Jack, trying to suss him out now we're away from his fan club. 'Cheers for coming with,' I say, trying to play it cool but my heart's going like the clappers. 'Thought I was going to go proper mental in there, tell you the truth.'

Jack flashes me a grin, running a hand through that messy hair of his. 'Ah, I was dying for a chance to stretch me legs! That Mandy's a clingy one - would've had me in a chokehold all night if I hadn't done a runner.' He mimes being strangled, tongue lolling out like a proper nutter. Gets a right laugh out of me.

Then those baby blues are pinning me in place, intense as anything. 'So, you're a southern boy, eh? Whereabouts you from then?'

'Surrey,' I reply, trying to keep my voice steady. 'Guildford way. You?'

'Liverpool lad, me. But I haven't seen that corner of paradise in donkey's years. Been living out here a couple years now, and before that, I was in LA for a bit.'

'And how's the Algarve life treating you?' I aim for breezy, even as my heart's doing double-time in my chest.

He shrugs, scuffing the toe of one battered cowboy boot on the pavement. 'Can't complain, I suppose. Beats going back to Blighty, don't it?'

'Too right, mate. And LA, though? Bet that was a trip and a half!'

'Bloody madhouse. Everyone's on the make, aren't they? Real cut-throat, the entertainment game. Felt like a little guppy swimming with them sharks out there.'

'Ah, but you've got the chops, Jack!' I insist, stretching the truth like taffy. 'That voice of yours? And the way you work a crowd? Magic, mate. Pure magic.'

'Listen to you, little charmer!' He's laughing now. 'Nah, I thought I had what it took to be a contender once upon a time. Had these daft notions of selling out Wembley, being the next Bowie or something? Been singing my heart out since I was a wee nipper. I have. But my dad, salt of the earth type... he always said I ought to keep my expectations low. I mean, the stuff I play at Hugo's, it isn't exactly Pyramid Stage material, is it? But you know how it is - punters want what they want, eh? A man's gotta eat!' He cuts me this significant look then, head tilted. 'I reckon you're a bit of a musician yourself, though. Saw you vibing to a couple of our numbers. Takes one to know one, and all that.'

'Too right,' I reply, flashing him the Raver Salute with a cheeky grin. 'Them electronic choons especially. I'm mad for it, mate.'

'Should've guessed from the getup, shouldn't I?' Jack snorts, eyeing me up and down like I'm glowing in the dark. 'You're a little raver through and through. You are. Clocked your sort, coming from a mile off!'

I shrug, sheepish. Scuff my battered Nikes on the cobbles. 'Ah, but I've got wide-ranging tastes, I have! Not just the old boots and cats, y'know.'

'Oh aye, I'm a man of eclectic interests myself,' he agrees, easy as you like. 'Got into grunge and all that when I was out in the States.

First time I heard 'Nevermind', it was like a bloody bomb going off in my brain! You know Nirvana, yeah? Kurt Cobain's a bleeding genius, swear down. Mark my words, that lad's got a long and bright future ahead of him. Grunge is the real deal - your Mudhoneys, Molly Peaches, all that lot. I could bang on about the Seattle sound 'til the cows come home, truth be told...'

'I know Nirvana, 'course,' I admit, 'but you've lost me with the others.'

'Ah! You're missing out!' Jack cries, clapping me on the shoulder. The brief touch sears me through my thin t-shirt, sparking up my nerve endings. 'Seminal stuff, that is. Tell you what, I'll educate you while you're out here. Broaden them musical horizons of yours. Fancy popping round mine sometime for a grunge crash course? How long you here then?'

'Three weeks,' I reply. 'Just touched down yesterday.'

'Sweet, we have plenty of time then,' he suggests breezy.

I'm nodding like a nutter, trying to get my head straight. But I can't stop staring at the way his hips move as he walks ahead of me, those tight jeans showing off every bit of his arse. Then he turns to push some branches out of the way, and watching his muscles shift under his shirt makes my mouth go dead dry. And just my luck, that's when he looks back over his shoulder - catches me right in the act of checking him out. But he just smirks, cocky git that he is. Like he's well used to leaving a trail of lovesick girls and lads wherever he goes.

'Yeah,' he goes on, 'for now I'm just killing time in this sunny paradise, ain't I? Waiting to see where life takes me next. Not giving up yet, mind. Still got big dreams, me.'

'I get that,' I stammer, my heart proper going for it the way he's eyeing me up.

We get to the petrol station, the fluorescent lights making everything look brutal.

Jack spins round to face me, grabs my shoulders, and fuck me - wasn't ready for that. 'So what about you then? What's the big dream hiding in that handsome head of yours?'

I just stand there like a plonker, mouth opening and closing before I shrug. 'Dunno, really. I...I'm not sure, to be honest.'

His grip on my shoulders gets tighter and his eyes go all fierce. 'Oi, don't waste your youth arsing about, mate!' he growls, giving me a little shake. 'Get out there and grab life by the balls, you hear?'

He laughs, squeezing my arms in a way that goes straight to my dick. 'Listen to me, sounding like some wise old man! I'll be going grey soon at this rate. Already racing through my 30s, ain't I!'

I stare at him, letting out this weird little laugh. 'Wait, how old are you, actually?'

'32, if you must know. Ancient, eh?' He wiggles his eyebrows, looking a bit manic.

'Practically one foot in the grave, grandad!' I give it back, trying to keep it light even though my head's spinning with the numbers. 32 to my 22... bit mad, that.

We both laugh, but it's well awkward, like we've run out of words. The bright shop lights can't come quick enough - and I can still feel his eyes on me as I walk inside.

Flat hits us like a proper rave - Laila's lost the plot to 'Groove is in the Heart', doing one in the lounge like she's at Ministry. Chris is giving it large from the couch, whistling fit to wake the dead. I grab a couple of tinnies from the fridge, chuck one to Jack, then crash next to Chris.

Course, it takes about two seconds for Mandy to be all over Jack again. Watching him suck her face has my jaw clenched so tight my teeth hurt. Then he looks up and catches my eye - gives me this proper intense look that goes right through me. I whip my head away sharpish, necking my lager like it's water. But I can feel him watching me while Mandy's grinding on his lap. Fucking hell.

Rest of the night's a blur of me getting more wound up by the minute while everyone's having it large around me. Then Jack's trying to peel himself off Mandy who's wrapped round him like ivy. Says he's got to head off, all his groupies giggling as they stumble for the door.

My stomach drops watching them go. Can't bear him just disappearing after getting me all worked up like this. Follow them to the door like some desperate twat, trying to look casual while Jack throws me one last killer smile over his shoulder. 'Cheers for a top night,' he goes, voice all rough. 'Catch you on the flip side, eh?'

And just like that, with a wink and that cocky grin, he's gone - back to his flock of birds as they all stumble down the stairs, shrieking with laughter. I'm left propped against the doorframe like a right muppet, trying to get one last look before he disappears. Even after I can't hear them anymore, I'm still standing there staring into the dark like a complete bellend.

Shamrock

We're sprawled out on the beach next morning, hanging off our nuts from last night's bender. Tell you what, if I never see another bleeding snakebite it'll be too soon. These kids next to us are showing us up, dead serious with their sandcastles and moats like it's proper architecture or something. Bit further out, you've got nutters throwing themselves in the sea, screaming their heads off when the water hits them. Place is rammed with red-faced tourists trying to sort some shade with whatever they can find - dodgy tents, deckchairs, brollies all over the gaff. And then there's the soundtrack - Crystal Waters pumping out someone's boombox, mixing with the waves and seagulls going mental in the wind. *La da dee, la dee da.*

Laila's licking her Sky ice cream, turns to Chris. 'So, what'd you reckon of Jack then?'

Chris has his head against her shoulder. 'Them girls were falling over themselves to get a piece of him, I saw. You fancy him an' all, babe?'

'Ugh, not even!' Laila scrunches up her face. 'Mandy gave me the lowdown on Jack, didn't she? Reckons he's a right dog - never goes back for seconds, always some new bit of skirt on the go.' She's chasing melting ice cream down the stick. 'Weak game, if you ask me. Quantity over quality, like.'

'Ah, he seemed alright to me,' I pipe up before my brain can tell my mouth to shut it. 'Good little performer, decent vibes and that.'

Chris shoots me a look. 'Bit long in the tooth though, ain't he? For dead-end pub nights?'

'Thirty-two, he said,' I reply, trying not to sound like I've been thinking about that all morning.

'Exactly,' Chris scoffs. 'Proper Peter Pan syndrome, still poncing about flashing his pecs for pissed-up tourists.'

'Oi, I reckon he's sound,' I argue, stung. 'Down to earth bloke, just trying to make a living.'

'Yeah, fair enough for some dodgy resort like this,' Chris shrugs. 'Probably got his fingers in a few pies too. Oi, reckon you could get him to sort us out with a bit of Charlie?'

I frown, feeling weirdly protective. 'I ain't going to ask the man for cocaine. Hardly know him, do I?'

'Why not? Probably keeps a stash backstage for after them sweaty gigs.'

'Well, he did say he spent time out in LA...' I say, thinking about how he'd looked at me in that petrol station, going on about his big dreams and that.

'There you go then! Might be right now that you can ask him.' Chris nods towards the waves.

I turn round to see what they're on about... and fuck me sideways. It's Jack, coming out the sea like something off Baywatch. Pure muscle everywhere, water running down him, and them red trunks ain't leaving nothing to the imagination.

He clocks us staring and throws up a wave, flashing that grin that could power up half of Portugal. Good job I've got this towel in my lap is all I'm saying.

We wave back as Laila mutters, 'Lorks, he's coming over.'

'Lock up your daughters!' Chris is proper laughing now. 'Here comes the Shagger of the Algarve!'

Can't even give Chris the evils properly before Jack's right there, dripping all over the place and smelling like salt water and oranges. Swear my teeth are gonna crack I'm clenching them so hard.

'Water's well good! Best thing for a hangover, bit of Atlantic, eh?' He drops down next to me on my towel, so close the water drops from his skin are hitting my leg. Trying my best not to think about... well. Chris and Laila mumble something about going for a swim, leave me and Jack sitting there.

Keep catching myself looking at him when I think he won't notice. He's different, ain't he? Proper grown-up face, not like the baby-faced boys I'm used to. Makes my stomach do weird flips, it does.

Then Jack turns them blue eyes on me, catches me right at it.

I'm blushing hard enough to fry an egg on my cheeks, but Jack just flashes me that effortless, friendly smile of his. Swear down, it could melt the Arctic from a distance. Then he lets out this little laugh and I'm coming up in goosebumps, even in this heat.

'Heading into town in a bit to have a dig through the vinyl shop,' he goes, eyes all crinkled up. 'Fancy tagging along?'

My mouth's saying yes before my brain's even caught up. Must look like a right muppet, nodding away like one of those dash-board dogs. 'Yeah! Proper sorted!'

'Sweet.' He stands up and suddenly I'm eye-level with... Christ. Them trunks ain't leaving much to wonder about. Try to look anywhere else but it's doing my head in - he's right there, and my face is going nuclear.

This close I can see everything - his trunks all clingy from the sea, and bloody hell, the way he smells. Sun and salt and whatever that aftershave is. Got me well dizzy.

Next thing, his hand's on my shoulder, massive warm palm sending sparks through me. He leans in and my heart's going mental, proper warehouse speeds, like some 150 BPM hardcore tune. Swear I'm about to melt right here on the sand.

'Oi,' he says all quiet like, 'better get some cream on you, mate. Sun's brutal - you're going pink.'

'Y-yeah, sound.'

He squeezes my shoulder. Just for a second.

'Right then,' he grins, stepping back. 'See you in a bit, yeah?'

Can't even speak now. Too busy watching him walk off - way his back moves, his arse in those wet trunks.

Then he's gone, lost in the crowd, and I can finally breathe again. Fucking hell.

When Chris and Laila come squelching back to shore, I'm already shaking out my towel, trying to act like I haven't just had the existential crisis to end all existential crises over a bloke's package.

'Going record shopping with Jack in a bit,' I chuck it out there, dead casual. 'Showing me his favourite spot.'

They trade a knowing look at that before they let out a laugh at my newfound friendship with an old geezer.

Double Diamond

I hop in Jack's battered Uno, still damp from the shower and stinking of Chris's uncle's posh aftershave. Christ, the seats are proper boiling - sun's been having a right go at them. Barely got my belt clicked before he's flooring it like a nutter, tearing through the narrow streets, riding everyone's arse who dares get in front. Some proper racket blasting out the tinny speakers - all screech and noise. Jack's loving it though, head going like he's at a metal gig.

'Oi, you hearing that riff?' he shouts over the din. 'That distortion? Proper filthy. All that percussion and that bluesy feel!'

I'm grinning like a right idiot. Haven't got a scooby what he's on about.

'Mudhoney, mate!' he goes, taking a corner so sharp I nearly shit myself. 'Banging track this - 'Every Good Boy Deserves Fudge.' Don't you reckon, Steve?'

'What?' I'm proper lost.

He just laughs, loud as you like, and cranks it up till the whole car's rattling.

When the noise finally dies down, Jack whips into a space between two tourist motors and bounces out like he's got ants in his pants. I follow behind, not exactly complaining about the view.

Walking these streets is like being in one of those naff postcards they flog to the tourists. Jack knows every alley like the back of his hand, while I'm just tagging along, taking it in - white walls going all flaky in the sun, cobbles worn smooth as glass. Old boys sat with their coffees give us these little nods as we pass, looking like they've been there since time began.

Got to keep my eyes peeled crossing roads though - steering wheel's on the wrong side here. Last thing I need is getting flattened by some mental Portuguese driver while I'm gawping at everything - well, mostly at Jack if I'm being honest.

Jack leads us deeper into this maze, dodging past all these tourists in their bum bags and Union Jack shorts. We turn down this tiny alley you'd miss in a blink, end up outside this proper dive. Sign says 'Vinyl Jorge's', looking as old as those geezers we passed. Jack's practically bouncing off the walls as he yanks the door, setting off these bells that sound like they're telling the whole town we've arrived.

Inside it's dark and cool, smells like old cigarettes and musty records. The shelves are stacked so full of vinyl they look ready to give up and fall over. I follow Jack through the tight spaces between all the crates and piles of records, till we get to this old fella behind the counter.

'Jorge, you daft old bugger!' Jack cries, pouncing on him with a bear hug that nearly sends them both flying. They jabber away in rapid-fire Portuguese, leaving me hovering like a right lemon.

Finally, Jack seems to remember I exist. 'Steve, this is Jorge - owner, operator, and all-around vinyl junkie extraordinaire.'

I give an awkward little wave, feeling about ten types of out of place. But Jorge just grins, dark eyes glinting behind his John Lennon specs.

Jack's already off again, burrowing into the stacks like a man on a mission. I tail after him, happy enough to ride shotgun on this little adventure.

'Oi, get a load of this!' He thrusts a record at me, bouncing on his heels like an overexcited puppy. 'Tad, mate. This is the real deal, proper sludgy stuff. Like audio tar, it is.'

I haven't got a clue what he's on about with all this music stuff. Every time his arm touches mine while he's digging through those records, it proper does my head in, like touching a live wire or something.

'It's more than just music, y'know?' he's going on, looking dead chuffed. 'It's a whole bleeding ethos. No pretence, no bollocks. Just raw emotion, splattered out for the world to hear.'

We're just stood there between the racks, and I'm trying not to lose my head over how close he is, the way his voice goes all deep when he's excited, how warm he feels next to me.

Then this gang of girls comes bursting in, all tanned and loud, and Jack's off like a shot. Doesn't even finish his sentence before he's over there, laying it on thick, giving it the full Jack charm offensive.

I'm left leaning against the wall, pretending to be super interested in this random Captain Beefheart album I've grabbed. But I can't help glancing over to where Jack's entertaining the girls, all of them hanging on his every word.

The lucky bastard makes it seem so easy - a wink here, a smile there, and they're nearly fainting into the sale section.

After what feels like an age, the girls finally disappear in a cloud of perfume and high-pitched titters. Jack wanders back over.

'Fancy grabbing a bevvy?' he asks, jerking his head towards the door. 'I'm gasping, me.'

And that's me done for. Not like I was gonna say no anyway.

The bar's dead nice after that mental sun - all dark wood and gleaming bottles, like something off the telly. Jack sorts the beers and we grab this rickety table outside under a knackered old Coca-Cola brolly.

'So, go on then,' Jack says, stretching out like he owns the gaff, and Christ - the way his shirt rides up... 'What's your story? What's a bright young thing like you doing slumming it with a clapped-out old rocker like me?'

I start faffing with my beer mat, trying not to stare at that strip of skin above his jeans. 'Ah, y'know. Uni. Studying law, trying to sort my life out. The usual 'what the bloody hell am I doing' bollocks.'

Jack takes a long drink, watching me over his bottle in a way that makes my insides go funny. 'Law, eh? Never had you down as the bookish type, what with all them raves and glow sticks.'

I can't help laughing. 'Yeah, well. Parents wanted something 'sensible', didn't they? Can't make a living off gurning and 5am jogs to the offie in just your pants.'

His laugh's proper filthy, has people looking over, but I'm starting to feel less like a right tit.

'Speaking of surprises,' Jack says, voice gone all rough, 'bet you've got all the birds in a right state back home, yeah? Pretty thing like you, must be beating 'em off with a stick.'

I nearly choke on my beer. Feel like someone's just kicked the air out of my lungs. 'Uh...nah, not really. No birds, no.'

Jack's giving me this look that burns right through me. 'A boyfriend, then?' he asks, voice gone dead soft.

And there it is. Right out in the open, innit?

I'm sat there proper stunned, heart going mental. How's he clocked me so quick? Am I that obvious?

'I...no boyfriend either,' I mumble, focusing on this bit of peeling paint on the brolly like it's the most fascinating thing I've ever seen.

Jack just looks me over, slow and deliberate, like he's taking his time about it. 'Aye, I reckoned as much. Nothing to be ashamed of, mind. I've been known to dabble m'self, time to time.' He leans in close enough I can feel his breath on my neck. 'Life's too short to limit yourself, innit?'

I'm sat there buzzing like I've dropped a pill that's way stronger than advertised. But before I can get my head straight, Jack's necking his beer and getting up.

'Right, best get a move on. Gotta sort myself out for the gig tonight - can't be giving the punters half-arsed Mick, can I?'

I'm stumbling after him, blood rushing in my ears. Can't stop myself checking him out - the way his muscles move under his shirt, them hip bones just visible above his jeans. Keep catching glimpses that make me dizzy.

'Get in, then,' he says, sliding into the driver's seat and messing with the stereo.

I make some noise that might be agreement and drop into the passenger seat, winding the window down and leaning back as Pearl Jam starts up. This is proper nice. Sun warming my face, music blasting, and Jack giving it large next to me.

'Oi, Stevie,' he goes sudden, and I turn to look at him. The sunset's lighting him up all golden, catching on his stubble and that killer smile.

'No gig tomorrow night. Fancy going on a bit of an adventure, just us? See what trouble we can get into.'

'Yeah,' I manage, trying not to sound as desperate as I feel. 'Yeah, sounds well good.'

His grin gets wider, and there's something proper dirty in the way he's looking at me that makes my mouth go bone dry. 'Sorted then. I'll pick you up at eight.'

I just smile back, trying to play it cool even though my insides are doing somersaults.

But then Jack gives me another one of those looks that turns my legs to jelly, and I know I'm absolutely done for.

Mad Bastards

Jack pulls up dead on nine, all sin in a ratty Zeppelin tee and those criminal jeans of his. We're bombing it down these mad windy roads - the kind that makes your stomach do somersaults just looking at them. He's totally calm, one hand on the wheel and the other messing with the stereo like he doesn't have a worry in the world.

'So, where we off to then?' I ask, trying to sound cool as a cucumber and probably failing miserably.

He just winks, the cheeky git. 'You'll see, Stevie boy. Got a real treat lined up for us.'

He sticks on this bootleg tape picked up in LA. Sublime, they're called. Insane mashup of punk, ska, and reggae. 'Think you'll like this one, Stevie,' he says, giving me a big grin. 'What with your fondness for the old green. Give 'Let's Go Get Stoned' a listen, yeah?'

It's magic, this. Tearing through paradise with a fit bloke by my side...don't reckon life gets much better.

We hit Albufeira's main strip and it's doing my head in - lights burning my eyes, music banging out from everywhere, geezers trying to shove flyers in our faces. But Jack just breezes through like he runs the place. Does this fancy handshake with the barman and bang - we've got cold beers in hand and these birds making eyes at him over their cocktails. It's like watching some pro at work, the way he works the room.

Tonight we're getting absolutely plastered, shots lined up on the bar like dominos. Standing in these bright lights, feeling well cocky with every drink and every laugh. Jack passes me another shot, his fingers brushing my arm, and I swear I could power the whole strip off that buzz. The way he looks at me over his glass, eyes all dark and mischievous in the flashing lights - I'm a goner. Following him about like some lovesick muppet, lapping up every word.

We're yelling bits of chat between rounds, trying to hear each other over the racket. 'Alright there, Stevie?' Jack shouts in my ear, his breath hot on my neck. I just nod, not trusting my gob, and he grins. 'Stick with me, kid. Night's just getting started!'

And bloody hell, ain't that the truth. Every time he 'accidentally' touches me, I'm falling deeper into whatever this is.

I lean in close, yelling over the music, 'This expat thing working out for you then?'

Jack just shrugs. 'Can't complain. Beats the pissing rain and miserable faces back home. Got my little spot at Hugo's keeping me in booze and birds. Could be worse, trust.'

I tilt my head, trying to read between the lines. 'What about winter though? When all the tourists bugger off back to their semis? Must get a bit... close quarters.'

Something flickers across his face for a second. His smile goes a bit tight as he leans in, shoulders hunching like he's cold.

'Turns into a right fishbowl, mate. Just us lot left here, sniffing around for any bit of gossip to keep 'em warm.' Takes a swig of his beer, tongue catching a drip. 'Feel like you're being watched all the time. Can't even take a slash without someone trying to make something of it.'

There's something tired underneath all his swagger, makes me want to... dunno, protect him or something mental like that. But before I can think too much about it, he's back to his usual cocky self, grinning like he knows something I don't.

'Tell you what, Stevie...' he says, smooth as anything, sliding closer. 'Fancy going somewhere a bit more... private?'

I nearly swallow my tongue at that. 'Lead on McDuff,' I rasp. 'Take me wherever you bloody like. I'm game.'

That smirk of his could make angels fall from the sky. It's blinding as he grabs my wrist, already pulling me through the crowd.

'Stick close,' he calls over his shoulder. 'Got a real treat in store for ya.'

And Christ, I couldn't fight it if I tried. The crowd's just noise and lights, and all I can see is Jack. The way his shoulders move under his sweaty shirt, his arse in those tight jeans. Fuck me, he's gonna be the death of me. And you know what? I don't even care.

'Easy does it, lad,' Jack laughs, catching me by the elbow as I stumble out into the fresh air, legs gone wobbly as jelly. 'Just breathe for us, yeah? In for a penny and all that!' I'm hanging onto his arm like some pissed-up koala, everything spinning.

He drags me down this alley where you can barely hear the music from the strip anymore, just this faint thump-thump. Through my beer goggles I clock this manky green door with a red neon sign above it. 'Alfonso's' it reads in dodgy writing, glowing like a warning light.

Jack spins round to face me, and his eyes have gone all intense. 'I'm trusting you with this, right?' he says, all serious even though I can smell the booze on his breath. 'This place... it's special. Sacred-like. So don't go running your mouth about it, yeah?'

I just nod, tongue tied up in knots. Bloody hell, what's he got planned?

Inside it's all dark corners and sticky floors, Wham's 'Club Tropicana' playing on some knackered old jukebox.

Then it hits me - everywhere I look, it's just blokes. Nothing but geezers, all over each other or in groups, getting right close. Not a girl anywhere.

'Jack,' I manage to get out, head gone west. 'Is this... this a gay bar?'

He gives me a wink, cool as you like. 'Welcome to Alfonso's - best kept secret in the Algarve!'

I'm following him in like I'm dreaming, taking it all in. Blokes just being themselves, not hiding nothing. Like every dirty thought I've had since I was sixteen, right there in front of me. Fucking hell.

Jack shoves a drink in my hand. 'Get that down you,' he goes, voice all rough. 'Bit of Dutch courage.'

Neck it without even tasting it. Too busy watching him watch me, looking at me like I'm his next meal.

Cher's giving it the big one about turning back time, fellas on the dancefloor proper going for it. Gets me so hot under the collar I have to shift about a bit.

'You alright there, Stevie?' Jack whispers, fingers drawing circles on my leg. He's that close I can feel him breathing on my face, his arm pressed right up against mine. 'Looking well shocked. First time in a place like this?'

Let out this nervous laugh, can't stop myself. 'Yeah, you could say that. Not exactly hitting Soho regular, am I? Been too much of a pussy to try it.'

Something passes over his face. Might be feeling sorry for me, but it's gone in a flash, replaced by this filthy grin that has my guts doing backflips.

'Fancy having a go then?' He nods at all them couples grinding away, denim on denim and tongues everywhere. 'Not bad at the old two-step, me. Could teach you a few moves, if you want.'

It's mental. Proper mad. Gonna end up making a right tit of myself. But I want it. Want him. Got this hunger for Jack that's eating me up inside.

So I down what's left of my drink, bang the glass down like I'm closing a deal. Squaring my shoulders, I take his hand, my heart going like the clappers and drowning out any last shred of common sense.

'Go on then, John Travolta,' I croak. 'Show us your moves.'

He laughs, this surprised sound that catches me off guard. Then he's pulling me onto the floor, right in the thick of it.

It's awkward as fuck at first, us two bumping about. Marvin Gaye's on about sexual healing while we're moving like a couple of saplings in a gale, Jack's hands burning through my shirt where they're gripping my waist.

Must be the crowd hiding us, or maybe it's the whisky making me brave, but I chuck my arms around his neck. Pull him in close till we're proper snug, hardly any space between us.

He makes this noise, a hot little 'Fuck, yeah' that goes straight to my cock.

Gets his hands on my lower back and suddenly we're moving together perfect - like something's clicked. He grinds against me, dirty as you like, that's got me seeing spots.

'Like that, do you?' he pants, his stubble rough against my jaw.

Can't even speak, just make this daft noise, lost in how good he feels.

We're moving well slick now, all rolling hips and heavy breathing. The tune's changed to 'Cream', Prince doing his sexy thing, and it's like chucking petrol on a fire.

Jack smells fucking amazing, all sweat and spice and something dead manly. I'm off my face on it, on him. He's at my neck now, snogging and licking like he's starving, leaving this trail that's got my toes curling in my knackered Nikes.

'Want to get out of here?' he says rough, mouth right on my pulse. 'Want to get you alone, yeah? See what you taste like with nothing between us?'

Nearly lose it right there, hanging onto his sweaty shirt like I'm drowning.

Everything after that's like some mad rush. Stumbling out into the hot night, snogging like we're gagging for it as we fumble for the car. Feels like the longest drive ever, him with his hand down my jeans at every red light.

Then we're falling through his door, ripping our clothes off like they're on fire. His hands are everywhere, rough and desperate, making me dizzier than all the whisky in Portugal.

Can't think, can't breathe - just need more of him.

Drops

Come round slow, my head fuzzy like I'm swimming through treacle. Sun's sneaking in through the blinds, and I'm aching in places I didn't know existed. Sheets are rank - stink of sweat and spunk and like a Lynx factory exploded.

Then it all comes rushing back - Jack's hands all over me, that filthy mouth of his, the way we went at it half the night. Just thinking about it has me tenting the sheets like some horny teenager!

Roll over for another go, but the bed's empty and gone cold. Prop myself up on my elbows, squinting against the bastard sun trying to blind me.

And there's Jack, perched on the windowsill in just his kecks, having a sneaky morning smoke. But something's off. He's all wound up tight, looking stressed as he puffs away. Sets me on edge just looking at him, even with the Portuguese sun doing its best to roast us alive.

'Morning gorgeous,' I rasp out, voice gone all scratchy from last night. Slide to the edge of the bed, not bothering to cover up. 'You gonna come back to bed then? Fancy another round before we face the world, I do.'

But he's shaking his head before I've finished, jaw clenched up like he's got lockjaw. 'Listen....' he starts, and my stomach drops. Know that tone, don't I? It's the one blokes use when they're trying to let some bird down gentle. Feel proper sick.

'What happened last night...' Jack takes this massive drag like he's trying to inhale the whole ciggie at once, then lets it out dead slow. 'That's just between you and me, yeah? Not a word to anyone else, capiche?'

I sit up straighter, sheet bunched round my waist. 'What, like we're in some spy film?'

He flicks his ash out the window bit harder than he needs to. 'A secret,' he goes. 'A one-off. Whatever you want to call it.' Another drag, won't even look at me. 'Just rather not have the whole bleeding town gossiping about what I get up to in bed, alright?'

'Thought we had something decent going here, though?' Meant to sound casual but comes out proper pathetic, if I'm being honest. 'Was hoping we might have another go, wasn't I...'

Jack murders his cigarette on the windowsill, chucks it down to the street like it's personally fucked him over. When he turns round, there's something in his face that makes my guts twist, lips gone all tight.

'This town's got...expectations of me, Stevie. Everyone thinks they know me.' Yanks at his hair like he's trying to pull his thoughts out by the roots. 'If people found out what I'm into, well. Make everything go tits up, wouldn't it?'

And yeah, I get it. Sort of. The sensible bit of my brain does. All these nosy bastards with nothing better to do than stick their beaks in everyone's business. Bloke's just trying to keep his head down, ain't he? Same as me with Chris and that lot, I suppose.

But my insides are churning something chronic, face gone all hot with shame. Feel like a proper mug. Lying here starkers, thinking last night was more than just a quick fumble between mates.

'So that's me then?' I manage to get out past the lump in my throat, trying for a laugh but it comes out wrong. 'Your dirty little secret, yeah?'

But before I can really start feeling sorry for myself, Jack's on me. Pushing me back into the mattress and snogging me stupid, one hand on the back of my head and the other shoving the duvet out the way. And bloody hell, just having him on top of me has me gasping like I'm gagging for it, hips coming up eager as he gets his tongue in my mouth all desperate.

'Too right you are,' he growls, biting at my jaw till I'm wriggling about mad. 'All mine, ain't you? Just for me...'

After that it all goes a bit wild, tell you the truth. Reckon this is Jack's way of shutting me up about the awkward stuff, getting me so worked up with his hands and mouth that I forget to worry about what happens next. And fuck me if it don't work perfect.

It's not until we're down the marina shoveling down a full English that my head starts doing one. To anyone walking past we're just two lads, hanging out with our hangovers and chatting bollocks over our eggs and bacon. Jack's got his public act down pat - all smiles at the waitresses, waving at randoms who pass by. But under the table, his leg's burning against mine. Just that one touch has my heart going mental, his boardies feeling well thin between us. Jack knows exactly what he's doing an' all, keeps giving me these right dirty looks over his tea. About as subtle as a kick in the nuts, but bloody hell if it ain't getting me going.

We're just walking onto the beach when I clock Chris and Laila sprawled out on the sand. Proper gutted - was hoping to dodge the Spanish Inquisition till I'd worked out what bollocks I was gonna tell them!

'And what time do you call this, young man?' Laila grins. 'Good night, was it?'

I duck my head, grabbing and fumbling with Chris's beach towel so I don't have to meet her eyes.

'Let the bloke alone, Lai!' Chris pipes up, levering himself onto his elbows. 'You're just narked he's getting his end away while you're stuck with my ugly mug!'

'Oi!' She swats at him, giggling. 'But no, really - you've got to give us the gossip, Steve! Who was the lucky girl that you spent the night?'

I open my mouth to spin some convincing lie, but Jack beats me to it. 'Francesca' He claps me on the shoulder, fingers digging in just a touch too hard for friendly. 'Let's just say our boy had himself a proper good time and leave it at that, yeah?'

Jack's hand slides off my shoulder, and I swear I can feel the absence of it like a brand. He's already turning to head for the surf, pointing finger-guns at Laila with a wink.

'Speaking of mystery and intrigue...I'm off for a dip. Care to join me, love? Could use a bit of help with the hard-to-reach spots, if you know what I mean!'

And he's off, Laila giggling her head off behind him. I watch him working his magic on these birds in their skimpy bikinis - all them air kisses and touches that linger too long. Makes my stomach turn, if I'm honest.

This is Jack in his element, ain't it?

Mr Bloody Charming himself. Just putting on a show though, isn't he? Getting everyone to look where he wants so they don't see what he's really about.

I'm face down on the beach towel, head pounding like the devil's own drum kit as the sun tries to boil me alive through my eyelids. Could murder a spliff right about now, take the edge off this bastard behind my temples.

'Oi, Chris...' I rasp, giving him a nudge. 'You holding?'

He just groans, fishing in his shorts pocket and lobbing a manky-looking joint at my head. I fumble for my clipper, spark up and breathe deep. I lie down and close my eyes, letting that first hit do its job. Feel all that tension start to drain right out of me, mixing with the sea air.

'So...' Chris starts, and I tense up all over again. 'You and Jack. Gettin' pretty cosy, ain't ya?'

I force a shrug, make some vague noise. 'He's an alright bloke, y'know? Bit long in the tooth maybe, but he's a laugh.'

A laugh. Bloody hell, if they only knew.

'Alright there, lad?'

I startle, blinking up at Jack looming over me. He's slicking his hair back, water running down his face like he's in some posh advert. Looks fit as fuck, if I'm honest, and I can barely remember how to breathe.

His grin's wicked, eyes following my throat as I gulp.

'Listen, I'm gonna head off - get myself ready for tonight's gig. You'll be there, yeah?'

I nod, hypnotised by his muscles in those tight trunks. He throws me a cheeky wink and he's off, swaggering up the beach.

Laila's watching me over her magazine. 'What about Francesca, then? She showing up tonight, or what?'

Oh, bollocks. Nearly forgot about my made-up bird. The fib falls out of my mouth, all tangled up with the ghost of Jack's taste still on my tongue.

'Nah, she's local, innit? Not one for tourist places.'

Laila's eyebrow shoots up, and for a sec, I'm bricking it. My heart's going like the clappers. Shit, has she sussed me out?

But she just sniffs and goes back to her mag. I let out a slow breath, flop back on my towel and shut my eyes, feeling like I've dodged a bullet.

I dig my toes in the sand, thinking about seeing Jack at the gig tonight. Proper mental, all this. But ain't like I've got much choice, have I? Just gotta ride it out and see where it takes me.

Adam

Every night at Hugo's is like some mad game of cat and mouse. Jack's up there doing his thing, proper swagger and charm, working the crowd like a pro. But I see the little looks he throws my way, them nods just for me. Like everyone else is getting the show, but I'm getting something special. Does my head in, that does.

After his set, he does his rounds - chatting up the regulars, dodging his fan club of screaming birds. But he always ends up right next to me at the bar, pressing up close enough I get proper dizzy off his aftershave. 'Mental in here tonight, eh mate?' he'll go, hand lingering on my arm just long enough to get me going.

Come closing time, I'm feeding Chris and Laila the usual bollocks. 'Off to see Francesca,' I tell 'em with a wink, the lie rolling off my tongue easier each time. They don't clock nothing though - too busy trying to eat each other's faces to notice what's what.

I hang about just enough to look normal, then I'm out of there like a shot. And there's Jack, waiting in the shadows, looking fit enough to stop traffic and cocky as you like. 'Took your bleeding time,' he'll say, giving it large.

Proper mental when you think about it. Half the birds in Portugal gagging for him, and here he is, sneaking off with me every night like some dirty secret. Sometimes I wonder if I'm just another notch on his bedpost. But then I catch him watching me when he thinks I'm not looking, and... dunno. This thing between us, whatever the fuck it is - it's doing my head in.

Days later and I'm still spinning from another night with Jack.

Can't settle.

Can't focus.

Just keeps playing in my head, making my whole body buzz.

Now I'm squeezed into this manky phone box by the marina, feeding more escudos into this greedy bastard than I've spent on booze all holiday. But fuck it - I'd sell a kidney for a proper chat with Gem right now.

When I hear her voice crackling down the line, it's like coming up on a pill. 'Oi oi, you slag!' she goes, and I can picture that massive grin of hers. 'How's it hanging? Tell me everything. And when I say everything, I mean all the dirty details, you mucky pup!"

I can't help grinning like a right numpty, leaning against the sticky glass of the phone box. 'Gem, you wouldn't believe me if I told you. Swear down, I've well and truly lost it this time...'

And just like that, the words are tumbling out of me in a giddy rush. All about Jack, this fucking force of nature that's turned me inside out. The buzz of sneaking about, the way my guts go funny every time he looks at me across the bar.

Gem, of course, is on it like a flash. 'Ooh, a secret lover!' she coos, gleeful as anything. 'Bet that's got your blood pumping, eh? Adds a bit of spice to the ole rumpy-pumpy!'

I just hum, tracing idle patterns on the graffitied wall. 'He's a bit of a ladies' man. No one's got a scooby, that he likes a bit of sausage on the side.'

'You're being safe though, ain't ya?' Gemma asks, and it's like a bucket of ice water down my spine. 'Not getting too carried away in the moment, are we?'

I swallow hard, throat gone tight. Because I haven't thought about it at all. Got so caught up in it all, the feeling of his skin on mine, I forgot to use my head. Been running on pure want, letting my dick do the thinking.

'Course, course,' I say, lying through my teeth. 'No mug, me. Got it all sorted.'

But it's bollocks and I know it. And from how quiet Gem goes, reckon she knows it too.

The rest of the call passes in a blur - me reassuring her I'm being good (another whopper), her extracting a solemn promise that she's still my number one girl (forever and always). But as I'm hanging up the receiver, her parting words snag like hooks behind my ribs.

'Take care of yourself, Stevie,' she murmurs, low and fierce. 'Don't go losing your head for a pretty face and a filthy smile, yeah?'

Too late for that, ain't it? Been too late since that first night.

ANGELS

So here I am again, sprawled out on Jack's bed - proper boneless and fuzzy, watching him work them guitar strings. He's a right vision, all tanned skin and wiry muscle. Every note goes right through me, makes my insides go funny.

'So,' he says casual as you like, flicking ash onto his bare chest. 'Your mates... they know you bat for both teams?'

I just snort, taking a swig of my lager. 'Nah. Chris has got his head so far up his arse, and Laila's only around cos she's shagging him. Gemma is the only one I've told.'

'This Gemma...' He tilts his head, considering. 'She ever been more than a friend? Ever had a go with her, then?'

The leer he shoots me is positively filthy, and I grin back like a loon. 'Once or twice, maybe. What's it to you, squire? Fancying a bit of competition, are we?'

'Pfft!' He rolls his eyes, all bravado. 'Take more than some bird to get me back up. Nah, just curious is all. Wondering what other secrets Stevie-boy here might be hiding in his closet, like.'

I scoff, chucking a pillow at his head. 'Mate, you are my sodding closet!'

He laughs at that, right loud one an' all. Puts his guitar down and leans forward, elbows on his knees.

'What about your folks, then?' He asks, voice gone soft and serious. 'They clued in on where you like to park your bike at night?'

I go quiet for a bit. Still does my head in, thinking about it. Makes me feel well sick - guilty one minute, angry the next, scared shitless most of the time.

'My mum... yeah, we close. But my dad...' I snort, trying to imagine my old man's face if he knew what I'd been up to. Christ, it'd be a sight. 'Mate, if my dad found out, he'd absolutely keel over on the spot. I'd have to scrape him off the carpet and bury him in the back garden. Might improve his personality, mind you.'

Jack huffs out a laugh, but there's something dead dark in it. 'Aye, I know that feeling all too well. My lot's so religious, they'd probably try to exorcise the queer right out of me. Tie me to a bed and douse me in holy water 'til I repent.'

'Kinky,' I quip, waggling my eyebrows. 'Didn't know you were into that sort of thing, Jacky-boy. Should I be worried?'

He swats at me, grinning. 'Cheeky git. Nah, I learned early on that I'm better off on me own. No one to answer to, no one to disappoint.'

'But doesn't it get lonely?' I ask, hating how small my voice sounds.

Jack looks at me then - never seen him look so... I dunno. Like he's really hurting underneath it all.

'Suppose it does, sometimes. But I keep myself busy, don't I?' And just like that he's back to his old self, all dirty grins and nudges. Trying to make a joke of it.

I allow it, for now. Let him tug the convo round to happier topics - first fumbles and celebrity shags, the music that lights a fire in both our bellies. It's nice, this. Comfortable as an old pair of trainers.

I scoot closer on the mattress until our knees are kissing. 'Fancy a snog?' It's barely a whisper, more felt than heard.

Something flashes in his eyes. Then his hands are dropping the guitar all careless.

'Oh, I fancy more than a kiss, pretty boy,' he husks, and the rasp of it zings white-hot down my spine. 'I'm going to take you apart with me teeth, ye daft sod, until you can't tell which way's up, 'til the only word you know is my name.'

And he's as good as his promise, isn't he? Bloody hell, I'm in for it now.

STAR

Sun's streaming through the curtains like it's on a mission before I've even opened my eyes. I'm in Jack's gaff, tangled up in his sheets that reek of sweat and shagging.

Last night comes flooding back. Brings a right cheeky grin to my face. Jack's hands all over me, his mouth leaving a trail of fire down my neck. The way he looked at me, eyes dark as sin, like I was the only bloke in the world worth a damn.

I stretch out, enjoying the ache in my muscles. Then it hits me - I'm off back to London tomorrow. Back to real life, while Jack stays here living it up in the Algarve.

Proper does my head in, thinking about all this being over. Makes me feel sick, if I'm honest.

I stumble out to the kitchenette, rubbing the sleep from my eyes. And there he is, bent over the counter looking fit as fuck. Christ, I'm gonna miss him, miss all of this.

'Alright?' I croak, sidling up behind him and wrapping my arms round his waist. But he's having none of it. Goes stiff as a board, twists away.

'Coffee,' he grunts, shoving a mug at me. 'Got to go to Loulé in a bit - pick up some records.'

I blink, thrown for a loop. This isn't like him. Usually he's all over me in the morning, hands wandering, grinning.

'Sound,' I mutter, taking a swig that burns my mouth. 'Fancy some company on the ride, or...?'

He just shrugs, staring into his mug like it holds the secrets of the universe. 'If you want, I s'pose. No time to faff about though - you'll have to make do with what you've got on. You can borrow a shirt of mine, if ya want.'

Feels like he's just walloped me one.

'Can I use your toothbrush maybe...?' I ask, careful like.

'Yeah, sure.'

'Right you are,' I say, voice gone all stiff. 'Gimme two shakes to grab my shoes and your shirt, and I'll be ready to roll.'

I hop in the shower quick, hoping he might join. But no dice. I towel off, throw on my jeans and his Rolling Stones tee, and find him on the sofa tapping his car keys on the table, staring at the stereo like it's personally offended him.

Seeing me, he jumps up. 'Ready? Let's get cracking.'

Blimey... what's crawled up his arse and died?

But I follow him to the car without a word, praying this icy vibe'll melt once we're on the road.

The drive is... fucking brutal. Jack's got the stereo blaring some depressing Pink Floyd shite about loss and decay. I try to catch his eye, crack a joke, anything to break this silence... but he's gone and shut down completely. Closed off in a way I've never seen before. By the time we get to the shop, I'm about ready to crawl out of my own skin, I'm that on edge.

I follow him inside, shuffling like a right muppet with my eyes on the floor, while he makes a beeline for Jorge.

They're off, yapping away, all jokes and poncy music talk that goes right over my head. Makes me feel like a right tit standing there. I wander over to the racks, pretending to give a toss about the records, just so I don't look like a complete numpty standing about with my thumb up my arse.

Feels like an eternity before Jack's ringing up his purchases, slapping ol' Captain Grateful Dead on the shoulder like they'll be sending out wedding invites any day now. I'm ready to scream by the time we stumble back out into the baking heat, Jack's arms full of crackly virgin vinyl.

We head to some poky cafe on a side street, air thick with the stink of old chip fat and coffee. Jack orders us both a beer and a couple of toasties, leg jiggling like he's fit to burst as we perch awkward on the rickety stools.

'So, er...' I clear my throat, take a swig of lager. 'What's the plan for the rest of the day, like? Thought we might-'

'Actually.' He cuts me off, grimacing. 'There's someone I need to meet up with in a bit. Alone. Shouldn't take more than an hour or two.'

I swallow hard round the sudden lump in my throat. 'Oh. Right. Well... d'you want me to just-'

'Nah, you're alright.' He's already standing, chucking a few crumpled escudos on the tabletop. 'Have another bevvy while I'm gone, yeah? My treat. I'll come find you after.'

And then he's off, the cafe door slamming shut behind him as he legs it up the street. Leaving me like a right mug, sipping at my piss-warm beer.

Bloody hell, this is...I dunno what this is. I keep mulling it over as I poke at my soggy chips, trying to suss out when it all went tits-up. When that easy spark between us turned into...this shite.

Was it something I said? Did I come on too strong?

I've got to get some air. Clear the stink of doubt and misery from my lungs before I choke on it. I settle up and head outside, gulping in great lungfuls of that salty wind.

I end up just...wandering. Drifting through the cobbled streets like a right plonker, chain-smoking till everything goes fuzzy. Trying to convince myself it's all in my head, this massive shift that's ripped a bloody great hole between us.

But time's ticking away. Slipping through my fingers as I loiter about like a spare part, no sign of his golden hair or that cheeky grin of his.

One hour turns to two. Then three. The shadows get long and the streets fill up with locals and lobster-red tourists, their happy babbling doing my head in. By the time I drag myself back to the cafe... I flop into a seat outside, head in my hands and feeling absolutely gutted.

I catch the rickety bus back alone. Jack's motor's long gone - just an empty patch of tarmac taking the piss.

Hopping off the bus, I make for Jack's flat, banging on the door like a man possessed. Nothing but silence. So, I set off on a mad dash 'round the area, looking for answers that don't bloody come.

JOKER

Later that night we rock up at Hugo's and there's Jack. Up on that tiny stage, giving it large for all those birds swooning at the front. Looks like the world's his bleeding oyster, not a care in his pretty little head. I'm trying to catch his eye over everyone's heads but he's not having it. Won't even look my way, just keeps scanning right past me like I'm not even there. My pint's gone proper manky, warm and flat, but I keep holding onto it anyway.

Waiting for my chance when he hops down to everyone cheering. Might catch him by the bogs, find out what the hell's got into him. But he just breezes past. Claps Chris on the shoulder, shoots Laila a wink with a promise to buy her a bevvy later. Me, I barely get a grunt. A tight 'alright.' that's it.

I'm standing there like a right muppet while he heads straight for the bar. Course he does - there's this bird there, all long hair and longer legs. His hand's on her back before he's even finished saying hello, making her laugh at whatever bollocks he's come out with.

Fucking hell. Think I'm going to be sick.

Laila nudges me, 'No hot date with your girl tonight then?'

I can't even look at her. Eyes too busy boring holes through Jack's skull, trying to work out what makes a man turn so cold so quick.

'What bird?' I mutter, distracted. Brain too busy tearing itself to shreds to keep up the charade.

Her and Chris give each other this look, like they're saying something without saying it.

'Ooooh, sounds like lover boy's forgot his squeeze already!' she crows, delighted. 'Holiday romances, eh? Blink and you'll miss 'em!'

I'm hardly listening. Too busy watching Jack with his hand all over that blonde bird at the bar, grinning like a right prat while she hangs off him.

'Yeah,' I croak out, tearing my eyes away. 'Turns out it was just a - a fling. Flash in the pan. No big deal.'

The words are acid on my tongue, stripping the skin clean away. Christ, is that what we were? A bit of slap and tickle, a sidepiece to chase off the cobwebs until he could find a better offer?

I dunno. I just...I believe in him, in us.

'C'mon,' Chris cuts in, slinging an arm round my shoulder. 'Let's go check out that club by the casino, yeah? Get you back on the horse, forget that silly bird.'

I let him steer me to the door, pasting on a grin I don't feel. One last look over my shoulder, confirming Jack is nowhere to be seen and neither is blondie. Stings like a bitch, that. Just wish he hadn't felt the need to carve his initials on my heart before he swanned off into the sunset.

The club's pure shite - all flashy lights and posers, music so loud it's making my fillings rattle. 'Kriss Kross, Jump' shrieking from the speakers. Soon as we're back home I'm finding a real banging rave again.

But the universe isn't done kicking me in the swingers just yet. We barely make it to the bar before I clock him - Jack bloody Hallowe'd Eve, draped over a stool with Blondie perched in his lap like a pedigree poodle. They're giggling and groping, all roaming hands and blatant snogs that leave precisely nothing to the imagination.

I'm frozen.

Can't look away, even as my lungs turn to stone and my heart feels like it's being squeezed through a mangle.

Course, that's when Chris spots them. Bellows out a greeting like the daft sod he is, waving them over with a grin.

Jack doesn't even flinch. Just keeps pawing at that plastic-looking bird, giving me this right nasty look while he's at it.

I'm done for. Shattered to pieces, choking on the shrapnel as he snogs her senseless mere feet away. Giving it the full all sly hands and knowing smirks. Jack wipes his mouth, satisfied. Pins me direct with a chilling, flat stare - the silent beat down cuts brutal as any blade straight through my chest. Then he's back nibbling her ear, looking real smug while everything crumbles to ash around me.

Ruined me, he has.

Can't even feel it anymore, that's how bad it is. Just stand there watching him drag her onto the dance floor, his hands all over her while they grind to some Billy Ray bollocks.

At some point Laila guides my sagging frame to a stool, pressing shots wordless into my quaking hands. I knock them back desperate - praying the alcohol might erase these blood red images of callous betrayal now seared across my brain. I just want to sleep. I need to leave. I need fresh air and space, need to be anywhere but here, stewing in my own embarrassment.

I'm out the door before Chris and Laila can stop me, cigarette already in my mouth as I leg it down the street. Just need to get away from it all. Can't stand seeing him like that, acting like nothing ever happened between us.

I'm a dead man walking. A ghost, rattling round the flat in the wee small hours with Massive Attack on my Walkman and a chest full of misery my only companions.

Dutch Barrels

A blaring car alarm drags me from restless sleep, my head pounding as last night comes rushing back.

Jack.

That bird.

But I haven't got time for wallowing. Clock's ticking on this doomed fantasy - I only have a few hours to get an explanation from Jack before I have to go back to England with nothing but crushed expectations as a memento.

So, I rally. Fling my shite in a case and snatch up Jack's manky Stones shirt like a holy relic. I cling to the lingering traces of sweat and Cool Water cologne as I pelt up the road toward his flat, pulse hammering in my ears loud as tribal drums.

Of course, the bastard isn't even in. I'm half-hysterical by the time his neighbour clocks me - probably look a right sight, all wild eyes and stress-sweat as I bang frantic on his door.

'He hasn't been back, love,' she says, all kind concern. 'Not since last night.'

And that...that hurts like hell. Because it's obvious where Jack has been. Who he's been with while I'm here getting upset on an empty doorstep.

Dunno how long I sit there like a mug, holding onto his shirt. Just sitting there breathing in the smell of him that's still on it somehow.

Then I hear someone coming up the stairs. My heart does this stupid little flip when I see who it is - Jack, looking like he's been dragged through a hedge backwards and then fucked six ways from Sunday. Still the most beautiful thing I've ever seen, even half-drunk and smelling of perfume.

'Alright?' I croak, levering myself upright as he blinks down at me. 'Thought I'd swing by and...y'know. Return your shirt and that.'

Weak as piss, but it's all I can force past the boulder in my windpipe. He just grunts, shoulders past to fumble with his keys.

'Grab yours while you're at it,' he says, cool as you like.

Soon as the door clicks shut, I hand over his manky Stones top, trying to act like I couldn't care less.

'Let me go fetch yours.'

He heads off to the bedroom and comes back with my T-shirt all balled up and creased. 'Sorry it's a bit rough,' he mumbles, looking everywhere but at me. 'So, you're off in a few hours, eh?'

I just nod. Keep waiting for him to say something, anything to make this feel less shit. But I can see it coming. That look on his face like he's about to be a right bastard about it all.

'Reckon you're making this into something it ain't.'

I stand there gawping at him like a right mug.

'Wasn't it?' I manage, hating how my voice goes all weird. 'Cos from where I'm standing, it felt like-'

'Like what, Steve?' he cuts in, real nasty now. 'Like we were gonna skip off into the sunset together? All happy families and that? Get real!'

I'm flinching from the venom in it, the casual scorn.

'I thought...I mean, it seemed like there was potential for-'

'For what?' He's laughing now, a jagged bark what's got not a lick of humour in it. 'A relationship?'

The way he's looking at me makes me feel like I'm nothing. Just some piece of shit stuck to his shoe.

'Those pills have scrambled your brain good and proper. This...' He gestures between us, all casual dismissal. '...was never more than a mutually enjoyable tumble. Fun while it lasted and that, but I ain't the flowers type. Thought you knew that, din't I? You're well mint,' he's blustering, cuffing my shoulder like we're nothing but pals. 'A right laugh, and a decent bit of stuff to boot. If you're ever back in the Algarve, deffo give me a shout for a redux, yeah?'

I can't fucking take it. The nerve of him, acting like what we had - what I felt in my bones was real - was just some quick how's-your-father in the grotty bog of a beachfront boozer, a sly handy round the back of Hugo's...

Something in me snaps.

'Now you fucking listen, Jack!' I grab his arms, squeezing till my knuckles go white, shaking him. 'I know you felt it too - this thing between us. Wasn't just some holiday fling to brag about down the pub. It was real. The kind of thing that doesn't come along twice.'

He's staring at me like I'm mental.

I'm breathing hard, searching his stunned face for a glimmer, a spark of what's been burning in my chest since I first saw him at Hugo's.

But there's nothing there. Just emptiness.

'I ain't a fuckin' poof, alright?'

The words hit me hard. I'm still trying to make sense of them when his fist connects with my jaw. Next thing I know I'm on the floor, mouth full of blood, room spinning. He's standing over me, face twisted like he's looking at something he's scraped off his shoe.

'There is no 'us', you deluded little sod!' The words are bullets, tearing through what's left of my wretched heart. 'Never was, never will be! So why don't you take a fucking hint and piss off back where you came from, eh? Chalk it up to experience and spare us both the bleeding melodrama!'

Can't even move as he grabs my shirt and drags me to the door like I'm rubbish that needs taking out.

Then I'm in the blinding sun, split lip throbbing with every heartbeat. Few people glance my way but no one gives a toss. Just another lad who got caught up in the Algarve nightlife and came off worse.

Should've seen it coming really.

&

Chris and Laila are already packed when I stumble through the door, cases lined up neat by the entryway. They clock me as I breeze past, a double-take that'd be right funny if I weren't so gutted.

'Oi, where you been?' Chris demands, all brotherly concern and barely-leashed nosiness.

I just grunt, ducking into the bedroom to grab my own shite. Can't bear to look at 'em head-on, not when I'm this close to cracking clean in two.

'Course, I'm not quick enough. Chris is waiting when I emerge, a low whistle escaping as he takes in the state of my mug.

'Fucking hell! Some geezer really did a number on you, din't he?'

I shrug, going for nonchalant. Failing miserably.

'This to do with some bloke, then?' His eyes are dead sharp now, like he knows something's up. Reckon he's starting to work it out - why I'm such a mess over all this.

But he just clears his throat, jerking his chin at my split lip. 'Her local fella catch wind of you sniffing round his turf, like?'

Jesus Christ. Almost laugh at how wrong he's got it, how much worse the truth is. Just look at him, feeling about a hundred years older than yesterday morning. When I was waking up warm and wanted, all tangled up in Jack's bed with his stubble scratching my neck, that cheap aftershave of his everywhere.

'Yeah,' I manage to get out. 'That's about the size of it.'

He makes this noise like he gets it, gives my shoulder a squeeze. Takes everything I've got not to pull away from his hand.

'Never mind mate, we're off home now ain't we? Leave all this Portuguese drama behind us.'

London's grey skies suddenly sound like heaven after all this fucking sunshine.

So I straighten up, wipe the blood off my nose best I can. Pick up my case and start walking, eyes fixed straight ahead as we head down these too-bright streets. Force myself not to look at that white building when we pass it, my gut turning over just thinking about Jack in there. Nearly chuck up right there on the street, taste of sick in my mouth. But I swallow it down, the burn of it almost feels right.

Taxi ride's doing my head in, Chris and Laila's enthusiastic yapping becoming background noise as I rest my forehead against the window. Watch the Algarve slip past - all that golden sand and sea, palm trees going by till it's just a blur of blue in the distance. I shut my eyes, letting the engine shake through me. It's almost a relief, the dull ache of it. Gives me something to focus on besides the ragged hole Jack's torn in my chest. Can't stop seeing it over and over - him spitting those words, the disgust in his face. The way his fist felt smashing into my face, blood filling my mouth.

It's not until we're flying, everything down below turned into this tiny patchwork, that I start breathing right again.

Blighty's a shock to the system when we land, the damp chill like a slap to the face after endless weeks of oppressive heat. For a mo' I just stand there, staring up at the grey sky while rain soaks my hair. Let the cold seep through my jacket, running down my back like some kind of baptism. Tip my face up, feeling the drops sting my eyes.

Rhubarb & Custard

'Alright listen up revellers. It's happening now and for the rest of the weekend. So, get yourselves out of the house and onto Castlemorton Common...Be there. All week-end. Hardcore!'

I'm tearing up this field at Castlemorton Common. Bank holiday weekend, and the place is pure mayhem - ravers off their tits left, right and centre. We're in the thick of it, grooving away in the DIY tent, music mental with beats so deep and dirty. Could be Sunday by now, but who's counting when you're buzzing off your nut on a cheeky double drop? My shirt's plastered to my back, sweat running in rivers as 'Papua New Guinea' pounds through the speakers. The crowd's giving it large, a writhing mass of limbs and grins, and I'm right in the heart of it all, exactly where I need to be.

Through the strobing madness, I clock a bloke who's the absolute spit of Jack. Same swagger, same pout and tousled hair. For a hot second, I think the pills have kicked my brain out my ears, but nah... just the ghost of him, haunting me even out here in the muddy back-end of beyond. I gravitate his way, pulling shapes until we're bumping shoulders in the sweaty crush. Swap these big, gurning grins like a pair of loons – he isn't Jack, not even close.

'Bloody Jack,' I mutter, shaking my head as I melt back into the writhing throng. 'Hi-Jacking all the space in my head, even when I'm miles from anywhere.'

He's been living there rent-free, tell you the truth. Ever since I touched back down in Blighty, it's been nothing but pining and winging. Three solid weeks of moping about, picking at the scabs... but not today. Not out here, lost in the glorious chaos of it all. Nah, today I'm here for a good time, not a long time - and with any luck, it'll be a belter.

Course, I can feel the sniffles creeping in, a dull throb kicking off behind my eyes. Reckon I'm coming down with the lurgy. Trying to fight off a stinking cold while I'm hurtling skywards... but that's the magic of the whole thing, I guess. The music and the medicine, all swirling together until you can't tell where the pleasure ends and the pain begins.

And I must look a right state - stripped to my waist, Ray-Bans jammed on my face, and this stupid white bucket hat (some bird gave me earlier) covered in gaudy yellow flowers. I'm a walking disaster, but who cares? I'm here to dance myself clean, sweat out the heartache until I'm shiny and new.

Just as I'm getting right into it, I spot Alex. The same Alex I was snogging in that chill-out room before Portugal. He turns and clocks me, eyes going wide, and I feel this massive grin spreading across my face. He's looking fit as, white vest showing off everything, jeans hanging low. Seeing him hits me like a rush, cutting through my pill buzz like a knife. Our eyes meet and bang - I'm back in that chill-out room, remembering how he tasted.

And then he's up against me, skin on skin in the crowd.

'Steve, right?' he shouts in my ear.

'Yeah,' I get out, heart going mad. 'Alex.'

His face lights up, eyes doing that thing that turns my legs to jelly.

'You look different without a dummy stuck in your gob!' he goes.

I burst out laughing at that, feeling my face go hot. My head's full of that night - his fingers on my lips, snogging him stupid in that sweaty little room.

He gets in close, nodding at the exit. 'Fancy a chat somewhere quieter?'

And I'm already turning towards the exit, towards fresh air and dark corners. Towards him, and whatever mad shit might happen next. We're pushing through this sea of sweaty bodies. Ducking and weaving, trying not to get smacked in the face or soaked in warm beer. But it's dead weird... everyone just sort of parts for us, like they know. Like the whole place is waiting to see what happens with me and Alex out in the dark.

We fall out into the cool air, and I can't stop laughing, my whole body tingling like electric. Everything feels fucking amazing.

Alex gives me this look that has my stomach doing somersaults. 'Been hoping I'd see you again,' he says, smooth as you like. 'Knew I would though, both of us being proper ravers and that. Like we were bound to crash into each other, innit?'

The pills make his words go off in my head like sparklers. Feel like I'm floating, I'm that buzzed.

We're walking past all these mental little stalls, taking in the chaos. Alex stops at this sweet stall, eyes going all bright at the selection.

'Fancy something?' he goes, already reaching for an Astro Pop and some space dust. Dead pleased with himself as he hands them over.

Our fingers brush when I take them, sending this electric shock right through me. Trying to tell myself it's just the pills making everything feel massive, like the whole universe is reaching out and touching me.

I'm arsing about with the Astro Pop wrapper, fingers all over the place. When I finally get the bugger open, I give it a proper go with my tongue till it's all wet and shiny. Being a right slag about it!

'Mmm, lush!' I go, pulling it out with a pop. 'Didn't have to get me nothing.'

Alex looks down, going all shy... but I can see him trying not to grin. 'What can I say? You stuck in my head. Can't just forget a snog like that, can you?'

'That right?' I say, heart going mental.

'Too right,' he says back, looking right at me. 'Been thinking about it loads. Well annoyed I didn't get your number after.'

My heart does this mad flip and I go all tingly. Can't believe he's been thinking about me - wanting me and that. Even when he's not mashed. Gets me well excited just thinking about it.

Quick as anything, I spin round and head for the bloke with the sweets, Astro Pop stuck in the side of my gob.

'Oi, mate!' I shout, giving him my best smile. 'Lend us a pen for a sec? Got something important to sort!'

He looks proper confused but chucks me this Sharpie. I grab it and spin round to catch Alex by the wrist before he can do one.

His skin's well hot under my fingers, can feel his heart going crazy as I write my Jane Hancock across his smooth dark skin.

'There,' I say, dead chuffed with myself as I give the pen back. 'Stuck with me now! Got my name on you and everything.'

Alex looks at his arm, grinning like a nutter.

'Looks like!' he says.

'Too right!' I say, bumping into him, feeling like I'm flying. 'I can be right stubborn when I want. And right now... I want to get to know you better.'

It's out there now. Just hanging between us, making everything feel electric.

We're just wandering about, letting the night take us wherever. Like a couple of candy fueled dreamers off our faces, going with the flow, seeing what turns up.

End up by these massive black trucks, all done up with silver and black flags everywhere. Music's gone proper mental now - that fast techno that feels like it's drilling into your skull, but I'm well into it. We climb up on the bonnet of one of the trucks, me helping Alex up like we're at some posh wedding or something. Lie back and bloody hell - the stars are doing bits tonight. Like someone's spiked the whole sky, putting on this massive light show just for us.

'Uni, yeah?' Alex goes out of nowhere.

'Doing law. You?'

'Politics. Gonna shake up the system and that.' He grins. 'Lawyer and a politician walk into a bar, eh?'

I crack up at that, how easy this is, like we've known each other forever.

Go quiet then, watching the stars do their thing. I'm losing the plot up here, swear I've slipped into another dimension with all the spinning and swirling going on up there. The Doves are doing me in proper, everything buzzing like it's alive. Having Alex warm against me just makes it all better, like the cherry on top of this mental cake.

'Puts it all in perspective, don't it?' he murmurs after a beat, sounding absolutely baked. 'We're just these tiny ants scurrying about, and the universe couldn't give a single toss about our merry little dance to the grave.' His eyes gleam as he looks at me full-on. 'Way I see it, that makes it our job to grab life by the proverbial and shake it till the pips rattle loose before our turn's up, you know what I mean?'

I'm totally with him. Like we're on exactly the same wavelength.

'Carpe the fucking diem,' I say, tipping the Space Dust right on my tongue. Bloody hell - it's like my whole mouth's exploding, making my head buzz even more.

Don't even think, just grab Alex's face and chuck some in his mouth too. He lets me do it, both of us lying there laughing like kids while it crackles away.

'So what about you then?' Alex goes after a bit. 'What's the big plan, eh? What's going on in that head of yours?'

'Nothing flash. Dead simple, me.' I look at him all shy, the pills making everything feel well intense. 'Just want to try everything, know what I mean? See it all, do it all. Get everything I can out of life before I'm done.'

He cracks up at that - this big gorgeous laugh that goes right through me. Can't help laughing too, can I? Next thing we're both in bits, taking the piss while that techno's banging away around us.

Fucking hell, this is mint.

We stay close for a bit - chatting shit, squeezing every last bit out of our mashed-up little moment.

Then Alex sits up quick, looking me up and down proper bold. 'Speaking of adventures... you're looking well tanned, you are. Like you've done one from our miserable country and been living it up in the sun!'

'Got it in one.' I'm grinning like a cat, right pleased with myself. 'Just got back from Portugal. Few weeks getting burnt and into trouble.'

'You lucky bastard!' He laughs, giving me this over-the-top nudge. 'Bet you had a right time out there!'

I shrug, trying to look mysterious. 'Was an eye-opener, yeah.' Pull a face and give this rough cough. 'Brought back this killer cold though. Throat's fucked, like I've been necking glass.'

Quick as you like, Alex cups his hands round his gob like he's on the telly. 'Spanish flu from Portugal! Patient zero's at Castlemorton. Leg it before the plague gets ya!'

I'm fucking dying, can barely breathe I'm laughing so hard. Alex is gone too, both of us creased up like right idiots.

Still giggling like a tit, I slide off the bonnet - bit messy, if I'm honest. Have to grab the side of the truck to stay up. Give him this look over my shoulder, half flirting and half taking the piss.

'Right then, Chuckles. You coming or what?'

Alex hops down all smooth. Proper showing off, moving like he's not even on one while I'm here trying to work out how my legs go.

He just gives me this smirk and follows me through all the ravers. Heading for this tiny tent we managed to get up by Chris's manky VW earlier - only clever thing we did before the pills turned us into right muppets.

There's a new sort of buzz building between us now. I can feel it. This crackling potential, like a live wire licking hot up my spine with every step. Alex' hand finds the small of my back as we walk, burning a hole clean through the thin cotton of my tee.

We get to the tent and Alex has to proper fold himself in half to get in, lanky bastard. Well tight in here, can't move without touching

- not that I'm arsed. Love having him this close, even if I am feeling proper Tom and Dick. Reckon I'm operating at 40% capacity, tops. Just flop back on the groundsheet, squeaking under me. Let my eyes shut and try to ride out this static in my head. Alex is rabbiting on about something but it's all fuzzy round the edges. Nice though, even with that bass still shaking the tent poles.

Nearly gone when Alex comes out with it, casual as you like. 'So, you only into blokes then, or what?'

'Nah, bit of everything, me.' Can barely get the words out through this massive yawn, eyes still shut in this warm fuzz.

Goes proper quiet for a bit. Then Alex shifts closer, can feel his breath on my mouth.

'Them mates of yours...' His voice goes all low in the dark. 'They know about all that? Or they getting the cleaned-up version?'

That gets my eyes open. Alex is right there, looking well intense in the dark. Like he's trying to work something out.

'Gemma, my best mate, she knows everything,' I admit, mouth gone a bit dry. 'The others... well, they get the highlight reel, don't they?'

'Right.' There's something in his tone that makes my stomach twist. 'And you're sweet with that, are you? Living your life in careful little edit?'

'Mate, I can barely keep my eyes open,' I try for light, but it comes out wobbly. 'Besides, it's not that simple-'

'Course it's simple,' he cuts in, really wound up now. 'Either they're your mates and they take you as you are, or they're just people you get pissed with. No in-between.'

Crack one eye, head swimming. 'Bit heavy for a party chat, innit? Could murder a Red Bull if we're having some big coming out crisis in this sweatbox.'

'Fair play,' he backs off. 'Reckon we could both use a breather from the heavy stuff.'

Just the bass going through the tent for a bit, people shouting somewhere. Then Alex's face changes - gets this right dirty look. Grabs my jaw and everything goes electric.

'Not one for the deep and serious, huh?' he says, mouth right there. 'Alright, I can adjust. How about we just snog until we can't think straight instead?'

Then he's on me. Proper going for it, tongue in my mouth like he's trying to map it out. And I just give in. Let it take over, buzzing from head to toe.

Could spend forever doing this - just grinding against him in the dark, hands everywhere on sweaty skin while the music pounds through the ground. Could get lost in it - his hot mouth, teeth nipping, tongue doing bits.

Course, that's when my body betrays me. Eyelids fluttering, limbs gone boneless, the whole box and dice. I've just got that wretched flu don't I, the double drop of pills, all of it dragging me under while this fit bloke's trying to snog my face off.

It's the ultimate cosmic joke, I swear, my poor neglected stiffy waving a tearful goodbye as I fade into the black.

Of all the piss-poor timing, this really takes the bleeding biscuit.

Wake up to some dickheads shouting outside. Head's killing me, throat feels like I've been eating glass, and my nose won't stop running. Right state, ain't I?

There's this manky Tesco receipt on my sleeping bag with a note: 'Hi sleeping beauty. Looked a bit rough so get some kip. Let's pick this up later - still got your number on my arm.'

He's left me a Mars Bar too, bit squashed but still.

It all comes back then - snogging Alex's face off like some horny teenager, everything well mint until I conked out on him like a total bellend. Fucking hell. How'd you even come back from something like that?

Can't help having a laugh at myself though. Trust me to cock it up that badly, proper making a show of it and all.

Stick my hoodie under my head and try getting back to sleep. Can hear some crusty on the bongos mixing with the techno somewhere.

Must've nodded off 'cause next thing, Gem's crawling in for a cuddle. Chris and Laila stumble in after, all pissed up and giggling. Their chatting sends me right off again.

Chris wakes us up taking the tent down. Feel well rough - flu and comedown both kicking my arse as we pack up. The whole weekend feels like some insane dream. Jack, Alex kissing me, that Mars Bar note... it's all mixed up in my head as I slump against the window.

The girls are chatting away in the back while I'm half asleep, thinking about what Alex said about not hiding who you are. Maybe he's got a point. But that's for later. Right now I just want to get home and sleep for about a week.

Triangles

This flu's doing me in proper after Castlemorton. Can't even face lectures, just hiding in my room with a stash of Night Nurse, Lucozade and Mum's chicken soup like I'm some invalid.

Wednesday night and the phone won't shut up ringing. Drag myself out there, ready to tell whoever it is to do one and let me suffer. Then I hear his voice, all warm and honeyed, and I'm grinning like a right muppet.

'Alright, Alex? Fair warning, I've come down with the lurgy. Hope I didn't pass it on.'

'Nah, mate, I'm fighting fit. Immune system of an ox, innit? But enough about my superior genes - focus on getting better, Sunshine.

We've got unfinished business, you and me.' My stomach does a little flip. Even half-dead, he makes me feel giddy as anything.

I shuffle to my room, pulling the phone cord while holding the receiver to my ear as I flop down onto my bed.

'Well, I'm chuffed you didn't lose my number, at least. Thought maybe you'd forget all about me once the buzz wore off. Just another pretty face in the crowd and all that.'

Alex makes this low noise in his throat. 'You having a laugh? As if I could forget a mug like yours. Got your digits permanently etched in my skin now, ain't I? Couldn't shake you if I tried.'

That has me glowing like mad.

'So,' I say after a bit. 'When'd you end up leaving Castlemorton, then? Thought maybe you'd gone full crusty, living in the mud and that.'

Alex laughs. 'Nah, bruv. Had to leg it Wednesday when the Old Bill started nicking everyone. Couldn't risk it, not with uni and everything.'

'Thought all that anarchy stuff would be right up your street. Sticking it to The Man and all that bollocks you go on about.'

'Oh, it was totally mental,' he says. 'Once in a lifetime that was. But much as I'd love to spend my life getting off my face in fields, got work to do, ain't I? Can't change things from the back of a police van, can I?'

'Yeah, remember you banging on about politics. All that changing the world stuff.'

'Ah, you were actually listening!'

'Course I was listening, you div. Hard not to with you going all Che Guevara on me.'

Alex proper laughs at that.

'Nah, don't reckon I could pull off the beret. But yeah, want to make a difference and that. Like my old man.'

'Your dad into all that then?' I ask.

'He's South African. Zulu fella. Met my mum when she was out there being all gap year, fell for her and came back here. But he's still dead serious about what's happening back home, you know?'

'Bloody hell,' I say. 'That's intense.'

'Anyway,' he says, bit lighter now. 'You'll have to come see it yourself sometime. Let me show you round.'

'What, South Africa?'

'Mate, it's something else. Sunsets that'll blow your mind.'

I close my eyes, thinking about it. Me and him watching the sun go down. Dead soppy, but I like it.

'Sounds well good,' I say, grinning like an idiot. 'Gem always says my hair's like an African sunset. Reckons it's my best bit, the ginger mop.'

'She's right there,' Alex says. 'Couldn't stop staring at it in the chill-out room. Prettiest boy I ever saw, no word of a lie.'

Thank fuck he can't see me going red as anything.

'Pack it in,' I manage. 'Gonna give me a big head.'

'Just telling it like it is, sunshine.'

I'm well beaming now, sinking into my pillows like some lovesick teenager.

'Actually,' he says suddenly. 'Fancy getting a pint when you're not all manky and diseased?'

'You asking me out?'

'Yeah, reckon I am. Up for it?'

'Wicked,' I grin.

'Get better first though, yeah? Want you fighting fit for our date.'

'I'll try not to be half dead this time,' I laugh.

'Better not,' he says, all warm like. 'No passing out on me again, sunshine.'

We keep chatting till my throat's too fucked to carry on, making plans between my coughing fits.

Even after we hang up I'm bouncing off the walls like some nutter.

&

Weekend drags on and I still feel like I've been twatted by a bus. Well gutted to miss the rave in Brighton, but no way I'm up for dancing, not feeling this rough. So I'm stuck on the sofa, getting baked off my face, letting Beavis and Butthead rot my brain with their special kind of stupid. That's when the itching starts up. My legs, my arms, my back - when I finally stop scratching long enough to have a proper look, I'm covered in these bright red spots. First thing I think: I've picked up some mental flea thing from Castlemorton. Just fucking perfect.

By next morning, these angry red dots are everywhere - arms, legs, chest, the whole bloody lot. Like I've been attacked by a nutter with a red pen while I was sleeping. Ring Mum proper freaking out. Her being her usual calm self just goes, 'Pop down to see Doc Marcus, love.'

So I drag my spotty arse to the doc, who's known me since I was a nipper. He has a good poke about, listens to me going on about the flu, Castlemorton, Portugal.

Then bang - out comes the diagnosis. 'Pityriasis rosea, my boy! Rare little bugger, this one. Couple of weeks, bit of cream and these pills, you'll be sorted. Not dying just yet, son!'

I wobble out of there, pockets full of creams and pills, head done in. Pity-what now? Since when did having a laugh in the sun come with so much grief?

On the train back to uni, bit of sun coming through making my head hurt less, I'm starting to feel human again. Even Chris has managed to get his arse to lectures, which is a right miracle. We have a chat about this weird rash I've got and what we're doing after summer.

'Got some interviews lined up in September,' he goes. 'Couple of internships and that, see what comes up.'

But I'm not really clocking what he's saying. My head's full of Alex - them shoulders, his eyes, that smile that gets me going something chronic. Proper buzzing for our date.

Starting to feel like my luck's changing, innit?

Dino

A week after that first call and I'm heading to meet Alex at the Odeon in Camden, bit paranoid I've overdone it with the aftershave. He's propped against the wall outside, ciggie hanging from those perfect lips, looking fit enough to cause a pile-up.

Me heart does this mental flip when he clocks me and grins. 'Alright, sunshine? Looking right tasty.'

I feel my face go red, but I laugh it off like the cool cucumber I'm not.

We get settled in our seats, knees knocking together, and I swear you could power the National Grid with whatever's crackling between us. Trying my best to be subtle about scratching this bastard rash but course he notices, don't he? But instead of doing one, he's well interested. Reckons the name sounds exotic when I explain it.

Batman Returns is playing but I ain't got a clue what's happening, too busy sneaking looks at Alex like some muppet. Can't help it though - he's gorgeous ain't he? All sharp jaw and them dark eyes.

Halfway through Batman saving Gotham for the millionth time, Alex's hand lands on my knee and I nearly jump out me skin. Heart's going mental while I inch my hand over to his thigh, trying to act casual. It's a miracle I don't spontaneously combust right there in me seat.

After the movie, we head back to his gaff. Soon as we're through the door, the stench of weed hits me hard, mixing with Wayne's World blaring from the telly. Alex's mates are sprawled on the sofa, passing a spliff about.

Alex pulls me to his room and Christ, it's something else. Massive tie-dyed sheet on the ceiling with this insane sun and moon thing going on. Free Mandela poster above his desk, and more books than the local library.

He catches me looking and comes up behind me. 'Cry, the Beloved Country,' he says, reaching past to grab a book. 'About apartheid and that. You can borrow it if you want.'

'Cheers,' I say, putting it aside for later. Hopefully much later, way things are going.

Then he's messing with the radio until he finds Pulse FM. The pirate radio tunes kick in, and suddenly the world shrinks to just me and him in this moment.

He grabs this wooden box from under his bed and sits cross-legged by the headboard, looking well fit and relaxed. His shirt rides up when he leans forward to skin up, and I get a right eyeful of his stomach. Dead distracting, that is.

'I'm well into the free party scene,' he says while he's rolling. 'If it weren't for uni, I'd be off with Spiral Tribe tomorrow. Join their convoy, live that traveller life.'

'For real?' I perch on the edge of his bed. 'You'd actually do it?'

'Course. Ultimate fuck you to the system, innit?' He grins. 'Better than getting some boring office job just because that's what everyone expects.'

He takes this massive drag, head tipped back. I'm trying not to stare at his throat, and failing miserably.

'Come here,' he says, patting the bed. 'Make yourself comfy. Won't bite.' Then he gives me this look that makes my insides go mental. 'Unless you want me to.'

I shuffle over next to him, our fingers touching when he passes the spliff. Even that tiny bit of contact has me buzzing. The Bouncer's playing now, bass thumping through the mattress, matching my crazy heartbeat.

Alex is looking at me, all intense now, like he's trying to work something out. He slides down onto his side and I copy him without thinking, because apparently my body's got ideas of its own.

'So,' he says, 'why law then?'

Bloody hell, right for the jugular. I try to think straight through the weed fog and the way he's looking at me.

'Dad's a barrister,' I say, shifting about. 'Just seemed the thing to do, didn't it? Follow in his footsteps and that.'

'Right,' he says slow, still giving me that look. 'But is it what you want?'

I take another drag, buying time. 'Never really thought about it if I'm honest. Can't all go chasing mad dreams, can we? Law's decent enough. Real job and all that.'

Even I can hear how weak that sounds.

Alex makes this noise in his throat, shuffling closer. Close enough I can feel his breath on my face. 'So you're just following the rules then?'

'Hook, line and sinker, mate.'

He stubs out the spliff careful-like, then he's propping himself up over me. 'Do us a favour yeah? Close your eyes a sec.'

'What you plotting?'

'Just trust me. Pretend you've got this magic genie, right? Saying you can do anything you want. Money's no problem. What's the first thing that pops in your head?'

It feels well intimate this, him hovering over me like that. But I do it anyway, let my eyes shut.

'Travel,' I say before I can stop myself. 'See everything, maybe even film it all? Show people back home stuff they'd never see otherwise. Different lives and that.'

I'm rambling now but can't seem to stop. It's like all these secret thoughts I never let myself think are just spilling out.

When I open my eyes, Alex looks... dunno. Soft? His hand comes up to my face, thumb stroking my jaw.

'Magic, that,' he says quiet. 'I can see it now, your own show on the Travel Channel. You'd be brilliant at it, I reckon. A total natural.'

I'm going red, can feel it. Then he's sliding between my legs and my brain pretty much stops working.

We end up chatting for ages - mad stuff about dreams and plans and what we'd do if the world was different. Can't stop looking at his mouth while he's talking, the way it moves. And his hands are everywhere, not that I'm complaining. Touching my face, my neck, like he's trying to learn me by heart or something.

The music changes at some point, goes all slow and dreamy. Alex makes this sound, then his hips sort of... shift against mine. Bloody hell.

'Perfect snogging music, this,' he says, and then his mouth's on my jaw, my neck, and Christ. I'm making these well embarrassing noises but I'm too far gone to care.

Then we're kissing and I'm gone. His mouth's doing things that should be illegal, stubble rough against my face. When his hands find their way under my shirt and his thumbs brush my nipples, I swear to god.

And I want to let it happen, want it bad. But Jack's still lurking in the back of my head like a bad penny. Plus this sodding rash is driving me mental, itching like nobody's business.

Takes everything I've got to pull back. Rest my forehead against his while we both sort out our breathing.

'Sorry,' I manage, voice all rough. 'Still a bit... you know. After someone. And this bleeding rash ain't exactly helping.'

Try to make it sound like I'm having a laugh but it comes out wrong. Alex just presses this soft kiss to my temple though, his hand warm on my face.

'Don't be daft,' he says right in my ear. 'We've got time, ain't we? I'm not going anywhere, sunshine.'

Something about that hits me right in the chest. Give him a quick kiss back, then tuck my face in his neck, breathing him in.

'Staying the night though, yeah?' he asks after a bit.

Like he even has to ask.

'Try and stop me,' I say, getting brave with my hands on his arse.

Next thing I know he's got me rolled over, spooned up behind me proper tight. One arm round my waist, other hand tangled with mine over my heart what won't calm down.

'Sweet dreams, gorgeous,' he whispers in my hair.

I drift off feeling safer than I have in ages.

I wake up to the sun in my face and the smell of coffee. Alex is already up, grinning like a nutter as he passes me a mug.

'Morning, Sunshine. Sleep alright?'

'Like a log,' I say, taking a big gulp. The coffee helps clear my head a bit - was pretty stoned last night.

We just chat shit while we drink our coffee, easy like.

When we're done, Alex grabs his jacket and we head out, walking to the station.

'Got Sunday dinner at my folks,' I tell him, my stomach rumbling just thinking about Mum's roast. 'She'll have gone all out with it, bet you anything.'

'Lucky git,' he says. 'I'm off to Wimbledon, seeing my uncle who's over from South Africa.'

It's different now, between us. Good different. But we're at the station before I know it.

Alex gives me one of them grins that makes my insides go wobbly. 'Top night, that was. Up for doing it again?'

'Fuck yeah,' I say, probably sounding too keen but I don't care.

Sort out next weekend quick as you like, and he gives me this filthy wink as our trains pull in. Watch him swagger off down the platform, can't wipe this daft grin off my face. Think I'm in trouble here - falling for him something chronic.

CALS

Train dumps me at Guildford and my brain's buzzing from the journey. Everything looks weird after being away, like someone's shifted it all a bit left. By the time I'm trudging up our path, gravel crunching under my feet, I'm about ready to face-plant right there in Mum's begonias. This flu's still hammering me something chronic.

'That you, Steven?' Dad bellows from the lounge, Sky News droning away like always.

'In the flesh!' I holler back, and here's Mum gliding out the kitchen looking dead posh in her white trousers and black top. She yanks me into one of them fierce hugs, all Chanel No5 and motherly concern. 'There he is! My favourite son.'

'Your only boy, more like,' I mumble into her shoulder, giving her a squeeze back.

Dad appears with his usual cheerful beam, clapping me hard enough to make me stumble. 'We were beginning to think you'd forgotten about us!'

The whole crew's complete when Claire comes tromping down the stairs, Jasper our daft golden retriever right on her heels as per. 'Well, well, the prodigal returns!' she goes, grinning while Jasper nearly knocks me over, soft git's that excited for a scratch behind the ears.

Mum's already herding me kitchen-ward, going full nurse mode. 'You look peaky, love. That rash any better?'

'Sort of,' I say, necking some juice straight from the carton till she clips me round the ear. 'Still itchy though.'

'Let's have a look then.' I lift my shirt, showing off the red patches which are doing my head in. 'Never seen anything like it.'

'Yeah, well. Keeps life interesting, don't it?' I try for a grin. 'Oh, and you'll never guess who I bumped into a few weekends back? That bloke I told you about.'

Her ears prick up at that. 'Tell me everything later,' she says, shoving a bowl of peas at me. 'For now, make yourself useful.'

We pile round the table in our usual spots - Dad at the head already eyeing up the Yorkshires, Claire in her spot by the window. I load my plate up - beef swimming in gravy, spuds, cabbage, and a Yorkshire pud big as my head. Sorted.

'Been to any banging raves, Stevie?' Claire asks, right cheeky mare.

I almost choke on my Yorkshire. 'What would you know about raves?'

'Claire went to one last weekend,' Mum drops it casual as you like, dishing out more spuds. 'Nearly gave your father a heart attack.'

Dad's fork hits his plate. 'I had no bloody say in it!'

'Hold up - you went raving at fifteen?'

'Went to Amnesia, didn't I!' Claire's sitting there dead proud of herself. 'Got right in with my mates. Thought I might see you there actually!'

'Christ,' I shake my head at Dad. 'World's gone proper crazy.'

Mum's trying not to laugh.

'Speaking of,' Dad starts, getting that look he gets when he's about to go off on one, 'all that festival nonsense in the papers...'

'Castlemorton?' I stuff in more beef. 'Just people having a laugh, weren't they?'

'Having a laugh!' He's going red now. 'Complete chaos! Police everywhere! Vandals and hippies, more like!'

'Just some travellers having a party,' I say through a mouthful. 'No one got hurt.'

Claire pipes up, 'That rave looked well good on the news!'

'Free party,' I correct her. 'And they're new age travellers, not hippies, Dad.'

But he's really going for it now. 'Call it what you want - nothing but trouble! People breaking in wherever they fancy, no respect for rules or safety!'

'Was brilliant actually,' I say just to wind him up. 'Best weekend of my life.'

'Public nuisance!' His fork's pointing my way now. 'And you, trespassing!'

'Public land, innit?'

He slaps the table. 'Thank god for that new law they're bringing in. Sort out all of those acid heads.'

'Yeah, because stopping people dancing to music is dead important,' I say. 'Real priority that.'

'We need these laws!' He's looking at me all serious now. 'Or it'll be more chaos like that gathering. Find yourself a real hobby, Steven.'

We're all cracking up at Dad going off on one. He looks round confused. 'It's not funny! Complete chaos... What's everyone laughing at?'

That just sets us off worse.

'Right,' Dad changes track quick. 'Your internship at Morton Turnbill. All set for September.'

'Need to get you a new suit,' Mum's already making plans.

'Thought I'd just rock up in my rave gear actually,' I say. 'Beatbox under my arm.'

Claire's howling now.

'Wouldn't put it past you,' Dad grumbles. 'Nothing surprises me anymore.'

'Oh hush,' Mum says. 'You still get surprised every time I make sticky toffee pudding.'

At the end of lunch, I shove the last spoonful of Mum's sticky toffee in my gob while they all carry on about suits and careers and proper jobs. Try not to scratch this bloody rash raw while my mind's somewhere else entirely - wondering when I'll see Alex again.

CROWNS

Nearly done with uni and Mum won't shut up about my 'bright future' but I couldn't care less. Can't think about anything except Alex, if I'm honest. Three weeks he's been turning my world upside down.

Squashed up against him on the tube now, getting proper light-headed off his aftershave. Cedar and smoke and just... him. We're off to some anti-apartheid rally - another one of his mad adventures, dragging me out of my comfort zone.

He leans in close, breath hot on my ear. 'You been keeping up with the madness in South Africa?' I shrug, not wanting to look like a complete muppet. Alex taps the graphic on his shirt. 'The ANC's fighting to give the land back to the people. That's what we're marching for today.'

We pile out at Charing Cross, dodging suits left and right. Alex is right there in the crowd, and I'm trying not to lose it every time we bump into each other. Haven't shagged yet, but Christ, the tension's doing my head in

Then we're off, joining the march. Never done anything like this before, but with Alex next to me, his voice raised with everyone else's... feels like I'm part of something bigger.

We end up in this proper dive after, squeezing round the last free table. Place reeks of cigarettes and spilled beer, but we're all still buzzing from the march. Dr Alban's 'Hello Africa' making the floor shake under our feet.

Alex drums his fingers on the manky table, eyes gone fierce. 'Africa... it's in my blood, you know? Been thinking about getting my master's out there someday. Proper immerse myself in the culture, the history, the struggle...'

The lager nearly comes back up my throat. 'You what? You're just gonna pop off to the savanna in the middle of all this apartheid bollocks?'

'Not the middle, Stevie.' His voice drops low, intense. 'The end. The racist wankers are losing their grip. The people are rising up, fighting for their freedom. I have to be there, see it with my own eyes.'

I'm sitting there like a right plank, trying to get my head round it. This mental gorgeous git who's turned everything upside down... and now he's talking about buggering off to the other side of the world.

'Blimey. That's... that's heavy. Well admirable, like.'

Flash of that wolfish grin. 'Well, I try.'

'So when's this big move happening then?' Words come out bitter as the dregs in my glass.

His head tips back laughing. 'Oh, not for ages yet. Just playing with the idea.'

Relief hits me like a rush. Time, then. Time to... what? Make him stay? Change his mind? Feels like I've got a brick in my gut just thinking about it.

'Besides.' He leans in close, voice gone smooth. 'Can't leave my best boy behind, can I? Who else is going to keep me out of trouble?'

My neck goes red hot and I duck my head. We go quiet for a bit, nursing our drinks while the pub carries on mental around us. Lager's working its magic now, making everything go soft round the edges.

Can feel him staring, burning holes in my skin. Don't dare look up - scared he'll see right through me, see how much the thought of losing him is doing my head in. But I shove it down, stick on a grin as I raise my glass. 'To changing the world, eh? One rally at a time.'

Alex clinks his glass against mine, smile gone all soft and sad. 'To changing the world. And to the poor sods who'll miss us when we do.'

We neck our drinks, that last mouthful proper manky. Alex slams his glass down, getting that look that means trouble.

'Right, fuck this depressing shit. Fancy that warehouse party in Brixton? Could do with a dance.'

'What, the one with all them lasers? Thought you said it was - how'd you put it? - "right wanky capitalist bullshit"?'

'Yeah well, that was before I got pissed, weren't it? Amazing what a few beers'll do to ya.'

He leans in close, beer on his breath. 'Plus I might need you to stop me falling on my arse later. Keep me from making a right tit of myself.'

Goes right through me when he gets this close. 'Oh yeah? Planning on getting proper messy then?'

His grin's pure mischief. 'Maybe. Stick around and find out, sunshine.'

Then he's up, grabbing his coat. 'Come on then. We ain't getting any younger.'

'After you, you crazy bastard.' Probably sound like a right soppy git. 'I'm right behind ya.'

Alex throws his arm round me as we push through the crowd, and bloody hell he's warm. I lean into him, trying to memorise how this feels. His heartbeat against my side, the way he keeps me steady. Could be all we get before real life kicks off again, before Africa or law firms or whatever comes next tears us apart.

Outside hits different after that sweaty pub - proper fresh, making my head spin less. Alex keeps his arm round me while we walk, and somehow we're moving at the same speed like we've been doing it for years. Past all these late-night kebab shops with their fluorescent lights making everything look well strange.

This warehouse party is mental - lasers cutting through smoke, bass so heavy you can feel it in your teeth. Alex is going mental, dancing like a proper nutter, and Christ he looks gorgeous. Can't take my eyes off him if I'm honest. When he's moving like that, all caught up in it, I forget there's anyone else even in the room.

&

We stumble into Alex's flat, bass still thumping in our bones. He's pulling me down the hall, giving me these looks that make my insides go wobbly.

In his room, I'm all over him straight away, can't help myself. He reaches past me to stick something on the record player, keeping one arm round my waist.

'Miles Davis,' he says against my neck. 'Real genius.'

I'm already half-gone as he starts moving us, his hands sliding under my shirt.

'Full of surprises, ain't ya?' I manage to get out. 'Thought you were just some raver bloke. But jazz? You're like them Russian dolls, one inside the other.'

'Just expanding your musical horizons, ain't I?' He's got his hands all over me now, sliding round to grab my arse through my jeans. Squeezing till I'm pushing back against him like I'm gagging for it. Which I am, if I'm honest.

'Educational, that what you're calling it?' My hands find his arse too, handful that it is.

He laughs against my neck, sending shivers right through me. 'Very educational.'

Then he's grinding against me, and Christ, I nearly lose it right there.

I'm on him before I know what I'm doing. Yanking at his shirt, getting my mouth on his jaw, his neck, anywhere I can reach. He makes this noise - half groan, half gasp - and tilts his head back, letting me at more of him. He tastes of smoke and beer and something else I can't place, something that's just Alex.

It's crazy how fast it all happens after that. Hands everywhere, clothes flying off, both of us desperate for it. My legs hit the bed just as the music goes all wild behind us.

We end up in a heap on his mattress, all sweaty skin and grabby hands. Can't think straight, not with Alex's mouth working its way down my body like that. When he bites my hip, I nearly come off the bed. Never knew I was into that sort of thing, but bloody hell.

Next thing I know he's sorting the condom, slicking us both up. Then he's pushing in slow, and fuck me, nothing's ever felt this good.

We're moving together now, really going for it. The bed's creaking something chronic, but I couldn't give a toss. Not with Alex hitting that spot over and over, making me see stars.

When it hits, it hits hard. Everything goes proper white for a second, like someone's stuck a lightning bolt right through me.

Afterwards, we're both knackered, trying to catch our breath. The jazz is still playing soft in the background, but all I can hear is my heart going wild in my chest.

And this is just the start, innit? Me and Alex. Whatever this is between us, it's only just kicking off.

Pink Calis

August melts into September and suddenly I'm round Alex's more than my own gaff. Days blur together - sprawled on his floor with books and records everywhere, hunting down dodgy kebabs at 3am, or losing ourselves in mental raves. Most times though, we're just tangled up in his bed for hours, learning every inch of each other like we're cramming for some exam we can't fail.

But last night I went and fucked it proper. Asked him to play it cool at today's picnic with Chris. No holding hands or nothing. Doing a right Jack on him, I was. Could tell he wasn't happy - his jaw went all tight, but he just pulled me close and kissed my neck. 'Anything for you, Sunshine,' he said, making me feel like the biggest tosser in London.

Now we're here, pretending to be just mates while everyone's sprawled about on blankets, necking warm beer and taking the piss out of Gemma's new bloke, Larry the Lad from Essex. Every time Alex's hand brushes mine by accident, my guts do this guilty flip.

Chris throws his arm round Alex. 'Reckon you've nicked my best mate spot, eh? Can't blame Stevie for spending all his time with you.' Alex's smile's not real. His eyes find mine over Chris's shoulder. 'Nah, you're still his best mate. Nothing to worry about.' I just sit there feeling like a right coward while Alex bleeds.

Tube ride home's dead quiet. Try to put my hand on his leg but he just shrugs it off, giving me this look that says it all.

Back at his, Alex slams on some Chili Peppers and face-plants on the bed. I'm stuck in the doorway like a right muppet, watching him fuming while Kiedis screams his head off in the background. Takes me ages to grow a pair and sit on the bed. Everything's wound so tight I reckon one wrong move and the whole world might snap.

But then Alex starts to soften up, bit by bit. By the time the record's nearly done, Kiedis must be working his voodoo magic because Alex has turned to me, his expression gone all soft.

'Come here,' he says quiet. I'm on him before he can change his mind, letting him pull me close.

'I'm sorry,' I manage, face pressed in his neck. 'Fuck, Alex, I'm so sorry...'

'Shh,' he says, running his fingers through my hair. 'I know. Just... it's shit, innit? Having to pretend we're nothing.'

Make some pathetic noise at that, holding him tighter.

'Stevie, I love you,' he says suddenly. 'You know that, yeah?'

'Love you too,' I choke out. 'More than anything.'

We just lie there for ages, wrapped up in each other. Should be perfect, this. Just me and him against the world. But there's this voice in my head, sounding like Dad, going on about what people might think. Keep telling myself I'll be braver tomorrow. Hold his hand in public, show everyone what he means to me. But tomorrow never seems to come, does it?

October hits like a freight train. One minute I'm off my face at raves with Alex, the next I'm wedged into a monkey suit for my internship at some posh law firm in Canary Wharf. Total head spin, that.

These glass towers are a different universe - all sharp suits and shiny shoes, making me feel like I'm playing dress-up in Dad's wardrobe. But three weeks in, it ain't all bad. My mentor Jeremy, this 40-year-old property lawyer with two kids and a mortgage, turns out to be a right laugh. He gets all my rave stories, trades them for tales about explosive nappies and projectile vomit.

Nights are different with Alex though. Like now, lying here starkers after a well good shag. Can't help staring at him - all muscle and dark skin, standing by the window. Still makes my heart go mental, every time I look at him.

'So...' he says casual. 'When you gonna introduce me to your folks then, eh?'

I damn near choke on my tongue. Wasn't expecting that one. 'Didn't know you wanted to meet them,' I mutter, suddenly fascinated by The Face magazine with the Stone Roses on the cover.

Alex just snorts, fixing me with one of his intense stares. 'Course I do, you daftie. They're your family. Wanna know where you get all your...' He waves a hand at me, 'Complications from.'

I pick at the corner of a page, keeping my eyes down. 'Well... we could do lunch with my mum, I suppose. She's been on at me to meet the 'nice young man.' I shake my head. 'God help us both, eh?'

Alex breaks into one of those grins that makes my insides flip. 'Brilliant! Just leave your mum to me. I'll have her oven baking for our wedding before the breadbasket hits the table.'

'You're a right cocky bastard, you know that?' I chuck a pillow at his smug face, but the twat just catches it one-handed like a bloody superhero.

'Ah, but you love it,' he winks, tossing it back. 'Keeps you nicely grounded, dunnit?'

I roll my eyes to hide my smirk, but then his face goes all serious, brows proper furrowed up. 'What about your dad, then? When do I get to meet him?'

My stomach drops like I've missed a step. 'It's... complicated,' I mumble, can't even look at him.

'You ever gonna tell him you like blokes too?'

I flinch, whole body going tight. 'Nah, can't see that going over too well. My old man's not exactly Mr. Progressive.'

Alex lets out this heavy sigh. 'So, I'd just be your 'mate' then, if I met him? Not your boyfriend?'

I nod, feeling like right shit.

'But what if things get proper serious with us? You gonna tell him the truth then, or what?'

I shrug, feeling well pathetic. 'Dunno... it won't be easy, that's for sure...'

'Why not?' His eyes are burning into me. 'You ashamed of me?'

'Course not!' I protest, but it comes out weak as piss.

'Then what is it, Sunshine? What's the bloody problem?'

I grab my ciggies, light one up just to have something to do with my hands, blow out the smoke. 'He'd just... be proper disappointed, wouldn't he? That I'm not the son he wanted.'

Alex' face goes sharp. 'Because of his expectations? Or because you fancy blokes?'

Let that one sink in, everything gone quiet...

'Honestly? Both, probably.'

Silence stretches out between us, making it hard to breathe.

'What's brought all this on?' I ask finally.

Alex comes over from the window, drops down next to me with a sigh. 'It's about us having a future, innit? Whether we've even got one if you can't be straight up with people who matter. Your best mate thinks you're some mega hetero, your dad's got no clue you swing both ways... when you gonna tell 'em the truth?'

I curl in on myself. 'Dunno... someday, I suppose. Just... not yet, alright?'

'Steve, it's not just about me and you!' he proper erupts. 'It's about being who you are! So what if you like blokes too? It's your life, Sunshine! Not your dad's, not anyone else's!'

His words hit me dead hard. I push for a subject change, anything to distract. 'If we so serious then can we start by ditching the condoms already?'

Alex groans. 'Not 'til we both get tested. I go every six months; you need to do the same.'

I roll my eyes dramatically. 'Seriously? We've been at it for months and neither of us is poorly, yeah?'

'You know HIV doesn't work like that,' he cuts back, voice gone low and serious. 'Just one tiny mistake can bugger both of our lives totally.'

He yanks me close, them dark eyes intense. 'This stuff hits different when it gets personal, yeah?' He looks away for a sec, then: 'My uncle Jeffrey back in South Africa... he's HIV positive, full blown AIDS now actually.'

My jaw drops. 'Bloody hell, Alex...'

'He's been ill a good while now.' Alex's voice goes quiet. 'Faithful bloke, squeaky clean. His partner of five years passed it on to him.'

I stub out my smoke, sliding closer. 'They still together then?'

'Nah. The bloke died last year.' Alex looks away, his voice going flat. 'HIV's rife over there, cutting through everyone gay or straight.'

'Shit, that's hardcore,' I mutter, my guts churning uneasily. 'Don't know what to say...'

'So, let's just get tested, alright?' His voice takes on a pleading edge. 'Soon as we've got the all clear, I'm ditching these johnnies for good.'

I look at him for a minute, then grab him for a proper kiss, one that says everything I can't. 'Alright, you win. If getting tested means I get to have you raw, I'll do whatever it takes.'

'Brilliant! I'll come with you to the clinic. There's one down Soho way.'

'Don't need a chaperone,' I shoot back cheekily. 'Let me handle this one on my own. Like I said, anything for a condom-free reunion with the Crown Jewels.'

He laughs, the tension finally breaking as he pulls me close. 'Christ, you're impossible sometimes. You know that, don't you?'

I grin back, waggling my eyebrows. 'Yeah, but you love me for it.'

'God help me,' he sighs, shaking his head. 'I really do.'

The next few days, it's like that game counting yellow cars on long trips. Only instead of motors, it's HIV ads. They're everywhere I look - posters, billboards, telly spots, all banging on about using condoms and getting tested.

I'm lounging on the sofa one night, trying to zone out in front of MTV. And this advert comes on, all moody and soft-focus, with a couple going at it hammer and tongs. Looks right romantic, until the bloke pulls out a gun and blows the bird's head clean off. Then it cuts to this plain white screen with 'SEX + HIV' plastered all over it in big black letters. Proper grim, put me off my crisps, that did.

So, I flip to the radio, hoping for some smooth tunes to take my mind off this heavy shit. But of course, the universe has other ideas.

First thing I hear is some bloke called Steve - already hitting too close to home - droning on about a holiday romance gone tits up.

'Thought it was just a bit of fun in the sun, din't I?' he's saying, voice all dramatic. 'But now look at me - Bob's your uncle and I've got HIV!'

I switch it off sharp, that little voice in my head whispering, 'That could be you, mate.'

Can't get Alex's words out of my head now. His uncle Jeffrey... keep thinking about how quick it can all go wrong. One mistake, that's all it takes.

Reckon I need to stop being such a pussy about this testing business.

New Yorkers

A week later, I'm on the Tube to the clinic Alex told me about, trying to look anywhere but at the people around me. Make the mistake of glancing up and there's this massive Benetton ad over some old geezer's head. He shifts and I clock the full image - a bare arse with 'HIV POSITIVE' tattooed across it. Proper grim, that.

By the time we pull into Warren Street, I'm half-tempted to stay put and let it whisk me off to the other end of the line. Far as I can get from this bloody mess.

But I can't do that, can I? Short walk to the clinic from the station, but feels like I'm running a bleeding marathon. Heart going mental with each step.

And then I'm there. Standing outside this nondescript little redbrick building, the kind you'd walk past without clocking. I stare at the 'Alex Pringle House' sign - had to be bloody 'Alex' didn't it? Universe having a proper laugh. The words go all wobbly and I swear I'm gonna chuck up right there on the pavement.

Hand's shaking as I reach for the door, about a million doubts doing my head in.

What if I've got it? What do I do then? How do I tell Alex? My mum?

This little voice in my head goes all reasonable, saying it's a long shot. Only been with a handful of blokes, and we've always been safe. Well... mostly.

'Cept for Jack, of course. Jack with his laddish grin and handsome cock. Jack who'd shag anything with a pulse, any minute of the day... Oh god.

All those nights I let him rail me raw, too off my face on lust to insist on a johnny...

I'm an idiot. A grade A, deluxe with all the trimmings, absolute moron.

I take a deep breath of that chilly air, clench my jaw hard, and shove through the door before I can lose my bottle completely.

Inside it's just wooden chairs and a sad bunch of flowers on the desk, like any other clinic really.

The receptionist smiles as I stumble in. 'Alright, love?' she asks, handing over a clipboard. 'Just fill these out and we'll get you sorted.'

I take the clipboard with a shaking hand, mumbling 'cheers' before scuttling off to the waiting room. I slump into one of the chairs in the corner and give the place a quick once-over. There's some fancy suit sitting ramrod straight, knuckles white on the arms of the chair. A scruffy group huddled together, whispering with wide, solemn eyes. Some bloke in an oversized red hoodie, face buried in a beat-up paperback. And an Adidas lad in the corner, jaw working frantically on a wad of gum.

Duck my head over the paperwork, trying to focus. Name, date of birth, contact details... all easy enough till I hit 'Reason for Visit'. That little box next to 'HIV Test' staring up at me like it's daring me to tick it. Do it quick and rough, like ripping off a plaster, then shove the clipboard back without looking at the receptionist.

Slump back in my chair, trying to zone out. Count the ceiling tiles, anything to keep my brain from going mental about why I'm here. That Adidas lad's still going at his gum like it's done him wrong, each snap making me jump in the quiet. Suit bloke's rustling through some manky old Time Out, pages proper crispy with age.

Then everything goes to hell in a handcart.

The door to the exam rooms swings open and this bloke comes stumbling out, face white as anything. Some nurse is chasing after him, trying to calm him down, but he's having none of it. He's completely lost it - crying like a kid, knocking stuff over as he legs it for the door.

When it slams behind him, everyone just sits there frozen.

You could hear a pin drop, I swear.

I look round at the others and we've all got that same thought written on our faces - that could be us in five minutes. Getting told we're dying, just like that.

I can't bear it a second longer. So, I mutter some half-arsed excuse, and stumble out the way I came in. I burst through the doors, gasping for air. Christ... what a total mind-fuck. What an absolute, gold-plated clusterfuck of a day.

I can see my breath pluming in the air in front of me now, my heart still rabbiting away in my chest like it's trying to bust free. I'm shivering, I realise. Shaking - and it's not just from the chill.

'Sod this,' I mutter, hands shaking as I light up. Reckon me and Alex will have to stick with johnnies after all.

I stamp out my ciggie and leg it to the Tube station like the devil's after me.

Yin Yang

The next few days, I try my best to forget the whole bloody circus. Focus on work, hit the pub with Chris, even tidy my flat like some functioning adult - anything to keep my mind off what a massive chicken I've been.

But the thing about running away from your problems? They've got this nasty habit of catching up with you eventually, usually when you're least expecting it. Like now, sprawled on Alex's bed with take-away curry going cold between us, his voice casual as anything: 'So, when're your test results due?' he asks.

My heart stops. 'Oh... didn't go actually.'

Can feel him looking at me.

'Why not, Sunshine? Thought we agreed it was important.'

I shrug. 'Changed my mind. Don't reckon it's necessary.'

Alex sits up. 'Something you're worried about? Is that why?'

'Look, the johnnies are fine,' I snap. 'Can we just drop it?'

Alex sighs but lets it go. We're just sitting there in this awkward silence when he shifts about.

'Got news,' he says.

My gut goes tight. Fuck it, what else could go tits up now?

'Remember me talking about maybe doing my Master's in South Africa?'

'Yeah?'

'Dad's sorted a recce for me to check out this uni in Durban. See if it's any good.'

Feel like the floor's disappeared. 'When?'

'Two weeks.'

'How long you going for?'

'Three months, give or take.'

Three months. Christ. We've only been together five months and now he's buggering off for three?

'Three months,' I say, voice gone weird.

'Not that long, Stevie,' Alex tries, but I can tell he's not sure either. 'Be back before you know it.'

I just stare at him. He can't be serious. Can't just piss off to the other side of the world after everything.

'And how long's this master's thing?' I force out.

He won't look at me now.

'Couple years, probably. But dunno if I'll stay that long. Nothing's set.'

'What about us then?' Hate how pathetic I sound. 'What happens while you're off finding yourself in Durban?'

Alex makes this noise and pulls me against him, holding on proper tight. 'Back before you know it,' he says into my hair. 'Not goodbye, just... a pause. That's all.'

He pulls back, hands on my face, wiping away tears I didn't even know were there. Well embarrassing.

'You're it for me,' he says, looking at me like he means it. 'You're my forever, Steve Bishopston. No amount of distance is gonna change that. Alright?'

I turn my face into his hand, breathing him in.

'Alright,' I manage. 'Alright, I believe you.'

And I do, that's the mental thing. Even with him about to disappear halfway round the world, I believe in us. Whatever the hell this is.

Third pint in at the King's Head with Gemma and Chris, and I'm still not pissed enough. Everything feels proper strange tonight - like I'm watching it all through someone else's eyes. Keep zoning out, my head stuck 6,000 miles away in bloody Durban.

Look up to find them both staring at me. Shit. Must be doing a rubbish job of playing it cool.

'What?' I mumble through a mouthful of cheese and onion.

Gemma leans over. 'You alright, Stevie? Gone dead quiet on us.'

'Yeah, mate,' Chris chips in. 'You're knocking those pints back like they're going out of fashion. Work doing your head in?

It's all there, right on the tip of my tongue - Alex, Durban, this whole mess. But I can't, can I? Not here. Not now. So I wash it down with another gulp of lager instead.

'Nah,' I say, draining my glass. 'All good.' Like I'm not counting down the days till the bloke I love buggers off to another continent. 'Just fucking perfect.'

Go to stand for another round, but Chris beats me to it, claps my shoulder. 'My shout, mate.' Gives me this worried look before heading to the bar.

Gemma's still eyeing me up like I've gone mental.

'What?' I shove another handful of crisps in my gob.

'What's eating you then?'

Crumble the empty crisp packet in my hands. 'Alex is fucking off to South Africa to do his masters in the sunshine, is all.'

'What? When's this happening?'

'Well, no decision yet. Going off with his dad in ten days to scope the place out while I sit here like a bloody war bride hoping he comes back.'

'Oh right. So just a trip then?'

Shake my head. 'Nah, Gems. I can feel it - this isn't good.'

'Bloody hell, you're dead gone on him, ain't you?'

I nod, feeling like a right muppet. 'Like you and Larry,' I try for a smile.

She throws her head back laughing. 'Not bloody likely. You're in way deeper than me and Larry. It's well obvious when you bang on about him.'

Glance towards the bar where Chris is almost at the front. 'You think Chris suspects?'

'So what if he does?' Gemma sparks up, passes me a smoke before lighting her own. 'About time you told him anyway.'

'He wouldn't understand,' I mumble.

She rolls her eyes. 'That's bollocks and you know it. He's your best mate, innit? Give him some credit. Besides, it's not like he's the one shagging Alex, is he?'

'I'm going to miss him,' I say quiet, feeling pathetic.

She squeezes my knee. 'I know you will. Just let him go. You know what they say - set someone free, and if they love you, they come back. And all that bollocks,'

I laugh as Chris appears with three pints balanced like some circus act.

Try to focus on Chris's mad stories about work, but my head's stuck on that calendar racing towards Alex's recce. Ten days. Might as well be ten minutes.

Each day's ticking by like a bloody time bomb. Going through the motions at work like some robot with dodgy wiring. Can't focus on the papers in front of me - might as well be reading Chinese for all I'm taking in. Everyone's nattering on around me but it's just noise. My head's stuck on Alex, on Durban, on this massive black hole opening up right in front of us. Nearly drowned my Weetabix in orange juice the other morning. Then got myself so turned around I ended up on some bus to nowhere, surrounded by faces I'd never clapped eyes on before. Everything's gone mental. Like someone's come along and kicked the world sideways, and I'm the only mug who's noticed.

I'm trying though. Dragging us out to whatever rave we can find, shagging till we're both raw, holding on tight enough to leave bruises.

Keep telling myself it'll be fine and dandy. That he'll get out there and realise Africa ain't all that. That good old Blighty's got more going for it - that I've got more going for it. But there's this voice in my head that won't shut up, whispering that I'm absolutely kidding myself.

Wagon Wheels

Night before Alex leaves, we're tangled up in his bed, my head on his chest, listening to his heart going. Keep wanting to say something - Don't go. Stay here. Stay with me.

But I can't do it, can I? Can't ask him to stay, to give up this chance. 'Cause I love the daft sod, don't I? And isn't that what love's supposed to be? Wanting what's best for your other half, even if it feels like your guts are being ripped out through your throat?

So I just hold on tighter, like if I squeeze hard enough he can't leave.

'You excited?' I manage to get out.

Alex runs his fingers through my hair. 'Yeah, bit nervous though.'

I look up at him. 'What, the great Alex Khumalo, nervous? Pull the other one.'

He laughs, but it's not real.

'You'll be fine,' I say, throat gone tight. 'Probably won't want to come back once you've seen them beaches.'

His arms go tight round me. 'Don't be daft. Nothing could keep me away from you, Stevie.'

I want to believe him, I really do.

We don't talk much after that. Instead, we let our bodies do the talking. It's different this time - slower, more desperate like.

'I love you,' I whisper against his skin, over and over.

'I love you, I love you, I love you.'

'Love you too, Stevie,' he murmurs back. 'Always.'

Don't sleep a wink. Just lie there watching shadows crawl across his ceiling, trying to burn every little detail into my brain - the soft whistle of his breath, the solid warmth of him pressed against my side, the faint thud of his heart under my palm. Keep thinking if I just stay awake, morning won't come. Proper childish, that.

But time's a right bastard, and soon enough there's grey light coming through his curtains. Morning's grim as anything - drizzle and grey skies like London knows what's happening.

Watch him pack with my stomach in knots, trying to memorise everything - the way he moves, that little frown he gets when he's thinking. Keep telling myself it's just three months, but it feels like forever.

His parents turn up early, and they're so nice it makes everything worse. All hugs and asking after work like everything's normal. His dad's practically bouncing about showing his son their homeland. And Alex... he's buzzing with it. Like he's finally found where he belongs. About as far from me as you can get.

Next thing I know, we're on the pavement and the wind's going right through my jacket. His dad's gets the car running, steam coming off it in the cold, while his mum fusses with his collar one last time. Street's dead quiet except for the rain and some dog kicking off nearby. Even the pigeons look miserable, huddled up like they know something's ending.

Alex pulls me close, holding on tight like he's trying to remember how I feel. I breathe him in - his cologne, that warm smell that's just him. Can't stop grabbing at his jumper.

'Don't want you to go,' comes out before I can stop it.

He just smiles, all sad, and puts his forehead against mine. 'Be back before you know it,' he says quiet. 'This ain't goodbye, alright? Just... see you later.'

Then he's kissing me, gentle like, right here on the street where anyone could see. Tastes of toothpaste and coffee and Alex.

But he's pulling away, slipping through my fingers. Watching him walk to the car feels like someone's kicking my chest in.

He looks back at me before he gets in. 'Love you, Sunshine,' he says, wind nearly nicking his words. 'No matter what happens, where I end up... that won't change, alright? Need you to know that.'

I just nod, scared I'll truly lose it if I open my mouth.

Door slams and I swear I feel it in my bones.

Stand there till the car's gone. Till there's nothing but an empty street and grey sky. Leg it then, hands in pockets, hood up 'cause it's fucking freezing. Can't look back though. If I do, reckon I'll proper crumble right here on the spot. A ginger pile of dust at that.

Get home and fall apart soon as I'm through the door. End up under the covers fully dressed, hiding like a kid. But you can't hide from this, can you? This massive Alex-shaped hole that's been ripped right out of me.

Lie there for ages, time gone weird. Keep drifting off and waking up with my face wet from tears I don't remember crying.

GHOSTS

True to his word, Alex rings me up the day after he touches down. Been staring at the phone like a right muppet when it finally starts jangling.

'Alright?' I manage, voice gone all weird.

'Stevie!' Alex sounds warm as ever even through all that crackling. 'You good?'

I shut my eyes, head back against the wall. 'Yeah, you know. London's still standing.'

He laughs and it hits me right in the gut. 'Thank god for that. Wouldn't want you getting bored without me.'

There's this pause, heavy with all the stuff we're not saying. Then he's off like a rocket, going on about his flight and some mental sunset that greeted him. Valley all lit up like a firework show, oranges and pinks and whatnot.

I'm making the right noises, ain't I? All 'sounds amazing' and that. But my head's somewhere else. Can't stop thinking about him out there while I'm stuck here in the pissing rain.

Keep telling myself to be happy for him. Trying to shut up that voice saying he's leaving me behind. That maybe... he won't come back.

Days after that first call, I'm walking round like I've been twatted in the head. Like someone's turned the world's volume down. Going through the motions at work, putting on a face for the lads, but really I'm just counting hours till I can crawl into bed and feel sorry for myself.

Alex rings every few days, but it's all short and crackly, eating up phone credit like nobody's business. We try to keep up with little chats but it's not the same, is it? Miss him like I've lost a limb or something. Going mental trying to find stuff to do, anything to stop thinking about him every five minutes.

Two weeks turns into three, then four. Calls get shorter, static getting worse between us. Still get that jump in my chest when the phone rings, but it's never enough - just bits of his voice, snippets of his new life that I'm not part of anymore.

Then this distraction comes clicking in on heels. I'm at my desk, exactly four weeks and three days into Alex being gone (not that I'm counting, like), when I clock the new temp. Proper stunner with these mental ginger curls everywhere. Can't help shifting about in my chair, trying to be subtle but she catches me looking and gives me this cheeky grin. Go red as anything and stare at my papers like they're the most interesting thing in the world. But there it is - something to think about besides Alex, even if it makes me feel like a right bastard.

Break time, I follow her casual as you like to the kitchen. Up close, she's even prettier, all freckles scattered across her nose and this smile that does funny things to my guts.

'Just fancied a cuppa,' I mumble, cheeks flaring when I realise I've grabbed Jeremy's naff '#1 Dad' mug instead of my own.

She bursts out laughing.

'Milk?' she offers.

'Brilliant, ta.' I try to play it cool. 'I'm Steve, by the way.'

'Lucy,' she replies with a smile. 'Bit different from all these old fogeys round here, ain't we?'

'Got that right,' I grin, chuffed she's chatting back. 'Just started here, yeah?' I wince at stating the bleeding obvious.

But Lucy just nods, unfazed. 'Yep, saving up for a big trip. You know, get the travel bug out of my system before life comes a-calling.' Her accent is pure Brummie, vowels all stretched out like toffee.

'From Birmingham way yourself, then?' I ask eagerly.

'Dudley born and raised!' she beams. 'Just outside Wolverhampton. You been before?'

'Once or twice, usually just passing through to get my rave on, ya know?' I confess with a cheeky wink.

Her eyes light up. 'No way, you're into the rave scene too?' She practically bounces with excitement. 'This is too good!'

I nod, buzzing on her enthusiasm. 'Is there anything better than losing yourself in the music? That feeling when the bass drops and the whole crowd just-' I mime an explosion with my hands.

'Yes! It's pure magic!' She's bouncing now, making it hard to keep my eyes up where they should be. 'London treating you well, then?' I ask, trying to keep my mind out the gutter.

'It's brilliant! I've wanted to live here forever.' Her smile's like sunshine after rain.

We natter on, me finding out she's living with mates in Wimbledon while I admit to my posh boy roots out in Surrey. 'Ah, knew you had to be a Surrey lad with that accent!' She winks, and my stomach does this weird flippy thing.

She goes all quiet when she spots Jeremy giving us the evil eye for skiving off. With a last grin, she heads back to her desk, and I try not to watch her go. Bloody hell, even just looking feels like I'm doing Alex dirty.

Jeremy shoots me this look as I slink back to my desk. 'Flirting on company time? With my mug, no less?' He raises one fuzzy eyebrow. 'Nice girl, though. Quite the looker for a young buck like you.'

'That she is, Jezza. That she is.' I slide his mug back, my head spinning with ginger curls and that Brummie accent while my guts churn with guilt.

McDonalds

Work ain't total shit with Lucy around. We end up by the photocopier most days, having a proper laugh. Makes missing Alex sting a bit less, if I'm being honest.

Then it all goes mental when Alex rings one night, sounding broken. His uncle's taken a turn, doctors saying he's only got weeks left.

'Fuck, Alex... I'm so sorry,' I manage, throat gone tight. 'Wish I could be there with you, do something...'

'You are helping, Sunshine,' he goes all quiet. 'Just hearing your voice... it's everything.'

We chat a bit more, him telling me about the family all crowded round the hospital bed, place stinking of antiseptic, death hanging about like a bad smell. Proper grim.

Next day at work I'm a right state. Lucy spots it straight off, corners me by the coffee machine.

'You look like death warmed up,' she says, pushing a chocolate digestive at me. 'Want to talk about it?'

I just shake my head, dunking my biscuit till it goes soggy. Can't exactly go telling her about my boyfriend's uncle dying in South Africa, can I? Plus something about her worried face just makes me feel like more of a tosser.

Alex rings again by week three - different from last time, all excited chat and going on about everything. Can't shut him up about this beach him and his cousins found, going on about the boiling sand and these weird fruits they're eating. Tells me about some mental storm coming in off the Indian ocean. I shut my eyes, let his words wash over me. For a minute it's like he's right here, all that distance just... gone.

Then the line starts going mental with static. 'Storm's coming,' he goes. 'Signal's going. Call you in a few days, yeah? Miss you, Sunshine.'

'Miss you too,' I say, but he's already gone.

Back at work, Lucy's become my shadow. During a rare lull, we're holed up in our usual spot by the printer, and I try to suss out her deal, relationship-wise.

'You ever been proper mad for someone?' I ask. 'All that hearts and flowers bollocks?'

She pulls a face. 'Nah, not my thing. Too much world to see before settling down.'

'But don't you want someone to share it with?'

She gives me this look that makes my insides go funny.

'Maybe one day. But I'm only 22. No point getting tied down now.' She leans in closer, and Christ, she smells amazing. 'Besides, why have bangers and mash when you can try the whole menu?'

Nearly choke laughing, going red as anything. 'Fair point.'

'Damn right,' she grins, shooting me a wink. 'Stick with me, Surrey Boy. I'll keep life plenty interesting.'

I know it's all just harmless fun, a flirty little game to pass the time. But can't help the way my stomach flips when she talks like that, nothing to do with the stuffy office air making me dizzy. It's playing with fire, I know it is - especially when I find excuses to brush up against her, to let the touches linger a few seconds too long to be strictly friendly.

But god help me, I just can't seem to stop myself.

Two weeks pass in radio silence from Alex. Each day without a word twists the knife a little deeper. Even my old standbys can't touch it -

been to three raves and they're all dead flat without him. Lucy keeps inviting me out for drinks after work, but I make excuses. Can't trust myself around her when I'm feeling this raw, can I?

Then finally, fucking finally, he rings me. But there's something off in his voice, like he's not properly there. Half arsing the chat while his head's somewhere else, probably on them sunny South African beaches. It's worse than when he wasn't calling at all, if I'm honest. At least then I could tell myself he was just busy with family and playing tourist. But now, hearing him give these vague answers, drifting off mid-sentence... it's like he's fading away, getting further and further out of reach.

I hang up feeling like shit. Can't face my empty flat after that, so I head into work early next morning, trying to keep myself busy. That's when Lucy catches me by the coffee machine, all bright smiles and worried looks.

'Fancy a drink after work?' she asks. 'Look like you could use one.'

And god help me, but I do. I really fucking do.

Flatliners

After that last half-arsed call from Alex, I start saying yes to Lucy's after-work drinks. Tell myself it's just mate stuff, nothing dodgy. But the way she looks at me over her glass, all heat and promise... it's getting harder to keep my guard up.

December rolls in like a right bastard, bringing nearly two months' worth of Alex-shaped emptiness and one office Christmas do. Perfect excuse to drown my sorrows in piss-poor mulled wine and maybe have a cheeky flirt with that fit redhead. The pub's rammed with our lot, all proper merry. Tinsel and fairy lights plastered everywhere, George Michael wailing about broken hearts under all the racket.

I'm watching the bar where Lucy's perched in this wild red dress, chatting to Janet. She spots me looking and grins, pats the stool next to her. I'm over there quick as you like, trying to ignore my stomach doing backflips as I sit down, our knees bumping.

'Oi oi, Surrey Boy,' she says. 'Didn't think you'd leave your cave.'

I catch the barman's eye for a pint. 'Your company was too tempting, wasn't it?'

Lucy snorts into her fancy cocktail. 'Surprised you got your eyes off my tits long enough to notice.'

'I'm wounded!' Slap my chest, playing it up. 'I'm a true gentleman, I'll have you know.'

'That right?' She leans in closer, voice gone all low. 'Not thinking about getting me naked then?'

Go bright red but try to cover it. Must be the drink making her more forward than usual. Not that I'm complaining.

'Guilty,' I say. 'Though that dress is doing half the work.'

Janet takes the hint and toddles off with this obvious wink. 'Leave you two to it!'

'Cheers, Jan!' Lucy waves her off before turning back to me. 'So go on then, spill - what's a posh boy like you doing slumming it with us common folk tonight?'

I snort into my lager, fiddling with a soggy beer mat. 'Not half as posh as all that, love. Surrey or no, I'm just another pleb pushing papers, same as the lot of you.' I shrug, taking a long swig.

'Mmm, dunno about that. That accent could slice bread - bet it gets you far with the birds, eh?' Her eyes are all mischief now, her smile sharper than a knife. Pure dangerous, that.

'Hasn't helped me pull you yet though, has it? Must be losing my touch.' I fire back, matching her smirk for smirk.

'Who says it hasn't?' She gives me this proper intense look, then her hand's on my knee under the bar. Can't mistake what that means.

For one mad second, everything just stops - the pub noise, the crowd, even my heart hammering away. Just Lucy's lips right there, and her eyes fixed on mine like she's trying to read my mind or something. I lean in, going proper mental inside. Close enough to see all them freckles on her nose. Then some prat lets out this massive laugh, snapping us both back.

Lucy blinks like she's waking up, sliding off her stool quick as you like. 'That's my cue to powder my nose. To be continued, Surrey...'

And then she's off, throwing these looks over her shoulder, and I'm just sat there like a right muppet, brain still catching up.

Takes me ages to notice Janet hovering at my elbow, looking dead pleased with herself. 'Well, well, well... if I didn't know better, I'd say our Lucy's got it bad for you, young man.' She's practically buzzing with new gossip.

That does it. Suddenly can't stand the packed pub, all that happy noise doing my head in. Alex's face pops into my head, and I feel proper shit.

Need to get out. Mumble some excuse about being knackered, down my pint and leg it, pushing through the crowd till the cold air hits me.

Spend the next week avoiding Lucy at work and trying not to think about what almost happened.

Next thing I know, it's bloody New Year's Eve, and I'm stuck at some overcrowded house party at Gemma's new gaff, feeling about as festive as a wet weekend in Skegness.

It's the same old song and dance - 'Auld Lang Syne' crackling out of knackered speakers like a dying cat, the floors already tacky with spilt beer and glitter, everyone well on their way to smashed by half nine. Gemma and Larry, are already wrapped around each other like octopi, snogging like the world's about to end right there in the middle of the lounge. I do my level best to ignore them, glugging cheap fizz straight from the bottle and keeping to myself in the kitchen like some sad Billy No-Mates.

Countdown kicks off, everyone steaming and shouting numbers. Can't hack it anymore - slip out the back before they hit one. Let them have their snogs and their soppy promises. I'm done.

Get home alone, head swimming with booze and self-pity. Spark up a spliff on the sofa, let the telly's bright colours and canned laughter wash over me. Proper shit substitute for the real thing though, innit?

Then the phone goes, making me nearly wet myself. Heart's going mental as I grab it - only one person it could be at this time.

'...Alex?' Comes out all croaky.

'Stevie.' His voice hits me right in the chest. 'Happy New Year, Sunshine.'

'Yeah... Happy New Year. You okay?'

The pause goes on so long I think we've been cut off.

'It's... it's not what I thought, Stevie.'

He tells me about the racism - all them looks and whispers everywhere he goes. How everything moves forward an inch then gets knocked back a mile. I'm making these pathetic little noises, feeling useless trying to help from the other side of the world.

'So...' Have to force it out, 'you not staying then?'

Static crackles between us before he lets out this heavy sigh. 'Need to check the uni first, get a proper feel. But being here... doing my head in, if I'm honest.'

'But you'll come back?' Sound like a right desperate twat. 'Promise?'

'Course I will, Sunshine. You're my home, ain't you? Don't matter where I end up... you're always gonna be my home.'

Sit there holding the dead phone, his words going round and round my head. Want to believe him so bad. But there's this voice in my head saying it's all bollocks. Try to picture his face and it's going fuzzy already, like trying to remember last night's dream.

Well, ain't that just fucking perfect?

Saturday 6 March

Doors open 6pm

SUNSHINE SESSIONS 1993

Paul Oakenfold
Pete Tong
Danny Rampling
Jeremy Healy
Sasha
Dave Angel
Justin Robertson
Nancy Noise
DJ SS

Bagleys Film Studios
York Way
Kings Cross
London
N1

License now granted

Dolphin

January's crawling by like torture, and that New Year's call from Alex is still doing my head in. Shuffling into work after another weekend of feeling sorry for myself, when Lucy bounces over, all curls and smiles, asking if I fancy a brew. Mental how quick everything brightens up - like someone's flicked a switch. Jump up to join her, trying not to look too keen. She's telling me about her mad night out while we walk to the break room, all about downing vodka shots and passing out at her mate's gaff. The old lot at their desks are giving us right dirty looks, probably shocked by all the talk about getting trollied. But I'm just grinning away, loving every minute of her stories, getting proper caught up in it all. When she asks what I got up to at the weekend, I make up some rubbish about a banging night out. Better than telling her I spent it moping about, staring at the phone waiting for Alex to ring.

&

Me and Lucy start having this thing going on as the days tick by. Catching each other's eye across the office, hands touching when we pass in the corridor, all that. Well electric, it is.

Thursday comes round and we sneak out for a smoke, huddling together under the shelter. February wind's freezing through my bones, making Lucy shuffle closer. Her perfume hits me - something sweet that goes straight to my head.

'Thailand first,' she tells me, grinning as she gets her lighter going. 'Got mates out there, gonna do a bit of island hopping and see where the wind takes me.'

'And after that?' I ask, trying not to stare while she takes a drag.

'Dunno, do I? That's half the fun!' She laughs, bumping my shoulder. Can feel it even through my jacket.

I shake my head, proper jealous. 'Wish I could do something like that. Just swan off into the sunset.'

'Why don't you?' Lucy stares me down fierce. Wind's whipping her curls about, and I catch myself almost reaching out to fix them. Something shifts in her face when she spots it, going all soft round the edges.

But before my head can get too carried away, Lucy's off on one about these Tribal Gathering tickets she's scored.

'You're coming, yeah?' She's got this look, like she won't take no for an answer. 'Gonna be absolutely wicked. It is. Can't miss it!'

And I'm nodding before I even think about it, couldn't say no if I tried. 'Yeah, 'course I'm coming. Wouldn't miss it for the world, would I?'

She just grins at me, and my stomach does this weird flip thing.

Rest of the day's just me and Lucy giving each other looks that mean something more, like there's this spark between us waiting to kick off.

Get back to the flat feeling proper shit about Alex - what the fuck am I even playing at? - when the phone starts going mental. My heart's in my mouth as I leg it to answer, already knowing it's him.

'Alex?' Comes out all breathless.

'Steve!' His voice goes right through me. 'I'm in Durban with my dad. It's bloody brilliant, Stevie!'

Try to keep steady. 'Seen the uni then?'

'Yeah, it's sound. Dead modern and that. Reckon I'll be one of the first black students through the door.' Goes quiet. 'Listen, Steve... I'm gonna enrol in politics out here. Do a year, then masters. Four-year commitment, all in.'

'Four years?' Words catch in my throat. 'So you're just... staying out there?'

'Stevie...' He sighs. 'If I do this... I won't make it back to England much.'

Feel all the air go out the room. Grip the phone tight, fighting these stupid tears. 'So that's it then? You're just fucking off to South Africa forever? Leave me here like some sad war bride?'

'It's not like that-'

'Isn't it?' Can't stop now. 'You're buggering off for your dreams while I'm sat here waiting for scraps?'

'Bloody hell, Steve, you're not being fair! I'm not doing this to hurt you! It's about my family, my history. My fucking birthright!'

Let out this mental laugh. 'Right, 'course. The great Khumalo legacy. Silly me thinking I could compete.'

'It's not a fucking competition!' He's shouting now. 'Christ, Steve, I'm not choosing anything over you-'

'Aren't you?' Words echo round the empty flat. 'Leaving me behind while you go play big man on campus?'

'I'm not-' He stops, and I can hear him trying to calm down. 'I could never just leave you behind. You're part of me, you know that. No matter where I go... you'll always be my home.'

Feel all the fight drain out of me. Slide down the wall, phone pressed against my ear so hard it hurts.

'We can make it work,' he goes, but he sounds desperate now. Like he doesn't believe it either. 'Long-distance and that. Loads of people do it. We'll write and call and visit-'

'And that'll be enough?' Voice comes out proper rough. 'Few shit visits, your voice down a crackly line? Watching you slip away bit by bit?'

'Please, Stevie. Please understand-'

'Fuck you, Alex.' Comes out broken. 'Just... fuck you.'

Slam the phone down so hard the plastic cracks. Next thing I know I'm curled up on the kitchen floor, crying like I haven't since I was a kid.

I cry till my head's pounding and my throat's raw.

He's actually doing it. Just ditching me like I'm nothing. And I'm not enough to make him stay, am I?

Well fuck him then. Fuck his big plans and his new life in Africa.

Don't need him anyway, do I?

Got my own stuff going on. Starting with Lucy and Tribal Gathering.

Eve

Finally, fucking finally, it's go time. Me, Chris, and Laila are crammed into his shitty VW Golf, flying down the motorway like bats out of hell. Got the wind ripping through my hair, some banging house tune cranked right up - getting me well hyped. Can't keep my leg still, bouncing about like I'm already on one as we watch London disappear behind us. All that grey concrete melting into countryside, and I swear I can breathe better already.

Passing this fat spliff between us, talking absolute bollocks, when I slip Lucy's name in there casual as you like.

'Met this fit bird at the office,' I go, taking a deep drag before lobbing it back to Laila. 'Gonna be hooking up with her at the rave, as it happens.'

Laila catches my eye in the mirror. 'What, this one you're not gonna keep hidden away from us like that girlfriend in Portugal?'

I know she's on about that bird I invented to cover for all them nights I was sneaking off to shag Jack. Feel my face flush hot at the memory, grateful for the cover of my shades.

Chris and Laila do that thing where they look at each other like they know something's up, but they leave it. And thank fuck for that.

Because the truth is, I haven't got a fucking scooby what I'm doing with Lucy. Just know I need something to take the edge off, don't I? Something to drown out Alex's voice in my head. The rest of it - that's tomorrow's problem. Right now I've got pills, music and a whole night of forgetting ahead of me.

The sun's melting into the trees as we pull up to the festival, sky gone mental with colours - like someone's emptied a pick 'n' mix across the clouds. Bass is already rattling through the ground, and there's hundreds of us lot queuing up. Everyone's got the full rave uniform on - whistles swinging, white gloves, bucket hats, looking well sorted.

Laila's got our treats stashed away in her knickers. Neck them quick behind the bogs, all pulling faces when that bitter taste hits.

Place is going off - ravers bouncing about with these massive grins, and I'm getting well hyped just being here. Weed smoke everywhere, mixing with Lynx Africa and sweaty bodies. Crowd's absolutely heaving, everyone going mental. Got this feeling in my gut like I'm about to take off.

Lose the others in about two seconds flat. Don't even care though, too busy looking for Lucy's red barnet in all this chaos.

Then bang - there she is. Looking fit as, hair gone wild, proper going for it with her mates. Feel a bit rough about Alex for half a second, then she clocks me and I'm done for. Legs moving before my brain's caught up.

'Oi oi!' she shouts, grinning like mad. 'If it ain't the Surrey boy!'

And then I'm there, close enough to touch, and she's launching herself into my arms like a heat-seeking missile. I catch her around the waist and lift her clean off her feet, spinning us both. She smells like coconuts and that fancy perfume they're always spritzing at the makeup counter in Boots.

We're off. Lucy's mates circle round as we spin and leap like possessed wind-up toys. Nothing exists but the music, the lights, and our sweat-slick skin sliding together. We dance till my lungs burn and my legs turn to jelly, the world blurring into pure sensation.

When Lucy mouths something about air, I don't hesitate. Grab her hand and start weaving through the sweaty mass of bodies. Time to see what tonight's got in store, innit?

We burst out into the night air like we've been underwater, gasping it down like we're dying for it. Proper heaven after that sweaty mess inside. Tell you what though - everything's gone well trippy out here. All these mental colours burning brighter than anything I've seen before. Got this buzz running through me, like my whole body's wired up wrong. Fucking hell, it's intense.

Lucy's hand is warm in mine as we wander past the stalls. Stop to watch this fire-dancer doing his thing, all mental with the flames. I pull Lucy closer, and she fits right against me.

Alex pops into my head then. Trying to shake him off but he's always there, innit? Fucking Africa. Fucking four years.

Lucy looks up at me. 'Wanna get out of here?'

And just like that, Alex does one. 'Cause Lucy's right here, solid and real, looking at me like I'm her last meal on earth.

'Yeah,' I manage. 'Let's find somewhere quiet.' Smooth, Stevie boy. Real smooth.

She shivers against me, her fingers tightening in mine like she's afraid I'll disappear. 'Lead the way, Surrey Boy. I'm all yours.'

So, I do, don't I? Like a man possessed, I lead her away from the circus of lights and noise, out past the fence where it's proper dark.

Music's gone all weird out here, like it's coming through water or something. Just us and about a million stars up there having a right laugh at us. We're both gasping like we've run a marathon, breath mixing in the cold air. Trees rustling about like they're watching us, probably taking the piss out of my pathetic attempts at romance.

Can't stop staring at her, can I? Like some soppy teenager at his first disco. But bloody hell - she's something else in this light. Moonlight's turned her all silver, hair gone mental wild, and those lips of hers...

Pull her in dead slow, like she might scarper if I move too quick. Get my hands on her waist, her hips, and Christ she feels good. Every bit of her's driving me mental, all soft curves pressing up against me.

'Fucking hell, Luce,' comes out all rough. 'You're something else, you are.'

She makes this soft sound that goes straight to my dick, her fingers tangling in my hair. And then we're snogging like our lives depend on it, deep and hot and desperate. Like we're both starving for it, drowning, and the other person is the only air for miles.

I pour everything into that kiss - all the longing, the confusion, the guilt. Let my fingers wander up her thigh, find those knickers of hers. She arches up against me with this gasp, and that's me done for.

Lower her down in the grass, losing myself in how warm she is, those thighs of hers wrapped round me, all the noises she's making. Moving together like we've done this a thousand times before, both of us getting well carried away.

Our eyes meet and she lets out this moan that sends me right over.

'You can come inside me,' she whispers, and I do just that, my whole world narrowing down to this moment, this feeling, this girl.

RED RUSSIANS

I'm pushing past prams and tourists on Oxford Street when I spot Gemma up ahead, looking fit in a sundress, her curls all wild. Been ages since we've had a real catch-up, just us two.

'Alright, gorgeous?' Pull her into a big squeeze, breathing in that familiar Gem smell. Just like that, we're off - chatting shit like we always do.

We're in Topshop when she gives me this look over the clothes rack. 'Bit weird though, innit? You actually sticking with a girl for once.'

I laugh, pausing mid-rummage. 'Settling down? Gem, it's only been a month!'

'Still though...' She's got that face on, the one that means trouble. 'A month with a girl. You. Who'd have thought?'

'Oi, what you trying to say? That I'm not boyfriend material?' Clutch my chest like I'm having a turn.

Gemma just smirks, giving my shoulder a playful thump. We move on, both lost in thought, but the conversation hangs between us, simmering under the surface.

The sun hits us hard outside. Fuck it - might as well get into it. 'Listen,' I mutter, 'Alex was something else, alright? But he's long gone, fucked off to the other side of the world. Least Luce keeps things breezy in the meantime. A bit of a laugh, nothing heavy.'

'So, she's just a distraction, then? A way to avoid dealing with Alex?'

Run my hands through my hair, getting proper wound up. 'Maybe, yeah. So what? I reckon I've earned a bit of distraction after the wringer he's put me through.'

'You can't just keep bouncing from one person to the next, Stevie, using them like human shields. First Jack, then Alex, now Lucy...'

'Why not?' I snap, throwing my hands up. 'Honestly, Gem, I'm fucking sick of feeling things, alright? Missing Alex... it's like having my guts ripped out through my nose every single day. I can't do it anymore. I need to just get out there and live a little, yeah? Have some uncomplicated fun.'

Her face goes all soft. 'I get it, babe. Just don't use Lucy to patch yourself up. Won't end well, will it?'

Something in how she says it makes me look closer. 'You jealous or something?'

Her cheeks go pink. 'Maybe,' she admits with a little shrug. 'Guess I just don't like the thought of her taking up all your time and attention, that's all.' Looks right at me. 'What about you? Get jealous over me and Larry?'

'Nah.'

'Really?'

'Course not,' I repeat breezily. 'We both know you're still mad for me, even with that boy-band wannabe sniffing around.' I poke her, grin going wicked.

She swats my hand, but she's smiling too.

'C'mon then,' I murmur, pressing a quick, fond kiss to her temple. 'Let's go grab a cheeky Maccies, yeah? All this feelings chatter's got me right peckish.'

For now, there's just greasy chips and my best girl's smiling face and the bone-deep relief of knowing that no matter what daft shit I pull, at least I'll always have her in my corner.

Can't ask for more than that, can you?

Gem's words are rattling round my nut as I head home. All that stuff about distractions and using people - stuck there like gum on my trainer. This bastard headache ain't helping neither, getting worse by the minute. By the time I'm fumbling with my keys at the front door, my head's pounding. Feels like there's a rave going on inside my skull, and I didn't even get a ticket.

Stumble into the kitchen and there's this postcard burning bright on the counter. Palm trees and a sky so blue it hurts my eyes. My heart does this weird flip when I see 'Durban' plastered across it. Turn it over with shaky hands to Alex's messy writing:

'Steve,
Write back or pick up the bloody phone, you wanker.
Alex.'

Can't help laughing. Cheeky git's got a point - been dodging his calls something rotten.

I'm lost in it when Chris shuffles in looking rough as. He spots the postcard and squints. 'Durban, eh? Looks well tropical, that does. Proper paradise.'

'Yeah,' I go, running my thumb over the picture. 'Paradise.'

Chris gives me this look. 'You miss him.'

Just nod, chest too tight for words.

Chris shifts awkwardly. 'So, listen... bit of grim news. Me and Laila... well, we've gone and split up, haven't we?'

'What? For real?' They've always been having it out but thought they were solid. 'What's happened?'

'She's getting too full on, banging on about weddings and kids. And I'm like, nah, not for me. I can barely decide on breakfast most days, let alone plan out the rest of my life, y'know?'

'Fucking hell,' I wince, clapping a hand on his shoulder. 'That's rough. You holding up alright?'

He shrugs, pulling this sad smile. 'Fancy the pub later? Could do with getting proper hammered.'

Should be meeting Lucy but... one look at Chris's face and I'm done for.

'Tell you what - let me ring Luce, see if she wants to join. Yeah?'

His face lights up. 'Legend, you are.'

Lucy's well up for it, and next thing we know we're all crammed in the pub with her flatmate Kiri, this mad Aussie bird. One pint turns into god knows how many, then Kiri starts with the Sambuca - proper getting us hammered. By chucking out time we're all in bits, weaving down to the kebab shop like a bunch of pissed-up penguins.

World's gone all wobbly now. Lucy's feeding me this massive kebab, giggling while I'm getting chili sauce down my chin like a right muppet. Keep looking at her face - going in and out of focus, but bloody hell she's gorgeous when she laughs.

Then we're stumbling home, her fingers tangled in mine, everything spinning like a fairground ride. Just flashes now - streetlights blurring, taste of kebab sauce, Lucy's warm hand in mine. Too pissed to make sense of any of it really.

Red Tulips

Feel like death warmed up. Someone's hammering buttons in the lounge, each click drilling through my skull. Drag myself in to find Chris and Lucy sprawled on the sofa playing Street Fighter, fresh as anything

Can't even make it through one round. Every punch and kick on screen's making my stomach lurch, that dodgy kebab plotting its revenge. One more 'Hadouken!' and I'm legging it to the bathroom, barely making it in time.

When I get back, Lucy's just pulled off some mental spinning kick with Chun-Li, sending Ryu flying. Chris is hammering his buttons like a nutter, trying to keep up, while she's got this smug grin on her face.

'Got ya, you muppet!' she laughs, giving Chris a dig in the arm. He just grins, still mashing them buttons. Always been a competitive git.

Match finally ends. Lucy wins, and Chris chucks his controller down with a groan, giving her this look like she's nicked his last Rolo.

'Looks like I'm on a winning streak,' Lucy says, sparking up.

Chris leans back, smirking. 'Don't go counting your chickens, love. I'll wallop you next round.'

While they're having their little moment, get this weird jeolous twinge in my gut. Try to shake it off. 'Oi, where's Kiri got to?'

'She buggered off home,' Chris says, not looking away from the screen.

'Fancy a cuppa then?'

'Nah, I'm good,' Chris says, starting another game.

Lucy finally looks at me. 'Yeah, ta. That'd be lovely.'

Put the kettle on, thinking tea might fix my head. Chuck some bread in the toaster even though food's the last thing I want. Take Lucy her brew but she doesn't even look up from the screen."

Try to eat my toast but that's a mistake - barely make it to the toilet before it all comes back up. Fucking kebab.

Clean myself up, stick my trackies on and go back in. Chris is smoking a fat one, and the smell's making me feel rough again.

'State of you,' Chris says, looking me up and down. 'You look like death.'

'Feel it. Must've been that manky kebab.'

Lucy don't even look over. 'I had one too and I'm fine.'

'Course you are,' Chris laughs, nudging her. 'You're Chun-Li, ain't ya? Take more than dodgy kebab to bring you down.'

Game's doing my head in so I neck some paracetamol and crash on the sofa. Must've dozed off 'cause next thing I know, I wake up in the dark, heads pounding, sweating like mad, throat's on fire.

Find a note by my cold tea: 'Gone to Ministry with Chris!' Proper kick in the teeth, that. Video machine says 3 a.m. - here's me dying while they're out having it large.

Wrap myself in the duvet, neck more pills, and drag myself back to bed.

Soft knock on my door. Crack open one eye - 9:04 a.m. Been out cold for six hours.

'Alright if I come in?' Chris, checking if I've snuffed it probably.

Look around but no Lucy in sight.

'Yeah.' Sounds like I've been gargling glass.

Chris perches on my bed. 'Still rough then?'

'Bit. Throat's fucked.'

He's scratching his neck, looking proper awkward. 'Listen mate... about Lucy. Need to tell ya something.'

'What?' Already know this ain't good.

'Thing is... me and her got chatting last night. She says you two ain't serious...'

Everything goes cold. 'Did you shag her?'

'Nah! Nothing like that! Just had a bit of a snog.'

'While I was in here spewing my guts up?'

'Come off it, weren't like that.'

'What was it like then?'

'You actually into her or what?'

'Nah.' Start shredding this throat lozenge wrapper, watching bits fall all over my duvet. 'But I was enjoying her company, weren't I? So you definitely didn't shag her?'

'Told ya - just a snog! Swear down.'

Stare at them bits of paper, feeling proper empty. Funny how something can hurt when it weren't even meant to be real.

'Do what you want. I'm going back to sleep.'

He gets up, hovers by the door. 'We're sweet though, yeah? Bros before... y'know.'

Door clicks shut and I'm on my own again. What Chris said feels like a right kick. Yeah, I'm well pissed off, but there's something else I can't work out. Like something's missing.

Close my eyes, room still spinning. Should laugh it off, pretend I ain't arsed. But I am well gutted. Not even about Lucy really, or Chris being a dick. It's about getting left behind again, ain't it? Me stuck here feeling like death while everyone else is cracking on with their lives.

Story of my fucking life lately.

Next morning, I'm dragging myself to work, feeling like the night bus ran me over. Head's banging. But bills won't pay themselves, will they? So here I am, looking like death, praying I don't chuck up over my desk.

Lucy's keeping her distance. Can feel her watching me though, eyeing me from across the office like she's waiting for something. When we finally end up cornered making tea, feels like the air's gone thick between us.

'Alright, Stevie?' she says, hands shaking as she sorts her tea bag. 'More human today then?'

'Well as can be expected,' I mutter.

She's tapping her rings on the counter, nervous like. 'No hard feelings, yeah? Didn't mean to cause no drama.'

Something in me snaps. 'Taking the piss, are you? Snogging my best mate while I'm passed out! But sure, Luce, no worries! Lunch later, is it?'

Janet waddles in before Lucy can answer, giving us the eye while she sorts her sandwich. We both faff about with our brews, kettle screaming between us like it knows something. Finally Janet does one.

'I weren't lying, Steve!' Nothing major happened with Chris, honest! Just a sloppy snog for a mo...'

Let out this proper bitter laugh. 'Not how Chris tells it.'

That gets her. 'Weren't planned, Steve... Got carried away, messing about. Thought we were just having a casual laugh, in't it?'

Get that familiar feeling - like with Jack and his 'just a bit of fun' bollocks. Same shit, different day. 'Think you and me are done here, Luce,' I tell her. 'If you want Chris, that's your choice. But I'm out.'

Walk away, leave her there with her tea going cold.

Next few weeks are awkward as fuck. Me and Lucy get good at dodging each other - quick turns in the corridors, different lunch breaks, that sort of thing. Even Chris keeps quiet about it all, though I catch him giving me these guilty looks sometimes.

Office feels weird now. Like when you're coming down and everything's just... wrong. Where there used to be us lot having a laugh, now it's just shuffling papers and silence.

Month later, Lucy's gone. Just like that. Comes in one morning, chucks her stuff in a box - that dead orchid she could never keep alive, her 'You don't have to be mad to work here' mug, all of it - and that's it. No big goodbye. Her chair's still spinning there empty, like she was never here.

And for the first time in ages, reckon maybe the quiet's exactly what I need.

KRYPTONiTE PRESENTS

Saturday 28th May

Doors open 6pm - 7am

MOONSCAPE ODYSSEY 1994

A JOURNEY THROUGH SOUND

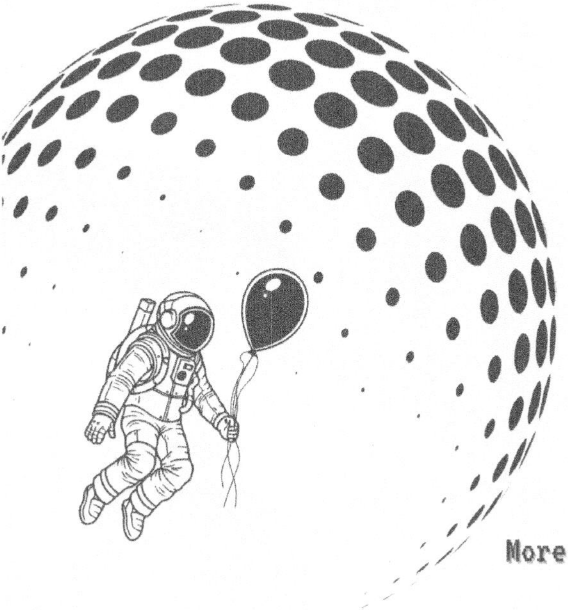

Tony De Vit

Andy C

Randall

DJ Rap

Jumping Jack Frost

DJ Die

Storm

Lisa Loud

Princess Julia

More names to be announced...

STATE OF THE ART SOUND SYSTEM

LASER SHOW

The Dielectric Club,

37-43 Rutland Street

Leicester

LE1 1RE

Mitsubishi

New year rolls in, same old bollocks with it. Gemma and Larry go tits up faster than a cheap firework. Just like that - bang - done. And then we're back to normal. The three musketeers, thick as thieves. Me, Chris, Gem. Sliding back into our routine like a pair of knackered old trainers. Days down the local turn into nights crashed out on the sofa. Spliffs and whatever crap's on the telly, cheap lager and taking the piss. Weekends lost to hard beats and sweaty clubs. Dancing 'til our legs give out, chasing that rush. Me and Gem, we keep it mates now. No funny business, even though we've pulled each other more times than I can count when we're off our faces. Better this way. Less aggro.

Alex and me, we're talking again. Shit phone signal and writing letters like we're banged up in prison or something. Him rabbiting on about beaches while I'm telling him about all the wicked nights out. We don't touch the heavy stuff, that thing between us just sitting there like some massive elephant. But I'm not poking that with a stick. Not yet anyway.

'Sunday Roast' is mental, ravers packed in like sardines. Been rough lately with this bastard flu doing my head in. Keep getting ill - probably all these raves and pills catching up with me. But fuck staying home.

That first Mitsi hits me like a train ten minutes after I walk in. I'm up there, buzzing, when this weird feeling crawls up my neck. Like someone's watching.

Christ, it's boiling in here. Can't get a breath through all these sweaty bodies. Room starts spinning and I nearly stack it, grabbing some bloke's shoulder to stay up. My heart's going mental, proper trying to burst out my chest.

Something's well dodge about that pill. Stomach's flipping and I'm fighting through the crowd, desperate to find Gem. Need her to tell me I'm not dying.

Spot her feathers bouncing and grab for her hand. She turns round, face proper worried. Can't hear what she's saying over the bass. She tries hugging me but it's too much - too hot, too tight. Everyone's crushing in and I can't fucking breathe.

'Gem,' I gasp, tongue feeling massive. 'Something's well wrong. The pill... I'm bricking it.'

She's saying something, rubbing my arm, trying to calm me down. Think I catch 'Just ride it out' and 'You'll be alright, Stevie' but my head's full of static.

Can't feel my legs now, like they're made of lead. Everyone's face is melting into one big blur. World's gone sideways.

Then they give in and I'm going down. Falling straight into the crowd, bass smashing through me like it wants to break me apart.

Last thing I see is Gem squeezing my hand before everything goes black.

Triple Five

The light's what hits me first, stabbing in like ice picks soon as I crack my eyes open. Fluorescents, glaring off-white walls and shiny lino. Christ, it's like being inside a lightbulb.

'Hello, my lovely? Are you feeling a bit better?' Voice makes me jump. Turn to see this nurse smiling at me through the curtains. 'Your friends brought you in the early hours,' she continues, bustling over to fiddle with the drip stand by the bed. 'Remember that?'

I shake my head. Brain's all fuzzy - just get bits and pieces. Lights flashing, bass thumping, pill grinding between my teeth.

'You're in Middlesex A&E. I'm Sophie. When you came in, you were badly dehydrated. The doctors have started you on a course of antibiotics to perk you up.' She moves closer to me. 'Have you been feeling poorly lately, even before your big night out?'

'Had a bit of flu,' I mumble. 'Nothing major.'

'Well, you've got a touch of thrush in your mouth as well, and your glands are up.' She checks behind my ears, under my jaw. 'But not to fret - a course of antibiotics and you'll be right as rain.'

She finishes her checks and straightens up.

'Now, do you think you can manage getting dressed and making your own way home? Or would you like us to call someone to come collect you?'

'Nah, I'll be alright,' I insist, pushing to sit up straighter.

She smiles at that. 'Alright then, love. I'll just grab your paperwork and a few bits for you to take home.'

She goes out, shoes squeaking on the floor. I'm just swinging my legs over the edge of the bed when she comes bustling back in.

'These are your antibiotics - take one three times daily with food.' She passes me a paper bag, then holds out a leaflet. Not the usual stop-smoking stuff. This one says:

HIV & AIDS: WHAT YOU NEED TO KNOW

I jerk back, clutching the pill bag.

'Why you giving me that?' Comes out rough, angry.

'It's important to be informed. If you're sexually active, you should know the facts. And if you'd like to get tested, there's information about-'

'I don't need a test!' Words echo round us. Then dead silence, just blood rushing in my ears.

She takes a step back. 'All right, Steven. It's just something to consider, that's all. No one's suggesting anything's wrong.' Her voice goes gentle. 'Now, shall we get you dressed?'

Twenty minutes later I'm in the lobby, staring at the grey day outside. Still in last night's clothes, reeking of sweat and smoke. Can't get her words out my head.

Sexually active... know the facts... get tested...

Makes me feel sick just thinking it.

Stumble out into the rain, cold air hitting hard. Standing there getting soaked, trainers full of water, and that voice in my head won't shut up.

What if, Steve?

What if?

That leaflet's heavy in my pocket. Can't look at it. Like maybe if I ignore it long enough, this'll all go away.

I fall through the front door and head straight for my room, kicking off my wet trainers and jeans. I yank the curtains shut against the grey light coming in. Shove my face in the pillow and try to switch my brain off. Just want some kip. Just want it all to stop for a bit.

But my head won't shut up. Just keeps going and going.

Testing positive for HIV doesn't mean AIDS straight off.

But it's a death sentence all the same.

No cure, no way back.

And how would I tell Mum? Alex, Chris and Gem?

I'm sweating again. Heart's banging so hard it hurts.

This is what being scared shitless feels like. Proper terrified. Never felt anything like it.

Can't just lie here thinking about it. Going mental. Need something else, need...

Someone starts hammering on the door and I nearly jump out my skin.

'Steve? Mate, you alright?'

Chris.

Try to answer but nothing comes out. Like my mouth's stopped working.

'What did the hospital say? Can I come in?'

I shake my head, even though he can't see me.

'Dodgy pill,' I manage to croak out. 'Just need to sleep it off.'

There's a beat of silence.

'Gemma's on the phone...She wants to know if-'

'Tell her I'm sleeping,' I cut in, gripping the sheets. 'I'm knackered. I'll call her later, yeah?'

He's quiet again. Then sighs. Footsteps going back down the hall.

Can't think straight. Everything in my head's going too fast, all these what-ifs getting worse and worse. Need to sort my head out, need...Alex.

I walk into the hallway, grab the phone and bring it back to my room. Ring after ring, the static hiss of distance, until:

'Alex?' I croak out, voice already thick.

'Stevie boy. What's up?' He sounds so close, so warm. Like he's just in the next room, not half a world away.

'Not too late to ring, is it? Can't kip, had to call you.'

'Nah, never too late. Always buzzin' to hear from you.'

'Sound.' I swallow hard.

The line crackles between us.

'So go on then,' Alex says softly. 'Talk to me.'

'Reckon I've caught the flu, or maybe got hold of some dodge pills. Bit of both. Ended up on ward and everything.'

'What did they say?' Sharp concern in his voice, makes my ribs ache.

'Dehydration, flu, swollen glands, thrush,' I rattle off, trying for casual. 'Hooked me up to a drip, bunged some antibiotics at me. So, no bevvies or big nights out for a bit.'

'Probably a blessing in disguise, Sunshine.' So gentle it hurts.

I fidget about, tapping the bedside table. 'Yeah, uh... funny thing though. The nurse, she slipped me this leaflet. About HIV testing. Well random.'

Silence down the line. I can practically hear him thinking. 'Did she say anything else?'

'Nah, just handed it over.'

'Christ...' He lets out this breath. 'Standard thought, innit? Nothing to worry about straight off?' Then, quieter, 'Have you been tested?'

I let out a heavy sigh, thumb picking over a groove in the tabletop. 'Tested for what, exactly?'

'Don't come the raw prawn with me, Sunshine. HIV, obviously. Might not be a bad shout to actually read that leaflet, get yourself down the clinic. Smart move for any bloke who likes a bit of sausage, or anyone on the scene, really.'

My jaw goes tight. 'I'm not exactly pulling left and right these days, am I? Been on my Jack Jones for ages now. What about you, have you been tested?'

'You know I get checked regular, if there's someone new in the picture. I'm careful like that.'

'Right, so if you're in the clear, stands to reason I am and all,' I shoot back.

'Doesn't quite work like that, but you already know that. 'Sides, you and me were always careful.' Softer now. 'Listen. Just go get it done, yeah? Put your mind at rest. I know it's scary, but you'll feel loads better once you've got a result to work with, trust.'

I rub the table, feel sick. 'Nah, I'll be fine. They just freaked me out, is all.'

'Steven.' Dead serious now. Full name treatment. 'Go. Tomorrow.' His voice goes funny with the bad line. 'Please, sunshine.'

'What if...' Can hardly get it out. 'What if it's positive?'

He's quiet for ages. Takes this deep breath.

'Well, you handle it, don't you? Get on the meds, start managing your health right.' Another breath. 'And if it's negative. You'll know for sure, can get on with your life. Either road, I'm here for you. No matter what, yeah?'

'I know you are.' Voice wobbling. But he's not here though, is he? Just a voice on a crackling phone line, memories fading away.

'I'm there in spirit, if nothing else. Always gonna be right there in my heart. You got that?' It sounds like a plea, raw and crumbling around the edges.

I grip the phone harder. Feel tears on my face. When did I start crying?

'I know,' I get out, words all sticky.

But he's going crackly. Breaking up into static. Slipping away bit by bit.

I stay on the dead line, breathing him in, till my face is wet and my ear hurts.

Only then do I put the phone down, gentle as anything. Curl up tight around the pain in my chest, the ghost weight of the phone still heavy in my hand.

When sleep finally comes, it brings no peace.

Dollars

Been two weeks since I talked to Alex, and I can't get what he said out my head. HIV test. Get it done. No matter what.

I'm on the Tube going to work. Just another face in the morning crowd. Stinks of coffee and sweat in here. Train stops. 'Warren Street,' says that voice over the speakers.

Something goes tight in my chest. Next thing I know I'm up, moving. Out onto the platform, running up the escalators. Burst out onto the street like someone's chasing me.

My legs take me down this familiar street, like muscle memory kicking in. End up outside the Alexander Pringle clinic - same spot I bottled it years back. Stand there staring at the buzzer, heart going mental, just like last time.

Don't want to be here. Really fucking don't want to be here.

The waiting room's grim as ever. Everyone huddled in plastic chairs, avoiding eye contact. Air stinks of disinfectant and tension. My hand's so sweaty the pen nearly slips while I'm scribbling my details on the form.

Try distracting myself with OK! Magazine while the receptionist keeps giving me these looks, like she knows. End up staring at some spread about Princess Di, willing my heart to slow down.

'Mr Bishopston?'

Nearly jump out my skin. Follow her down the corridor like I'm walking to the gallows. The exam room's tiny, walls plastered with posters about condoms and jabs.

The counsellor's dead calm, but it's not helping my nerves. She runs through the questions, gentle but quick.

Status of partners? Nah.

Unprotected sex with blokes? Once or twice... or more.

She's good though, don't judge.

'Testing positive doesn't automatically mean AIDS,' she tells me, but it's just words. All I can think about is them posters, the adverts, people wasting away...

'Do you feel ready if the test comes back positive?'

I shake my head. Ready? How can you ever be ready?

She's watching me careful now, spots my bouncing knee, the tears I didn't know were there.

'We can always reschedule,' she says. 'If you need more time...'

'No.' Voice comes out weird. 'Let's just... let's get it done, yeah?'

Next room's a blur. Snap of rubber gloves, tourniquet pulling tight. Can't get my breathing right, disinfectant burning my nose. Needle goes in quick - watch my blood swirl into the vial. Proper red. Red for danger, red for stop, red for...

'All done.' Nurse tapes a cotton ball to my arm. 'Now, try not to worry...'

I'm gone before she finishes, hugging my coat tight. Past all the scared faces in the corridor, following the exit signs. Out into the cold, gasping for air.

Start walking fast, head down. Then jogging, then running flat out down the street. Lungs burning, heart going mental.

For one mad second, reckon I might just outrun all of it.

Then I'm home, crashing onto the bed still in my coat, trying to breathe normal. Two weeks. Two weeks before I know if...if...

Need a cuppa. Hands shaking while I flip through my Filofax. Ring old shags, old flames. Patrick sounds fine on the phone. Gary's banging on about his new bloke. Both of them healthy as anything.

End up on the sofa after, holding a mug gone cold. Brain's gone quiet, just staring at nothing.

Catch sight of the vodka bottle in the kitchen. Sitting there like it's got all the answers. Promising to make everything stop. Just for a bit.

Seal breaks with a crack, first gulp burns all the way down. Drink till the room starts spinning, till the panic ain't so sharp.

Just need to forget for now.

Pick up the phone, dial Gemma.

'Gem? Yeah, love. Listen, fancy a trip over the channel, you and me? Reckon the 'Dam is calling our name, and I ain't talking windmills and tulips...'

She gets it. Course she does. My girl always knows what's what.

AK47

Two fucking weeks of not knowing. Been doing my head in, proper.

Can't keep still. Jump like a twitchy twat every time the phone rings. Brain won't shut up - keeps spinning out these scenarios, each one more mental than the last.

Tried keeping busy. Me and Gem had a proper mad one in the 'Dam, got absolutely trollied. Helped for a bit. But then I'm back here, throwing myself into work, into going out. Anything to stop thinking about what might be in my blood, eating away at me.

Sleep's gone to shit. Lie there sweating, sheets soaked through like I've been on one. When I do drop off, get these dark nightmares. All hospitals and funeral parlours and Mum crying. Wake up gasping like someone's sitting on my chest.

But I'm keeping it together, ain't I? Got this face on like everything's sweet. Can't have people asking questions. This one's all mine to deal with.

And now, here I am. Back at the clinic. Can't keep still in this waiting room chair, knee bouncing while I keep wiping my hands on my jeans because they won't stop sweating.

Place is dead quiet but everything's too loud. Every creak of the chairs, shuffle of papers, that bastard clock ticking away.

Try looking at a magazine but can't focus on the words. Pictures all swimming together. Chuck it back on the table.

To keep from losing it completely, I start making up stories about the others waiting. Old bloke in the corner in his tweed - Albert, maybe Harold. Should be feeding ducks somewhere, not stuck in here. Young girl next to him, can't be twenty, big scared eyes - Daisy, something like that.

Mad what your brain does when you're bricking it.

Then she appears. Same woman as before, kind eyes and gentle smile. Sarah, says her name tag. Catches my eye, nods me over.

Get this tiny flicker of hope. Maybe it's alright. Maybe I've been worrying for nothing. She wouldn't smile if it was bad news. Would she?

Legs gone wobbly as I follow her down the hall. Feels like the longest walk of my life and no time at all, trainers catching on the cheap carpet with every step.

Her office door clicks shut behind us. I perch on the edge of the chair she offers, ready to leg it like a scared kid.

There's a folder on her desk. Can't stop staring at it, like it might explode. My whole life sitting there in a few bits of paper.

She opens it up and I swear I can hear the pages rustling over my own breathing. The way she settles back in her chair to read... It's like them films where they're trying to defuse a bomb. Red wire, blue wire. Life or death hanging on what comes next.

That's me right now - pulse going mental while Sarah reads the results. Can't even get a proper breath in.

And then she looks up at me, something in her gaze that makes my stomach drop clean through the floor. A terrible, aching softness that speaks of sympathy. Of pity.

Oh god. Oh fuck.

'Steven...' She clears her throat gently, folds her hands on the desk. 'I'm so sorry. But your test results came back positive for HIV.'

Positive.

The word hangs there between us. Echoing in my head like a gunshot.

Positive.

I'm positive.

I've got the virus.

All the breath leaves my body in a single, punched out whoosh. I feel my chest caving in, my lungs shrivelling up like raisins. There's no air in here, I can't... I can't bloody breathe...

Sarah's going on about something, her mouth moving. Medications and CD4 cell counts and support groups and... It's all just white noise, innit? Static hissing between my ears, pressure building and building 'til I'm sure my head will pop.

This ain't happening. Not to me. I'm not... Fucking hell, I can't be...

But I am, ain't I?
The test doesn't lie, does it?
It's in there now, in my blood, doing whatever the fuck it does. No getting rid of it neither.

How long have I got?
Weeks, months?

How long 'til I start to fall apart, 'til I'm nothing but skin and bones and sores?

How long 'til I just...

A bin. I need a bin. I'm going to spew. I can't...

'Steven? Steven, look at me.'

Sarah's voice cuts through the panic, firm but gentle. Force myself to look at her, fighting back tears.

'I know it's a shock. I know it's the last thing you expected to hear today.' She pushes a box of tissues towards me, but I don't move. Too scared I'll fall apart if I do.

'But this isn't the end of the world, alright? You're not alone in this. We're going to figure it out together, one step at a time.'

I want to laugh at that. Or scream. Or put my fist through the nearest wall. Because she's wrong, isn't she? It is the end of the bloody world. My world, at least. The world where I was just a normal bloke with normal problems. The world where my biggest worry was getting to work on time, or if Spurs would make it past the semi-finals.

The room's gone grey, with Jack's fingerprints smudged all over it.

I don't realise I'm crying 'til I taste the salt on my lips. Big, ugly sobs ripping out of my chest like they've got a mind of their own

Sarah just sits there; calm as you like. And ain't that just the final kick in the nuts? Her pitying me, comforting me. Like I'm some poor sod she can make all better with a few kind words and a pile of soggy Kleenex.

I shove my chair back sharp, metal legs screeching on the floor. Wipe my face with my sleeve, this mad laugh bubbling up.

'Right then. Suppose that's that. Stick a fork in me, I'm done.' Voice comes out raw. Doesn't sound like me at all. Like someone else using my mouth.

Sarah starts to stand, hand out.

'Steven, wait. Please, just...'

But I'm already moving, stumbling for the door. Need to get out. Need proper air, not this stale bollocks choking me. Need...

Don't know what I need. Time machine maybe. Go back, do it different. Not be such a stupid kid.

But I can't, can I? Stuck here, in this moment. In this body, with this virus eating through me.

Light hits me hard when I burst out the clinic doors. Have to dig in my pocket for shades, hands shaking like mad.

Mum. Oh Christ, Dad. How do I tell him? Better to say it's cancer or something. Anything but this.

No. Stop. Can't do this here. Can't let the panic swallow me whole right in the middle of the street like some nutter. Just need to get home. Go to pieces in private, like a good lad.

One foot in front of the other. Keep breathing, keep moving. Head down all the way to the tube, sure everyone can see it written on my face. Carved into my skin like a brand. Infected. Unclean. Jack's dirty secret.

Drop onto a seat, gagging. Shove my face in my trembling hands and bite back this scream that's trying to claw its way out.

Doors hiss open and I'm vaguely aware of some birds piling in. One of them's done up like a goth Barbie, eyes me up something fierce.

'You gutted over Kurt Cobain dyin' an' all?' she asks.

I just blink at her. Like she's speaking bloody Martian.

She shrugs, turns back to her mates. 'Reckoned he was bummed about it, din't I? Well cut up, poor bloke...'

Their chat fades to nothing, just noise in my head. Close my eyes, press my forehead to the cold glass. Wish I could disappear through it.

Walk from the tube to the flat's doing my nut in - buildings looming over me like they might topple any second. Everything's gone weird - too bright, too loud, like someone's cranked the world up to eleven and broke the dial off.

By the time I get to the flat I'm drenched, shaking so bad I can barely get my key in the bleeding lock. Drop the bastard twice before I manage it.

Chris is there when I stumble in, clutching some post, giving me a right worried look.

'You alright mate? Looking proper rough.'

Try to say something but my gob's not working. Words all jammed up in my throat like I'm choking on them.

End up just snatching the letters off him. Grunt something that might be thanks. Hear him leaving. Thank fucking christ for that.

Alone at last, I go through the motions. Filling the kettle, slamming bread in the toaster. Mechanical, like I'm some wind-up toy soldier. Tea goes cold, toast untouched.

Then it hits - need to clean.

Everything.

Grab the scrubbing brush, attacking every surface like it's done me wrong. Scouring and scraping till my muscles burn, skin gone red raw.

But it's not enough, is it? Never fucking enough. Flat reeks of bleach and Dettol but I'm still manky inside. Like it's worked its way right through to my bones.

Strip off, stumble to the shower. Crank it hot as it'll go till the room's thick with steam. Step under and it's like boiling oil, but I welcome it. The pain, the heat. Maybe it can burn away what's inside me.

Scrub and scrub till my skin's angry pink. Till it feels like I'm taking layers off, trying to get at what's underneath. But there is no beneath, is there? No escaping what's in my blood. It's part of me now, innit? No going back from this.

After, I towel off, pull on joggers and a ratty t-shirt, I collapse on the sofa and whack the telly on, needing some noise, distraction. Anything to drown out the screaming in my head.

MTV flickers to life, George Michael giving it large about freedom. The irony burns like bile in the back of my throat. Freedom? What a laugh. I'm in a prison of my own making, ain't I?

Everything's gone weird - colours all washed out, world moving like some dodgy pirate video. Can't focus on Beavis and Butthead, or Kurt Cobain's memorial choking up Seattle.

Can't even take it in. Not my world no more, is it?

Then a bloody HIV testing advert comes on. Christ, can't escape it even here, can I?

Back in the bathroom. More soap, more scrubbing. Going at it 'til my skin's proper raw and my joints are screaming, water gone freezing ages ago.

End up curled up on the floor like some kid. Rocking back and forth, making this noise I've never heard come out of me before. Like a wounded dog or something. Then this animal sound rips out of my throat, bouncing off them tiles. This awful howl that keeps getting louder and louder, filling up the tiny bathroom.

Can't stop screaming. Tears mixing with the water still running. Scream 'til my throat's wrecked and there's nothing left in me. 'Til I'm just this empty thing, shaking on the wet floor.

Time's gone mental, skipping like a scratched record. I surface enough to ring work, spinning some bollocks about measles.

I hang up.

Measles. I wish. What I wouldn't give for a nice, normal, curable disease right about now.

Gotta get out. Get away. Can't stand these four walls closing in on me anymore.

I throw on yesterday's jeans, a jacket that reeks of stale smoke. Stuff wallet and keys and ciggies in my pockets, a man on a mission.

Down the offy, I grab a bottle of Grouse. The cheap shit, hardcore. A few packs of Mayfair, a handful of gum to mask the stench. Might as well go all out, eh?

The cashpoint spits out a wedge of notes, crisp promise. I shove 'em deep, don't even bother to count. Who cares about money when your days are numbered?

Then I get on the bus, destination Bagley's.

Boomerang

Started at Bagley's with that bottle of Grouse burning in my gut, and haven't stopped moving since. Eclipse, Sanctuary, Diehard - it's all one long blur now. Pills and powders, uppers and downers - anything to keep reality at bay.

Coventry, Milton Keynes, Leicester, Liverpool, Manchester. Following the music like breadcrumbs, letting it drown out everything else. The fear, the diagnosis, the death sentence hanging over my head.

Carl Cox, Sasha, Judge Jules, Lisa Lashes - they're spinning the soundtrack to my life. Bass thumping through me, like it's replaced my heartbeat.

Flyers and roaches stuff my pockets, while club stamps crawl up my arms like war paint. Microdots and MDMA, strawberry acid on my tongue. Sweet as sin, bright as anything. I'm flying, I'm falling. Spinning out into nothing.

Sometimes I surface long enough to stagger home. Stuff myself into the shower, sluice off the sweat and glitter. But mostly I'm a vagrant, a ghost. Crashing wherever, whenever, the crash comes.

I hitch a ride with some ravers in a jeep called Whistling Rufus, bass shaking the whole thing. The driver's off his nut, going on about Goan full moons and thousands dancing until dawn. We nearly roll the thing, veering off the road. I'm laughing, euphoric. Cheating death, giving it the finger. What's the worst that could happen? I'm already a dead man walking.

Brighton next, trailing a gaggle of glittered up birds. They take me to their flat, put me in a bubble bath, and paint my face with makeup. Give me a shirt that says 'NO ONE KNOWS I'M A LESBIAN.' I wear it like a shield, like a sick joke. Dance for days in that getup, sweat pooling in the small of my back.

Orbit's mental, like nothing I've ever seen. Sven Vath on the decks, whipping the crowd into a frenzy. I'm just another body, another vessel. Throbbing with the bass, the relentless beat. Some bloke tries to catch my eye, all smouldering looks and that.

I brush him off cold, spit the words like venom. 'Sorry mate, I'm straight as they come.'

Must be day 15, or 20, who's keeping score anymore? I'm at Sanctuary, propping up the wall like a broken doll. Lost in the throb of the music, the press of sweaty bodies. Familiar faces keep popping up, spotting me too - flashing knowing smiles, warm hugs on the dance floor.

And then, through the lights and haze of smoke, I see him. That bloke I've been eyeing up for weeks, tall and lanky, with a slash of cheekbones and full lips.

He glides past, then just stops dead, those bright blue eyes locking onto mine. A vision he is, like Cobain reborn or Ziggy resurrected. Comes closer, each step dead deliberate, all these bracelets jangling as he moves. Checking me out through the haze.

Then he's right there, so close I can feel the heat off him. His hand ghosts over my skin, making me shiver. Leans in close, lips right against my ear.

'Don't fret so much, darling,' he says soft. 'It might never happen.'

Quick kiss on my cheek, then he's gone, disappeared into the crowd. Like something I imagined.

But later, on the dance floor, he finds me again. Comes out of nowhere and pulls me close, arms round my waist. 'Open wide,' he whispers, pressing something against my lips. Pill's bitter on my tongue as I swallow. Like taking communion, like being forgiven.

I hold onto him tight, face buried in his neck. Breathing him in - smoke and sweat and something else I can't place. Everything else just... disappears. There's only him, only this moment. Then I blink and he's gone again. Like magic, like he was never there at all.

The comedown hits like a hammer, everything gone grey and fuzzy round the edges. End up on the early train to London, squeezed between all these office types in their suits. Must look a right state in last night's clothes, reeking of smoke and sweat.

Nick a bottle of OJ off someone's doorstep, down it in one go. Leave a quid though - like that makes it any better. Like anything could make any of this better.

Home's a bloody tomb. Got messages stuck all over the fridge - Mum, Gem, work. Alex. Can't face hearing them worry about me, can't deal with the pity when they find out. Chuck the NHS letters straight in the bin without opening them. Work's sacked me too - extended absence, they say. Don't even care, if I'm honest. Not like I'm planning on sticking around long enough for a pension, am I? Might as well let it all go to shit. Nothing matters anymore.

I force myself through the motions. Shower, a change of clothes. A piece of toast like cardboard in my mouth. Gotta keep moving, keep shaking off the rigor mortis. Can't let it set in, stiffen my limbs and stop my heart.

I'm in the thick of it at AWOL, bodies all crushed together, moving to the beat. Air's thick with sweat and tiger balm, lasers cutting through the smoke. Then I spot him - that silver vision from Sanctuary, all long limbs and grace. He's at the bar chatting up some bloke, wearing chrome so tight it leaves nothing to the imagination.

I try to act like I don't give a toss, pushing through the crowd like I'm heading nowhere special. Then these long fingers grab my wrist, pulling me back.

'Brett, get a load of this stunner!'

He slings an arm around my shoulders, easy as you please, like we're old mates instead of near-strangers in the dark. Up close, he's proper gorgeous - all angles and grins, skin gone silver under these lights.

'What's the damage then, beautiful? What should I call you?' His voice goes right through me, making me shiver.

'Steve,' I mumble, ducking my head, feeling about five years old. Can feel myself going red, thank christ it's dark in here.

'Basil,' he replies, his grin widening. He leans in close, as he whispers, 'Charmed.' Says it like he means something else entirely, something that makes my chest go tight.

And then he's pulling away, dropping a scorching kiss on my sweaty cheek.

'Catch you on the floor, yeah?'

Then he's gone, twirling off in a cloud of glitter. Leaves me standing there dazed, like I've been staring at the sun too long. Can't help touching my cheek where he kissed it, skin still burning.

I lose myself in the music after that, let it carry me away from everything - my failing body, my spinning head. End up with this Scottish lad, all cheekbones and stubble. Do some lines in the bogs, getting off against the door. Hands down pants, teeth on skin, both of us proper desperate.

He comes back to mine, but then I remember - I can't, I can't. The virus in me, poison in my blood. Could kill him with a kiss, with a touch. Drop to my knees instead, praying it's enough. Praying I can keep him safe from the horror show in my veins. It's over quick - he finishes, zips up, gives me a pat on the shoulder and he's gone.

I wake to an earthquake. Chris hammering on my door.

'Steve! The hell is going on? Where's the bleeding stereo?'

I peel my face off the pillow, stomach churning and head stuffed with cotton wool. There are glow sticks round my wrists, a rainbow of chemical hues. The Scot. He must've swiped the stereo on the way out, the cheeky git.

I'm gearing up to shout back, to tell Chris to piss off and let me wallow in peace. But then it hits me. Gemma. Oh, Christ, Gemma. When was the last time we...? Before Jack, or after? I scan back through the mental rolodex, flipping through memories like case files. But it's all a jumble, a tangle. I can't remember. I can't remember. And now she could be... I could have... No. No. Not her. Anyone but her.

The door flies open, hinges screaming. Chris, storming. He beelines for the window, rips back the curtains. Throws it wide, letting in a blast of icy air.

'Smells like a crack den in here,' he scoffs, taking me in with hard eyes. 'When was the last time you surfaced, eh? Last time you saw daylight, you mole?'

I'm gaping at him. Brain stuck on a loop, a record scratch. I slept with Gemma. I slept with Gemma and I can't remember when and now she might be sick, might die, and it's all my fault. Oh god, oh Christ...

'And the rent, Steve? You owe me a small fortune, you muppet. Been covering your arse for weeks while you've been out raving like a right fiend.'

Rent. He's talking about rent, about the bloody stereo. Like any of those matter, like any of it means a single goddamn thing in the grand scheme of this cosmic shit show. I might have killed my best friend. Might have snuffed out her shine, her boundless light. With one careless mistake, one roll of the viral dice.

I want to scream. Want to put my fist through the wall, my head through the window. Want to tear the entire world down around me, raze it to ashes and dust. But I can't. I can't do any of that. Because Chris's still looking at me, brow furrowed and eyes dark with worry.

'Yeah,' I rasp out, tongue thick and useless in my dry mouth. 'Yeah, I'll sort the rent. And the stereo. Promise.'

He sighs, a gust of pure exasperation. Scrubs a hand over his stubbled jaw, his close-cropped hair. 'And work, mate? They've been ringing off the hook, threatening all sorts. You can't keep blanking them. They'll give you the boot, no messing.'

I almost laugh at that. Planning for the future, worrying about careers and references and keeping my nose clean. When I won't even have a future, not really. But I can't say that.

'I'll sort it,' I mumble instead. 'I'll call them today, grovel a bit. It'll be fine.'

Chris is not convinced; I can tell. 'Right then. Have a shower, yeah? Scrub the crust off. I'll rustle us up some breakfast, put the kettle on.'

He's gone before I can argue.

The shower scalds, pinking my skin and sluicing away the dried sweat, the flaking glitter. I stand under the spray until it runs cold, till I'm shivering and raw. I dress in a daze, tugging on trackies and a ratty band tee. Can't look at myself in the fogged mirror. Don't want to see what I've become. Monster. Murderer.

In the kitchen, Chris's plating up a full English. Sausage and beans, fried bread glistening with grease. He slides it in front of me.

'Get that down you,' he says gruffly, nudging the ketchup my way. 'Put some colour back in your cheeks.'

I try. I really do. I manage a few mechanical bites, washing it down with tea that scours my tongue.

'Pub later? Gemma's been asking after you.' Chris's voice is deliberately casual, but I can hear the note of pleading underneath.

I paste on a smile, a gritted-teeth grimace. 'Course. Sounds ace.'

He gives me a wink and buggers off, leaving me alone with the overwhelming silence. I turn on the taps more for the white noise than the washing up, if I'm being honest. Anything to drown out the sound of my own thoughts.

My hands are shaking as I pick up the phone. Take a few deep breaths, try to get it together. Dial mum's work number while my leg won't stop bouncing.

'Hi Mum...' I croak out when she finally picks up, voice scratchy and small.

'Steven?!' Her tone is a cocktail of worry and relief. 'Oh, thank god! Where on earth have you been, sweetheart? I've rung and rung, but Chris always says you're out and about. Are you alright, my love?'

'M'fine, Mum,' I mumble. 'Just... been having a bit of a rough patch, that's all.'

There's a pause.

'Well, where exactly have you been keeping yourself, then? You're working at the office.'

'I am working still, Mum. Promise. Just been... y'know, busy with cases and... and hitting the clubs after hours to unwind. That's all.' Even to my own ears, the excuse rings hollow.

'Well...you know how I fret when my best boy goes off radar for too long!'

'Best boy' hits me right in the gut. Makes me feel sick with guilt. Better get this over with before I bottle it.

'Actually Mum, I was hoping to ask a bit of a favour...' I trail off, trying to get the words out. 'See, I'm... I'm a bit short on funds this month for the rent. Would it be possible for me to borrow a few quid off you until I'm back on my feet again? Just to tide me over until the next pay comes through.'

Silence.

'Yes, yes, of course I can help you out, my love. But Steven... sweetheart, please. I need you to be honest with me now. What's really going on with you?'

My eyes squeeze shut.

'This isn't like you, darling - avoiding my calls for weeks on end, always out at all hours and dodging questions about work.' A pause. 'Please, Steve...please just tell me what's wrong so I can try and help, yeah? I'm your mum. It's my job to fuss over you.'

The tears spill over before I can stop them, hot and shameful.

'Nothing's wrong, Mum,' I force out at last. 'I told you already...e verything's fine. Don't go fussing yourself.'

She lets out a soft, wounded noise at that. 'Sweetheart, when can I see you next?' she asks, delicate. 'Maybe...maybe we could plan a little getaway soon, just the two of us? Your aunt Amanda says we're welcome to use her Paris flat for a weekend if we'd like to pop over...'

And that...that undoes me completely in a way nothing else could. Can't stop this noise coming out of me, like something's being torn right out of my chest.

'Y...yeah, Mum,' I somehow force out between wheezing gulps of air. 'That sounds...th-that sounds absolutely brilliant. Count me in, okay?'

'Steven?' Her voice is rising in pitch now. 'Steven, my love...what is it? What's happened?'

But I can't go there, can't let the words leave my lips. 'I...I've got to go, Mum,' I choke out, hardly aware of what I'm even saying at this point. 'But thank you, SO much for the loan, yeah? You're an absolute lifesaver, honest. I'll be in touch about those Paris plans within the next couple of days, I promise.'

'Steven, wait!' She's panicking now.

Can't take any more. Slam the phone down so hard it rattles.

Just stand there for a bit, trying to breathe while the tears come. Can't even wipe them away.

Later, I'm at the pub with Gemma and Chris, necking pints and chatting bollocks. But my mind's miles away, spinning like a broken record. I turn to Gemma, trying to sound casual. 'Oi, Gem. You get sick much?'

She blinks at me, confused. 'What you on about?'

'You know, like some people are always down with something. You been poorly lately?'

Gemma shakes her head, glancing round the dingy pub. 'Nah, not really.'

'Right, so you're pretty healthy then,' I mutter, taking a long swig of lager.

She frowns now, looking worried. 'Suppose so. Why, you feeling rough, Stevie? Coming down with something?'

'Nah, not feeling too bad. Just curious, is all.' I force a grin, but it feels as fake as a three quid note.

Gemma's not having it. 'You ought to slow down on those parties, though. All those late nights are gonna do you in eventually.'

I scoff, waving her off. 'Yeah, yeah. Chris is always banging on about that.'

'But you know it's true, don't you?' She leans in, all serious. 'You can't keep going like this. Something's got to give. You need to look after your health.'

'My health?' I let out a laugh that sounds more like a bark. 'Funny you should mention that. How long's it been since we last... you know?'

'Since what?' She lets out one of her beautiful laughs, the ones that make her freckles dance. It hits me like a punch to the gut, thinking I might've sentenced her to death.

'You know what I mean,' I say, wiggling my eyebrows and throwing her a wink, trying to keep it light.

'Oh, since we shagged?' She grins. 'Don't tell me you've forgotten. Was I that forgettable?'

I pinch her arm. 'You? Forgettable? Never. Just wondering, is all.' I shrug, picking at my beer label. 'Was it before I went to Portugal in '92?'

Gemma nods. 'Yeah, definitely before then. I remember it clear as day.'

Relief washes over me. Before Jack, before the virus. She's safe, untouched by my mess.

'You're acting weird, Stevie.'

'I'm fine, Gem.'

She frowns, but lets it drop. Later, we're sprawled on the sofa. Some rubbish film's on the telly, volume low. Gemma's head's on my chest, her hand gripping my shirt like she's afraid I'll vanish if she lets go.

Next morning, I pop into the post office. Flipping through the Dudley phone book, I scan for Lucy's family name. Only a few listings - I jot the numbers down quick, hoping one reaches her mum at least.

Back home, I start dialling. First number - nothing. Second - same. On the third try, a Brummie voice answers. Not Lucy, but her mum. Says Luce is still off travelling. I leave my number, asking her to have Lucy ring me soon as she can.

I try ringing Hugo's Bar in the Algarve too. Some bird there tells me Jack's buggered off to Tenerife, no forwarding address. Probably for the best - what was I gonna say to him anyway? Thanks for the death sentence, mate?

Seized by a sudden, desperate impulse, I stab out another number. Familiar as my name, my heartbeat.

'Steve, that you? Where the bloody hell have you been?'

'Raving.' The word is jagged glass in my throat, lacerating. 'Just been out raving, ain't I? Non-stop, like a fucking machine.'

There's a pause. 'For six weeks!!!' It's not a question.

'Steve?' He's really worried now. I can hear it, even through the shitty connection. 'Stevie, talk to me. What's going on?'

I can't speak. Can't form words.

'You got your results.' A sigh. 'Fuck...'

I can't. I can't do this, can't bear it. The pity, the grief. The useless platitudes, the hollow comfort.

'I'm dying, Alex. It comes out flat, toneless. 'I'm... I'm dying.'

'No!' His voice is shaking. 'No, don't say that. We'll figure this out. We'll get you on the meds. You'll be alright, you'll-'

'I won't.' A harsh croak. 'I won't be fucking alright. Don't lie to me, don't you dare!'

'Steve, please...' He's crying now, little hitching sobs. 'Please, we'll sort this. Together, like always.'

'There is no together!' I'm yelling, spit flecking the handset. 'You're in bloody Africa, Alex! Oceans away, building a new life. A life without me.'

'That's not true.' He's choking on it, words wet and clotted. 'It's not, I swear. I'm here, I'm right here. I'll always be-'

'You left me.' It's a broken whisper. 'You left, and now I'm alone. And I'm so scared. I can't stand it.'

'I know. But you're not alone, not ever. I'm with you, I'm here. Even when I'm not.'

I'm crying now. Deep, wrenching sobs that feel like they're tearing me in two. Feel like I'm being ripped in half. Want to believe every word he's saying. Want to let him make it all better like he used to. But he's not really here, is he? Just a voice crackling down the phone from the other side of the world.

'I have to go.' I'm gulping, hyperventilating.

'Steve, wait-'

But I'm slamming the phone down. Wrenching the door open, stumbling out into the watery light.

Rain's bloody freezing, soaking through my clothes in seconds. Shove my hands in my pockets and start walking. Don't even know where I'm going. Just need to move, need to get away. Feel like I'm disappearing with every step.

I stumble into Helter Skelter at Sanctuary, the world already tilting off its axis. The bass throbs through the soles of my feet, the strobe lights searing my retinas. It's like walking into a fever dream, reality blurring at the edges. Someone presses a baggie into my hand. Ketamine, they shout over the pounding beat. A one-way ticket to oblivion. I don't hesitate. Just dip a key and bring it to my nostril, snorting deep. Once, twice, three times. The bitter drip hits the back of my throat and I gag, eyes watering.

Then it slams into me like a racehorse has trampled me. Can't even stand straight anymore, just sort of melt against the wall while my fingers try to grab onto bricks that keep moving about. The lights have gone mental - all these neon trails making patterns I've never seen before, faces turning into watercolours around me. Someone's laughing somewhere, sounds like it's coming from underwater or outer space or both. Look at all these beautiful people dancing, all of them with their whole lives stretched out in front of them like some glossy magazine spread. Jobs and mortgages and marriages and sprogs - all that normal stuff that's never gonna be mine. All I've got is right here, right now, this chemical holiday from being me. Just me and my death sentence, having a party.

My knees buckle, my arse hitting the sticky floor. I let my head loll back, let my eyes flutter shut. Everything's spinning out of control. Can't catch my breath, can't think straight. But the fear is gone, the dread and self-loathing. Burnt away in the whiteout blaze of the high.

'Bunny? You alright?'

The voice is soft as molasses. It filters through the static, the clamour in my skull. I force my eyes open. And there he is. Basil. Bare-chested and beaming, a beret sat on top of his curls. He crouches down next to me, and Christ - I can smell him, all sweaty and leathery. Something cold gets pushed into my hands - water bottle.

'Drink up, love. It'll help.'

Can't make my hands work right, everything's gone all weird and floaty. Finally get the cap off, manage a few swigs. Feels like heaven on my mangled throat.

'Ta,' I croak. 'M'alright, yeah?'

Basil chuckles, low and honeyed. 'More than alright, I'd say. You're in the stratosphere, bunny. A million miles from here.' He leans in close, his breath a hot tickle against my sweat-damp skin. 'When you're done exploring the cosmos,' he murmurs, voice like velvet, 'come find me, yeah? I'll be waiting.' Then he's gone, leaving nothing but a wink and that smile that does things to me even when I'm this twisted.

Takes me about a year to get to my feet, world going mental around me. But I've got one thing on my mind now - Basil.

Proper mission getting to the dance floor, like trying to walk through soup. Everything's gone weird, faces all blurry, lights making patterns I have never seen before. But it's like there's this rope pulling me forward, straight to him.

And there he is, right in the middle of it all, like some sort of rave angel. No shirt on, just these silver kecks hanging off his hips, showing everything. Got this massive tattoo on his back - pair of wings that look real under the strobes, like he might just take off any second.

He clocks me coming, gives me that grin that does funny things to my insides, and holds out his hand. Next thing I know, he's pulled me in close, and Christ, he's burning hot, all sticky with sweat.

'Alright, bunny,' he says all soft, holding my face in his hands like I'm something precious.

Then we're dancing, if you can call it that. More like we're melting into each other, his hips against mine, moving to the bass that's thumping through us both. His hands are everywhere - my back, my sides, and I just let go. Let myself forget about everything except how good this feels, how right.

He's got his mouth on my neck now, whispering stuff I can't hear over the music, but I can feel it. When he finally kisses me... bloody hell. Better than any pill, better than anything. I'm kissing him back like he's air and I'm drowning, like maybe if I kiss him hard enough, all the bad stuff might just disappear. And he's giving it right back, matching me movement for movement.

Don't know how long we stay like that, could've been minutes, could've been days. When we finally come up for air, both of us panting like we've run a marathon, everything seems brighter somehow, more real. He rests his forehead against mine, and I can feel him breathing all fast and shaky.

For the first time in ages, I am not scared.

Never been kissed like that in my life. Never want to be kissed any other way again.

PINK PANTHER

I'm at my folk's place, still feeling that 4 am pill mixing with the virus inside me. My roast dinner lay practically untouched at the table– lost my appetite somewhere on the dance floor. Dad and Jasper have gone off for a walk, while Claire's upstairs, playing 'Wonderwall' on repeat.

Head's still fuzzy as I slump onto the wicker couch. Mum's perched there with her wine, staring out at the garden.

I'm grasping for the right words, something to soften the blow.

'Mum, I'm... I'm HIV positive.' The words tear out of me.

Her wine glass stops dead, knuckles gone white. 'What did you just say?'

'I'm HIV positive.'

'What are you on about? You have AIDS?' She's panting now, each breath a sharp little gasp.

I flinch at the word. 'My CD4 count is still alright. I don't have AIDS. Yet.'

'What the bloody hell does 'CD4 count' even mean?' She lurches to her feet, red wine sloshing over the rim of her glass.

'What do I tell Dad?' My hands shake like a fucking leaf.

'Oh, to hell with your father. From who? How? When?'

I look down at my lap. 'This bloke I met in Portugal a few years back.'

'Some random bloke?'

'His name's Jack. He's in a band.'

'A band?' Her voice goes mental high. 'You slept with a boy from a band in Portugal with no condom? Have you absolutely lost your mind? What on earth were you thinking?'

She's muttering now, words tripping over themselves. 'Jesus fucking Christ!' Over and over, like she's gone mental. 'We can fix this! We need to get you the best medical treatment. I'll ring Dr Marcus immediately, see if Patricia has any tips on alternative medicine.'

'Mum, it's going to be alright.' Load of bollocks, but she needs to hear it.

She stops dead, like she's just remembered it's me who's dying. The way her face crumples does me in completely. 'Oh Stevie...my darling boy...'

Next thing I know she's got me in a bear hug. Can feel her heart thumping against my chest, the way she's trying not to cry.

'That's why you've been distant. I see it now, love.' Her voice is all muffled in my shoulder, grip tight as anything.

What can you say to that? Nothing, that's what.

She pulls back, grabs my face in her hands. Makes me look at her. 'Please. Talk to me.'

Throat's gone tight. 'I'm scared Mum,' comes out barely a whisper. 'I'm so fucking scared.'

And then I'm breaking down, these massive sobs ripping out of me. Tears and snot everywhere, looking a right state. And Mum just holds on, saying my name over and over like it might fix something.

'I know you're scared,' she soothes, even as her own voice wobbles. 'I am too. Oh my God, Steve. My beautiful boy.'

But there's no making this better, is there? We're both just drowning here, clinging onto each other like we might go under.

'I'm sorry, I'm so sorry...' she keeps saying, rocking me like I'm still a kid. But sorry doesn't mean shit now. Can't change what's coming.

The room goes proper silent. Mum gets up slow from her wicker chair, making this horrible creaking sound. Her hands are shaking something awful as she digs out this ancient pack of Silk Cut from the drawer, can barely get the lighter going. Tops up her wine, takes this desperate drag like it's keeping her upright.

Front door slams. Jasper's bells jingling away like everything's normal. Dad walks in, stops dead when he clocks us - Mum with mascara everywhere and ciggie hanging off her lip, me looking like absolute shit.

'What's all this then? Janice, why you smoking?'

Mum just sits there, mute. Takes this deep drag on her ciggie and pours herself another massive glass. I'm willing her to say it for me, but she can't get the words out either. Room's heavy with all the stuff we're not saying, just the snap and crackle of her cigarette burning.

She doesn't even look at Dad. Just reaches for the ashtray with shaking hands and shifts closer to me on the sofa. 'Sit down, dear,' she finally gets out. Waves her ciggie at the empty chair. 'We need to talk.'

I'm squirming while Dad lowers himself down, eyes bouncing between us. Jasper drops at his feet, happy as Larry.

'Steven's got something to tell you.' Mum just crumbles then, all noisy sobs. 'Oh God, Nicholas.'

Dad looks at me, face gone all desperate.

Deep breath. 'I've got HIV.'

'You have what? I don't think I heard you right, son. What did you say?'

Mum slams the ashtray down. 'Oh, for God's sake, Nicholas, you heard what he said! Steven is HIV positive.'

'HIV? How... how did this happen? I mean, how did you get it, son?'

She cuts him off, voice gone harsh.'That doesn't matter right now. We need to focus on getting him the support and treatment he needs.'

For a sec, I reckon Dad might do a runner. Just grab the scotch and pretend none of this is happening. But he gets up slow instead, all stiff-like. Shuffles over to sit beside me on the couch, dead quiet.

Mum pulls me in tight like she thinks she can protect me from it all - from the tiny bastards eating me up from inside.

Then Dad's hand lands warm and heavy on my knee.

So we just sit there. Breathing. Let that tinny Oasis tune drift down from upstairs, while all this pain and shock and fear just hangs there between us.

For the next week, Mum's fussing over me constantly. Worried about my 'lifestyle choices' and trying to steer me away from the rave scene. About as subtle as a sledgehammer, she is. But it's nice, I guess. Her popping round with homemade food and taking me out on little shopping trips. Makes me feel loved, even if it's a bit full-on at times.

She comes with me to see Dr Sher at Middlesex Hospital too. We get ushered into his little office after the nurse has drained about half my blood. The place gives me the willies - it stinks of disinfectant and the harsh white walls under them flickering lights make my head hurt.

Dr Sher's this old bloke behind a desk that's about to give up under all his medical books. Got a comb-over that's hanging on by a prayer, bit like the rest of us in this cheery little setup. He peers at my notes through these thick glasses, gives us both a polite smile. 'Let's see how we're getting along then...'

Flips through his papers, humming away. 'CD4 count is over 500 - just where we want you.' Feel my shoulders drop as he adds, 'But we'll need to do monthly blood tests to keep an eye on things.'

Mum's got her pen ready, looking worried, like she's going to write down every word that comes out his mouth. Asks what happens if my levels drop below 500. Dr Sher just says straight up we'd have to start me on meds then, but for now I'm stable. My guts still doing backflips though.

Can't help myself. 'How long have I got, Doc?'

Mum goes dead still next to me, staring at him.

'Current prognosis is around eight years,' he says, voice gone soft.

Watch Mum's face fall to bits and it does me in. She doesn't deserve any of this shit.

Then he starts on about these new drug trials in America and Europe. Some treatment called antiretroviral therapy that's working well so far. Mum's ears prick up at that, scribbling in her Filofax like mad. Wants to know if it might help me.

'Potentially yes, quite significantly actually,' Dr Sher nods. 'It's still a few years away from mainstream access though. In the meantime, Steven's health is stable, so we'll carry on monitoring things closely.'

Let out this breath I've been holding, feel my insides unclench a bit.

As we're heading out, Dr Sher gives my shoulder a squeeze. 'We're making great strides all the time,' he says. And I nearly believe him.

Me and Mum drift down Oxford Street after, arms linked, not saying much - still shaken from the hospital. Dead weird being out here with all these normal people doing their shopping. They've no clue what we've just heard, what's ticking away in me. Part of me wants to grab them and scream it in their faces. But then... Christ, part of me just wants to pretend I'm still one of them. Just for a minute.

She drags us into Borders, starts loading me up with books. Trying to get her head round it all, I reckon. Or maybe just needs something to do with her hands. She's picked up 'And the Band Played On' and this well cheerful looking thing called 'The AIDS Book - Creating A Positive Approach.' Bit much for me right now, if I'm honest. I've grabbed a few 'Living with HIV' books and stuff for newly diagnosed people.

We don't really talk about it straight up over the next week. Just read and mark bits, pass notes back and forth. I'm trying to figure out what's going on in my body now. Found out that flu and rash at Castlemorton was it starting - virus having a go at my immune system. Turns out loads of people get ill a few weeks after catching it. So that's one mystery sorted.

Dad even digs out his pile of Guardian newspapers with some bloke called Oscar Moore writing about having AIDS. Tries to be funny about it. Fucks with my head though, reading that. Like looking in some twisted mirror at what's coming. Makes me bounce between thinking I can handle it to being scared shitless in about two seconds flat.

But least I'm not on my own anymore. Me and Mum, we pass our books back and forth, desperate for answers or just something that makes sense in all this mess. Like we're trying to do this massive jigsaw in the dark. For now, all we've got is each other and these piles of books. Suppose that'll have to do.

Olympics

I finally work up the nerve one Friday to tell Chris and Gemma what's going on with me. We're just hanging out in the lounge after I threw together some pasta for dinner. Sun's going down, we've cracked open a few beers, and everything's gone quiet.

Chris asks if I've got any raves lined up for tonight. I just shake my head and say, 'Nah, not really feeling it.' They both stare at me like I've grown a second head.

Gemma jokes, 'What, our Stevie ain't out raving? You feeling alright?'

'Yeah mate, You coming down with something?' Chris chuckles.

I shift in my seat. Might as well just say it. 'Uh, yeah, could be... got back positive test results for HIV, actually.'

Chris forces an uneasy laugh. 'Come off it, mate.... that's not funny.' He takes a slow drag on his cigarette while Gemma grips her cider can tight, eyes darting between us.

I meet Chris's gaze. 'On my life. I swear I'm not taking the piss here. I don't muck about with health stuff. This is the straight truth.'

Room goes dead quiet. Some car alarm's kicking off down the street, proper doing my head in. Gemma's gone all pale, like she's seen a ghost or something. Chris just sits there gawping at his ciggie like it might tell him what to say.

Finally he looks up, face all twisted. 'But how'd you... I mean... how?' His voice has gone weird, like he's trying not to yell.

Gemma's hand finds mine, squeezing tight. Think she knows what's coming.

'I got it from someone I was sleeping with,' I say, watching Chris careful. 'A bloke.'

The silence after that feels like it goes on forever. Then Chris stands up slow, like his body's not quite working right. 'A bloke,' he repeats, voice gone flat. 'You're having a laugh.'

'Chris-' Gemma starts, but he cuts her off.

'No, hang on. So what, you're telling me you're...' He can't even say it, just stands there tugging at his hair.

'Bi. I swing both ways.' Might as well get it all out now.

He starts pacing, quick angry steps. 'How long?' When I don't answer straight away he practically spits it: 'How fucking long, Steve?'

'Always, I reckon. Just took me time to figure it out.'

His face is all shock. 'Are you taking the actual piss, Steve?!'

'Oi, what's your problem?' Gemma snaps, all hard edges now.

'Problem?' He turns on her, grabbing his jacket. 'You both knew about... THIS,' he gestures at me, 'and never bothered mentioning it?'

'Woah, easy, ...' I try to calm him down, but I know it's pointless.

'Piss OFF, the lot of ya!' he shouts, and something breaks between us that I reckon might be permanent. He storms out, kicking over the ashtray as he goes. It shatters on the floor, scattering butts and ash everywhere, door slamming so hard the windows rattle.

Fuck. This is exactly what I was afraid of. Years of friendship gone just like that. Part of me wants to run after him, explain everything. But what's the point? He's made up his mind about me already, hasn't he? Christ, what a mess.

Gemma's across the room before Chris's footsteps fade, wrapping me up tight. I hold on, feeling sick thinking my best mate's just walked out of my life.

'Fucking hell, Steve,' she mumbles into my t-shirt. 'What you gonna do? They got you on something for it?'

I squeeze her tighter, breathing in that familiar Gem smell - bit of her perfume, bit of smoke. 'Can't talk about it right now, yeah? Let's just breathe for a bit.'

We stand there in the dark, candles making shadows on the wall, holding each other like after those heavy nights when everything got too much.

'Come on,' she says, voice wobbly. 'I'm staying over, alright? No arguments.'

She takes my hand, and we get into my bed fully clothed, wrapped around each other like always. Just lying there quiet in the dark, listening to the world going on outside - some cat having a row, distant sirens, the old pipes creaking. Her arms are tight round my middle like she's scared I might disappear if she lets go. Been ages since we've done this, must've been that night after Danny Thompson broke her heart at the Christmas do. Different now though, innit? This time it's not just some bloke, it's my whole life gone to shit.

'Love you, you daft cow,' I whisper as she drifts off, meaning it more than ever.

I'm lying there in the dark, Gemma's soft breaths tickling my neck, when I hear Chris stumbling past my door. Must be gone two. I ease back the covers dead careful, trying not to wake Gem, and creep over to his room. Door's cracked open a bit and I peer in, heart going mental, not sure what I'm gonna find.

'Chris... you awake?' My whisper sounds proper loud in the quiet. Few tense seconds, then a grunt. 'Yeah.'

I slip in his room, just the orange glow from the street light coming through. It's dark in here, like some cave. Park myself on the edge of his bed, no bloody clue how to fix this weird thing between us.

Finally, Chris shifts and lets out this long breath. Rubs his hands down his face, sound dead loud in the quiet. 'Shouldn't have flipped my lid back there,' he says, voice all rough. 'Just didn't know how to wrap my head around it, you know?'

'Trust me, I get it. Been running from this shit ever since I found out.' I stop, trying to swallow past this lump in my throat. 'But no matter how far I leg it, it's always there, waiting for me.' Voice goes a bit wobbly, but I blink back the tears threatening to come.

I can tell he's struggling to find the right words, so I just wait it out.

'Do you know where you... caught it?' His voice goes all quiet like.

'Jack. From Portugal.'

Long silence, then Chris lets out this low whistle. 'Bloody hell. Suppose that explains why you were following him round like a lost puppy the whole time we was out there.'

He clears his throat. 'So, uh... what's it feel like? The HIV?'

'Can't feel nothing yet. But that 'yet' does my head in every bloody day.' Wipe my face quick. 'Up here though...' tap my temple, 'it's always there, innit? Like this shadow I can't shake.' Can't stop the tears now, no matter how hard I try. 'Makes me feel... dunno, dirty or something,' I get out, voice cracking. 'Like I'm not proper human anymore, just waiting to fade away.'

'Don't be daft. Could happen to anyone.' He puts his hand on my shoulder, something he only does when he's proper mullered at a rave. Makes me look at him, even through the tears. 'Don't matter why or how - this bastard virus ain't picky about who it gets.'

We sit there for a bit, just listening to some car down the road blasting 'Glory Glory Man United'.

'Bet you're proper bricking it though, eh?' Chris says quiet.

'Mate, I'm absolutely shitting myself.'

He goes quiet, then sits up straighter. 'But you've got to keep the faith, Stevie. They'll sort this out someday. It's the 90s, innit? Science is moving like mad - they'll crack HIV too, you watch. Can't give up now. Don't you dare go checking out early on me.' His voice goes all raw. 'Way you're facing this... you're the hardest bloke I know. Ten times braver than me.'

I snort at that. 'More like hanging on by my fingernails, mate. Proper scared most days.'

'Nah, you're still standing though, ain't you? Still fighting.' Goes quiet for a bit. 'Remember that time at Dreamscape when them dick-heads started on Gem? You didn't even think, just jumped straight in. Always been the one leading the charge, you have.'

Feel something warm up in my chest then. First proper smile in weeks. 'Cheers, mate,' I whisper. 'Dunno what I'd do without you lot.'

It's not fixed, not by a long shot, but it's a start. And right now, that's enough.

Saturday 28th April

6pm - 8am - gates open 5pm

CELESTIAL CIRCUS 1995

20 000 CAPACITY

MASSIVE SOUND SYSTEMS

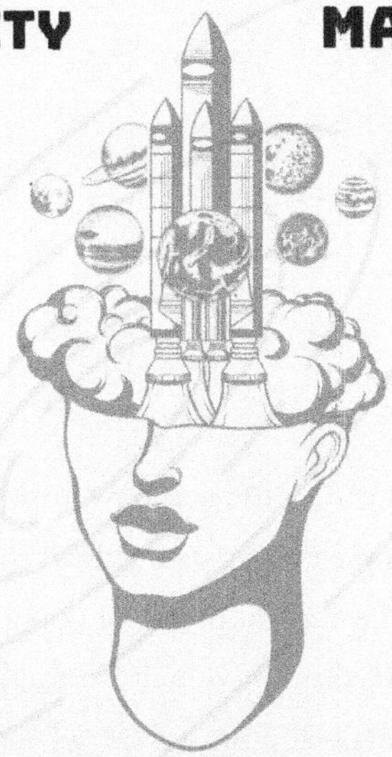

Alex P

Lisa Pin-Up

Nicky Blackmarket

DJ Phantasy

Judge Jules

Boy George

Tall Paul

John Kelly

Brandon Block

SECURITY ON SITE

CHILL OUT ZONES

Brafield Aerodrome Fields

Horton road

Brafield

Northampton

GORBACHAVS

Trying to get my head round this new normal, whatever that means. Found myself a part-time gig at this tiny law firm - dead quiet, just me and towers of musty old books. Got a window that looks over the park though, which isn't half bad. Makes me feel almost like a normal person most days, when I'm not thinking about it all.

Had to drag myself down the DWP for my disability. Bloke sorting my claim's built like a brick shithouse - arms about to burst through his shirt and everything. Fit enough, if I was bothered. According to their rules, HIV diagnosis gives you six months to live. Which means I get a decent wedge of cash. Proper laugh - I've already lasted twice that! But suppose the joke's on me, innit?

Finally managed to kick the cigarettes too while I'm at it. Still smoke the odd spliff here and there, hit the occasional rave... but I'm making more of an effort to eat right and get outside regular. Chris joins me for a game of squash down the leisure centre when our schedules line up. And we have a kick about in the park sometimes too.

Can't just sit about feeling sorry for myself though, can I? Got to keep moving or this virus'll catch me with my pants down. Still rough at night though. That's when the dark thoughts creep in - picturing these nasty little buggers having a party in my blood, spreading about like they own the place. My own body turning traitor, the sneaky bastard.

Not been with anyone since that mental snog with Baz at the rave. It's not like I don't want to - Christ, do I want to. But having to explain all this... how I got here, what it means... feels too heavy to dump on someone new.

'Relationships are still very possible, Steven,' Doc Sher reminds me gentle-like. 'You've still got needs, same as any young man.'

Nowadays, I'm a regular at his office—check-ups and the occasional game of backgammon, oddly enough. Get on well with the old boy. I suppose he's the only one who truly gets what I'm dealing with day in, day out.

This time Sher brings up my non-existent love life while trouncing me again on the backgammon board. Cheeky sod.

I squirm like a worm on a hook. 'But how do I tell someone about all... this?' I wave a hand vague at myself.

He ponders, moving his piece. 'For non-penetrative activity, you've no obligation to disclose your status.' He hops two pieces cocky. 'Obviously, any fluids exchanged means protection's essential. I'd advise against oral without.'

I wince, thinking of that Scottish bloke who nicked Chris's stereo.

'Many positive people end up dating within the community.' His voice goes stern. 'But repeated infections only weaken your system further. I've seen patients become 'super-spreaders' having unsafe sex with other positives.'

I let out a nervous laugh at his superhero phrasing, but his point hits home.

'Did you have a partner after finding out?' He nicks another of my pieces, the bastard.

'Yeah. Always played it safe,' I say, thinking of Alex while trying to catch up.

'And he's negative?' Doc moves again.

'Thank Christ, yeah.' I grab one of his pieces. Small wins.

'So you kept him safe.' He nods. 'See? Relationships work if you're careful.'

'Been having weird symptoms though.' I stop caring about the game. Feels daft pushing bits around while I'm falling apart inside.

He looks up. 'Like what?'

'I can't breathe.' The tightness hits my chest immediately.

'Is it pain in your lungs?'

'Nah, it just feels like I can't catch my breath. Like I'm suffocating.'

'Do you also feel overheated?'

'Yeah.' I'm bricking it now. This is it, I think. The beginning of the end.

'Sounds like a panic attack - probably anxiety about living with HIV.'

'So, it's not the virus?'

'Anxiety is understandable after a diagnosis like this.'

He bangs on about meds, counselling and support groups. I swerve the last two sharpish - bare my soul to a room full of strangers? Do me a favour.

Clutching my script tight, I pass the Broderip AIDS ward. Grim looking doors. Can't help thinking I'll end up behind there one day, just another skeleton. But Sher's words nag at me - doesn't have to go that way. Just got to hang on in there. Still here though, ain't I? Still kicking. Promise myself I'll fight tooth and nail to stay out. Come on then, you microscopic bastards. Let's have it.

Outside, weather's being a right git. Pissing it down, matching my mood perfect. This virus follows me everywhere now - bus, kitchen, work. Can't escape it or the panic bubbling under.

Shove the anxiety script in my pocket and splash through puddles to the chemist's. Meeting Chris and his new bird after - Tanya, barely left school and already raving like there's no tomorrow. That's his type these days. Kids who think nothing bad'll ever touch them.

Tanya's perched all possessive on Chris' lap, denim skirt riding up her curves as she babbles loudly with her mates. Matching skirts, little crop tops, giggling nonstop about some upcoming rave. Meanwhile

I'd rather be home watching Discovery on mute. This Sarah bird beside me is chatting me up hardcore. Pretty enough I suppose, but her being all up in my face just makes me antsy. I can barely focus or breathe right with her all over me. I force politeness, though, try to act normal. Everything feels proper wrong... fake. Like I'm watching it all happen from somewhere else. Doc Sher's chat about relationships rings hollow now.

'Remember Donavan, that fit bloke from the gym?' Sarah says, vodka and lime in hand.

I take a pull of my bitter, half listening.

'I was at the steppers today and clocked him by the treadmills, all sweaty.' Sarah giggles through her straw. 'So, I 'accidentally' dropped my towel in front of him, had to really slowly bend to pick it up...'

Tanya squeals, 'Get in! What happened then?'

'Well, don't go after Donavan is what I'm saying,' Amanda stage whispers. 'I think he might be a bit of a poofter, eh? You seen them tiny shorts he wears!'

More cackling erupts round the table.

I paste on this tight smile while my guts turn to water.

'I don't mind if he's a bender though, do I?' Sarah considers. 'Bit sexy really!'

Another round of screeching laughter. 'I mean he is well fit!'

'Just hope he ain't got the AIDS or nowt!' Amanda suddenly bellows.

And the pack of them loses it completely, howling and carrying on without a thought. I feel my face flush, hands gone clammy as pins and needles creep into my fingers. My lungs are seizing up and I can't catch my breath.

Chris shoots me a worried sideways look. 'Alright, pack it in. It ain't funny.'

They just shriek louder until Tanya stage gasps - 'Oh but AIDS ain't funny though, is it!' - sending them into fresh hysterics.

They go on about 'dirty AIDS people' and such. Crass, callous stuff. I push violently back from the table, nearly toppling my chair. Without a word I bolt for the exit, the walls closing in on me.

I stumble out into the freezing night, chest heaving something painful. Fumbling for the anxiety meds, I try wrestling off that bloody child-proof cap with shaking fingers. Finally, it pops free and I quick jam a tablet under my tongue.

Chris steps out, immediately sparking up with a deep drag. 'Alright, mate?'

I just nod, not able to get the words out.

'They uh...they don't know, obviously,' Chris mutters, all apologetic.

'Shouldn't chat that sort of bollocks,' I rasp finally, still struggling to breathe right.

'No, they bloody well shouldn't.'

We shut up. Just my ragged breathing and Chris flicking his lighter in the wet dark.

Eventually he grinds the smoke out under his boot. 'So, coming back in then?'

I shake my head adamant, shoving my fists deep into me coat pockets.

'Nah. Heading home, I reckon.'

Chris looks worried but doesn't push it. We part with an awkward pat on the shoulder that we both know doesn't make up for anything. As I pick up his still smoking ciggie butt and chuck it in the bin, the tightness in my chest slowly starts easing off. By the time I'm rounding the corner towards home, the meds have kicked in and I can finally suck in a proper lungful without feeling totally suffocated. Small victories, I suppose.

&

I let out this shaky breath as I stumble in the flat, digging in my coat pocket for them diazepam. Chuck my jacket on the rack and collapse on the sofa, already feeling round for the remote. Whack the telly on, flicking through channels till I find Attenborough going on about big cats hunting and that. Proper calming, his voice. Like some warm bath for your brain. Pop another pill, let that fuzzy feeling creep in while I zone out to this lioness stalking zebras. She's all muscle and murder, ain't she? Dead set on her tea. Wouldn't want to be that zebra, tell you that for nothing. My mind starts drifting, all the sharp thoughts about death and being sick going soft round the edges. Nice break, even if it won't last.

Lost in all that African stuff, I start thinking about Alex. Been a month since we had a proper chat. Reach for the phone and dial his number without even thinking, watching this lioness pick out her dinner while it rings.

'Alex.'

'Stevie-boy.' His voice warms through the fog in my head.

I sink back into the cushions. 'What you up to then?'

'Slogging through this thesis.' A good-natured grumble. 'You know how it is.'

'Ah, the glamorous life of a scholar. Making any progress, at least?'

'Some, yeah. Slow going, but I'll get there.' Rustling on his end, like he's shifting the phone. 'What about you? What you getting up to this fine evening?'

'Oh, you know. Just watching a bit of your homeland on the telly.'

'Oh yeah?' The grin carries in his voice. 'What's Attenborough banging on about this time?'

'Lion in the bush. Stalking her prey, all majestic like.'

A low, warm chuckle down the line. 'Hate to break it to you, Sunshine, but there ain't too many lions roaming the streets of Durban. Least not last time I checked.'

'Well, that's a right disappointment, innit?' I match his playful tone. 'And here I was, thinking you were out there wrestling big cats on the daily.'

His laugh comes bright and surprised. 'Nah, mate. The only predator prowling these city streets is the one in my trousers.'

'That right?' I settle in. 'Well go on then, give us the gory details. What sort of fearsome beast are we talking here?'

And just like that, we're off to the races. Alex spinning proper mental stories about the untamed wilderness of his pants, me cackling like a mad bastard and egging him on. Slips right back into place, don't it? That old rhythm of ours. Everything else just... fades out. For a bit, it's just me and him, talking absolute shite and cracking each other up.

I lose track of how long we natter on, the minutes ticking by, every penny worth it for this moment of peace. The diazepam's got me proper floaty now. Alex's voice mingles with Attenborough going on about lions, and I'm wrapped up in it all, safe and warm. Just drifting here on my sea of benzos while this lioness wanders off into the sunset, all orange and glowing like.

Anker

By my next appointment with Doc Sher, I'm down to the dregs in that little amber bottle of diazepam. Have to sheepishly admit I maybe went a bit over the recommended dose...been necking a handful through the day, two at night to try and get some kip. Like bloody Smarties, they were.

Sher levels me with a look. 'That was meant to last three months, Steven. You made it one.'

I just fidget uncomfy. 'I know...I just, it really helps, yeah?'

'It numbs,' he counters gentle. 'Doesn't truly help, I'm afraid.'

He reluctantly scribbles me more, along with adding some antidepressant called Prozac too. He mentions counselling again, but I wave it off as always.

Prozac takes the edge off, at least. Gets me through without going insane. Then after a month, nurse says I've dropped six pounds without trying. Kicks my guts in - could be the virus causing it? Tell Sher, but he says it's just the meds, happens all the time. CD4 count's still decent. Small wins, yeah?

After the check-up, I can't face my empty flat. Just me and the silence and the waiting... do my head in proper.

End up in some pub, telling myself just one quick pint to settle my nerves. But one turns to three, then four. The booze warming my belly, pushing back that icy dread that's been hanging about. Each drink makes everything lighter. Future stops mattering so much. Can't stand the thought of home now. Need noise, need chaos, need out of my head for a bit.

Next thing I'm proper mullered, stumbling into 'The Gardening Club' just as Jeremy Healy kicks off. Place is mental - packed with sweaty bodies going absolutely nuts. Still got my work gear on like some city wanker, but I've undone my buttons and I'm getting right in there. Lasers cutting through smoke, bass proper rattling my ribcage, whole place stinking of sweat and beer and weed. Everyone squeezed in tight, moving as one. My shoes are getting absolutely battered, tie's wrapped round my head like a proper nutter, but I couldn't give a flying fuck.

First time in ages I'm not thinking about dying. Just beats and bodies and feeling proper alive. Part of something bigger than all this virus bollocks.

Keep dancing, I tell myself. Even when it's just in your head. While you're moving, you're living. Has to count for something, don't it?

By the end my feet are raw and I can barely stand. Stumble out into the freezing morning, ears ringing, heart still going mental. Knackered and half-cut and feeling... dunno. Something like hope maybe.

I'm hobbling home as the sun's coming up, shoes in hand and socks stuck to my feet like I've stepped in glue. A right mess, this. Flat's empty, Chris's likely over at Tanya's, lucky sod. I peel my socks off, slow as anything, and pull a face as a blister pops. After a quick hop to the shower to wash off the grime, I carefully plaster them up.

Just then the phone screeches like a banshee. I one-leg hop to answer, pulse kicking up imagining maybe it's Alex. But there's only fuzzy static on the line, crackling like a bonfire.

'Uh...hello?'

More crackling silence. I wait a long moment just listening to the pops and hisses and then the voice isn't Alex deep and familiar, it's a girl that answers.

'Alright! It's me - Lucy!'

I freeze, blood turning to ice in my veins.

'Luce?'

'My mum told me you've been ringing, and she gave me your number. I don't even know what time it is over there.'

'Where are you?' I manage to ask, mouth dry as sawdust.

'Koh Samui,' she replies, 'Thailand.'

'You're still out there?'

'Yeah, it's been almost a year now. Bostin' here, been going to trance parties and working at a bar on the beach.'

'It's been ages since I saw you,' I sink onto the couch, heart going mental as I try to get the words out I've practiced about a million times. 'Luce-' But before I can get it out, she's off like a rocket.

'Yeah, Thailand's been crackin', except for this crazy thing that just happened.'

I pause. Anything's better than the chat I know's coming. 'Go on then - what happened?'

'Well,' she begins, 'I was seeing, not really seeing, having a bit of a thing with this Dutch bloke, Jannis, and a girl who'd been with him tested positive for HIV.'

My heart stops dead in my chest. 'And?'

'So, she told me straight out I need to get tested too 'cause he musta passed it to her.'

I swallow hard.

'So... what happened then? With the test?'

'Here's the mad bit,' she says, almost laughing. 'It came back positive! Mental, innit?'

My guts drop. Worst fears come true. Grip the phone tighter, trying not to spew.

'Christ, Lucy...'

But she's all breezy. 'Got to be a cock-up. Everyone knows Thai clinics balls up results. False positives all the time.'

'But your mate tested positive,' I say weak as piss.

'We're both fine! Healthy as anything, even with all the raving. Tests are dodgy.'

I squeeze my eyes shut, guts churning with guilt and panic. If she only bloody knew.

'Lucy, listen,' I try again, desperate now. 'What if it's not wrong? Get tested again, yeah?'

'Don't stress, Steve! Results are bollocks. I'm fine - was with Jannis ages after you anyway. Nothing to worry about!'

Her words hit like a brick to the chest.

'Luce, please,' I choke out. 'You don't get it. I'm...'

Static cuts in, mangling everything. Lucy's voice fades in and out.

'...test when I'm back home... no stress...'

Line starts beeping.

'Phone card's dying,' she shouts over the noise.

'Lucy, listen!' I'm yelling now. 'Can't wait for England! Go tomorrow! Need to know now!'

'Just leave it... handle it my way, alright?'

'Are you hearing me?! I'm begging... Lucy, I'm positive! I've got HIV!'

Silence. Then the line dies, taking my confession with it.

I slump back, still gripping the phone like it might bring her back. She's gone. And here I am, truth stuck in my throat like broken glass.

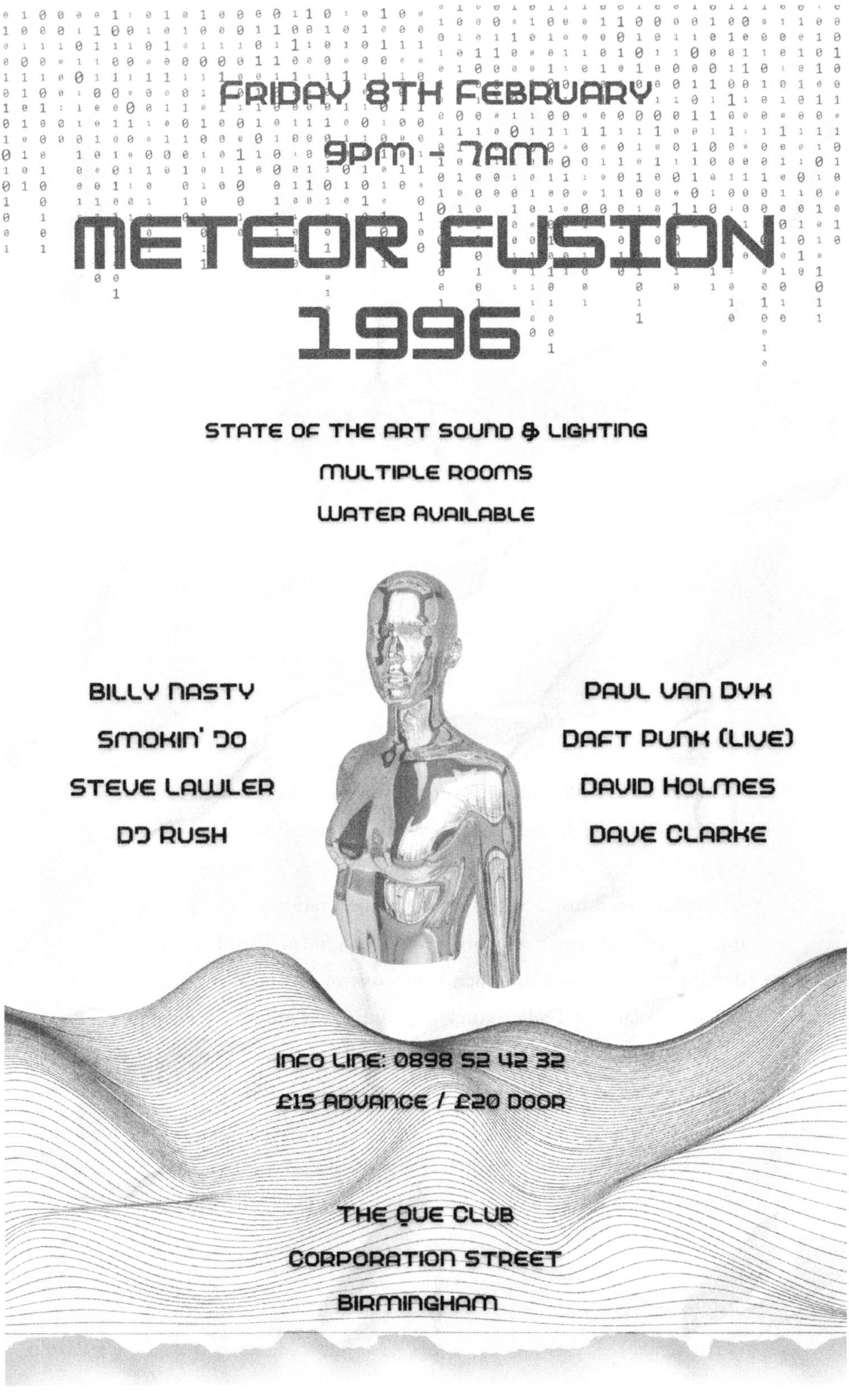
FRIDAY 8TH FEBRUARY
9PM - 7AM
METEOR FUSION
1996
STATE OF THE ART SOUND & LIGHTING
MULTIPLE ROOMS
WATER AVAILABLE
BILLY NASTY
SMOKIN' JO
STEVE LAWLER
DJ RUSH
PAUL VAN DYK
DAFT PUNK (LIVE)
DAVID HOLMES
DAVE CLARKE
INFO LINE: 0898 52 42 32
£15 ADVANCE / £20 DOOR
THE QUE CLUB
CORPORATION STREET
BIRMINGHAM

Rolls Royce

Day started off well nice - sun showing off like it was getting paid for it, sky as blue as anything. I'm wandering through the park back to work, shades on to hide from all the happy sods walking by. Had lunch with Gemma earlier, rabbiting on about Ibiza plans with her new work mates. Just normal stuff, yeah? Another boring Tuesday. Then bam - out of nowhere, my guts decide to wage war. End up stuck groaning in the office bogs until I can make a wobbly break for home, feeling like I've gone ten rounds with Mike Tyson.

A few days in and everything goes tits up. Wake up with my glands swollen like golf balls under my arms and in my groin. Throat's so raw

I can't even get water down without wanting to cry. Like my body's just decided to boot me in the bollocks non-stop.

By Friday I'm bricking it. Deep down I know what this is - the virus making its move while my immune system waves the white flag like a right coward. I'm curled up miserable on the sofa trying to get my head round how quick it's all changed. Few days back I'm with Gem planning Ibiza, now I'm wondering if I'll make it to September.

Proper head-fuck, that.

Ring Mum in a panic and she comes flying over, Dad double-parked outside like some getaway driver. They help me down from the flat, and there's this weird relief hitting as we drive away from the city. Like going home might fix everything somehow. Like Mum's soup and Dad's awkward hovering is gonna fix this mess.

What happens next is proper hell, just a blur of feeling rough as fuck. Brain's on fire with fever, cramps folding me in half, and this headache like someone's taking a sledgehammer to my skull. Mum's buzzing round like some worried wasp, trying to get soup and water down my manky throat while I'm drifting in and out of these mental fever dreams. Can hear her begging Doc Marcus on the blower to come round - but he's not having any of it. We both know my CD4's gone to shit, but neither of us says it out loud, like keeping quiet might make it not true. But I see it in Mum's eyes, same fear that's doing my head in. Through the fog, I catch Mum and Dad having this massive row. She's pleading to keep me home so she can look after me, but Dad's not having it. Never heard them kick off like this before, then

Dad's voice cuts through clear as anything: 'Damnit Janice, I'm ringing the hospital myself!'

Next thing, it's Doc Sher on the line - dead calm but urgent like, telling them to get an ambulance sharpish.

Front door nearly comes off when this swarm of uniforms charges in like the cavalry. Get me strapped on a stretcher and wheel me out into the sunshine, and ain't that a kick in the teeth - all that gorgeous freedom out there while I'm trapped in this broken body. They're jabbing me with painkillers before we even hit the road. Skip the local hospital, bombing it straight to Middlesex instead. Ambulance screaming through traffic, every bump making me wince, strapped down and staring at the ceiling while some paramedic keeps checking my vitals.

Then my trolley's rattling like mad as they wheel me through these stark halls. The fluorescent lights making everything look worse than it is. I can feel everyone's eyes on me - doctors, nurses, visitors, all of them. These strangers don't know me from Adam, but I'm convinced they can tell exactly why I'm here. That I'm contaminated. Dying. My guts are churning with pain and fear, and I'm fighting back tears like a big man. Can't handle their looks, so I just stare at their shoes, trying to block everything else out.

They whisk me behind these curtains, everything going mental with confusion and panic. I'm thinking, this it? This how I go out, in some fluorescent-lit cubicle without a friendly face in sight?

But then, like some guardian angel in a white coat, there's Doc Sher. His face kind behind them thick glasses of his, giving my shoulder a squeeze that does more than any medicine could. 'You're not dying, Steven,' he says, calm as you like. 'Just a nasty infection, we'll get that fever down and you'll pull through this.' Another pat and he's gone, leaving me clinging to that promise like it's the last pint in London.

As the meds kick in and the fever breaks, everything starts going fuzzy round the edges. I'm sliding into this deep sleep at last, grateful to just check out for a bit.

&

I wake up groggy, head stuffed with cotton wool while the ward's making a right racket - all snoring and sniffling and that. Takes me a minute to focus under them harsh lights, trying to make sense of the faces around me. Everyone's lost in their own little worlds, monitors beeping away steady as anything while sheets rustle and nurses chat in whispers.

Bloke by the window's got all these cards and this heart balloon bobbing about - bit sweet that, in a naff sort of way. Over in the corner there's this poor sod in a wheelchair looking half gone already, bald as a cue ball with these dark marks all over, IV dripping away like it might make a difference. Couple of blokes across the way keep giving me the eye, whispering when they think I'm not looking - one's got bleached hair with blue bits stuck in, his mate's got a ponytail down to his arse. Even got a vicar in the far bed, which ain't exactly filling me with confidence.

My throat feels like I've been gargling glass, and I'm gagging for water something chronic.

Then this tiny nurse bounces in, all neat bob cut and pressed uniform. She does a quick sweep of the room before heading over to Mr Heart Balloon's bed, giving him this big hug while she grins at his soppy decoration.

'This one's from Sergio then?' she says, making him go all shy while she reads his card.

She works her way round the room, stopping here and there for hugs like she's everyone's favorite auntie. By the time she gets to my bed, I catch this whiff of CK-One.

'Alright, love?' She gives my shoulder a squeeze. 'I'm Margaret, I'll be looking after you while you're here.' Another smile as she pats my hand. 'Let's get some brekkie in you, yeah?'

'Just water'd do me,' I manage to croak out, but she's having none of it, going on about needing proper food for strength and that. Then she's off to the next patient, trailing that perfume behind her like some fancy cloud.

The bloke next to me sits up sudden, grinning like he's won the lottery of hospital beds. 'Morning, mate! I'm Jason - what's your name?'

'I'm uh, Steve,' I mumble, still feeling like I've been proper done over by a bus.

Before I can even get my head straight, Jason's jumping out of bed, pulling on this vest and these bright white socks that could probably guide planes in. Next thing I know he's got Kiss FM blasting away, which gets them two across the way perking right up.

'Oi, I fackin' love this choon!' Blue-hair shouts, already dancing about like a right muppet. Waves over at us like we're in some club instead of a hospital ward. 'I'm Gary, by the way! This here's Mikey.'

As the beat drops, those two start shuffling around, getting everyone laughing - even the vicar's cracking a smile at their antics.

Margaret comes back in with breakfast trays, giving our little ward rave this look that's trying to be stern but comes out dead sweet instead. She puts my tray down careful - teapot steaming away, water jug, and this bowl of strawberry yoghurt that looks about as appetising as wallpaper paste.

'That fever still needs sorting,' she tells me, fussing with my pillows. 'You really must drink something, love.'

'Cheers,' I manage to get out. Down the water like it's the last drink on earth, then force down some of that yoghurt before I'm knackered again. Let my eyes shut as everything starts fading out - all that happy chat and house music floating around me while I drift off.

When I surface again, Doc Sher's at my bedside, checking me over and giving my shoulder one of his trademark squeezes. His face has gone all serious, which ain't exactly filling me with confidence.

'Your CD4 count's dropped,' he says, straight to it. 'Down to 296. And you've got CMV - that's what's causing your throat and stomach pain. Caught it early, but we'll need to watch it.'

My guts turn to ice at that. I know about CMV - nasty little bastard that can mess with your eyes, your insides, the lot. This it then? Start of the downhill slide I've been dreading?

Doc must clock my panic 'cause he goes all reassuring. 'We'll get you on IV antibiotics, sort this out. You'll need to stay in for a while though.' He gives me this confident smile, like he's got it all sorted. 'Getting you on the new antiretroviral combo too. You're in safe hands, Steven.'

Gives me a pat and leaves, calling back about 'plenty more backgammon to come!' like that's supposed to cheer me up. I let out this shaky breath, trying to believe him while Margaret fusses about with my pillows, chatting away about nothing and everything.

She sorts my IV quick smart, getting the needle ready with practiced hands. 'Just a little prick, love!' she says, all innocent like.

Michael shouts from across the ward before I can even wince, 'Well, that's a shame, innit?'

The lads start proper howling at that, Jason joining in with, 'Never been fond of little pricks myself!' Even Margaret's trying not to laugh while she sorts me out.

Soon as I'm hooked up, she gets this look I'm starting to recognise. 'Right then, young man. Up you get!'

I groan like I'm dying (might be, to be fair), but she's not having any of it. Next thing I know I'm on my feet, wobbling about like some pissed uncle at a wedding while she steadies me.

'Bit of movement will do you good,' she says, all cheerful. 'Get your strength back.'

So here I am, clutching my IV pole like it's keeping me alive, shuffling down this endless corridor with Margaret nattering away beside me. We pass this makeshift lounge where some lads are huddled round a portable telly, tinsel wrapped round the bunny ears like that might actually help with the reception. One bloke's buried under about six blankets, looking proper fed up with whatever's fuzzing in and out on BBC1.

The nurses' station's absolute chaos - phones going mental, staff rushing about with folders and charts while some volunteer sorts through magazines like she's in her front room, not arsed about the mayhem around her. Get well cards everywhere, and this massive board full of photos - patients grinning, nurses pulling faces, like some mad family album.

Then I see it - this room done up in black satin instead of those sterile white hospital sheets. Some bloke's on the bed chatting to visitors, then he looks up and my legs go to jelly. That messy hair, that pretty-boy face with the turned-up nose, them blue eyes that could stop traffic. Can't be... But it bloody well is. Basil. Same Basil I've been thinking about since that snog at the rave, feels like another lifetime ago now.

My mouth goes desert dry as Margaret steadies my elbow, probably thinking it's just the fever making me wobbly. He clocks me and grins that same cheeky grin, and I'm proper done for. Can barely hear Margaret asking if I'm alright as she steers me past, my head spinning something chronic.

Can't stop wondering if he remembers me, and Christ - is he sick too? Try focusing on staying upright, but that smile of his is stuck in my head, that spark in his eyes still there even here. Like seeing my old life walking about - fit as ever and turning up in the last place I expected.

Proper head-fuck, that.

Little Grape

Gemma turns up the next afternoon, clutching a pack of Maltesers. We settle into the corner lounge, just me, her, and some middle-aged bloke snoring away by the window, mouth gaping like a stunned fish. She offers me one of the chocolates but something tastes off - sort of chemical, like I'm licking a car battery. I let it sit dissolving in my dry mouth rather than try to swallow the thing. Trying to steer conversation away from my health, I mention spotting Basil from the raves here too.

'Trust you to pull in hospital, you absolute muppet!' She's proper creasing, eyes all crinkled up happy.

When she mentions Chris sends his love, I'm all ears straight away. 'Yeah? Tell him same back, will you? Any chance he'll pop in?'

'You know what he's like with hospitals...'

Fair point that. We share this look, says more than words could really, before she gets that glint in her eye. 'Least you've got your fit raver boy to keep you entertained!'

I feel my face going red, trying to play it cool and just enjoy having a bit of normal for five minutes. Before she heads off though, I press Alex's number in her hand.

'Give him a bell for me? Just say I'm in hospital but doing alright.'

'Course I will, you daft sod.' She squeezes my hand tight, then can't help herself: 'Want me to mention your new boyfriend while I'm at it?'

'Shut it, you.'

She plants one on my forehead and buggers off, leaving me with just the human foghorn for company. Catch myself straining to hear Basil's voice from his room, wondering when them eyes of his might appear again.

Don't get much chance to think about it though - Mum, Dad and Claire show up not long after, Claire grabbing the seat by my bed like she's claiming territory. She holds my hand dead gentle, like I might break. Dad's perched on his chair stiff as a board, twitching and looking anywhere but round the ward. Mum's fussing over me, brushing my hair back with trembling fingers. Can feel the worry coming off her in waves.

Dad glances about before whispering, 'This ward only for AIDS patients?'

'Yes, Nicholas, it's the Broderip ward,' Mum says, lips tight.

Dad sort of crumples in on himself at that, and I catch the fear on his face - cuts right through me, that does.

Mum chatters away while Claire goes on about her new music on her walkman, voice too bright. But Dad's locked in his head, won't even look my way. When they leave, Mum hugs me so tight my ribs hurt. Her Chanel No. 5 lingers after they're gone.

Ward goes quiet come evening, lights dimming down like we're all in some separate little world. I'm thinking about another wander, maybe accidentally-on-purpose bump into Basil, when wouldn't you know it - in he strolls looking fit as ever, trackies riding low, wearing this daft smiley face top. Even knackered with them dark circles under his blue eyes, he's still gorgeous.

He swans over to Balloon Man's bed like he owns the place. 'Why hello, darling Malcolm.' Does this sweep of the ward, clocks the bloke in the corner. 'You alright, Bruce?'

Bruce manages the tiniest nod before nodding off again. Basil mutters 'bloody hell' under his breath, then catches me staring.

'Well, hello stranger!' His grin lights up his whole face. 'Back with us then? Out for days, you were. Steven, right?'

I just nod like a muppet, tongue gone dead useless. His smile gets wider. 'Couldn't forget a gorgeous face like yours, could I?'

Throws me this wink that sets my heart going absolutely mental. Christ, I'm like some kid with their first crush all over again.

He turns back to Malcolm, voice gone all gentle. 'My darling, time to make you even more exquisite for that divine boyfriend of yours.'

Malcolm sits up and I get a proper look at him - handsome bloke underneath it all, with sharp cheekbones and green eyes still full of spark. Hair's thinning but neat as anything. Got these black spots scattered over his skin though, nasty big one right on his neck.

'Sergio's going to fall in love with you all over again,' Basil says, whipping out concealer and this fancy brush from his track pocket. Gets to work, chatting away while he covers the spots. Can't help watching his hands move - dead precise, like he's done this a thousand times before.

He catches me looking, gives me this cheeky smirk. 'See something you like, darling?'

I go bright red as he gives me a slow once-over. 'What brings a tasty morsel like you here? No offence, love, but you don't look half dead yet.' His grin's infectious. 'I mean, I don't either, though apparently I'm 'fatally ill'.'

'CMV,' I shrug, nodding at my IV. 'Got me on the good stuff.'

'Welcome to the club, dove! Such fun, eh? Live here more than my flat now - got half my wardrobe stashed about.' Strikes a pose that makes me want to laugh and snog him all at once. 'Still look fabulous though, yes?'

'Too right,' I blurt before I can stop myself, making him preen like some right peacock. His wink sets the butterflies in my chest going mental again. Mad how he makes even this place feel alive.

Few more brush strokes and he's done. 'Perfection, darling. Sergio'll go weak at the knees.'

Malcolm checks himself in the mirror, the nasty marks barely visible now. The way his eyes light up - gets you right in the throat, that does.

Then Basil's at my side quick as anything, his cologne hitting me as those blue eyes sweep over my face. He grabs the bed rail, leaning in with this look that spells nothing but trouble. Heart's going mental as he hops up on my bed, long legs swinging next to mine. Like we're kids on a park bench, except there's nothing innocent about the heat between us.

'So! Have we properly introduced our little family yet?' He nods at the other patients, but I'm barely listening, too busy taking in every bit of him. His hair's all messed up golden curls, cheekbones sharp enough to cut glass, and that mouth... Christ. Then there's those eyes - reckon a bloke could drown in baby blues like that.

Right weird having all his attention on me. The ward, the virus, everything else just... disappears. Nothing matters except him right here, close enough I can feel the warmth of him.

He points out sleeping Jason first. 'That's Jason, resident DJ and all-around cheeky monkey.'

'The one who does the ward raves?' I ask, remembering the Kiss FM incident.

'That's him! Spends his days kipping and his nights spinning vinyl at some club round the corner in Soho. We should go sometime.'

My stomach does this flip at the way he says it - like there's gonna be a sometime.

Next, he nods at the bloke in the corner, slumped there with just his IV for company. 'And over there, that's Bruce. Poor lamb, he was an English professor at Queen Mary before all this nastiness.' His voice goes all soft. 'His mum comes every day, bless her. Before work, after... doesn't matter. She's always here, holding his hand and reading to him. Poetry, mostly. Keats, I think.'

Something in how he says it makes my chest go tight. Can't help wondering about his lot at home - if they know where he is, if they give a toss. But I keep my gob shut about that one.

Basil shakes it off quick as he turns to Malcolm. 'And of course, you've met our darling Malcy. Quite the dish, isn't he? Hard to believe he used to make his living off that pretty face.' He pauses, winking. 'Well, that and a few other choice assets.'

Malcolm gives him this eye roll, but you can tell they're proper close. Funny how being stuck in here does that to you.

'His Sergio is a lucky man,' Basil carries on. 'Comes round every evening like clockwork, he does. The very picture of devoted love.' He fans himself dramatic. 'You'll see for yourself soon enough - they're both so disgustingly gorgeous, it's bloody offensive.'

Can't help laughing at that. Then he's moving on to Mikey and Gary, who're bent over some manky old Smash Hits like it's the Bible.

'Ah yes. Tweedledee and Tweedledum, joined at the hip and thick as thieves. I'm convinced they were separated at birth.'

They look up together when he blows them a kiss, all dopey-like, then go straight back to their magazine like they're sharing one brain between them.

'The rest are new to me,' he waves at the fresh faces. 'But give it a day or two, and we'll be bosom buddies. That's how it goes in here.'

He says it casual, but there's something about it that proper gets to me. Because he's right, ain't he? This virus that's dragged us all in here... it's made us family in some mental way. Stuck together whether we like it or not.

'Funny, isn't it?' Basil says, gone all quiet. 'The way the universe has chucked us back together again. Like... like there's some plan. Pattern we can't see yet, but it's there.'

'You reckon it's fate?' I ask. 'Us being here?'

He leans in close enough I can feel the heat of him through my manky hospital gown. 'Darling, I don't believe in coincidences. Not for the big stuff. This?' His finger trails between us. 'You and me? That's fate.' His face goes all soft. 'How you really doing, love?'

And just like that, it all comes pouring out. 'Don't know how to do this. How to be sick, be... dying. I'm twenty-six, for fuck's sake. Should be out there living, not stuck in here.' Can feel myself shaking but can't stop. 'This is proper shit, innit?'

'Oh, darling.' He strokes my hair gentle like. 'I know it feels like the end of everything.'

He takes my face in his hands, those blue eyes of his going right through me. 'But listen to me, Bunny. You hearing me?'

I nod, couldn't look away if I tried. He smiles, all fierce and tender at once.

'This is not the end. Not even close. You are so much more than this disease, do you hear me? So much more than the hand you've been dealt.'

Try to argue but he puts a finger to my lips. 'No talk of dying. We're gonna grab life by the bollocks, squeeze every bit of joy out. That's what we deserve.'

The way he says it - can't help believing him, just for a bit.

'That's my brave Bunny,' he whispers.

His lips brush my forehead, sending this spark right through me. 'Never stop believing, never doubt...'

Then he's gone like smoke, leaving me dizzy - heart still racing, skin tingling where he touched me. Takes a minute to notice the ward again - the machines beeping away, people chatting. Been lost in whatever that was, like waking up from some dream.

Gary's grinning over from his bed with this look that says he knows exactly what's running through my head. I can feel my face going red as anything - getting all worked up over someone in hospital, what am I like?

'Basil, king of Broderip ward,' Gary says, still wearing that cat-that-got-the-cream smile.

'Got it sorted, he has,' Mikey chimes in. 'Even got his own private room.'

Malcolm's voice comes weak from his pillows, 'Funniest bloke I ever met... one of a kind.'

Jason stirs just to add his two pence: 'And fit as anything!'

Mikey cracks up at that, setting us all off like we're back in school.

'Absolute life and soul, that one,' Gary says, voice gone all soft and fond.

Can't help laying here playing it all back - the way he looked at me, touched me, going on about fate and stars like some mystic down the market. Like something I never thought I'd find in here of all places. Let myself get lost in it, that kiss on my forehead still burning there like some mark.

Little Rocket

Days blur into this dull routine. Wake up to an IV cocktail, then those stiff walks round the ward that feel more pointless every time. I peek in on Basil's room sometimes - mostly empty now, all dark corners. When I catch him kipping in those black satin sheets, he looks different. Like someone's nicked all his sparkle.

Lunch ain't bad though – bit of normality when me, Gary and Mikey can mess about like we're down the pub. Telling stories and talking rubbish, trying to forget where we are for a bit.

Mum shows up after work, fussing like mad. We dance round the big stuff careful, both of us trying to keep it light.

By tea I'm knackered, too done in to be sociable. Just sip at the watery soup and let the others' laughing fade into background noise till I'm nodding off.

Next morning it all starts again - more drips, more shuffling about feeling rough as anything. But I hang on tight to each new day, hoping there's something better coming through all this darkness.

&

Day five and Alex rings - just hearing him down the crackly line makes everything feel closer, more real. I'm in the tatty armchair by the window, IV stand next to me. Heart's going mad just from his voice.

'Steve...?' Careful, like he might break something.

My hand trembles on the receiver, knuckles going white. 'Alright, mate?'

'You holding up?'

Let out a long breath, trying not to let the dark thoughts in. 'Okay as I can be. Stuck in here anyway.'

I look round at the ward, fingers drumming against my knee. Not exactly five-star.

'What's happened?'

'Just a CMV flare-up.' I fiddle with my IV line, watching the liquid drip steady. 'Got me on the good stuff now, so...' Trail off, not knowing how to finish that one.

'CMV? What's that?'

Drop my voice, leaning further into the corner. 'Form of herpes virus, minor strain.' Pick at my gown, hands needing something to do. 'Nothing to worry about, yeah?'

'Bloody hell...'

'So!' My voice comes out too bright, too forced. 'How's uni? Still winding up all them posh boys?' Try to picture him in some fancy lecture hall.

'Fuck uni. Don't care about that. Just want to know if you'll be alright.'

'I'll be fine.' Try laughing but it comes out weird and hollow. 'You know me - tough as old boots. If this does me in, least they might name a ward after me - Steven Bishopston Memorial Wing for the Terminally Fabulous.'

'Don't.' His voice cracks. 'Don't joke about that. I'm worried sick.'

I close my eyes, fighting tears. The silence between us weighs a tonne. My grip on the phone's so tight my fingers are going numb.

'I promise, I'm fine. Honestly.' Don't even believe it myself.

'Just...be careful, yeah? Take your meds. No tough guy act.'

'Scout's honour. Model patient, me.'

'I mean it, Steve.' His voice breaks. 'I can't lose you. I can't.'

'You won't.' Throat tight. 'Not going anywhere.'

We just breathe together over the line. I watch the weak sun through the window making patterns on the floor. Peaceful, in a way. My hand's shaking so bad I have to press the phone harder against my ear.

'Should go. Let you rest.'

'Yeah.' Barely more than a whisper.

'I'll call again soon. Check you're behaving.'

'I'll be by the phone.'

He laughs soft - can picture his eyes crinkling.

'Get some sleep, you daft sod. Doctor's orders.'

'Aye aye, captain. Sweet dreams, yeah?'

'Sweet dreams, Sunshine.'

Line goes dead. I sit there holding the phone, not ready to let go yet. The plastic's warm where I've gripped it too hard, leaving marks on my palm.

Finally force myself up, legs gone wobbly. Drag myself back to bed with a sigh

'Ah, Steven! There you are, my boy!'

Doc Sher's voice booms through the room, snapping me out of it. He's grinning, old backgammon board under his arm.

'Just finished my rounds. Fancy one last game before I head home?'

Can't help grinning back, mood lifting already.

'You're on, Doc. Warning though - feeling lucky tonight. Gonna absolutely beat you this time.'

He chuckles, wheeling the tea tray over. 'We'll see about that, young man.'

We set up the board, pieces clacking, dice rattling. While we play and take the piss, all the heavy stuff fades away - the fear, missing Alex, all of it.

Doc lands some killer moves at first, but after some choice words and bit of luck, I pull ahead. When I win, let out a right cheer. Doc beams at me like he's chuffed.

'Well, I'll be!' He shakes my hand. 'About time you beat this old dog!'

His eyes go all warm and fatherly as he packs up. Gives me a wink and promises to win his title back next time.

After he's gone, I sink into my pillow. First time in days I feel almost normal. Almost like myself again.

TWINS

Week two and looks like the meds might finally be doing their job. The thrush, that bastard gut rot... all of it easing off, bit by bit, thank Christ.

Malc's chipper today, perched by the window with his cuppa, going on about Paris clubs and mental weekends in Ibiza like he's flipping through some photo album in his head.

'Wouldn't change a thing,' he says quiet, watching the city buzz about below us. 'Lived the dream, didn't I? No regrets, not a single bloody one.'

Mikey's hanging on every word, proper star-struck. 'You had it all, mate. Seeing the world, travelling in style... that's living, that is.'

Malc just gives this soft little smile. 'Yeah, took it all for granted though, didn't I? All that good health.' He touches his cheek, checking himself in the window's reflection. 'Maybe not my usual dashing self, but I'm feeling alright, you know?'

Gary's gone all thoughtful, rubbing his chin. 'Wish I'd been straight, if I had my time again.'

Mikey nearly chokes on his tea, giving Gary a dig in the ribs. 'Straight? Mate, you're bent as a nine-bob note and you bloody know it!'

That sets us all off - laughter bouncing round our little corner of the ward like we're down the pub or something.

Even Malc's beaming now as he spins these tales of his glory days. All them sunsets chased, cities painted red, not a care for the shadows creeping up behind. Gets you right in the chest, that does.

Door bangs open and in comes Baz like a whirlwind, all baggy jeans and this pink 'BOY' shirt. Loud as anything and cheeky with it. Can't help staring. He looks... bloody hell. None of that hospital grey about him today - he's glowing, bouncing about like he's got springs in his shoes.

'Gossiping about me again, are we?' he trills. 'Well, don't stop on my account, darlings! You know how I love being the centre of attention!'

Throws us a dramatic wink that has Malc chuckling and shaking his head. 'Oh, we know, Baz. Trust me, we know.'

'Now now, Malcy! Don't be jealous just 'cause you've been stuck in that bed since before I was born!'

Malc lets out this shocked gasp. 'You cheeky sod!'

Baz just grins wider. 'Might be a bit wobbly on my pins, but I'm still all about the sex, drugs, and rock 'n roll. Well, maybe not the rock 'n roll - can't be doing with that racket. House music or nothing for this glittery queen!'

Then his eyes land on me and I swear my heart stops. 'There you are, my little rave bunny! Up you get - no point moping about in bed all day. Unlike Malcolm and poor Bruce in the corner, you can still shake that cute arse of yours!'

He's waving his hands about all dramatic like. 'Come on, bunny. Time to live a little - got trouble to cause, parties to crash, hearts to break!'

I'm lost. 'Wait, what? We going somewhere?'

His grin gets even bigger, if you can believe it. 'Course we are, darling! You think I'm just here for the scenery? We're breaking out of this depressing dump, even if it's just for a few hours!'

That's all I need to hear. I'm grabbing my green flannel shirt before my brain's caught up with what's happening, feeling excited for the first time in ages. Turn round to see Gary and Mikey standing there looking like kids at Christmas.

'Can we come?' Gary's practically bouncing.

'Course you can, my loves!' Baz claps his hands like he's conducting an orchestra. 'Get your coats though - we're doing a runner! Adventure awaits!'

He's skipping about while we're all scrambling for coats and that. 'Let's show this place how it's done, shall we?'

Then we're off, trailing Baz like ducklings. Margaret catches us at the nurses' station, giving us a 'be back for meds' warning with a knowing smile.

Out the ward, down the stairs, into the city's heart. Baz throws his arms wide, breathing deep. 'God, it feels good to be out in the world again! Smell that smog, feel that grime!' He shepherds us across the road, cooing and fussing all the way. 'Careful now, mind the traffic! Look both ways, there's a love!'

Mikey and Gary exchange smirks, rolling their eyes at the theatrics. But they're loving it too, I can tell. Loving being part of Baz's mad little crew.

We dive into the Oxford Street madness, dodging past shoppers, blokes flogging tat, and buskers making a racket. Complete head-spin after the quiet hospital - lights everywhere, horns blaring, people yelling about their bargains. Baz just glides through it all, grinning like a loon. Leads us down till we hit Tottenham Court Road where it's a bit less chaotic.

Between two jeans shops, these dodgy stairs lead down to this tiny ticket window. Bloke inside clocks Baz straight away, gives him a nod, takes his cash and hands over a little bag. Few more quick deals for the rest of us and then we're in, smoke and bass hitting us as the door swings wide. It's well cosy inside - velvet benches everywhere, Pearl Jam playing soft through the haze.

Gary pipes up, eyes wide as Baz rolls a spliff neat as anything beside me, his leg pressed right up against mine. 'What's this gaff then?'

Baz just grins, all cat-that-got-the-cream. 'This, my doves, is our little escape hatch. A puff of the good stuff, a few cheeky drinks, a chance to just let ourselves breathe for a moment. No nurses, no meds, no hospital smell following us around.'

Mikey's proper twitchy, keeps looking over his shoulder. 'But what if Old Bill turn up?'

'Oh, I hope they do, darling. Liven things up a bit, wouldn't it?' He holds the smoke in his lungs like it's precious. 'Now hush and trust your Uncle Basil, loves. I've got you.'

Passes it to Mikey who takes the tiniest puff and nearly coughs up a lung, setting us all howling. Even Mikey's grinning once he can breathe again. Baz tuts playfully, retrieving his craftwork. 'Steady on, darling. Can't have you turning blue on us now, can we? No doctors or nurses around here to save you.'

The spliff makes its rounds, and we're all getting well settled. Baz launches into stories of Soho's seediest spots, all sly grins and waggling eyebrows. Mikey's eyes are nearly popping out while Gary's just zonked, blowing smoke rings.

'That's proper mental,' Gary mumbles. 'Most exciting thing I've done is kip in the chill-out room.'

'You mean to tell me there are actual real live gay men who've never been to a sex club?' Baz's jaw drops all dramatic. 'What a travesty!'

Then he's giving me this look that sets my stomach doing flips. 'Tell me you're a bit more debauched than these two, Bunny.'

Go bright red at that, can't help it. 'Not really.'

'Oh, you sweet summer children!' He claps his hands together. 'Never mind, darlings. Plenty of time to corrupt you yet.'

We're all getting well loose now, chatting about raves and that. First proper time since being in here I've felt almost human.

Baz leans forward, eyes sparkling like he knows something we don't. 'But the common thread uniting us all is surely our love of raving, oui?'

'Them tunes were a lifeline for me.' Mikey's gone all deep and thoughtful. 'When everything was going tits up, least I had somewhere to go.'

'Best nights of my life under them strobes,' I say, catching Baz's eye.

'Dance floor's a church, darling. A holy place. Somewhere I truly belong, even if it's just for a night.'

We all go quiet after that, lost in memories of them mental nights. The smoke's well thick in here now, and I can feel the spliff wearing off, all that hospital reality starting to creep back in like a tide.feel the spliff wearing off, all that hospital stuff starting to creep back in.

Baz must sense the shift in mood because he suddenly sits up straighter, clapping his hands together. 'Right, my ducklings! I don't know about you lot, but I'm starting to feel a bit cooped up in here. Fancy a bit of fresh air?'

Gary perks up at that. 'Ooh, yeah. Could do with stretching my legs a bit.'

'Brilliant idea!' Baz cries. 'Let's take this party to the park, shall we? Soak up some sun, cause a bit of mischief...' He waggles his eyebrows, winking outrageously. A bit of vitamin D will do us all some good. Doctor's orders!' He grins, pulling Mikey to his feet.

As we're sorting ourselves to leave, Baz gets all close, can feel his breath on my ear. 'Ice creams on me, darlings! Can't have a real day out without a 99 Flake, now can we?'

We're all proper giddy as Baz herds us out like some fabulous mother hen. Sunlight hits me right in the face after that dark club - proper blinding - but once I can see straight again, can't wipe the stupid grin off my mug. First time since being banged up in that hospital that I feel like me, you know? Even if it's just for a bit.

Baz is going mental out in the sunshine, swanning about, leaving bits of glitter everywhere he goes. We end up queuing for ice cream, all elbows and taking the piss while that sweet smell gets my mouth watering. Find this spot under this massive old oak tree, sun coming through the leaves making patterns on our skin and that. For a minute there, it's like... like we're just normal lads having a laugh on a sunny day. No hospital, no virus, no worried mums or doctors pulling long faces. Just us lot, being alive.

But then Mikey shifts about, fiddling with a daisy. 'My mum don't know,' he says quiet, eyes fixed on the flower. 'About the diagnosis, I mean.'

'You gonna tell her?'

'Nah.' He gives this little shrug. 'Can't do that to her. She's better off.' His voice drops even lower. 'I'm ashamed. Dirty.'

Baz goes dead still, ice cream dripping forgotten down his fingers. 'You think this is punishment? God smiting us?'

'I dunno. Maybe?' Gary's gone all red. 'Reap what you sow, in't it?'

'A loving god condemning folks for joy?' Baz lets out this bitter laugh. 'Sounds more like the bollocks my father would spout.'

Goes quiet after that, all of us sat there with our own demons for company. Give Baz a little nudge with my elbow, trying to pull him back from wherever his head's wandered off to. He blinks a few times, then slaps on that smile of his.

'Sod that for a game of soldiers!' He springs up like he's been shocked. 'I'm done letting narrow-minded wankers dictate my happiness. We're here, we're queer, and we're not going anywhere. So, let's bloody well make the most of it, yeah?'

A ragged cheer goes up, Mikey and Gary both getting caught up in Baz's fire. He grins, fierce as anything, and reaches down to haul me up. 'C'mon, Bunny. Let's go cause some chaos.'

And so we do. Swagger down Oxford Street, arm in arm, taking the piss and not giving a toss who's looking. Baz drags us into HMV, making a beeline for the listening booths like he's got something planned. Next thing I know he's got me pressed up against him in this tiny space, Leftfield pumping through the headphones.

'Dance with me, Bunny.' His hands are everywhere - my hips, my sides, the back of my neck. The bass is pounding through us and Christ, he feels good. Can barely think straight with him moving against me like that, his breath hot on my neck.

Just as things are getting proper heated, someone bangs on the glass. Gary's face appears, grinning like a right tosser. Baz just laughs it off while I'm trying to sort myself out without being obvious about it. Bloody Gary.

We stumble out the booth all flushed, and there's Mikey and Gary looking well pleased with themselves. 'Alright, lovebirds?' Gary's got this proper shit-eating grin on his face.

Baz just throws him a kiss, grabs the Leftfield album from the counter and slips it into my hand. 'Jealousy is so unbecoming, darling,' he purrs, leading us back out into the street.

Baz leads us on a merry dance through the streets till he spots M&S, and gets this look in his eye that spells trouble. Swans in like he owns the place, heading straight for the booze aisle.

'Right then, my darlings!' He's practically bouncing. 'Time for a bit of the old five-finger discount.'

Me and Gary exchange looks while Mikey goes white as a sheet. But Baz is already in motion, smooth as anything. He's got this system worked out - gets Gary chatting to the security guard about football, has Mikey accidentally knock over a display near the tills, all while he's slipping a bottle of champers under his baggy top quick as you like.

'Come along, ducklings!' He breezes past us toward the exit. 'Nothing suspicious about a few queens browsing on a Tuesday afternoon!'

We burst out onto the street, hearts racing, trying to look casual while Baz is practically skipping. Once we're round the corner, he whips the bottle out with a flourish - proper expensive stuff and all.

'And that, my loves, is how it's done!'

Gary looks like he might faint. 'Fucking hell, Baz!'

'Stick with me,' Baz winks, passing the bottle to Gary to stash. 'I'll show you how to really live.'

And Christ, I believe him. I'd follow this mad, beautiful, impossible boy anywhere.

As we head back to hospital, Gary keeps checking his coat where the bottle's stashed, looking like he might have a heart attack. Mikey nudges him, grinning. 'Oi, mate. Calm down, yeah? It's just hospital, not Pentonville.'

Gary manages a weak laugh, but he's stiff as a board in the lift, eyes darting everywhere like he's expecting Old Bill to jump out at any second.

'Let's neck it now!' he whispers, desperate. 'Get rid of it before we're back on the ward!'

Baz looks up from checking his nails, all casual like. 'Honestly, darling. Where's your sense of adventure?' Gives Gary's shoulder a playful shove. 'Buck up, soldier. Night's still young!'

He sways out ahead as the lift opens, blowing kisses at the tutting nurses while we follow him in a wobbly line to his room. Then he flings the door wide with his usual drama.

'Champagne for everyone!' he announces, voice ringing through the ward.

We settle in cross-legged on the floor, clinking plastic cups and giggling like kids at a sleepover. Then Sophie catches Gary and Mikey mid-laugh, eyebrow raised.

'Are you lot high?' she asks, trying to look stern. 'Drinking on your meds? Very unwise...'

But Baz just grins, innocent as anything. 'Don't be a spoilsport, Soph!'

She huffs and sweeps out while we laugh ourselves stupid. Everything's brilliant until Gary suddenly groans, face going grey. He clutches his stomach, legs wobbling beneath him. Mikey's right behind, looking just as rough, and they both bolt for the loos.

And then it's just me and Baz. The room goes quiet - just machines beeping somewhere and the last of the bubbles fizzing in our cups. He shuffles closer until our shoulders touch, his warmth proper distracting. The day's catching up with me now, making everything feel soft round the edges.

'Bad timing, poor Gary,' he says, sipping his wine. 'Better here than Oxford Street though.'

Can't help smiling. Trust Baz to find the bright side.

He turns to me, eyes gone dark and hungry. 'So, Bunny. Did you enjoy our little adventure in the big wide world?'

I'm leaning in, lips almost touching his, when Sophie bustles back with supplies.

'Right then, love. Transfusion time!' She snaps on her gloves, smirking. 'Would've been here sooner, but someone was off gallivanting, wasn't he?'

Baz beams up at her, not moving an inch away from me. 'Guilty as charged, Sophie darling. And it was simply marvellous!'

He chatters away while she sorts his IV, but his free hand finds my knee, thumb stroking slow circles that's driving me mental. I settle against his side, trying to act normal while Sophie works.

'To healthy blood!' He raises his plastic cup.

'To healthy blood,' I echo, bubbles tickling my nose.

Baz watches me soft-like. 'Thank you for today, Bunny,' he says quiet under Sophie's fussing. 'For... well, for everything, really.'

My throat goes tight. 'Pleasure's all mine, Baz. Truly.'

We clink cups again, making a silent promise to grab whatever joy we can.

Back in my bed later, ward's gone quiet except for the machines beeping and nurses doing their rounds. Can hear Sergio next door, voice all choked up. 'Please, love. Don't leave me alone in this...'

Makes my chest hurt hearing that. I grab my headphones quick, put on that Leftfield CD from Baz. First beats take me right back to that cramped booth, him pressed close against me.

Let myself get lost in it - those wild curls, that wicked smile, those eyes that see right into me. Track fades and I'm drifting deeper, wondering what tomorrow might bring.

If tomorrow comes at all.

Rolex

Chris shows up Saturday night, clutching a packet of Haribo like some sort of peace offering. We settle in for England vs Scotland - the ward's usual racket of beeping machines and shuffling nurses our backdrop.

Jason's faffing about with the telly's bunny ears, trying to fix the wonky reception when Chris pipes up, voice all nervous, 'So, uh, is this the Broderip ward? The one Princess Di opened back in the 80s?'

I just shrug and tear open the sweets, shove a pink gummy bear in my gob. 'Did she?' We both glance over at Jason, still waging war with the antenna.

'There's a plaque up front, I think,' he calls over his shoulder. 'But it got covered by some dodgy flower painting years ago. Proper eyesore, that is.'

'Why is it covered, then?' Chris asks, motioning for Jason to adjust the bunny ears to the right.

'Some patients' families don't know they got HIV.' Jason explains, finally getting a clear signal before flopping onto the sofa beside us as the match kicks off. 'Can't have their folks cottoning on when they pop round for a visit, now can we?'

Chris is well twitchy, bouncing his knees about. Looks like he might do a runner any second.

As soon as halftime starts, Jason's snoring loudly next to us, mouth hanging open like a landed fish. Chris snorts. 'Bloody hell, he's out like a light!'

In the quiet bit, I want to ask how he's really doing. If we'll still be mates after I get out or if he'll do a disappearing act. But can't get the words out, just pass him a Haribo instead.

Some random Walkers advert comes on with a nun on a bench eating crisps. Chris barely looks at it before dropping casual like, 'So yeah... Tanya and me are getting a place together now.'

The Haribo's gone all sticky in my mouth, can hardly swallow it. Ref's whistle goes for second half but I'm stuck staring at Chris like a right muppet. Feel proper winded, like he's just kicked me in the gut.

'You're moving in with her?' Can barely get the words out. 'As of when?'

'Next week,' Chris replies, eyes glued to Shearer's opening drive. 'But don't stress about the flat, yeah? I paid my share for next month already, so you're sorted there.'

Can't get my tongue working right. 'You're just telling me this now?'

'Come on, lads!' Chris bellows triumphantly as a goal goes in, fist-pumping hard enough to take someone's eye out. Even Jason joins the cheering, momentarily revived from his coma-like slumber.

As the replay starts, Chris finally meets my stare head-on. 'I'm just trying to move forward with my life, yeah? Me and Tanya are serious now.' He scrubs a hand through his hair rough like. 'I'm not the one dying here, mate. I've got to keep living...'

Everything goes proper wobbly as Chris gives me this awkward pat on the shoulder. 'We're still mates though, right?'

I force out this smile that probably looks as fake as it feels. Then our attention snaps back to the match just as Gazza scores a blistering goal and hits the turf, with Sheringham rushing over with a water bottle, tipping it into the madman's mouth as he writhes on the pitch in ecstasy!

The final whistle blows and we're on our feet, roaring over England's triumph! I turn back grinning, riding the high of victory, but Chris's already grabbing his jacket like his arse is on fire.

'Oi, where're you off to?'

'Meeting Tanya,' he mumbles, bolting out without a backwards glance.

'Wanker...' Jason mutters as the doors flap shut behind him.

I just stand there feeling empty as anything. Course he couldn't stick around - might have to face what's left of our friendship, wouldn't he? All those years together, gone just like that.

With a laugh that tastes proper bitter, I drag myself to the phone to ring Mum. She'll need to fetch my stuff from the flat now. Just another bit of my old life crumbling away - another casualty of the virus, I suppose.

Can't get my head straight after Chris. Mind's going mental, so I wander down hoping for a chat with Baz. But his room's empty when I get there, just rumpled black satin sheets and that poncy cologne of his hanging about. Fuck it. Nothing for it but to drag my sorry arse back to the common room.

That's when I spot Malcolm. Christ. He's breathing like he's got a whole brass band stuck in his chest, his eyes all sunken and dead-looking. Just this morning we were having a laugh, and now... Part of me wants to leg it. Can't help thinking this is what I've got to look forward to, ain't it? But I force myself to go over, close enough to feel every rattling breath he takes.

'Alright, Malc?' I manage to get out, trying not to sound as scared as I am.

He sucks in this wheezy breath, waving me over with a finger that looks like it might snap off if you breathed on it wrong. 'How...do I look? For when Sergio gets here...'

Fucking hell. The way he's looking at me, all desperate, trying to hold onto his dignity. I grab his shoulder, gentle as I can.

'Looking stellar,' I lie through my teeth, trying to sound cheerful. 'Bloody gorgeous you are.'

He lets out this whisper of a laugh that's barely there. Pats my hand while his eyes start closing, knackered. I stay put while he drifts off, like I'm some sort of guard dog keeping the Grim Reaper at bay.

Time's going as slow as shit until Sergio bursts in looking like he's been through the wars - eyes all red and puffy, hair a right state.

He goes straight for Malc's bed. Just... folds in on himself, really. Grabs hold of them twiggy hands of Malc's and then... bloody hell. The noise that comes out of him.

I'm rooted to the spot like a right muppet, no clue what to do while Sergio's whole world falls apart right in front of us. Marge tries doing the decent thing with the curtain, but it's no use - can't block out the sound of someone's heart breaking, can you? Goes right through you, that noise does. Like something wild and wounded.

Grab for my headphones quick smart, slam on that Leftfield CD, desperate to drown it out. But his crying cuts through the bass like it's nothing. No escape from it.

Yank them off just in time to catch Sergio: 'No, please...I'm not ready! Please God no, not yet...'

Can't get any air in my lungs. Look round and Gary's gone and curled up tight as anything, hands clamped over his ears. Poor Mikey's disappeared under his blanket.

And Sergio just keeps going, his grief bouncing off the walls and taking chunks out of us with every sob. Squeeze my eyes shut but it's fucking pointless. All I can hear is him falling to pieces while Marge tries her best to hold him together.

Feels like we're stuck in this nightmare forever, every sob ripping through the place like barbed wire. It's too much. Making my skin crawl, desperate to be anywhere but here.

Keep thinking I should say something, anything. But what the fuck do you say to make this better? There are no words for this kind of thing, are there? So I just sit there, letting it all sink in, wondering if this is what we've all got coming.

Then Baz shows up, thank fuck. Just puts his hand on my shoulder, solid as anything. Doesn't say a word, just nods at the door with this serious look I've never seen on him before.

I'm up and following him before my brain's caught up, Sergio's crying fading behind us as the ward doors slam shut like we're making a break from the worst fucking place on earth.

VIP

Air hits me when we step out - all disinfectant and floor wax catching in my throat. Lights are doing my head in, bouncing off that shiny lino like nobody's business. Everything feels wrong out here, too clean and harsh.

Baz is all fidgety beside me, fingers tapping against his thigh.

'Reckon this place is haunted?' he stage-whispers, all dramatic like. 'Victorian ghosts rattling chains - oooOOOooo!' Then he's off, dancing about like a nutter at some mental rave.

'Bugger off,' I snort, aiming a kick at his ankle. But I'm grateful really - him trying to get me out of my head.

His ghost voice turns into snickers that echo down the empty halls. 'Honestly though, I'd die again of boredom if I had to haunt these stuffy corridors every night,' he says once we've caught our breath.

We wander down the corridor past all these framed photos hanging wonky on the walls. Stern-faced nuns and hospital big-wigs looking down their noses at us. Like they're judging us for daring to breathe their air.

Baz stops by this big glass door, looking all ghostly in the moonlight. 'Imagine if we did haunt this place together though,' he says, eyes going soft. 'Bunny and Baz, the ghostly gays of Broderip ward!' Does this dramatic swoon like some Victorian lady.

The thought of forever with Baz makes my chest ache with hope.

He leads me into this hidden garden, feels like we've found a quiet spot away from all the hospital chaos. After the stuffy ward, the night air hits me proper cold. Look up at the endless sky stretching over us, making me feel tiny under all them stars. We drop onto a bench next to some scrawny tree in a pot, its leaves barely rustling in the breeze. Before I can get my bearings, Baz has pulled out a spliff from nowhere and lit it up quick as you like.

'Mate, really shouldn't be...' I start, but he just gives me this cheeky grin.

'Oh hush, Bunny. What are they gonna do, kill me faster?' Takes this deep drag, hollowing his cheeks. 'I'm dying either way, aren't I?'

Feels like a punch to the chest, hearing it put out there so blunt like that. I take the spliff with trembling fingers, desperate for the escape.

'You alright, though...?' Baz asks, voice gone all quiet.

I shrug, trying to act like I'm not falling apart. 'Just been a head-fuck of a night.'

Baz nods, staring off into nothing. 'I've seen too much of this shit, Bunny. All the death, the goodbyes... Must be over thirty funerals I've been to now. All in a few short years.' Lets out this laugh that sounds more like breaking glass. 'You never really get used to it. Losing them. Watching them slip away.'

He drags hard on the spliff. 'Malcolm didn't deserve that ending. Can't imagine what Sergio's feeling right about now...'

We both look up at the moon looming over us while Baz goes, 'You frightened, Bunny?'

My mouth's gone dry, like I've been chewing cotton. Have to swallow hard before I can get anything out. 'Terrified.' Feel this shiver go right through me, cold sweat starting at the back of my neck like some horror film. My hands are going mental, clenching up tight while I force the rest out. 'Seeing what happened to Malc... it's like looking through some window at what's coming for me. No way round it, is there?'

Baz's hand finds mine, all cool and steady. 'They'll find a cure,' he tries, but it comes out hollow as anything. 'These new meds, all these combos... there's hope.'

'So they keep bloody saying,' I rasp. 'Doesn't change what's happening though, does it? We're stuck in here.'

Baz lets out this sigh that seems to come from his bones. 'Been clinging to that cure hope for years - in and out of hospital, one scare after the next. But I'm out of time now, out of chances. Reckon this is my last dance with these lovely corridors...'

I make this noise like I've been gutted. Baz squeezes my hand. 'Made my peace with dying itself. But the how... the suffering at the end. And what comes after - that's what turns my blood cold.' His eyes are burning into me. 'What do you think happens when it's all over?'

'Fucked if I know,' I answer, feeling raw. 'Like to think our souls shoot off somewhere else. Some new adventure, away from all this bollocks.'

Baz hums, tips his head back to the stars. 'Think we live on in the hearts we leave behind. In memories. Little fragments scattered into the world.' Gets this soft smile playing on his lips. 'Sort of immortality, if not all fluffy clouds and harps.'

'Poetic sod,' I tell him, but I'm grinning. 'Proper Wordsworth of the ward.'

Baz snorts, leaning into me. 'Speaking of poetic ends... I want to go out dancing. Die right there on the dance floor.'

Can't help but smile at that. 'I'll be there, front row, making a right spectacle. Rain down glitter while you go out blazing.'

'Got an epic funeral planned already. Promise you'll come, Bunny.'

'What happened to all that poetry?' I laugh, giving him a shove.

Baz changes track quick. 'Always wanted to get to Japan.'

'Why Japan?'

'It's mental there. All that neon, mad fashions...' His eyes go distant. 'Place where you could lose yourself completely.'

'I'll go,' I blurt out, surprising myself. 'To Japan. For you. Stuff my face with sushi, make a tit of myself doing karaoke. Take a bit of you everywhere.'

Baz's head whips round, eyes gone wide and shining. 'Yeah?'

'Yeah. The whole bloody works.'

'Oh, Bunny...' He breathes it like it's sacred.

We get chatting about love - him and his wild stories, me and all my mess-ups. Can feel him warm against my side, his fingers making me shiver.

'Oh darling, I'm simply mad for love,' he hums, shoulder pressed to mine. 'That delicious thrill when someone sweeps you off your feet.'

His fingers brush my wrist. 'Rather brave though, isn't it? Risking your heart again and again. After getting ill, I thought that part of life was finished - all blood tests and no romance. Never imagined I'd feel that spark again.'

He leans in till our heads touch. Makes me tingle all over.

'And then you saunter in,' he says, playful. 'My gorgeous Bunny, right when I'd given up hope.'

Touches my face and I lean right in.

'One last deliciously scandalous affair,' he giggles.

We sit there holding hands, just breathing together. Then dead slow, he turns his hands over and links our fingers. Feels right, that does.

'That kiss at the rave...' His voice goes all smooth. 'Remember that night, Bunny?'

'Course,' I manage, caught in those blue eyes.

He flashes that smile. 'I remember the first time I saw you at Sanctuary. Leaning against the wall, lost and wrecked. But even then, your beauty cut through the dark like a beacon.'

His hand comes up gentle to my face. 'You were just divine.'

I shiver at his touch, his words washing over me. Our faces close now and he murmurs, 'Every moment of that kiss is seared into my memory. The heat of you against me...'

We're both lost in it for a minute. Then: 'Kiss me again, Bunny?'

'Abso-fucking-lutely,' I breathe, already going for it.

When we kiss, it's like everything clicks into place. World goes quiet except for Baz's soft mouth on mine, our tongues meeting, these little sounds we can't help making. All that fear and sadness just melts away - like we've found this perfect moment in the middle of all the shit.

I let him take control, loving how his fingers tangle in my hair, getting me exactly where he wants me. Can't stop touching him - his waist, his shoulders, anywhere I can reach. Feel well electric between us, warming me right through.

Lost track of time, just know it ends way too soon. When Baz pulls back his lips are all red and swollen, looking well kissed. I'm about to dive back in for another go when he stands up, taking my hand and pulling me with him, our fingers still tangled together.

We walk back through the quiet hospital, not saying nothing but not needing to. End up in his bed like it's the most natural thing. He wraps round me and everything else just... fades away. Like all the heavy stuff can't touch us here. Just me and him in the dark.

Curl up against him, feeling peaceful as I drift off. Even half-asleep, know he'll be there when I wake up. Whatever this is between us - it's ours for now. For as long as we can hold onto it.

Apples

Marge breezes in like a gust of spring air, yanking open the curtains. Summer light floods in quick as you like, warming me straight through.

'Got a new lad joining us today, gents!' she announces, all chipper as she sets to work on Malc's old bed. Christ, you'd think she was prepping for the Queen, the way she's faffing about with them sheets. Every last wrinkle smoothed out like it's some posh hotel.

'Poor love's been through the wringer, from what I hear,' Marge says, dropping her voice to a conspiratorial whisper. 'But we'll soon have him right as rain, won't we, boys?'

Suddenly she stops, peering out the window with a face like she's seen the second coming. 'Well, I never! There's a fire down there! Firemen rushing about...'

'Firemen?!' Jason perks up.

'Are they fit looking, Marge?' Gary adds.

'Oh yes, a few of them. I rather fancy that tall one...'

Well, you've never seen a bunch of half-dead blokes move so fast. A right stampede to the window, except for Bruce who's dead to the world as usual.

And wouldn't you bloody know it - Marge was right on the money. There they are, bunch of firefighters standing about like some calendar photo shoot, all broad shoulders and proper fit jaws like they've walked straight off the Chippendales stage.

We're all hanging out the window like right pervs, when Jason lets out this dreamy sigh. 'I do love a bloke in uniform...'

'Me too!' Marge chimes in, sounding just as thirsty as our Jason.

'Christ, look at that one though,' Jason goes, setting us all off giggling like kids. Mental really - bunch of grown adults acting like we're back in school, getting hot and bothered over these poor bastards just trying to do their job. But when you're banged up in here going spare, reckon you'll take what entertainment you can get, won't you?

And wouldn't you know it, in waltzes Gemma herself, proper perfect timing. Fresh off the plane from Ibiza, them silver bangles of hers jangling away like always. Looking well golden, all sun-kissed with new blonde bits in her hair.

Should've been our holiday together, that. Before I got banged up in this glorified petri dish. But seeing her face light up when she spots me... almost makes me forget about missing out. Almost.

She damn near squeezes the life out of me with that bear hug of hers, going on about how healthy I'm looking. And you know what? I'm feeling alright myself. So much so that when we head down Oxford Street, I'm actually starving for the first time in ages.

Got my heart set on a cheeky Maccies, but Gemma - bless her cotton socks - steers us towards Pret instead. Reckons a sarnie and soup's better for me. Haven't got the energy to argue, have I? Though I'd murder a Big Mac right about now.

Sun's playing hide and seek while we're wandering about, hand in hand like some loved-up teens. Pop into HMV and Topshop, and them familiar smells hit me right in the chest - memories of when everything was simple, before my body decided to do one on me.

By the time we hit Hyde Park I'm absolutely knackered. Legs feel like I've been hauling cement blocks about, lungs burning. Collapse onto the grass like some sack of spuds. Gemma's still full of beans though - settles in next to me with that look she gets.

'You doing alright there, you muppet?' she asks, giving me a gentle shove.

I muster a grin, shaking my head. 'Getting there, Gem. Just need a mo' to catch my breath, that's all. Blimey, when did walking become an Olympic sport?'

We end up on the grass watching everyone. Couple of rollerbladers showing off in the distance, Fugees playing from their boombox.

Grass is wet under my hands, all fresh and green. Some bloke's throwing a ball for his dog - energetic thing, barking its head off. Got more life in it than I've had in ages, lucky bugger.

Gem rolls onto her side next to me, arm bumping mine.

'So how was Ibiza then?' I ask casual, twirling a blade of grass between my fingers like I'm not dying to hear about the holiday I missed.

'Mental. Wild parties, loads of booze,' she smiles. 'Wicked fun though.'

'I saw Chris few days back, popped by to watch footie,' I tell her, scanning the clouds for shapes. Anything to avoid eye contact for this bit.

'Oh yeah? How'd that go?'

'He told me he's shacking up with Tanya now.' I keep picking at the grass.

'Yeah, he mentioned. Alright with that then?'

I shrug. 'Wasn't like we'd room together forever, I guess. Just happened quicker than expected is all... And he was a bit cold about it. Like I'd gone and caught the plague on purpose just to inconvenience him.'

'That's our Chris. So, what's the plan for you now, yeah?'

I look over at her, bit shy. 'Think I'll stay at Mum's when I get out. Maybe do some travelling after...'

Can't help thinking about Baz - the way his eyes crinkle up when he laughs, all that. Makes my chest go tight, thinking about leaving him behind.

Shake it off, try for a grin. 'Come with me, Gem?' Nudge her shoulder. 'We could backpack round the world together. You be my nurse and I'll be your handsome patient.'

Her eyes light up quick. 'I'd definitely consider it! After Ibiza, I'm down for anything.'

I playfully poke her side. 'C'mon, really now—just you, me, and the open road?'

She laughs, nudging me back. 'Stevie, you know I'd follow your sweet arse anywhere.'

Grinning, I tuck a loose gold curl gently behind her ear. 'I mean it, Gemma... see the planet together?'

'I'd love to. Really would...'

'Wicked,' I beam.

But can't help another face filling my head as I say it. Baz. My beautiful, mental, impossible Baz.

I drag Gemma back to meet Basil. He's sprawled out reading in bed, but his whole face lights up when we come in. Looks ready to jump up and tackle us, but Gemma gets there first, wrapping him up in one of her crushing hugs. Swear I hear his bones creak.

Even in that manky hospital gown, Baz looks like he's stepped off a magazine cover. Hair's all artfully messy - bet that took him ages - and there's something different about him today, something bright in those eyes of his. Still too skinny mind, can see his collarbones sticking out, but he's got this energy about him that not even this shit disease can knock down.

'Got yourself a stunning tan there,' Baz says with that cheeky grin of his.

Gemma's practically glowing. 'Just back from Ibiza! The parties were mental!'

That sets him off, getting all misty-eyed about some club night back in '94. 'Manumission at Ku Club,' he says. 'Three days straight of absolute madness. Ended up starkers on the beach with a bunch of drag queens, waving club flags about, off our faces on whatever we'd taken. Best weekend of my life!'

But I can see he's flagging - breathing's gone all ragged and he's sweating now. Typical Baz though, putting on a show for Gemma like he's not half dead. Makes my chest hurt, watching him push himself like that.

Then he turns to me with that eyebrow thing he does. 'What about you then, Bunny? Ever been to the White Isle?'

I just shrug, feeling a bit left out if I'm honest. 'Nah, never made it.'

But Gemma jumps right in, arm around my shoulders. 'We're planning an adventure soon though, aren't we, Stevie?' Subtle as a brick through a window, our Gem.

Baz looks proper made up about that. 'Brilliant! You've got to take him to Ibiza, Gem. Get him to Manumission. It'll change his life.' Throws me a wink that has my stomach doing backflips, the git.

I plonk down next to him on the bed, shuffling close till we're pressed together. Gemma settles in on his other side, and we're off - chatting about any old rubbish, taking the mick out of each other, having a laugh.

At some point, his hand finds mine on top of the blanket. Just a little thing, but it feels big somehow. Like everything's slotting into place.

I'm just sat there grinning like an idiot at my two favourite people. Wish Alex was here too, though that might be a bit awkward. Still, I've never felt luckier than I do right now. Funny how things work out.

When Gem's got to go, she hugs me extra tight. Can feel her shaking a bit.

'Just want you sorted, don't I?' she says, all wobbly. 'Want you to be happy again.'

I pull her back in, hide my face in her hair so she can't see I'm about to start blubbering myself. 'I am happy, Gem. Swear down, happiest I've been in ages.'

Watching her leave, I get this weird feeling. Happy, yeah, but something else too. Bit scared maybe? But then I look back at Baz and he grins at me, and everything feels right again.

End up tangled together that night, trying to keep our laughing quiet so we don't wake the whole bloody ward up. When he finally drops off, face peaceful against my chest, I make myself get up.

Shuffle back to my own bed, cold and empty without him in it.

But lying there, staring at the ceiling... I can still feel where his hands were. Still feel his breath on my neck.

Medusa

Next day, Mum springs me for lunch. Over a heaping plate of pasta - appetite really is making a comeback - I mention Malcolm's passing. Mum makes all the right noises, but changes the subject, quick as you like.

'Your dad sends his love,' she says, sipping her wine. 'Hasn't quite wrapped his head around everything yet, but he does worry.'

I let out this snort before I can stop myself. No point picking at that particular scab though, is there? Instead, I just blurt it out: 'Met someone actually. At hospital.'

Mum's eyebrows shoot up but she's trying to play it cool as anything. 'Patient?'

'Yeah,' I manage. 'Not some nurse or doctor or nothing.'

We both crack up at that, tension breaking a bit.

'Basil,' I tell her, feeling my face go all hot but pushing through anyway. 'Early days and that... but I really like him, Mum.'

Her face goes all soft round the edges. 'Well you know all I want is for you to be happy, love. Everything else is just details.'

Later on the ward, I'm bricking it about Mum meeting Baz. I was worrying for nothing though - one flash of that killer smile of his and she's well smitten.

'You must be the famous Basil,' she beams, pulling him into a hug before I can even do introductions.

'The very same,' he drawls, shooting me a wink over her shoulder. 'Though I must say, Steve failed to mention his mum was such a stunner.'

And just like that, he's got her eating out of his hand. Watching them together, heads bent close as they swap embarrassing stories about me. Something clicks right then, watching them. Like finding the last bit of a jigsaw you thought the dog had eaten ages ago.

Mikey's heading home end of the week. We all crowd round his bed while he packs up his stuff, grinning like he's won the lottery. Marge is over with Doc Sher sorting paperwork - she's already been round his flat, made his bed up and aired it out.

Can't help wondering why this new med combo that's worked so well for me isn't doing the same for Baz.

We follow Mikey down to the doors, sending him off like right mugs.

After watching him disappear down the street, end up jingling coins in the foyer. Figure I'll ring Alex, make this day proper complicated.

Picks up first ring, eager sod. 'You out of hospital yet?'

'Nah, not yet. Still enjoying the five-star accommodation and gourmet cuisine, ain't I?' Lean against the booth while some old geezer in a wheelchair's giving me the eye, nosy bugger.

'Listen... I've actually met someone here.'

'Yeah? Where at?'

'Around the ward.' Brace myself for it.

'Another patient you mean?'

'Yeah, he's a patient here. Didn't fancy any of the doctors. Too healthy-looking, you know?'

'And...? What's he like then?'

'Really great. Funny, charming... makes me feel proper good.'

'Is he... ill?'

The bloke in the wheelchair's having a right good listen now. 'You asking if he's got AIDS? Because if you are, I've got news for you about this ward...'

'Well... yeah.'

'Not too healthy... but this new med combo is working wonders for the rest of us. Could help Basil buy more time.'

'You really think getting involved with someone that ill is wise?'

'He's still fighting. Besides, when have I ever done the wise thing?'

'Right, but...don't get too attached, alright? I don't want you getting hurt when...'

Let out this breath. 'Makes me happy though, don't it? Or what - you rather I just sit here being miserable, watching bloody Eastenders and choking down this hospital shit they call food?'

Line goes all fuzzy. 'Alex?'

'Here, mate. Here... Just be careful, yeah?'

Feel my hackles going up proper. 'Oh right, so I'm not allowed to be happy now?'

'Course not! Want that for you, Steve, always did...'

'He makes me feel good though, Alex! Truly good—first time since you and me, even.'

Silence stretches out.

'I just want you happy. But getting attached to someone else in that ward... don't want to see you hurt again when...'

'Like how you hurt me, you mean?' Feel that old wound opening up, bitter as anything.

'Yeah... reckon so.'

Nod even though he can't see. 'Guess we can't outrun our hearts, eh?'

'Suppose not... Just...be careful, alright?'

Squeeze my eyes shut tight. Alex means well, soppy git that he is.

'Right then.' Slam the phone down before he hears my voice crack.

Turn back to the ward and everything's gone heavy now - even the air feels thick with it.

Bruce goes quietly, just... stops breathing. No drama, no fuss. One minute he's there, the next he's not. Never thought death would be so quiet.

His mum's holding his hand the whole time, watching her boy slip away. Makes my throat tight just being there, like I'm intruding on something private.

The nurses get on with it, calm and professional. Handle him gentle though, fixing his hair, straightening his gown. It's those little things that get to me - how careful they are with him, even now. Can't look away even though I want to.

They pull the curtains round, giving Bruce and his mum some privacy. Ward's gone dead quiet except for his mum crying soft. Even the hospital smell seems stronger somehow. Outside the curtain, machines keep beeping away like nothing's happened.

Hear the porters coming, wheels squeaking on the floor. Coming to take Bruce wherever we go after all this is done.

Want to go to Baz, crawl in next to him and hold on tight. But I can't wake him up. I don't want to see his face when I tell him about Bruce. Some things you just want to protect people from, even if it's only for a few more hours.

Been a week since Bruce, and now Gary's standing here with his duffel packed, grinning. His mum sweeps in, smile bright as anything. He comes over all secretive, tells me he's staying at his mum's for a bit, then him and Mikey are getting a flat together. Says it's just mates and that, but I'm not thick - can see the way he goes all soppy when he mentions it. Our Gary's in for more than just sharing the leccy bill, I reckon.

His mum's tall and skinny like him, bit of grey in her hair - but she's got that same cheeky grin when she's fussing over him. Proper funny watching Gary turn from ward clown to mummy's boy in about two seconds. He's squirming away from her pinching his cheeks, acting all embarrassed but loving it really.

Can't help looking at Gary's empty bed though, even with all the happy families bollocks going on. We're all thinking the same thing - who's next in... or out. Marge tries going on about how nice it is having a free bed, but we all know better in here, don't we?

By evening there's some new bloke being wheeled in. Another scared face, just like I was when I first landed here, no fucking clue what he's in for.

Dennis The Menace

Christ, just when I'd gotten used to the hospital routine - the beeping machines, the squeaky trolleys, the endless waiting - Baz decides to cause chaos. Should've known better, really. Can't have a quiet minute with that one about.

He comes strutting in like a man on a mission, hands on hips, striking a dramatic pose. 'Bunny!' he trills. 'We're going on a shopping spree down Oxford Street to find some smashing new looks for tonight!'

I blink at him, confused. 'Shopping? What for?'

'For the rave tonight, obviously! Keep up, darling!' He rolls his eyes, looking at me like I've gone soft in the head.

'Rave?' I echo, sitting up slow. 'Baz. You sure that's a good idea? I mean, you're not exactly...' I eye up his skinny frame.

'Oh, pish posh!' He waves me off. 'I'm feeling fab-u-lous today, Bunny! Positively bursting with energy!' Does a little shimmy. 'And we simply must look the part for our big night out!'

I sigh, doing up my trainers. 'Alright, you mad bastard. Lead the way then.'

'Yay!' He grabs my hand, practically bouncing. 'Let's go paint the town red! Or glittery rainbow, as the case may be!'

We pass the nurses' station, Baz blowing kisses. 'Don't wait up, ladies!' The nurses just hide their smiles, shaking their heads. That's Baz though - makes everything feel special.

Out on Oxford Street, it's mental - crowds everywhere, music blaring, like some sort of carnival gone wild. Baz is weaving through the masses like he was born for it, all graceful like, while I'm stumbling about like a right elephant, constantly going 'sorry, mate' as I bounce off people.

Topshop's even worse - bass thumping so hard my teeth are rattling. But Baz is living for it. Eyes all bright, cheeks flushed, darting between the racks like he's had about ten Red Bulls.

'Bunny, we simply must get you out of hospital grungy casual!' He keeps holding stuff up against me, giving me this proper critical look. 'Hmm, yes. This blue really brings out your eyes! Oh, and this silver top - absolutely divine with your colouring!'

I'm just standing there feeling like a right plonker. 'Baz, I can't afford none of this.'

He looks at me like I've gone mental. 'Oh, don't be silly! It's my treat, of course!'

Try to argue but he shuts me up with a finger to my lips. 'I insist, Bunny. Let me spoil you a bit, yeah? Besides, I won't live long enough to pay off this debt!' Says it with a grin, but something flickers in his eyes that makes my chest go tight.

We end up squeezed in the changing room like a couple of naughty school kids. Having him pressed up close like this, feeling his ribs sharp against me - makes me want to wrap him up and keep him safe from everything.

He catches me staring and gets that look. 'See something you like, Bunny?'

Can't help myself - just have to kiss him, try to say all the stuff I can't get out in words. He kisses back proper hard, fingers digging into my hips, pushing me against the wall. His tongue's in my mouth and Christ, he tastes amazing. His whole body's pressed against mine now, all angles and heat. Makes these little noises that drive me mental when I slide my hands under his shirt.

'Bloody hell, Bunny,' he breathes against my mouth. 'You're going to be the death of me.'

'That'd be one way to go,' I manage, making him laugh all breathy before he's kissing me again.

Then he's off, all energy and sparkle in his leather and sequins. Follow along behind him, can't quite believe my luck really.

Baz ends up choosing these mental leopard print trousers with a black top and biker jacket. Looks like he's stepped right off some catwalk, makes it look dead easy. For me, he picks out this blue boilersuit - top half tied round my waist all neat, white vest on top. Chuck on my flannel and Vans, feeling scruffy next to him.

But the way he looks at me... makes me feel like I might be something special after all.

We head out, Baz bouncing around. 'Tonight's going to be mega, Bunny!' Throws his arm round my shoulders. 'We're going to dance until dawn, until we're dizzy with it!'

And yeah, I believe him. Course I do.

Back at the hospital, we come swanning in like celebrities, arms full of shopping bags. 'Hello, darlings!' Baz trills, 'The beautification committee has arrived!'

We dump our bags on the bed, and Baz whips out this massive makeup case from nowhere, looking well pleased with himself.

'Right,' he says. 'Let's get to work, shall we? Going to make us the most gorgeous couple at the rave!'

He pats the bed and I perch on the edge, bit nervous as he lays out all these brushes and that. But then he takes my face in his hands, and I forget everything except them bright blue eyes and how gentle his fingers feel.

'There,' he says after ages, sitting back looking well chuffed. 'Utter perfection, if I do say so myself.'

He shoves the mirror at me and bloody hell - is that really me? Look decent actually - eyes all smoky, cheekbones looking well sharp.

'Baz,' I get out, 'This is mint. You're bloody good at this, ain't ya?'

He just grins, smug as anything. 'Oh, I know, Bunny. The fashion world's been my playground for years - models, music videos, drag queens. I've painted them all, darling.' Then his lips are on mine, breath hot against my skin. 'But you, my sweet... you are the most exquisite canvas of all.'

Sends shivers right through me, that does.

'My turn now!' He's practically bouncing. 'Prepare to be dazzled, darling!'

And bloody hell, am I ever. Never seen anything like it - the way he works them brushes, turning himself into something magical, all sparkle and sass.

While he's at it, he's telling me stories - about his first paid job at eleven, spending every penny on makeup from Boots. How he'd do secret makeovers for girls at school, turning them from ugly ducklings into swans.

'Course, had to keep it quiet at home,' he says, rolling his eyes. 'Couldn't have the parents catching on about my fabulous alter ego. But in the clubs?' His grin goes wicked. 'Let my freak flag fly high and proud!'

He spins round all dramatic like. 'Well? What's the verdict, Bunny? Am I a vision, or am I a vision?'

Can't do nothing but stare. Those cat-eye flicks, the way his lips look all done up - he's something else entirely.

'Baz,' I manage. 'You look... fucking hell. Just look at you.'

His face lights up bright at that. Leans in and plants one right on my cheek, leaving a purple lipstick mark behind.

Just as Baz is adding the final touches, Marge strides in, spots our bizarre makeup setup - IV bag in one hand, extra meds tucked under her arm. 'Alright, you two, what's this then?'

'Why darling, we're off to hit a rave of course!' Baz throws her his most dramatic look. 'Care to join in the revelry?'

She chuckles, getting started on Baz's IV. 'In another lifetime perhaps.' Her smile goes a bit sad. 'But don't forget - meds for Basilton first. And more antibiotics for you as well, Steve.'

Feel my stomach drop at that. Nothing like a reminder of why we're really here. But then Baz squeezes my hand tight, looks right at me. 'Not tonight, Bunny,' he says fierce. 'Tonight, we forget all that, alright? Tonight's about being alive.'

Marge looks us up and down proper careful, then this grin spreads across her face. 'Well, you can't go raving with those hospital tags on, can you? Not with all that glitter.' Next thing she's got these little scissors out her pocket. That snip when she cuts them off... feels like breaking free of something.

'There,' she says, pocketing the tags. 'That's better.' Gives us a proper look over, trying to hide her smile. 'And make sure you eat something before you head out!' she calls back as she leaves.

Catch Baz's eye in the mirror then - both of us looking well fierce now, nothing hospital about us at all. Mental really, but feels right. Tonight we ain't patients - just two blokes having a laugh.

We spill out the taxi absolutely wired, can't stop grinning. Club's like some cave - all dark and dripping with sweat, that bass smacking you right in the chest moment you walk in. Everyone seems to know Baz, all hugs and kisses like he's some celebrity, but he keeps his fingers locked tight with mine through it all. Sweet-talks the barman into sorting our water dead quick, that smile of his working its usual magic. Then he's got a pill on his tongue and pulls me in for this snog that's all heat and chemicals.

'Bottoms up, Bunny,' he says with a wink, tapping his water bottle against mine. 'Let's get this party started.'

Hit the dance floor just as the DJ drops this filthy house track, bass coming up through my feet. Been ages since I've done this - just let go and moved. But with Baz against me, way he moves like he was made for it... feels like getting something back I thought was gone forever. Just let it all take over - the bass in my bones, sweat on my skin, that lime-green pill dissolving sweet.

Can't stop grinning at each other like kids, nicking kisses while the music pounds. Pills are coming on strong now, everything going soft round the edges.

'Feel amazing, doesn't it?' Baz shouts. 'Like nothing can touch us!'

He's right. Feel like I could do anything. Maybe I'm just some sick bloke who's forgotten how ill he is for a bit, but right now I don't give a toss.

And Baz... bloody hell. Got his whistle between his teeth, fists in the air, them curls all wild in the lights. Looks nothing like that pale bloke in the hospital bed. Like the music's brought him back from the dead or something.

When he pulls me in close, it's all need and heat and kisses that say everything we can't put into words. Like if we get close enough, nothing else matters.

Heat gets too much after a bit. Pills are proper rushing now, making everything feel mental. We end up outside, still holding hands, cold air hitting like heaven after that sweatbox.

I lean back against the wall, head tipped up, eyes shut. Everything's gone well intense - rough bricks digging in my back, music still thumping away inside, air proper cold on my face. Like someone's turned all my senses up to eleven.

Baz slides down beside me, all warm against my side. 'Careful there, Bunny,' he says, voice gone all soft. 'Get too comfy, you might just melt right into the wall.'

I laugh, roll my head to look at him. He's giving me this grin that sets me on fire all over again.

'Might do,' I manage, tongue feeling too big for my mouth. 'Could just stay here forever. Be part of the building. Steve the Human Brick, that's me.'

Baz leans in close. 'Gonna take you back in there, sweetheart. Dance with you till there's nothing left but us and the music.'

Gives me this proper filthy laugh and a quick kiss on the jaw.

'But first,' he says with a wink, 'water. Can't have you turning into part of the architecture.' Pushes himself up trying to hide the wince, but I clock it - that flash of pain crossing his face. Moment's gone before it really lands though.

Then he's off into the crowd, throwing me that cheeky grin of his. Watch him disappear into all them bodies, this daft smile still stuck on my face. Even with the pills making everything feel magic, can't help that little twist in my gut - knowing this night can't last forever, knowing what's waiting for us back at the hospital. But for now... for now we've got this.

Still propped up against the wall, pills hitting just right. Everything's buzzing beautiful when Jay appears - one of mine and Chris' old school mates - heading over with this big grin on his face.

'Stevie boy! Been bloody ages, hasn't it?' He drops down next to me, throwing an arm round my shoulders like old times. 'You still hanging about with Chris then?'

Can't help grinning back, everything feeling well lovely, thoughts all floaty and warm. 'Yeah, bit and bob. You know how it is.'

'Mental seeing you here - remember behind them posh tennis courts? Getting absolutely cunted on that cheap cider?'

'Christ, don't remind me. Still can't look at White Lightning without feeling sick.'

He laughs, digging in his pocket. 'Speaking of...' Pulls out some gum. 'Here, sort yourself out. Minty fresh, with a little kick in the centre. Perrrrfect for a night like this.'

Shove it in my mouth grateful, let that cool tang wash away the cotton mouth feeling. Been like I've been chewing sand all night.

We chat about nothing much for a bit, then his voice goes all serious, forehead getting all crinkled up while I'm still riding this nice wave. 'Tell you what though, Stevie...been meaning to say. You're not looking yourself lately. Dropping weight like it's going out of fashion.'

Jay's still nattering on, voice going all concerned big brother while I'm trying to hold onto my buzz. 'Now, I know we don't run in the same circles much these days. But listen, if you're in trouble...if you need help kicking the gear, or checking into rehab or something...I'm here for you, yeah? Ride or die, just like old times.'

And I dunno what it is - maybe his serious face, maybe just how insane this whole thing is with me feeling this good - but I completely lose it. Start laughing so hard I can't breathe, tears running down my face. Can't remember the last time I laughed like this, probably look like a right nutter.

Jay's looking at me like I've gone mental, his concern turning to proper worry now. 'Steve...you alright? What's so funny?'

Try getting it together, wiping my eyes as the giggles die down, cheeks aching from grinning. 'You reckon I'm on gear or something?' And his baffled face just sets me off again. Oh, if he only knew. If he only bloody knew.

'I mean, yeah, Stevie? Shit, I'm off my face myself now, ain't I? Just seems like maybe you're doing too much, is all. Going a bit overboard like.'

'Jay, mate...' I manage, still chuckling. 'I'm not on gear. Well, I am right now, but that's not the real problem, yeah?' Give him a tap on the nose, everything still feeling well sparkly and warm.

He blinks at me confused. 'But... the weight loss? What else could it be?'

Feel the laughter drain away even through the rush. Even with the pills making everything lovely, can feel the weight of what I'm about to say.

'I've got HIV, Jay.'

The music and laughing around us just makes it worse somehow. Like dropping a bomb in the middle of this perfect high.

He just stares at me, mouth hanging open like a goldfish. 'W hat...like AIDS?'

'Nah, not AIDS. HIV. It's...it's different.' Different, but heading the same way, I think but don't say. No need to completely do his head in all at once.

Jay's still looking at me like I'm speaking Chinese. 'But...how? You been sharing needles or something? Didn't reckon you were using hard stuff, mate. Just the party fare.'

Let out a breath, run my hands through my hair, all sweaty from dancing. Christ, he's about as quick as a concrete milkshake. 'No, Jay. I got with this bloke, yeah? Someone I trusted; someone I reckon I loved. Ended up with HIV instead.'

His eyes go massive. Can almost see his brain trying to work it all out through his own pill haze.

'Wait...you're telling me you're a bender? And you caught the bug from taking it up the arse?'

Feel myself flinch at that, even with everything feeling soft round the edges. But I just nod. 'Yeah, Jay. That's about the size of it.'

He slumps back against the wall like his strings have been cut. 'That's... that's a lot to take in, mate.'

Just shrug, feeling dead calm suddenly. Like the pills have wrapped everything up in this weird peaceful blanket. 'I know it is. But it's the truth. And I'm done hiding from it.'

Give his shoulder a squeeze, feeling stronger somehow. But my head's already racing ahead, knowing soon all our old crew will know everything I can't hide anymore.

Then Baz appears through the lights like some glittery angel, all swagger even now. And something just clicks into place. Give Jay's shoulder one last squeeze, then take Baz's hand firm in mine. Everything's still sparkling but it's not just the pills anymore.

We head back to the dance floor, and I know there's no going back after tonight. But with Baz's hand in mine, feeling this good, reckon I'm okay with that.

&

We spill out into early morning, hanging onto each other like a pair of pissed penguins. Flag down a cab under grey London skies - few cyclists about, adding to the quiet morning sounds. Thank fuck it's overcast - eyes couldn't handle the sunlight right now.

Through the cab window, watch it all fade away. Reality proper hits then. The hospital beds waiting for us, Baz gone all pale and done in. My own body giving me grief, reminding me we're both on borrowed time. Can hardly breathe in here.

Get out and the cold morning air slaps us. We've barely made it round the corner when Baz doubles over, chucking his guts up. He hits the wall hard, heaving into the gutter, shaking all over.

I'm there quick as anything, rubbing his back and talking any old rubbish to keep him going. 'That's it, get it all up. You're alright, I've got you.' Christ, we must look a right pair. Two sparkly messes spewing on a London street at dawn. If this ain't love, dunno what is.

Goes on forever, but finally he's just dry heaving, nothing left to chuck up. He falls against me and I just grab hold, don't care about the sick on his shirt or people giving us funny looks.

'Sorry,' he gets out, voice gone all rough. Tries wiping his mouth with shaky hands, looking well rough. 'Guess I'm not the invincible party monster I used to be, eh?'

'Nah, you've just got smarter,' I tell him, trying for a laugh. 'Now you're the invincible party monster who knows when to pack it in. Or at least wait till morning.'

He lets out this snort but I can feel him leaning on me now, letting me take his weight. Makes my chest go tight, seeing him like this - my beautiful mad Baz, still fighting even when he's knackered.

'Come on,' I say, getting a better grip. 'Let's get you back, yeah? Get you cleaned up and that. Might even nick some of that industrial mouthwash from the nurses' station.'

He just nods, too done in to argue. So we start the slow walk back, holding each other up every step. Must look a right state - clothes all messed up, faces gone grey, clinging on like the world might tip over if we let go.

Push through the revolving doors and get hit with that hospital smell straight off. Like that - all the magic of the night just disappears, back to reality proper quick.

Marge is there faffing with Baz's drip, doing her usual efficient thing. 'So, did you enjoy your night out then?' she asks, dead kind. I just nod from where I'm perched, trying not to let these walls get to me. All that white closing in, making everything feel too real again.

'We had a fabulous time, Marge!' Baz pipes up, still full of beans even though he looks rough as anything. 'Dancing all night with my gorgeous Bunny here.' Throws me a wink, grinning away.

'Long as you didn't lead our Steven too far astray,' Marge chuckles, sorting his arm out.

'Oh no!' Baz goes all innocent. 'Bunny was finding his own trouble, wasn't he?'

Both grab at the sleeping pills Marge offers like they're gold dust. Give Baz one last squeeze before I go, and he hugs back just as tight. 'Bunny, we smashed it! We raved so hard we ended up in hospital!'

'That we did, love,' I say quiet, giving him a quick kiss. 'That we did.'

Drop into bed like a sack of spuds, letting everything go fuzzy. That track from VTrax still going round my head as I'm nodding off - can still feel Baz's lips on mine, us two lost in the music together. Last thing I think before I'm gone is me and him on that dance floor. Just us, no hospitals, no being sick. Pure magic that was, even if just for one night.

Superman

Few weeks on and I'm watching Doc Sher going through my charts. He's practically bouncing while my guts are doing backflips between hope and bricking it.

'This is excellent news, Steven. Your results are very promising.'

Never seen the old boy so animated, going on about this new antiviral combo working brilliant. Gets proper excited telling me how patients like me could get better, not worse. It's doing my head in a bit - after months of doom and gloom, this sudden burst of hope feels dangerous. Like if I lean into it too hard, it might all come crashing down.

'So, how are you feeling? Any concerning side effects?'

'Feel good actually.' And it's true - haven't felt this alright in ages. 'Though there's this weird thing where I'm constantly starving. Can't seem to stop eating!'

He chuckles at that. 'Well, a good appetite is certainly a positive sign!'

Goes off on one about some AIDS conference in Vancouver and breakthroughs with the medicine I'm on, but I find myself drifting. Then his words snap me back: 'As such, I see no reason to keep you here any longer. We can discharge you as soon as this afternoon if you'd like.'

'You... you saying I can go home today?' The words feel foreign in my mouth, like they belong to someone else.

'Yes, indeed! I'll have Margaret sort your release papers.'

As it starts to sink in, my thoughts immediately turn to Basil, just three doors down, still fighting for every breath.

'But how come Basil isn't on this treatment, too?'

Doc Sher's face falls, and he settles on the edge of my bed with a sigh. 'It's complicated with Basil's case, I'm afraid. He's been ill for a long time now. Sometimes, the body can only take so much.'

'Have you tried getting Baz on the full dose yet, though?'

The look he gives me is full of such gentle pity I want to look away. 'We're doing everything we can for him, Steven. I know how close you two have become.' His voice goes soft. 'We're doing our best to keep him comfortable.'

I squeeze my eyes shut at that. Don't want to hear the kindness in his voice, don't want to face what 'keeping Baz comfortable' really means.

Doc heads off, going on about future backgammon matches, and I'm sat there stunned. Can't even get excited about going home now, not when Baz is stuck here without me.

Haul myself out of bed, need to find him. Need to see him, touch him, make sure he's still here, still fighting. Spot him chatting with Sophie by the nurses' station and make my way over.

Sophie smiles and shifts over. I sit next to Baz, and he rests his head in my lap while I run my fingers through his curls. Try not to think about how this might be one of the last times we get to just... be.

'So. Doc reckons I can go home this afternoon.'

Baz tries for a smile but it's all wrong. 'That's smashing news, Bunny.'

'I'll be here every day though,' I say quick, like that'll fix everything. We both go quiet, just the usual ward noise around us.

'Hey Baz... Fancy coming round mine for Sunday roast?'

He opens those beautiful eyes again, a flicker of light returning. 'I'd love to meet your family, Bunny.'

I lean down to give them curls a quick kiss, like I'm sealing the deal between us. Something to anchor us while everything else goes to shit around us.

The car buzzes with nervous energy as we head home. That hospital smell's still clinging to my clothes - bleach and sickness and hope all mixed up together. Feels weird watching the world zip by after months of staring at the same four walls. Mum's nattering away but my mind's still back on the ward with Basil.

'I've got your room fixed up nice, all your bits from your old flat so it doesn't feel like a teenager's room anymore.' Her voice has gone all bright - probably because she'd been bricking it when they first rushed me to hospital months back.

'Thanks, Mum.' I stare out the window as towns roll by. It's doing my head in a bit. After months in the ward, everything feels proper strange, like I'm watching it through thick glass.

'So, is it alright if Basil joins for Sunday roast?' Try to keep it casual.

'Course love!' Mum latches on quick. 'I'll make my famous beef plus all the sides!'

Catch Dad's eyes in the rearview, his knuckles going white on the wheel. 'And who might this Basil be exactly then?'

Tension in the car goes up about ten notches.

Mum touches his leg, voice gone low but pointed. 'He's a new friend of Steven's from hospital.' Way she says 'friend' makes me want to crawl under the seat and die.

Watch Dad exhale slow, like he's counting to ten in his head. 'I...see. Well, that's uh...that's rather nice.'

Turn back to the window, hiding a smile. No explosions yet. Suppose that's progress, of a sort.

Walking into the house throws me - everything's exactly the same but feels different somehow. Reckon I'm the one who's changed though. Stand there proper lost until Jasper comes bounding over, all wagging tail and slobbery kisses, and suddenly I'm back in my body again. His familiar greeting helps ground me a bit. Claire's quick hug before she disappears upstairs is so familiar I have to blink back tears. The quiet hits me after months of constant hospital noise. But then Dad's flipping on Sky News, familiar drone of the presenters filling the air.

As I demolish a plate of Hobnobs (Christ, I've missed these), Dad turns to me, face gone all careful. 'So, you're feeling quite improved?'

'Right as rain now, I'd say,' I tell him, reaching for another biccy.

Something in his face softens then, eyes suddenly bright. 'Very glad you're home safe now, son.'

Don't usually get that from Dad, catches me right off guard. Have to swallow hard past the lump in my throat. I squeeze his shoulder, hoping he gets all the stuff I can't say.

We turn back to the telly – something about a cloned sheep in Scotland now – and for just a moment, with biscuit crumbs on my lap and the familiar sounds of home around me, it feels like any other night from before. Like maybe, just maybe, everything might turn out alright after all.

'Alex...'

'Steve.'

'You back home then...?' His voice is thick with sleep - past midnight there in South Africa.

'Yeah, my old teenage room.' I'm wrapped in shadows and pillows, comfort of home still feeling weird.

'Let me guess - young Steve had Sam Fox all over his walls?'

'Nah, was more Simon Le Bon if I'm being honest.'

He lets out this sleepy chuckle. 'Showing your hand early there, weren't you? Must've been a right treat for teenage you.'

I lean back into the pillows. 'Dead quiet now - no hospital racket or weird smells. Though sharing space with all them blokes was mental.'

'Well, I always found those communal scenes quite appealing myself.'

We both laugh at that, proper fond.

'Got used to it after a while. Became like home.' I listen to Robbie Williams blasting from Claire's room, Mum and Dad pottering about downstairs, Dad's Sky News droning on in the background.

'You're feeling healthier these days, then?'

'Like you wouldn't believe! These new meds are magic. Doc says they could add years onto my life.' My throat goes tight. 'Can't say for sure, but just getting through each day is like a gift now.'

'How's your friend holding up?'

'Basil's...hanging in there.' Let out this bone-deep sigh. 'Actually, he'll be over Sunday for roast with the family.'

There's this surprised pause. 'Your house for dinner with your family? Your dad too? Colour me impressed!'

Can't help but smile. 'Thought you might be. I'm...nervous, but hopeful it'll go smooth.'

Another stretch of quiet between us, loaded with everything we've been through.

'This Basil bloke must be well special to get the invite over.'

I squeeze the phone tighter. 'I should have had you round back then, done it right.'

'Yeah.' He exhales soft. 'But we got time now, eh?'

Silence again, then his voice comes warm down the line. 'That's the important thing, Sunshine. However much or little, we're still here. Still kicking. Still with chances to live life full up, yeah?'

I nod to the empty room. 'Yeah, reckon you're right.' My voice has gone all wobbly. 'Few months ago I was preparing for the end, and now...'

'Now you've got a whole lot of more time ahead of you. It's a lot to wrap your head around, eh?'

'You're telling me.' Let out this laugh that's half crying. 'Christ, what am I supposed to do with all this... this future?'

'Well,' and I can hear him smiling, 'I reckon you start by living it, Sunshine. One day at a time.'

Ringing off, those words stick with me. One day at a time. Laying in my old bed, listening to the house creak and settle, I feel something I haven't had in ages - hope.

Scary as fuck, that, but in a good way.

BATMAN

Saturday rolls in bright as you like. Pull up to find Baz waiting under the awning, and my heart does this funny little flip. He's looking well fit - pressed trousers, shirt with the top buttons undone just so, wine and flowers in hand like some. My Baz.

I grab him in a tight hug, breathing in that familiar scent that still makes me dizzy. Even through his shirt I can feel the jersey underneath - his way of hiding how the illness is eating at him. Makes my heart ache, knowing why he's layered up in this heat, but I push that thought away. Just focus on having him here, solid and warm against me.

His pale skin's got a touch of foundation - something only I'd notice. Trying not to freak my folks out too much on first impressions, I reckon. But despite everything, just being with Baz makes me feel proper chuffed. No more hiding or pretending, just us two together. For today at least, everything feels perfect.

Mum's driving us home with the windows down, all of us chatting about sweet nothings. But it's all just background noise compared to having Baz here with me, laughing and looking gorgeous. Then she catches his eye in the rearview mirror, giving him this warm smile, and that's when he turns on the charm.

'Everyone at the hospital's so impressed by Steven's progress,' he tells her, balancing the wine and flowers careful. 'Dr Sher uses him as an example for the other patients, banging on about how well he's doing on the new meds. It's giving everyone such hope.'

He winks at me in the mirror, cheeky sod. We both carefully dodge talking about his own health for now.

Dad's waiting all wound up when we get in, but Baz steps forward smooth as anything. 'Pleasure to meet you, Mr Bishopston,' he says, proper posh, extending his hand.

Baz follows Mum to the kitchen where she's got a roast on. She won't hear of him helping, just hands him the wine to open instead. I hover by the door bricking it, but Baz works his magic quick as that. Before I know it, he's got Mum giggling like a schoolgirl while they sort the wine.

Then he drifts to the lounge, pouring Dad a drink, and suddenly they're deep in chat about ditching pounds for euros.

Mum's outdone herself with this spread - roast beef so tender it's falling apart, swimming in gravy. Roasties crisp as you like, Yorkshires puffed up massive. A feast fit for a king, or at least for my Baz.

'This is absolutely delicious, Mrs Bishopston,' Basil says, all polite, though he's barely touching it.

Mum smiles warm. 'Oh, do call me Janice, dear. And please, eat only what you can manage.'

Baz just nods and gives her one of those smiles that has her beaming.

Then he turns to Claire, curious. 'What music were you playing upstairs, love? I don't believe I've heard them before.'

'Spice Girls,' Claire chirps back.

Just like that, they're off, taking the mick out of the group's nicknames and songs. We all join in, laughing and teasing.

Then Dad gets this look on his face, like he's tasted something off. 'So, Basil. Where are you from originally?' he asks, pushing his Yorkshire pud around the plate.

'Wick,' Baz says smooth as anything. 'Too quiet for me by far. I'm more of a city chap.'

Dad nods, slow. 'And your father, what does he do out there?'

I feel my stomach drop, not wanting Dad to start his twenty questions. Mum and Claire exchange worried looks across the table.

'He's a tradesman,' Baz says, polite as ever.

'Ah, honest work that,' Dad nods. 'Does your mother work as well?'

Something flashes in Baz's eyes. 'She did, once. These days, I couldn't say.'

'Couldn't say?' Dad's voice goes sharp, fork clattering against his plate. 'Bit odd, not knowing what your own parents are up to, isn't it?'

Claire tries to cut in with something about the gravy, but Dad's not having it. The temperature in the room drops about ten degrees. Mum's frozen with her fork halfway to her mouth. Claire's looking between Dad and Baz like she's watching a car crash in slow motion. I'm gripping my fork so hard my knuckles have gone white, wanting to say something, anything, to stop what's coming.

But Baz just takes a deep breath and squares his shoulders. The look in his eyes - I've seen it before. 'The truth is, my parents and I haven't spoken in a few years,' he says.

Dad shifts in his chair, running a thumb along his collar. 'Really?' he says. 'Why on earth not?'

'Dad, please,' I manage to get out. 'Not now, yeah?'

But Baz just squeezes my hand under the table. 'It's alright,' he says quiet. 'My father and I, we didn't see eye to eye. Especially after I came out. He took it rather badly. And when I fell ill... well, that was the final straw. They cut me off completely.'

The silence after that's so thick you could cut it with a knife. Dad looks like he's been slapped. Mum's got tears in her eyes.

'Oh, Basil love, I'm so dreadfully sorry,' Mum whispers.

'It's not right!' Claire bursts out. 'Cutting off your own child like that. It's absolutely horrid!'

Dad rubs at his jaw, something he always does when he's thinking hard. 'No, it's not right at all. I'm terribly sorry to hear that, son. No one should have to go through that. Especially not from their own parents.'

Baz just shrugs, all resigned. 'I gave up trying with them ages ago. But I've got my friends now, my chosen family.' He looks my way as he says it. 'They're the ones who really matter, at the end of the day.'

'Well, I'll drink to that!' Claire says, lifting her glass. 'To friends and found family!'

We all join in, clinking glasses. The tension in the room starts to fade. I catch Baz's eye over my glass, and my heart does this funny little flip.

Baz turns to Mum and Dad then, all serious. 'I just want to say, the way you've supported Steven, loved him through all this... it's something truly special. I can see where he gets his strength from, his kindness.'

'To Steven,' Baz says then, not looking away from me. 'For being not just an extraordinary son, but an extraordinary man, full stop.'

Dad clears his throat again, but this time there's a hint of a smile on his face. 'I'll second that,' he says, raising his glass. 'To our Steven.'

And I'm just sat there, grinning like a right muppet, feeling like I might burst from all the love in the room.

Mum's proper crying now, dabbing at her eyes with her napkin. Even Dad looks a bit misty-eyed, though he tries to hide it.

I reach for Baz's hand under the table, holding on tight.

After pudding, we all drift to the sunroom like any other Sunday afternoon. Late sun's streaming in, making everything golden and warm. Baz settles into the wicker chair, already deep in a chat with Mum and Claire about Kate Moss while I head out with Dad and Jasper for a walk in the field behind the house. Jas is proper loving it, nose to the ground, sniffing out God knows what.

Dad breaks the quiet after a bit. 'It was brave, bringing Basil round today.'

Keep my eyes on Jas, trying to play it casual. 'Didn't want to hide him away, did I? Like he's something to be ashamed of.'

Dad comes to a stop. 'I'm proud of you, son. Really proud. The way you're handling all this, on your own terms... it's admirable.'

He clears his throat, looking a bit awkward. 'I know I can be a stubborn old man sometimes. Set in my ways. And perhaps I don't agree with all your choices.' This little smile creeps onto his face. 'But I want you to know, Steven... the man you've become? I couldn't be prouder. I really couldn't.'

Takes me a minute to find my voice. 'That... that means a lot, Dad. More than you know.'

We walk on quiet for a bit. 'This Basil of yours... he seems a good chap.'

'The best, Dad. Didn't think I could ever feel like this again, if I'm honest. But Baz... he just makes everything brighter.'

'He's quite ill himself though, isn't he?' Dad says it gentle.

'Yeah,' comes out barely more than a whisper. 'Yeah, he is.'

Dad stops walking, hand on my shoulder. 'I just want to see you happy, son. Want you to be with someone who brings out the best in you. Someone who lights up your life.' His smile's wobbly but real. 'And Basil, he seems to do just that for you.'

Then he's pulling me into a hug, tight as anything. Can feel him trembling a bit as he says, 'Thought I might lose you, son. Really thought you were slipping away from us.'

We just stand there for a bit, holding on. Both of us with tears in our eyes, not that we'd admit it.

Something's shifts between us. Like maybe, just maybe, we're starting to get each other at last.

Love

The drive back to London's a right mix. Easy chatter one minute, comfy quiet the next. Dad keeps eyeing Baz in the rear-view, proper charmed by his witty chat about everything from the scenery whizzing by to the latest chart-toppers crackling on the radio. But underneath all that, I clock how knackered Baz looks, the way he sags when he thinks no one's watching. A reminder of the shit waiting for us, lurking just round the corner.

We're not heading straight back to hospital, thank fuck. Nah, we're off to Baz's place in Maida Vale. Fetch more clothes, show me where he lives when he's not stuck in Broderip. I'm just chuffed to get more time alone with him, if I'm honest.

As we pull up outside his flat, Dad reaches over and gives Baz's shoulder a warm squeeze. 'You're a good bloke, Basil,' he says, all gruff but dead sincere. 'Been a pleasure getting to know you.'

Baz ducks his head, cheeks going all pink. 'Likewise, Mr Bishopston,' he murmurs, shooting me a cheeky grin. 'Your son's not half bad either, I s'pose.'

Dad barks out a laugh, shaking his head as he climbs out to see us to the door. One last rib-creaking hug, and then he's off.

And suddenly, it's just us two. No parents or beeping machines or watchful nurses hovering. Bit weird, that.

'Welcome to my humble abode!' Baz declares, faffing with the keys. 'Bit out of practise,' he jokes when the lock sticks. 'There we go!'

Christ, walking in is like being wrapped in pure Baz - he's everywhere, even with a layer of dust coating everything. He runs a finger along a side table, pulls a face at the grey smudge. 'Sorry love, hospital's been keeping me rather occupied,' he says, wiping it with his sleeve.

Place is still gorgeous though - all jewel colours and posh fabrics, old bits mixed with new. Proper him.

'So, what d'you reckon?' Baz has gone all shy, chewing his lip while he watches me take it all in. 'Bit over the top? I do have a flair for the dramatic, as you might've noticed.'

'Baz...' I grab his hand, tangling our fingers together. 'It's perfect.'

His face lights up brighter than Piccadilly at night.

'Too right,' I say, pulling him closer, breathing him in - that cologne of his mixing with warm leather from the car. 'Mind you, those gold curtains are a bit naff...'

'You philistine!' he squawks, giving me a slap. 'Those are genuine Versace!'

We end up howling, holding each other up as the buzz of the day, of just being here together, hits us full force.

Eventually, Baz sorts his hair out, gives me this saucy wink. 'Right then. Fancy a tour of the boudoir? I promise to behave...'

'Like I'd believe that for a second, you cheeky sod.'

His bedroom's like something out of a posh magazine - all fancy fabrics and bits arranged just so. But you can still spot the real Baz underneath. Tatty paperback of 'Maurice' by the bed, about fifty eyeliner pencils scattered over his dressing table.

Baz is already buried in that massive wardrobe of his, clothes flying everywhere. 'Got it!' he shouts, waving this sparkly leopard print thing at me. 'This'll look perfect on you, Bunny!'

Then he's off, playing dress-up with me like I'm his personal dummy. Keeps loading me up with all these designer labels - Westwood trousers with more straps than sense, some see-through Gaultier thing, these wicked green McQueen boots that could blind you. Mental seeing his world like this. But it's the way he's showing it to me that gets me right in the gut. Every time he grins, every time his fingers brush against me while he's sorting out them clothes... feels like something precious I want to bottle up, save for when things get rough later. Christ, listen to me - turning into a right soppy git.

We end up sprawled on his bed, can't breathe from laughing so much. All these clothes scattered around us like party decorations. Baz curls up next to me, resting his head on my shoulder, and something shifts in the air. Goes quieter somehow.

'Love this bed of mine... Come here then, darling...'

I scoot closer, catching how his face has changed. That daft grin from before's gone, replaced by something that makes my heart squeeze.

'There's something I need you to know. Something I need you to remember, after.'

'Baz...' I reach for him but words get stuck in my throat.

'No, Bunny. Let me say this, yeah?' Takes a breath, eyes not leaving mine. 'I'm dying. We both know it. This body...' Glances down with this little smile that breaks my heart. 'Time's running out.'

'Please. Don't, I can't...'

'Shh...' His fingers on my lips, gentle as anything. 'I know it's hard. I know.' Traces my mouth so soft. 'But you need to hear this, alright? When I go... when this heart stops...' Takes my hand, puts it right over his heartbeat. 'Part of me stays with you, Bunny. Right here in your heart.'

My eyes are proper blurry but I keep blinking - can't miss a second of his face.

'Was half-dead before. Just waiting to die. But you, Bunny... you made me feel alive again.' His voice catches. 'First time ever, I know what it means to really love someone. Want to give them everything.'

Can't help the noise I make, but Baz just smiles - so beautiful it hurts to look at him.

'You've made me so happy. Happier than I thought I could be.' His thumbs catch the wet off my cheeks. 'Being with you, loving you... easiest thing I've ever done.'

When he kisses me, I can taste salt - hello and goodbye all mixed up. Christ, he's everything. Just everything.

I hold his face when he pulls back, trying to burn it all into memory.

'I love you,' I get out, meaning it more than I've ever meant anything in my life. 'Love you so much, Baz.'

His eyes close, one tear sliding down. 'Oh, Bunny...'

I wipe the tear away, can't stop the words pouring out. 'And I'll love you forever, you hear? Till I'm gone too.'

'I love you. My gorgeous Bunny, my once-in-a-lifetime boy.'

Then we're kissing again, slower this time. Sweeter. Taking our time with it, like we're trying to memorise every little bit. Moving together slow, getting lost in how he tastes, how he smells of vanilla and spice. It's gentle, like we're both scared of breaking the moment. No need to rush. Because we know time's running out. Makes you want to hold onto every second.

Getting my shirt off with one hand, trying to undo Baz's buttons but my fingers won't stop shaking. Need to feel him close, need to remember exactly how he feels. Like I'm learning him by heart, keeping every bit stored away safe.

We get each other's clothes off between kisses, can't stop touching. Baz runs his fingers over my shoulders, down my back, making me shiver. His skin's so warm under my hands, just perfect.

'Drawer...' he breathes against my neck, and I reach over all unsteady, finding the condom. His eyes stay on mine the whole time, looking at me so intense it makes my heart stutter.

Then we're together, like two pieces that were always meant to fit. Moving with each other while the sunset turns everything gold. Never felt anything like this before, like my heart might burst from feeling too much.

'I love you,' comes bursting out of me, couldn't hold it in if I tried. 'Love you so much, Bunny. My beautiful boy...'

We fall apart together, holding on tight while everything else just... disappears. Just us, just this - breathing hard, hearts racing.

After, we stay wrapped up in each other. Touching, kissing, trying to remember everything. Don't want to let go, not even a little bit, trying to grab onto every second we've got left.

Today, I keep him close. Memorising every detail - his warmth, his heartbeat, the way he fits against me.

Today, nothing else matters. Just us. My Baz.

Love Double Drop

Bedside clock's glowing just past 11pm as Baz shuffles from bed.

'Just need the loo, Bunny,' he mumbles, giving me a sleepy kiss. 'Won't be long.'

He makes his way to the bathroom, hand against the wall to steady himself.

Feels well nice, this - like we could stay wrapped up in our own little world forever.

I slip quiet into the darkened kitchen, stomach growling like a right beast. All I find in the fridge is some manky old gherkins and a bottle of fizz. End up scoffing the gherkins anyway, wash out the jar after. Some gourmet feast, that.

Head back to the bedroom, but Baz is still in the bathroom. Spot one of his white BOY jumpers in the mess of clothes everywhere. Pull it on - still smells of that vanilla shower gel he uses, feels like being wrapped up in him.

Get caught looking at the photos on his dressing table. There's him with his best mates, Ricky and Ian, grinning like mad. Another one of him on holiday somewhere, holding up a glass of wine, looking all golden in that Mediterranean sun. Then at some club - silver trousers with a studded belt, lights catching while he dances. Can see that angel wing tattoo across his back. Last one's well old - a blonde woman smiling on this flowery sofa. Little Baz sat on her lap, proper chuffed with this toy train he's holding. Got the same blue eyes as her. Christ, he was a cute kid.

It's gone too quiet, and Baz has been in there way too long. Call his name and my voice comes out all wobbly, nothing but dead silence coming back. Press my ear against the bathroom door, desperate to hear something, anything.

Heart's going mental now as I knock once, then again harder when there's nothing. 'Baz...?' Silence stretches out, horrible and heavy. End up hammering the door, panic rising while the empty hallway echoes back at me.

'Basil!' Fists pounding wood, heart in my throat, palms gone all slick with sweat. Handle won't bloody budge, so I slam my shoulder against it again and again till something finally gives.

My heart just... stops.

There's Baz on the bathroom floor, all crumpled up where he must've dropped. His face has gone this horrible grey color, lips turning blue, barely getting any air in.

'Baz!' Drop down beside him, hands shaking something fierce as I grab his face. His skin's like ice under my fingers. 'Come on love, please...'

He stirs just enough to crack those blue eyes open, gives me this tiny smile that rips my guts out. Then his eyes flutter shut and he goes heavy in my arms.

'Got to get an ambulance.' Scrambling up, watching him fade right in front of me. 'Just hold on, Baz, please...'

Fingers trembling so bad I can hardly work the phone.

Woman answers all calm while my whole world's falling to bits. 'Emergency, which service?'

'Ambulance!' Comes out proper strangled. 'My boyfriend's collapsed, he's not breathing right!'

Spot an envelope on the table, his address right there. Thank fuck for that.

'It's Basil... Basil Harlett! 14 Warwick Avenue, Maida Vale. Please hurry!'

She's asking more questions but my mind's gone blank.

Then it hits me. 'He's got AIDS,' the words burning my throat. 'They need to know that, yeah? For safety?'

Can barely hear her over my pulse roaring in my ears.

Everything's gone weird, like them nightmares you can't wake up from, except this is real. This is happening. Baz is dying right in front of me and I can't do a bloody thing about it. Keep thinking about losing him, about those blue eyes closing forever, and it feels like someone's reaching in and ripping my heart out. Want to scream the place down, but there's no time. Baz needs me. Got to hold it together even though I'm falling to pieces.

Chuck the phone down and rush to find clothes, but my hands are shaking so bad I can hardly grab anything. When I get back, try to be gentle as I dress him. His arms are dead weight as I work them through the sleeves, head lolling against my shoulder. Like dressing one of them shop dummies, except this one's my whole world, and he's slipping away with every breath.

Waiting for the sirens feels like forever. Keep him close, can't stop the words tumbling out, begging him to stay. 'Come on, love,' rocking him gentle. 'Don't you dare leave me now. We've got so much left to do, you and me. All them adventures waiting. You can't check out, you hear me? Won't let you.'

Outside, London's just carrying on like nothing's happening - traffic humming away, some pissed lot singing rubbish, bass thumping from the pub down the road. But in here, all I can focus on is Baz fighting for each breath and my heart going like a drum. His skin's gone all clammy under my fingers, that vanilla scent turned sour now, mixing with something sharp and medical. Floor's freezing under my knees but I couldn't give a toss, just counting each breath like it's precious gold.

Can feel him slipping away bit by bit. Nothing to do but hold on tight and pray for sirens, for miracles, for anything that'll keep my Baz here with me just a little bit longer.

White Dove

Sat by the window, watching everyone down there just getting on with their day. Like nothing's happening up here. Like my Baz isn't dying right above them. Branches keep tapping against the window, proper miserable, rain dripping off them against the grey sky. Feels about right, that. Inside, them monitors just keep beeping away, cold and sterile, counting down each heartbeat while I'm sitting here watching him slip away.

'He was so excited to meet your family,' Marge whispers, almost to herself. 'Laughing as we dashed out to grab a bouquet for your mum, a nice bottle of wine for your dad.' She looks over at me gentle. 'So, was it a nice visit?'

Glance at Baz and try for a smile. 'Most beautiful day of my life.'

He stirs a bit at my voice, this weak smile flickering across his face while I cling to his fading warmth.

'Just hours ago, he was fine.' Memories of us tangled together still fresh in my mind. 'He seemed alright then... How'd this happen so quick?'

'It's the nasty nature of this disease,' Marge says quiet, prepping another round of meds for his drip. Then she gives me a proper look. 'You've been here all night, haven't you? And what about your own medication?'

Just shake my head, numb to everything but Baz. Marge crosses her arms, gives me that look of hers before heading out. Back in a minute with those familiar pills.

'Here, surplus from another patient. Dr Sher's away at an AIDS conference in Vancouver, but the fill-in will replace them...' Rests her hand on my shoulder all kind, passes me some water. I neck the pills without thinking.

'Dr Sher's gone? What about Baz? He knows his history...' Feel my guts twist with panic.

'We'll manage. But please, Steve, look after yourself too—it's what Baz would want.'

Give her a half-hearted nod, but my focus is glued to Baz.

More tests follow—blood draws, x-rays, all showing the pneumonia's getting worse in his lungs. Margaret rings up Ricky and Ian, listed as next of kin since his mum won't acknowledge her dying son.

Baz is asleep when they arrive. Ricky brings his best single malt, winking as he touches a whiskey-dipped sponge to Baz's cracked lips. A faint smile crosses Baz's face at the taste. More mates filter in, gathering round his bed while I stare at the scuffed linoleum, rubbing at marks with my shoe. Like I could scrub away all the suffering these walls have seen.

We're caught in this loop, the DJ scratching the same three beats like a knackered old record. Baz goes downhill by the hour - pale as milk, breaths shallow, body withering away to nothing. He drifts in and out, shivering with a cold no warmth can touch. I murmur about daft little things. Trying to remember everything about him. His face, his voice, all of it.

Every so often, he stirs weakly, whispers, 'Still here, Bunny...' in that broken voice before drifting off again. I just hope wherever his mind takes him, he isn't scared. That maybe he's seeing us together, dancing under rainbow lights without a care.

When Sophie offers food, I barely manage two bites before pushing it away, my stomach in knots.

'Why aren't you eating, Bunny?' Baz asks faintly, eyes flickering open.

I press my lips to his cheek, run my fingers through his curls, trying to show him everything I feel.

'You really must eat,' he insists, still fussing over me even now.

'I will, Baz, I swear it, just not now,' I choke out, stroking back his hair. Like if I keep touching him, he'll have to stay.

'Bloody parched though,' he mutters.

I hold his water glass, guide the straw between his cracked lips.

He takes the smallest sip before turning away, knackered just from that.

Jason sets up his decks, careful like. Spends the afternoon playing all Baz's favourites, saying goodbye the only way he know's how.

Can't stop looking between Baz - so pale and still in that bed - and those bloody monitors tracking every breath. Nurses keep saying it won't be long, but won't tell me straight. Doesn't matter though - I'm not going anywhere. Going to stay right here holding his hand, making sure he knows how loved he is.

Sophie drags in a thin mattress, tucks it up against Baz's bed. Sorts out a blanket and pillow for me, not saying a word. She knows.

I ring Mum; she comes with spare clothes, like when I was the one in hospital - feels like another lifetime now. Gives me a squeeze before heading off quick, knowing there's nothing else to say.

I shower, change, and get back to Baz. Settling in for whatever comes next. He's my whole world now, and I'm not letting go.

There's nothing pretty about this. No peaceful drifting away like in films - just Baz in agony, thrashing about on the bed, being sick into the dish Sophie's holding. Marge comes in and sorts his pillows, tries to make him comfy. Brings the morphine that's meant to help with the pain tearing through him. Dabs at his sore, cracked lips with a damp cloth, like that might do any good.

'I just... I just want my mum...' Baz mutters between heaves.

'I know, love, I know...' Marge says softly.

'Can you call her...see if she'll come...'

'I will, Baz love, I promise.' Marge's voice is gentle, though we both know it's hopeless—his mum won't budge. I follow her out, trying to keep up as she tells me, 'His mum won't return my calls. And his dad says his son is already dead to him.'

'He needs quiet, Marge. This place is too noisy; he can't get better with all this racket.'

I'm proper desperate now. 'If I can just take him home, back to mine, he'll be alright. He can recover there. You can bring his medicine, visit. He just needs peace and quiet.'

But she stops, tears in her eyes. 'Steven...' Her words cut deep. 'It's not the noise. Basil is dying. Do you understand?'

I try to argue, but she squeezes my shoulders.

I'm not listening because I can't face what I already know.

'Are you hearing me? There's nothing you can do but be there, make him comfortable.' She pulls me into a tight hug while I sob. 'Now go to him. Hold him. Just be together. That's all we've got left.'

I take a deep breath and head back in.

Carefully, I shift closer on the narrow bed. Baz barely makes a dent in the mattress now - he's gotten so thin there's plenty of room for me to slide in beside him. I curl round him like I could somehow shield what's left, and his eyes crack open just enough to give me this tiny smile while I hold him.

His hand trembles as he reaches for mine, and I grab it tight, desperate for any bit of connection. We just lie there together, not saying nothing, just breathing. Don't need words - just being here, feeling each breath against each other. I try to match my breathing to his, scared that once he's gone, I'll forget how it's meant to sound.

Hours blur past until a nurse comes to check on him. But she lets me stay wrapped round him, even though we both know I can't keep him here.

Can't tell how long I'm there - it all blurs together. Just watching Baz breathe, listening to the machines beep, hearing footsteps in the corridor. Keep nodding off but never let go, scared he'll slip away if I do.

Marge gets me up in the end, giving my shoulder a gentle shake. 'Come on, love. Let's get some air, yeah? Just for a minute.'

I try saying no - don't want to miss a single second. But the room's getting smaller and smaller, and I can hardly breathe through the hospital smell. So I let her lead me out, legs gone wobbly, squinting at the brightness.

Outside, the sun's going down, turning everything orange and pink. Air hits my lungs sharp after all that hospital staleness. Feels wrong somehow, being out here while Baz is in there, hanging on by a thread.

Marge gets out a cigarette, the lighter clicking in the quiet. Wind brings over the smell of smoke, mixing with the hospital still stuck to my clothes.

'Didn't have you down as a smoker,' I say.

She narrows her eyes mid-drag. 'Why's that then? Cos I'm a nurse?'

I nod, seeing her tap her foot to some internal rhythm while inhaling deep.

'Always wanted to be a nurse,' she says distantly. 'Played at it as a kid—bandaging up my brothers, pretending to save them. Helping people feels good, you know?'

But her face goes stormy with the next puff. 'This nightmare tho ugh...didn't sign on for this bollocks. Not a damn bit.'

And I know exactly what she means.

'My parents think I work ICU,' she says, blowing smoke aside. 'Can't tell them it's the AIDS ward, or they'd fret about catching something or me getting ill.' She shakes her head. 'Load of old tosh.'

'Yeah,' I sigh hollowly, feeling that deep.

She looks at me closely. 'You alright, Steve?'

I shrug half-heartedly, barely holding it together.

'Dead brave you are,' she whispers, 'caring for Baz and yourself.' She stubs her cigarette out heavily. 'I'm so terribly sorry about all this.' Squeezing my shoulder firmly, she adds, 'Love can be a right mess sometimes, eh?'

'Nah, it ain't, I swear,' I reply adamantly. 'It's still flipping beautiful as anything.'

She smiles warmly then reaches up suddenly to cup my chin, yanking me into a fierce hug.

'You really are something special, Stevie,' she whispers, choked on tears. 'Wish to heaven there was more I could do...'

'Me too, Marge,' I confess back rawly, my voice cracking.

I follow Marge back, heading for Baz's room while she hurries off somewhere. He's lying there dead still when I come in, breathing so shallow you'd hardly notice, face peaceful like he's just having a kip. I touch his arm gentle-like, then catch sight of something mental out the window - the sky's gone and exploded into colour, all orange and pink bleeding into purple round the edges. Most beautiful sunset I've seen in my life.

'Baz... you've got to see this sunset!' I try, but he doesn't move. Just lying there like a statue, only those tiny breaths showing he's still with me. Can't have him missing this. Not this.

'Come on, wake up!' My hands are on his bed now, pushing hard enough to make the wheels squeal against the floor. Everything goes flying as I crash towards the window - the side table toppling, monitors screaming their heads off, IV lines stretching like spider webs. 'It's fine, I can sort this...' Stumbling round, trying to get everything lined up right, because he needs to see this. Has to see this. It's the most beautiful sunset I've ever seen and my Baz is missing it.

'Baz, look!' Pointing at all them colours painting the sky, but his eyes stay shut. Nothing. Not even a flutter.

Then it hits me, this ice-cold feeling right through my chest. My hand's searching for his heartbeat, the way I've done a hundred times before, but there's nothing. Just silence where his heart should be.

World goes proper weird then, like someone's stuffed cotton wool in my ears. Everything sounds far away and close up all at once.

This can't be happening. We were meant to have more time. More sunsets, more laughs, more of everything. More Baz.

Can't breathe properly. Can't think straight. Keep waiting for him to open his eyes and give me that cheeky grin of his, tell me I'm being a right drama queen.

'Just breathe, please,' words coming out all broken between sobs. 'Don't leave me here on my own.'

Tears are proper streaming now as I scream, 'Breathe! Just one more...' Getting louder with every word. 'Baz... BAZ wake up and breathe, one more breath will do! BREATHE!'

I'm shaking him but his head just flops about like one of them rag dolls. He's gone. He's actually gone. Keep screaming, sobbing, kissing his face between begging him to come back.

Marge has to pull me away in the end, holding me while I keep saying 'He just needs to breathe...' over and over like a broken record.

That beautiful sunset disappears same time as Baz's last breath, everything going grey and lifeless.

Holding onto Marge for dear life now, legs gone to water, chest so tight I can't get air in. Been so desperate trying to make him breathe, I've forgotten how to do it myself.

Sonic

I sit with Baz until the porters come. Try following but lose them down some corridor. Then I'm just... lost. Walking past people laughing, past sad little bunches of flowers wilting in their vases. Past empty chairs and gurneys all piled up. Spot that Bowie portrait Baz always loved - swear those eyes are following me. Keep walking, head down, trying not to hear Baz's voice in my head calling 'Bunny...'

Find an exit sign, push through into the dark. Door slams behind me with this bang that makes me jump like a right tit.

Outside hits me hard - freezing as anything. Some taxi nearly takes me out, horn blaring. Can barely keep my feet under me as I stumble to the bus stop, gripping my travel card so tight it's creasing.

The 16 pulls up. Drag myself on, collapse into this manky seat with stuffing coming out. Press my head against the window, engine vibrating through my skull. Through the steamed-up glass, everyone's just getting on with their day - postie doing his rounds, some woman with a pram, bloke selling papers. Like the world hasn't just ended. Like my Baz isn't...

Don't even know which stop's mine. Just get off when it feels like I can't sit still another second. Need to keep moving or I'll fall apart right here on this bus. Stumble through streets I don't know, trying to find Baz's road. Eyes stinging, hands shaking as I dig his keys out - been holding them so tight the brass has gone warm.

Hits me like a punch when I open his door - that smell of him. Vanilla and that posh aftershave he loves. Loved. Makes me want to spew, knowing I'll never smell it on him again.

Three steps in and my legs give out. End up on my knees on his carpet, this noise coming out of me like a wounded animal. Can't stop it. Can't breathe right. Everything's going dark round the edges while I'm trying to get air in my lungs, but it's not working. Just these rough sounds I can't control.

Don't know how, but I make it to his bedroom. Face-plant on his bed, our smell still on the sheets. Kicks me in the guts - they're still stiff from the other night, when everything was alright. When he was still here. Can't tell what I'm feeling anymore. Like everything and nothing all at once. Keep grabbing at bits of him - his shirt collar, the warmth left in his bed - scared I'll forget how he felt, how he smelled. End up crying into his blue shirt till I pass out.

&

Two days of this. Living in my head where me and Baz are still together, still laughing and touching. Then reality smacks me in the face again, leaving me crying like a baby, feeling like someone's put my heart through a cheese grater.

I fumble for the phone, dialling Alex's number without thinking - know it by heart, don't I?

'Alex...' My voice comes out all mangled.

'Stevie? What's wrong?'

'It's Baz...he's gone. He's dead.'

Long pause, just Alex breathing shaky down the line. 'Oh, Stevie. I'm so sorry, love. God, I'm so sorry... Tell me what you need. Anything, Sunshine.'

Try to pull myself together, end up sniffling like a kid. 'Just... just talk to me, yeah? Need to hear your voice. M'calling from Baz's pho ne... no one left to pay the bill, is there?' Let out this mental laugh that sounds all wrong.

Hear him moving about. 'Gimme a sec. Going out on the balcony.'

'Tell us what it's like there.'

'It's warm out here. Smells like salt and petrol, bit of them sweet flowers they've got everywhere. Moon's barely there, keeps hiding behind clouds. Bit like that night in Blackpool, innit? Us under that manky blanket, passing spliffs till morning.'

Makes me laugh, even if it's weak. 'That's when you nicked my last Dunhill, you wanker.'

'Borrowed, mate.' Can hear him grinning. 'Not my fault you fell asleep.'

We go quiet for a bit, just breathing.

'What else?' My voice goes all scratchy. 'Tell us more.'

Alex makes this thinking noise. 'Got these palm trees opposite, all bent over in the wind. Still standing though, ain't they? Bit battered but keeping on.'

Throat goes tight, getting what he means. 'Like us then? Couple of stubborn gits.'

'Too right.' His voice goes dead soft. 'Storm's coming in. Sky's gone dark, clouds all twisted up.' He lets out this little laugh. 'Even the weather's feeling it tonight.'

Hear thunder in the background.

'Look, Stevie... reckon we get more than one love if we're lucky. Few chances to find someone who gets us, really gets us. Hurts like hell when it's over, but that's how you know it meant something, innit? Each one changes you a bit. Gets under your skin. And if we're lucky, we get to feel like that more than once before we're done.'

Massive crack of thunder makes me jump. 'Bloody hell, what was that?'

Alex just laughs, bit mental. 'Absolutely pissing it down now! End of the world type stuff!'

'You daft sod, get inside! You'll get struck by lightning!'

'No chance, sunshine! Feels too good - letting it soak me through. We're still here, ain't we? Still going. That's what matters.'

Just hear the rain for a minute.

'You still there, Stevie boy?' His voice goes all quiet. 'Love you, you know that? Always have, always will. We'll get through this. Together, like always. You're the strongest bloke I know.'

'Love you too, you mad bastard.' Come out half-crying, half-laughing.

'Just take it slow, yeah? Hour by hour if you have to. Let Gem look after you a bit.'

'Should probably go. This call's gonna cost Baz's estate a fortune.'

'Sod the bill,' Alex scoffs. 'What they gonna do, chase him down in heaven for it? Pretty sure being dead gets you out of paying BT.'

Can't help laughing, bit hysterical. 'Watch it, or I'll ring you every hour, do your head in. Spend my days chatting rubbish like some mad old git.'

'That a threat or a promise?' He fires back. 'I'll be here anyway, sleeping with the phone under my pillow.'

'Alright, keep your hair on. I'll ring tomorrow, yeah? And the next day, and the next. Every day till you're sick of me.'

'You better, Sunshine. Or I'm getting the first flight to Heathrow.'

'I will, Alex. Promise. Now get in out the rain, you muppet. Catch your death, then where will I be?'

'Yes, boss,' he says, trying to sound sarky but coming out soft instead. 'Go on, try and get some kip. And eat something, even if it tastes like cardboard. Keep your strength up.'

'Sir, yes sir,' I say back, meaning to take the piss but sounding well fond instead.

Line goes dead with a crackle. Can still hear his voice in my head though, keeping me warm. Keeping me here.

Speckled Dove

Ring Gem after. She turns up with this rucksack, slips into the bedroom, quiet-like. Watch her sort through it - my meds first, lined up on the nightstand. Then some clean clothes, socks and that.

She just kicks off her shoes and gets in bed with me, like it's the most normal thing. Sheets still smell of me and Baz, his clothes everywhere. Next thing I know she's got her arms round me, holding me like a kid, and I just... break.

'I've got you, Stevie,' she keeps saying, holding me tight. 'You're not alone, not while I'm here.'

Must've passed out after that, proper knackered from all the crying.

Keep thinking I can hear Baz's voice echoing round the flat as I drift in and out. Like this is all some sick joke and he's still here, getting better.

But when I finally drag myself to the lounge, it all hits again.

Gem's on the sofa with Ian and Ricky. Ricky jumps up, gives me this massive hug, and I'm off again, crying like a baby.

They're here to sort Baz's final wishes. Ian drags in this scarlet suitcase from the wardrobe. 'My Fabulous Funeral' written on it in Baz's messy writing. Have to laugh - trust him to label his own send-off like it's some West End show.

Inside, there's his playlist - all camp classics and dance tunes. Then the outfit. Pure Baz from head to toe - silver leather trousers, studded belt, fishnet vest. Even the cowboy boots, one last 'up yours' to all the small-minded gits. We pass it round, hands shaking, laughing and crying cos it's so bloody perfect.

Find these old photos underneath. Baz before all this AIDS shit - little cherub with ice cream all over his face, beaming on some fairground ride. One with his dad that makes my chest hurt. Then him in full drag - blue glitter on his cheeks, pink lips pouting like he owns the world.

At the bottom, envelopes for everyone - Ricky and Ian, Marge and Sophie. His mum. And me. Hold mine tight, along with the ones for the nurses and his mum.

Funeral's going to be at this community place near Ricky and Ian's. No church stuff. Only rule is no black - banned it outright, he did. Didn't want any boring suits ruining his fabulous send-off.

Ian's left a message for Baz's mum, but we not holding our breath. She's missed out on years of her boy being brilliant. Can't see that changing now.

Can feel myself going again. A right leaky tap these days.

After they go, end up rummaging through his wardrobe. Don't even know what for. Just need to feel close to him, I guess.

Chuck some bits in my bag. His leather jacket that's gone all soft. BOY London t-shirt that smells of his fancy oils. This absolutely mad leopard print waistcoat that's so him it hurts.

Nick a few photos an' all. Just little reminders for when it gets rough.

Stand there for ages, just looking round his flat. Trying to take it all in - the mad colours everywhere, all his bits and pieces. His life, sitting here waiting for someone who ain't coming back.

Finally make myself sit down on the sofa. The envelope's burning a hole in my pocket. Been avoiding it, scared of what's inside. What last words Baz might've left me.

Take it out slow, hands shaking as I break the seal.

Inside there's this plane ticket. Have to read it twice to believe what I'm seeing. Round-the-world thing from British Airways, looks dead expensive. Sort that makes you stop at all these exotic places - Thailand, Australia, the lot.

Then I read his note, that familiar messy writing making my heart stop:

'My Bunny,

Let's jet off together and see this mad old world, you and me. My treat, and my deepest dream. I'll love you beyond the horizons, always.

Your Baz x'

Just sit there gawping. Even dead, he's still pulling stunts that knock me sideways.

Hands are shaking as I hold it. Like he's reached out and grabbed hold of me. 'Come on, Bunny,' I can hear him saying. 'One last adventure.'

Want to laugh and cry and scream all at once. Typical Baz, always going over the top.

Close my eyes and I can see him clear as day. That cheeky grin, them blue eyes sparkling. 'Don't you dare waste this, Bunny. Want you to live, truly live. For both of us.'

Hurts so bad I can barely breathe. But there's something else there too. This tiny bit of... dunno. Hope, maybe?

Hold the ticket against my chest. 'Alright, Baz,' I whisper, all choked up. 'You win, you daft sod. One last grand tour.' Have to swallow hard. 'I'll see it all for you, my love. Promise.'

Not saying I'm okay with any of this. But it's a start. Wobbly as anything, but a start.

Stick the ticket in my wallet next to that Ibiza photo of him. Take a deep breath and head out.

Gem's waiting outside. Takes one look at my face and links her arm through mine.

We've only gone a few steps when she stops dead. 'Oi Stevie,' she goes, dead surprised. 'Look at that rainbow. Ain't it mental?'

Look up where she's pointing, sun in my eyes. And there it is. Biggest, brightest rainbow I've ever seen, right across the sky.

Magic against all that grey. Every colour you can think of, all running into each other. Like Baz has spread those angel wings of his one last time, painting London up, as anything.

Makes me think of that sunset at hospital - the last one he never saw. But this feels different somehow. Not like an ending. More like... something else.

Like Baz giving me a wink from up there. Writing me a message across the sky.

Alright Bunny? it's saying. Chin up, love. Sun's still there, even if you can't see it yet.

Tip my head back, let the wind mess up my hair. Take this deep breath of cold air, feeling it fill up all them empty spaces inside me.

First time since losing him, I can breathe again.

Snowball

We're all packed into the taxi in our brightest gear - pure Baz style - but, fuck me, it hits different without him here. Keep catching myself looking for him, like he might bounce in any second with that laugh of his, spinning some tale about a miracle cure. But he won't though, will he? This grief's dug in real deep now, ain't going nowhere.

Mum keeps banging on about 'closure,' like this funeral's meant to fix everything. Make it all better somehow.

'Don't want closure,' I tell her, voice gone all rough. 'Because then it's really over, innit? He stays alive, sort of, long as I keep our story going.'

Gem squeezes my knee, gets it without me having to explain. Makes me think of Alex and all those late-night calls. My rock through all this, talking me down when missing Baz gets too much. 'You matter more, Sunshine,' he keeps saying about the phone bills. 'I've got you, long as it takes.'

Pull up at the community hall to find Marge and Sophie waiting with Doc Sher, faces already wet, as anything. They fold me into this massive hug, and I breathe in Marge's CK-One, trying not to lose it while I hand over Baz's letters.

Inside's wild - packed with every face, from every dive bar, and dance floor Baz ever lit up. His world. Each one holding a bit of him we can't let go.

Lights go down and there he is on screen, larger than life - laughing under that Ibiza sun, telling stories round beach fires, lost in the music. Just these little glimpses of him being so... alive.

When 'It's My Life' kicks in, can't help but laugh. Dramatic bastard.

Ricky and Ian get up first, voices all wobbly while they share stories of Baz at his best - all those wild nights, quiet moments, times he sorted them out when they were being daft. I'm lost in my own memories when Ricky waves me up. Somehow get to the front, throat so tight I can barely speak, trying to explain how Baz made everything brighter just by being in it. Not enough words for that, but I try anyway.

Back in my seat when 'Seasons in the Sun' starts playing and my heart just... breaks. Trust Baz to twist the knife one last time.

Everything goes bit blurry after that. We're all there laying silver roses on his glittery coffin, tears proper streaming while someone starts humming along to the music. Then another voice joins in, bit stronger, and another. Sadness catching in our throats turns into something else - like Baz's spirit is rising up through us, pushing back against all that grief. The music takes over then, bass thumping through the floor, lights going mental, and suddenly we're all up moving. Dancing through our tears, holding each other up, letting Baz's energy flow through us one last time. Even Dad's having a dance, bless him.

It's absolutely mental.

It's perfect. Pure Baz.

Finally spill outside, 'Insomnia' still banging through the walls. Everyone's got their silver balloons, ready to let him fly. That's when I spot her - this slash of black against all our colour. Baz's mum. Sat there on her own, trying to make herself small on some bench.

My feet are moving before my brain catches up. Stand there with this daft balloon dancing between us, while she stares straight ahead like she's made of stone.

'You look just like your photo,' comes out before I can stop it. Voice sounds weird, like it ain't mine. 'The one Baz kept by his bed. You holding him when he's about four, both of you beaming. Before you knew what he was, eh? Before he turned into something you couldn't stomach.'

See her jaw go tight, eyes squeezing shut. Good.

'He called for you.' Gets harder to speak, like words are cutting my throat. 'Right at the end, when the pain was worst. When he was scared and hurting and needed his mum. But you couldn't even pick up the phone, could you? Couldn't face seeing what AIDS had done to your beautiful boy.'

She's shrinking with every word, but I'm past stopping now.

'Should've seen him though - even then, even dying. Still cracking jokes, still lighting up the whole bloody ward. Still Baz. Nurses loved him. His mates never left his side. But his own mother...' Have to swallow past this lump in my throat. 'His own mother couldn't get past her shame long enough to say goodbye.'

Everyone's gone dead quiet. It's not just Baz hanging over us now - it's all of them. All the sons and daughters who had to die alone cos their families couldn't get past their church or their pride or whatever bollocks kept them away.

'You missed it all,' my voice is cracking now. 'Every time he lit up a room just by walking in. Missed loving one of the best people to ever walk this earth. And why? Because he dared to love different than you wanted? Cos he didn't fit your perfect little picture?'

Hands shaking as I pull out his letter. 'He wrote this. Before. Still trying to reach you, right till the end. Because that was Baz - heart bigger than any of us deserved.'

Think she might ignore it, but then her fingers come up all trembling, taking the paper like it might bite.

'That's me done.' Step back, that silver balloon still bobbing between us like some mad joke. 'Rest is yours to live with. All the stuff you did. All the stuff you didn't. All the love you were too scared to give.'

Turn away, leave her with her regrets and that letter - Baz's last gift to someone who couldn't love him enough to stay.

Silver balloons catching what bit of sun we've got, bouncing wild against the grey. This is it then - Baz finally getting shot of that body that did him in. Feel like the whole world's holding its breath.

Fingers gone all shaky on the ribbon. One more second with him.

'Go on then, you daft bugger,' I manage, voice gone to shit. 'Show the lot up there how to have a party.'

Watch them all go up together, like Baz has chucked his last load of glitter all over London's miserable sky. Stand there till they're just little silver dots, eyes stinging something fierce.

End up at Ricky and Ian's, squeezed between Gem and Claire, passing round pills and spliffs and memories. Find myself going on about feeling Baz everywhere - like he's pure energy now, buzzing through everything.

They get it though. Through sniffles and nods, they feel him too. Our Baz, still causing chaos, changing everything he touches. We hold onto each other all night, dancing and crying and laughing, keeping him alive between us. Trying to catch him in our rubbish words and shaking hands.

He's in every tune that drops now, every belly laugh. In the scratch of stubble and the sweet hit of pills. He's the fizz in our blood, the fire in our guts, the steady hand when it all gets too much.

Our beautiful, gorgeous Baz - bet he's up there now in those platform boots and fishnets, throwing glitter at the angels. Too bloody brilliant to stick around down here with us lot.

Month crawls by. Learning to carry Baz with me - in sudden laughs, in bits of music, in the way light catches glitter on a dance floor. Grief's weird though. Just when you think it's utterly flattened you, hope sneaks in through the cracks.

Like when Dad bursts in waving the paper about that AIDS conference in Vancouver. About these new HAART drugs changing everything. Doc Sher had it right - this mix of pills they've got me on is kicking it, like you wont believe. Blood tests getting better, not worse. First time since diagnosis, I am not just hanging on - actually thinking I might have a future.

Hovering by the phone, heart going mental as I dial those familiar numbers.

'Alright, Alex?' His voice warms me right through.

'Sunshine! What's the latest?'

Can't help grinning. 'Me and Gem land Johannesburg Saturday, half seven your time...'

'Wicked! I'll be there. We can do the Valley first thing!'

'Been too long. See you soon...'

He clears his throat, voice going soft. 'We still taking Baz's ashes to Japan next month?'

'That's the plan. Then just... see where the road takes us. Whatever adventures come up.'

Can hear his grin matching mine. 'World's ours for the taking, innit.'

'Too right. Open road ahead...'

And somewhere, swear I hear Baz laugh, feel him wink as he whispers, 'Go live, my Bunny.'

Acknowledgements

I would like to extend my heartfelt thanks to those who helped me understand and honour the HIV/AIDS crisis of the 1990s: Paul Coleman for the wonderful afternoon of conversation and hours of informative stories in the archives of the National HIV Story Trust; Professor Ruben Sher, the grandfather of AIDS, for his tireless work in South Africa; and Barbara Von Barsewisch for her care and work in Broderip Ward and the decades after, as well as for sharing such heartfelt, bittersweet memories with me.

Jane Bruton's insights into her years at Broderip, her extensive ongoing work with AIDS patients, and her explanation of the '90s HIV test process were invaluable. Oscar Moore's book 'PWA' ('Person With AIDS') was instrumental in understanding the lived experience of those with the condition. I am indebted to Martin Burgoyne, whose life inspired the character of Basil, and to Gideon Mendel, whose photographs of Broderip Ward helped me visualise hospital life.

My deepest appreciation goes to everyone who worked in the Broderip Ward at Middlesex Hospital, and all the carers and medical staff who supported AIDS patients during the pandemic. To the mothers who lost children, to the long-term survivors, and to those we lost – your stories and strength have been a constant inspiration. To the Terrence Higgins Trust for their crucial work, and to TheAidsMemorial social media group for always remembering.

I often think of the two young men on the bus to Amsterdam in 1992, who had just learnt they were HIV positive. Your story has stayed with me.

In capturing the spirit of the era that frames this narrative, I owe thanks to Aaron Trinder, whose documentary 'Free Party a Folk History' captured the raw energy of the movement. To Harry Harrison and the DIY Team, thank you for the parties. To Mark Harrison and Spiral Tribe, everything is aligned exactly as it should be.

Big thanks to the Waterboys for 'Whole of the Moon.'

For support along the writing journey: Lisa Mcdonald, my dear friend who read the first draft and still offered encouragement, and Sian Cook of HIV Graphics, for unearthing an early '90s advertisement. To my son, Lleyton, for listening to me talk about this book endlessly.

Finally, to all the ravers of the '90s: we will always be the glitter on the dance floor. I love you!

Rave on!

About the Author

Jessi Morris is a fresh voice in contemporary fiction with her debut novel, 'Whole of the Moon'.

At home in the picturesque city of Bath, Somerset, Jessi embodies a spirit that is wild, free and always in motion. When she's not crafting stories that pulse with energy, you're likely to find Jessi losing herself in the rhythms of nature or the beat of the latest underground track. She believes in the power of words to transport, transform and transcend, much like the euphoric rush of a perfect dance floor moment.

Jessi's writing, like her spirit, refuses to be confined. She draws inspiration from the rolling hills of Somerset, the pulsing euro dance scene and the raw, unfiltered experiences of individuals navigating love, identity and purpose in an ever-changing world.

'Whole of the Moon' is more than just Jessi's debut - it's a declaration. A promise of stories to come that will move you, challenge you and maybe even inspire you to dance under the stars.

Printed in Great Britain
by Amazon

57891495R00209

To Richard
and Anthea
from Nick and Jolien

Vila Nova
September 2017
with love

GRONINGEN VAN BOVEN

Groningen from the sky

Photographed by Koos Boertjens

Inhoud

Contents

Colofon / Colophon

Fotograaf / photography: Koos Boertjens

Piloten / aviators: Tom van der Meulen en Matan Izhar

Vormgeving, layout en beeldresearch / design, layout and photoresearch: Ruurd de Boer, DBD design

Teksten / text: Bill Mensema

Eindredactie / edited by: Anton Scheepstra

Dank aan / thanks to Jannie Kroes, Lilian Zielstra

Druk / print: ÈPOS PRESS, Zwolle

2e druk 2016

ISBN 97890 5452 290 4
NUR 520

Voorwoord

Groningen van boven. Groningen vanuit de lucht. Groningen zoals we het kennen maar zelden zien. Kronkelende rivieren, rechte kanalen, akkers en weilanden, snelwegen en landweggetjes, klei en zee, dorpen en boerderijen. En vanzelfsprekend ook de stad. Want Groningen is Stad en Ommeland, twee verschillende maar complementaire grootheden, die samen de provincie vormen, samen de provincie zijn.

Groningen is een wonderlijk, weemoedig gebied. Niet voor niets blijven fotografen, schilders en dichters het telkens weer vastleggen, met alternerende zware en lichte kleuren, zoals het land is, zoals het land voelt.

Dit boek biedt een uniek perspectief. Het is een blik vanuit het zwerk. Het is een blik die ook een overzicht toont en verbanden blootlegt. Er is een verhaal in te zien – niet compleet en zonder einde – van land en zee, van mensen en dieren, en hoe de Groningers in de loop der tijd hun wereld hebben vormgegeven.

Op de grond is het niet altijd goed waarneembaar. Soms moet je afstand nemen om het beter te zien.
Soms moet je de lucht in om de volle schoonheid van Groningen te ervaren.

Introduction

The Dutch province of Groningen from above. Groningen from the sky. Groningen as it is known but rarely seen. Winding rivers, straight canals, fields and pastures, highways and country lanes, clay and sea, villages and farms. And of course the City. Because Groningen is Country and City, two different but complementary quantities, which together form the province.

Groningen is a beautiful, wistful area. This is the reason why photographers, painters and poets try to capture it time and time again, with alternating heavy and light colours. As Groningen is. As it feels.

This book offers a unique perspective. It is a view from the sky. It is a look that also reveals an overview and connections.
There is a story to see – not complete and without end – of land and sea, of people and animals, and how the people of Groningen have shaped their world in the course of time.

On the ground you cannot always see it well. Sometimes you need some distance to get a better picture.
Sometimes you have to get up in the sky to experience the full beauty of Groningen.

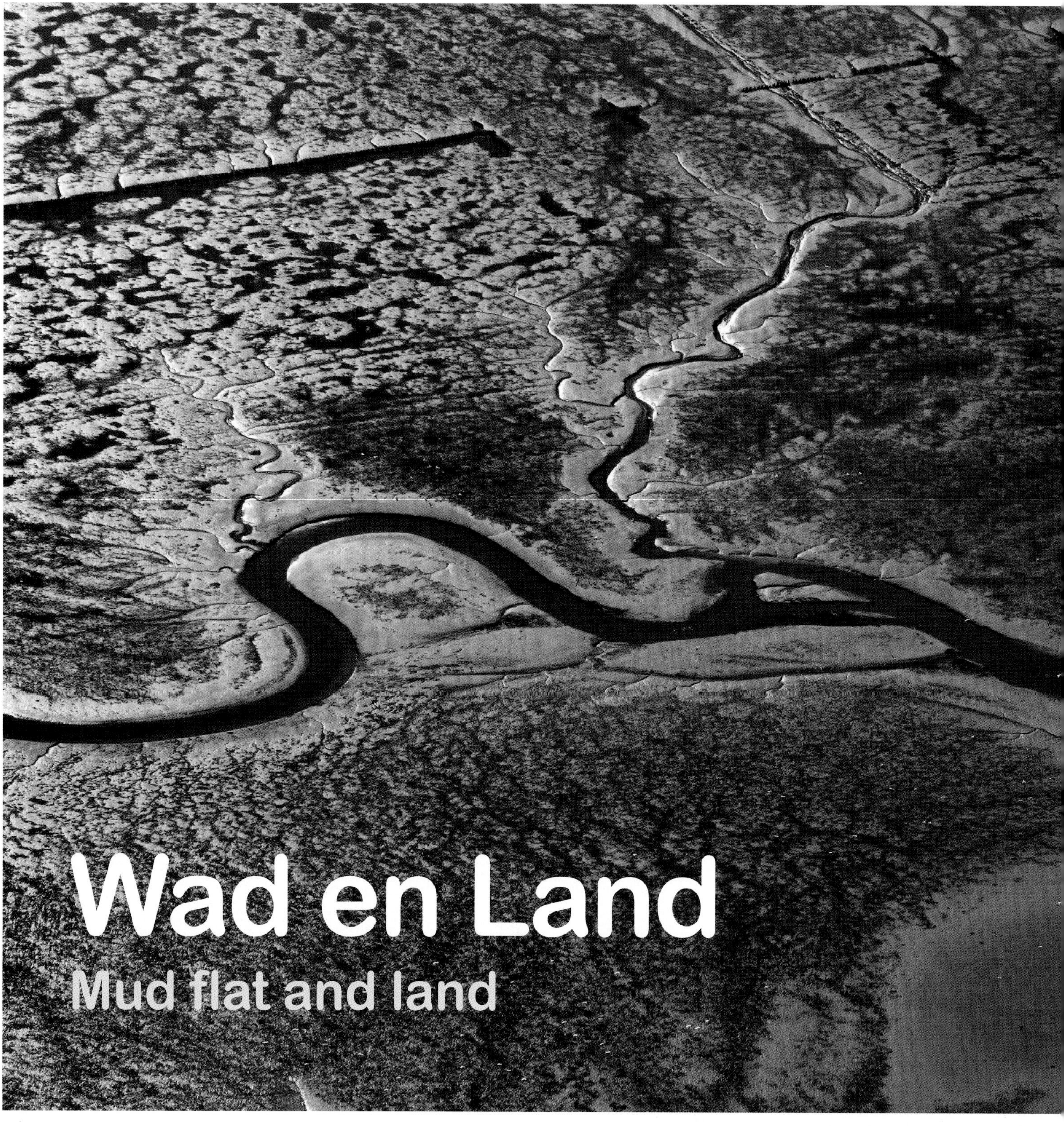

Wad en Land

Mud flat and land

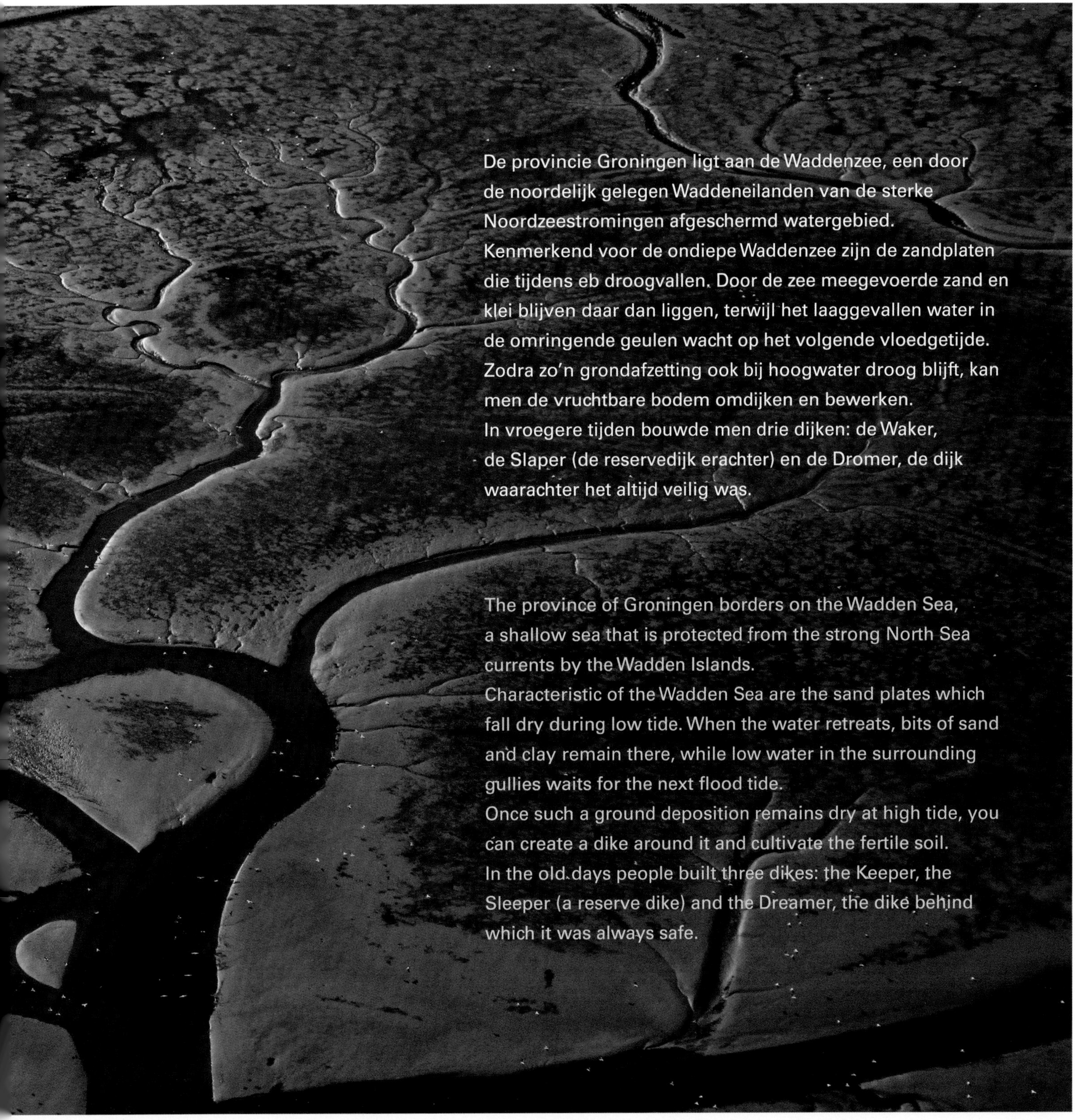

De provincie Groningen ligt aan de Waddenzee, een door de noordelijk gelegen Waddeneilanden van de sterke Noordzeestromingen afgeschermd watergebied.
Kenmerkend voor de ondiepe Waddenzee zijn de zandplaten die tijdens eb droogvallen. Door de zee meegevoerde zand en klei blijven daar dan liggen, terwijl het laaggevallen water in de omringende geulen wacht op het volgende vloedgetijde.
Zodra zo'n grondafzetting ook bij hoogwater droog blijft, kan men de vruchtbare bodem omdijken en bewerken.
In vroegere tijden bouwde men drie dijken: de Waker, de Slaper (de reservedijk erachter) en de Dromer, de dijk waarachter het altijd veilig was.

The province of Groningen borders on the Wadden Sea, a shallow sea that is protected from the strong North Sea currents by the Wadden Islands.
Characteristic of the Wadden Sea are the sand plates which fall dry during low tide. When the water retreats, bits of sand and clay remain there, while low water in the surrounding gullies waits for the next flood tide.
Once such a ground deposition remains dry at high tide, you can create a dike around it and cultivate the fertile soil.
In the old days people built three dikes: the Keeper, the Sleeper (a reserve dike) and the Dreamer, the dike behind which it was always safe.

Landaanwinning

Bij vloed voert de zee slib aan. Wanneer het water zich weer terugtrekt, blijft er steeds een beetje liggen. Dit is nieuwe modder. Nieuwe klei. Zo ontstaan de kwelders. Zo ontstaat het vruchtbare land.

Land reclamation

At high tide, the sea moves sludge to the shore. When the water withdraws, it leaves a little behind. This is new mud. New clay. This way salt marshes are shaped. And so – eventually – the fertile land is created.

Termuntenzijl/Dollard

Aanvankelijk was visserij een belangrijke vorm van levens-onderhoud. Eeuwenlang voeren kotters vanuit havens zoals die van Termunterzijl de zee en de Dollard op, om daar vis en garnalen te vangen.

Initially, fishing was an important form of living. For centuries cutters would sail from ports such as the one of Termunterzijl to the sea and the outland water bosom of the Dollard to catch fish and shrimp.

Lauwersoog

Na de indijking is het Lauwersmeer uitgegroeid tot een van de mooiste natuurgebieden van Nederland. Kolganzen en grutto's broeden er en 's zomers geven rietorchissen het land een paarse gloed.
In 1969 ontstond op het midden van de dijk het visserijdorp Lauwersoog. De spuisluizen net ten westen van het dorp verzorgen de afwatering, via de schutsluizen kan men de Waddenzee opvaren en vanuit de haven vertrekt de veerboot naar het waddeneiland Schiermonnikoog.

After its damming, Lauwersmeer became one of the most beautiful nature reserves in the Netherlands. In summer Greater White-fronted geese and godwits breed there and the Reed orchis gives the area a purple glow.
In 1969 the fishing village of Lauwersoog was founded on the middle of the dike. The locks to the West provide drainage of the reserve, the locks in the village offer a passage to the Wadden Sea and there is a ferry to the Wadden Island of Schiermonnikoog

Reitdiep

Via het Reitdiep vaart men door een van de oudste cultuurgebieden van Europa de provincie in. Ooit was het Reitdiep de enige verbinding van zee naar de stad Groningen. Totdat er een sluis bij Zoutkamp werd aangelegd, waren de getijden ook in de stad merkbaar.

Reitdiep River

Sailing on the Reitdiep River, one enters the province through one of the oldest cultural areas of Europe.

For a long time the river was the only connection from sea to the city of Groningen. Until a lock at the town of Zoutkamp was built, the tides were also noticeable in the city.

Land

Het aan de zee onttrokken land wordt door de mens bewerkt en beheerd. Er vindt grotendeels landbouw plaats: akkers en weideland, soms doorsneden door brede, bochtige sloten… de geulen van weleer, de geulen van het Wad.

The land taken from the sea is now cultivated. It's mainly agriculture: fields and grassland, cut by ditches and small, winding rivers called Maren. They are the gullies of yesteryear, the gullies of the Wadden Sea.

Van klei naar steen

From clay to stone

12.000 jaar geleden leefden er al mensen op de zandgronden in het zuiden van de provincie. Ze lieten hunebedden na, zoals die in Noordlaren.
Toen de zeespiegel begon te rijzen, ontstonden er vruchtbare kwelders in het noorden. Door het opwerpen van wierden kon men deze gebieden bewerken.
Het oosten bleef nog lange tijd onherbergzaam met zijn oneindige moerassen en verraderlijke venen. Totdat men het begon te ontginnen. De afgegraven turf was veelgevraagd. En het ooit zo woeste landschap veranderde in een knap geordend lijnenspel van akkers, wegen en kanalen. Ook dit was mensenwerk, met opgerolde mouwen en een schop in de handen.

12,000 years ago people lived on the sandy soils in the South of the province. Dolmens were left behind, such as in Noordlaren.
When the sea level began to rise, fertile salt marshes were shaped in the North. By erecting hills to live on, called Wierden, these areas could be cultivated.
The East remained inhospitable for a long time with its infinite swamps and insidious fens. After it was drained and the remaining peat was dug off, the once ferocious landscape changed into handsome organized lines of fields, roads and canals.
All of this was done by people, with sleeves rolled up and a shovel in the hands.

Wierden

Stevige kwelderwallen en natuurlijke verhogingen op uitlopers van de Hondsrug werden door mensen aangevuld tot wierden, die bij hoogwater droog bleven. Het vee graasde in het laagland en op de wierde verbouwde men granen, zaden en bonen.

Solid salt marsh walls and natural increases on foothills of the Hondsrug formed the base of the Wierden hills, which at high tide remained dry.
The cattle grazed in the lowlands while on the hill grains, seeds and beans were produced.

Borgen

Oorspronkelijk versterkte steenhuizen van herenboeren, die rechtspraken bij geschillen, raakten borgen als luxueus buitenverblijf vooral in de 16e en 17e eeuw in zwang. Van de ooit ruim 200 borgen zijn de mooiste bewaard gebleven.

Originally fortified stone houses of gentlemen farmers who ruled in the event of a dispute, these small castles became luxurious country residences, especially in the 16th and 17th century. The most beautiful are preserved.

Kloosters

Kloosters zoals die in Aduard en Ter Apel waren ook zeer belangrijk voor de vroege landontwikkeling van de provincie. Ze deden veel aan waterbeheersing, veenontginning en turfafgraving, waarbij de monniken zelf ook flink de armen uit de mouwen staken.

Monasteries

Monasteries such as those in Aduard and Ter Apel were also very important for the early land development of the province. They organised water management, soil drainage and peat extraction. The monks themselves laboured hard at this.

Vestingen en schansen

De vesting Bourtange is een van de fraaiste historische attracties van het land. Ze ziet er tegenwoordig eindelijk uit zoals ooit gepland.
De drukbezochte, jaarlijks nagespeelde Slag om Bourtange heeft overigens nooit plaatsgevonden.

Fortresses

The fortress Bourtange is one of the most beautiful historic attractions of the Netherlands. Nowadays it finally looks like it once was planned.
Actually, the annually performed Battle of Bourtange, which is always well-visited, never really happened.

Dorpen

Het land langs de kust werd ingedijkt en de wierden werden dorpen. Daarbuiten weidde men koeien en schapen en ploegde men de akkers. Verderop verschenen de eerste boerderijen.
Zowel in de Veenkoloniën als in het Westerkwartier werden de barakken van de veenarbeiders vervangen door kleine huisjes aan de lange, rechte kanalen, waarover het turf naar de stad werd vervoerd. De opkomst van de voor deze streken typische lintdorpen was in gang gezet.

Villages and towns

The land along the coast was dammed and the hills became villages. Outside cows and sheep were grazed and fields were ploughed. The first farms appeared.
Both in the West and the so-called Peat Colonies in the South-East, the barracks of the peat workers were replaced by small houses along the straight canals, on which the much sought-after peat was transported to the city. So, the typical Ribbon villages of these areas were created.

Landschappen

De provincie Groningen herbergt diverse landschappen. In het Westerkwartier treft men er het coulissenland aan, waarbij de velden zijn omringd door boomrijen. In het noorden – in de landstreken Hunsingo en Fivelingo – het ruime wierdenlanc Aan de kust kwelders en ingedijkte polders. In het oosten de rechte lijnen – kanalen en wegen – van de Veenkoloniën en het Oldambt. En zowel in Westerwolde als in de gemeente Haren vindt men er esdorpen en bossen.

Landscapes

The province of Groningen is home to a variety of landscapes. In the West, the fields are surrounded by tree rows. In the North, the land around the hilled villages is spacious. On the coast, there are salt marshes and dammed polders. In the East, the land is shaped in straight lines, with similar canals and roads. And in the far East, as in the municipality of Haren in the Soutl the soil is sandy and forests dominate the landscape.

Groningen is veruit de grootste stad in Noord-Nederland, met zo'n divers aanbod dat men geregeld een dagje gaat shoppen in Stad (zoals men de stad liefkozend noemt).
Groningen is een eigenzinnige stad. Altijd al geweest. Ver van de machtscentra ging de stad vaak haar eigen gang.
Er werd overzeese handel gedreven en de investeringen in veenontginning en infrastructuur betaalden zich ruim terug.
Groningen is dan ook een slimme stad die inzet op uitstekend onderwijs. Studenten komen er graag, ook omdat Groningen een culturele stad is met voor ieder wat wils.
Groningen is een stad die te midden van het Ommeland groeit en bloeit.

The city of Groningen is by far the largest city in the North of the Netherlands, with such a diverse offering that people often come to town.
Groningen has always been a very headstrong city. Far from the centres of power, the city mainly operated on its own.
Oversees trading and investments in the mining of peat and infrastructure created a lot of wealth.
Groningen is a smart city that offers excellent education. It attracts students from everywhere, also because Groningen is a cultural city with something for everyone.
Groningen is a prospering city in the middle of the country.

Stad

The City

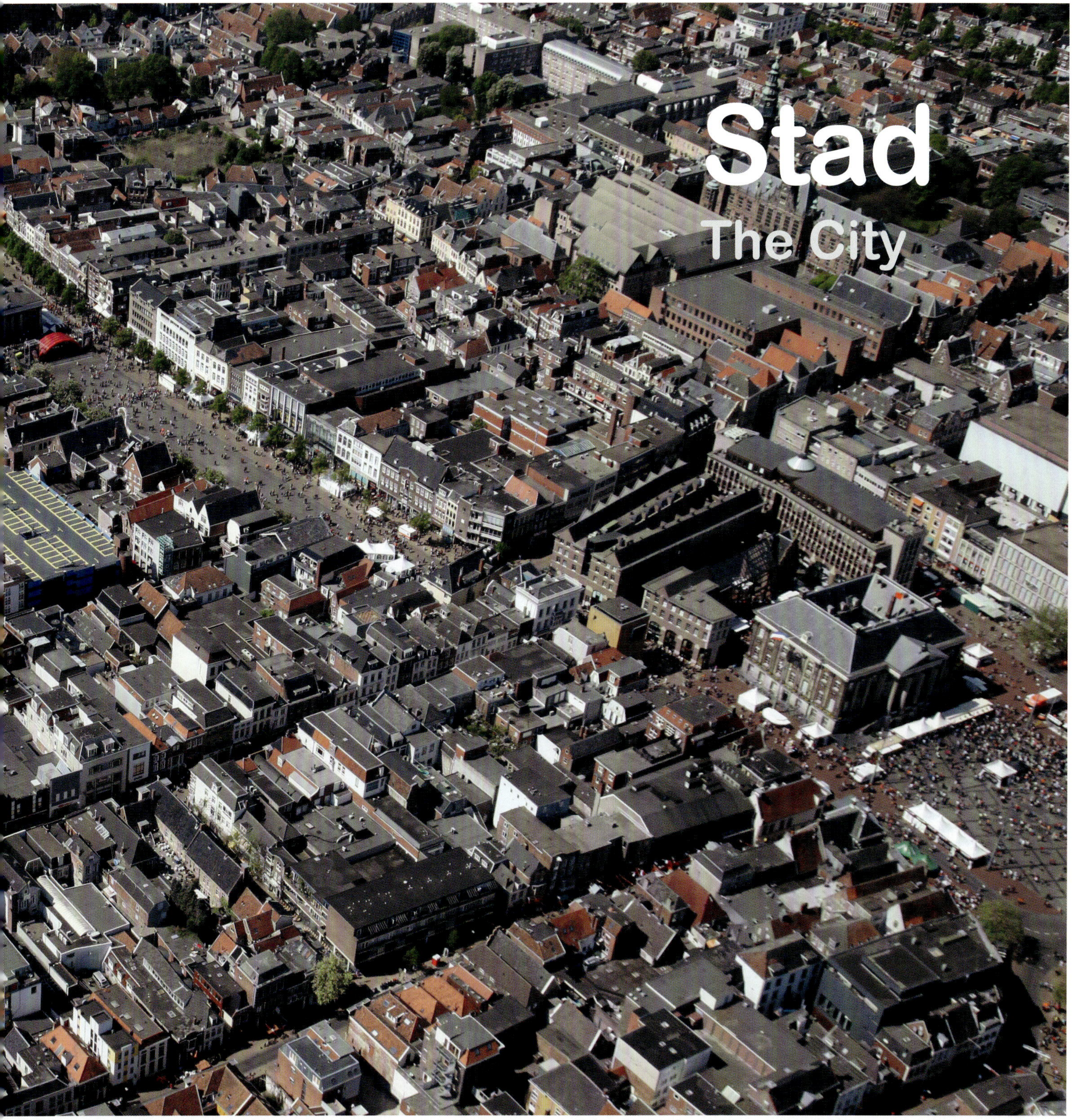

Diepen

De Diepenring is de grachtengordel rond de stad Groningen. Vroeger waren dit de loskades voor de schepen die via het Reitdiep naar de stad voeren. Toen was het nog een getijdenhaven waar afhankelijk van het getij op verschillende kades werd gelost.

Canals

A ring of canals surround the centre of the city of Groningen. This used to be the bays for the ships that enter the city via the Reitdiep River. When it was still a tide port, depending on the tide the cargo would be discharged on different bays.

Centrum

Dominerend boven de bedrijvige stad is de bijna 100 meter hoge Martinitoren, ook wel d'Olle Grieze genoemd vanwege de kleur van het Bentheimer zandsteen waaruit de toren is opgetrokken.
Met mooi weer is de toren tot ver in het Ommeland te zien.

Centre

Dominating above the bustling city is the almost 100 meter high Martini Tower. It is also called The Old Grey, due to the colour of Bentheimer sandstone which was used to build it.
On sunny days, the tower is even seen in the coastal region.

Indrukwekkend

Groningen is altijd een stad geweest om iets te laten zien: wat je geteeld hebt, wat je gefokt hebt, wat je bedacht hebt, wat je ontwikkeld hebt, wat je gemaakt hebt.

Kortom, een stad om te laten zien wat je waard bent.

Impressive

Groningen has always been a city to show things, what you have grown, what you have bred, what you have developed, what you have created.

In short, it's a city to show what you're worth.

Evenementen

Groningen kent veel evenementen zoals de Meikermis, de KEI-week (om eerstejaars studenten wegwijs te maken in de stad) en Noorderzon, een elf dagen durend podiumkunstenfestival in het Noorderplantsoen, met internationale en regionale artiesten.

Events

The yearly city events include the May fair, the KEI week (to introduce first-year students in the cit and an eleven-day performing arts festival called Noorderzon ('Sun o the North'), with international and regional artists.

Wonen in stad

Vroeger beluisterde men een elpee op een met draden aangesloten stereo. De elpee werd cd, werd mp3, werd stream. En alles werd Wi-Fi.

Alles verandert. Ook de wooneisen. De stad Groningen heeft daar altijd adequaat op ingespeeld

Living in the city

One used to listen to an LP on a wire-connected stereo. Then the LP became CD, became MP3, became stream. And everything became Wi-Fi.

Everything changes. So do the living requirements. Groningen has always met the new standards adequately.

Vanouds wordt alles wat buiten de stad Groningen ligt het Ommeland genoemd. De toon is er anders. Er staan lange boomrijen aan de heiige horizon. Er trekken majestueuze wolken over het land, nu nog omgeploegd maar straks weer vol in bloei. Er is een oeroud ritme voelbaar voor mens en dier. Er is de geur van mest. Er is de geur van aarde.
Men groet elkaar met een simpel 'Moi'.
De verbindingen zijn er goed en anders fietst men wel. Vaak met wind tegen, maar daar word je alleen maar sterker van.

Everything outside the city of Groningen is called the Country. The tune is different. There are long rows of trees on the hazy horizon. There are majestic clouds floating over the ploughed fields. There is an ancient rhythm palpable for humans and animals. There is the smell of manure, of Earth.
One says 'Moi' instead of Hello.
There are busses and trains, and otherwise there is always the bicycle. In the country, cycling is often against the wind. It's tough, but it makes you strong.

Ommeland
The country

Oost-Groningen

Het oosten van de provincie is een enorm, wijd open land, met velden vol graan, aardappelen en koolzaad. De wind waait er vrij over de Dollarddijk en houdt de lucht schoon en fris, net zoals het land is.

The East

The East of the province is a vast wide open country, with fields fu of grain, potatoes and rapeseed. The wind blows freely over the Dollard dike and keeps the air clean and fresh, just like the land is.

Stadskanaal

Stadskanaal is een van de belangrijkste regiocentra van de Veenkoloniën, met tal van winkels en voorzieningen. Het kanaal waarover vroeger turf naar de stad werd vervoerd, vormt nog steeds de ruggengraat van het tien kilometer lange lintdorp.

Stadskanaal ('Canal of the city') is one of the most important centres of the Peat Colonies, with many shops and amenities. The canal on which the former brown gold was transported still forms the backbone of this ten kilometres long Ribbon village.

Winschoten

Het centrum van het Oldambt is Winschoten, ook bekend als de Molenstad. Er staan er verschillende, zelfs op rij. Eentje is de hoogste van de provincie, na in 2004 te zijn verhoogd aangezien een nieuw appartementencomplex de wind belemmerde.

The city of Winschoten is the centre of the East. It is also known as Mill City. There are different mills, even in a row. One mill is the highest of the province, after it was increased in 2004 due to a new apartment complex that obstructed the wind.

Noord-Groningen

De radiale structuur is ongewijzigd gebleven, maar er is wel iets veranderd in de wierdendorpen van weleer. Middels moderne media houdt men ook hier stevig de vinger aan de pols en dankzij de verbeterde mobiliteit haalt men elk gewenst product zo in huis.

The North

The radial structure has remained the same, but something has changed in the hill villages. Due to modern media everyone here is up-to-date and thanks to improved mobility one can possess any product one thinks of in no time at all.

Appingedam-Delfzijl

Twee verschillende plaatsen die samen een kleine agglomeratie vormen. Appingedam met zijn historisch centrum, waar het Damsterdiep als een gracht doorheen stroomt. Delfzijl met zijn fabrieken en werven, waar de rivier in de gemoderniseerde haven uitmondt.

Two different places that together form a small conurbation. The historical city of Appingedam, where the Damsterdiep River runs through like a canal. The port of Delfzijl with its factories and shipyards, where the river ends in the modernised harbour.

Wonen in Groningen

'Niet slecht' is Gronings voor 'prachtig'. Toch zijn de stugge Groningers verknocht aan hun land. Degenen die weggaan, blijven het missen en hoe mooi het elders ook is, velen keren weer terug. Het is nu eenmaal hun stee.

Living in Groningen

In Groningen, one says 'Not bad' when something is really beautiful. It's the stiff nature of these people, who remain hooked on their country.
Those who leave the province, keep missing it. And often they return.

Economie
Economy

In de belangrijke landbouwprovincie Groningen worden veel graan, suikerbieten en aardappels verbouwd.
Ook zijn er locaties voor gaswinning, sinds 1959 een pijler van de Nederlandse economie.
De bouw van kustvaartschepen bij Hoogezand-Sappemeer heeft een historische basis, toen in de 19e eeuw meer turftransport nodig was. Evengoed traditioneel is de stedelijke verwerking van suiker en tabak.
Andere aanjagers van de Groninger economie zijn Delfzijl (haven en fabrieken), de Eemshaven (centrales en energie) en de zakelijke dienstverlening (ICT en Life sciences).

In the important agricultural province of Groningen grain, sugar beet and potatoes are widely grown.
There are also sites for gas extraction, since 1959 a pillar of the Dutch economy.
The construction of coastal ships at Hoogezand-Sappemeer has a historical basis in the 19th century, when more peat transport was needed. Also traditional is the processing of sugar and tobacco in the city.
Other boosters of the Groninger economy are Delfzijl (port and factories), the port of Eemshaven (power plants and energy) and the business services (ICT and Life sciences).

Landbouw

In Groningen wordt ondermeer koolzaad verbouwd, geschikt voor biodiesel. Vooral in het Oldambt kleuren de velden dan geel. De rijke grond leent zich ook uitstekend voor tuinbouw, zowel binnen als buiten de kassen.

Agriculture

The grown crops in Groningen include rapeseed, suitable for biodiesel. Especially in the East, these fields will colour yellow. The rich soil is also ideal for horticulture, both inside and outside the greenhouses.

Scheepsbouw

Aan het Winschoterdiep worden met name coasters gebouwd, maar ook bijzondere sleepboten en zelfs Rijncruiseschepen. Nadat zo'n schip te water is gelaten, wordt het via het Eemskanaal naar zee gevaren.

Shipbuilding

Typically, at the Winschoterdiep Canal coasters are build, but also special tugboats and even Rhine cruiseships.

After such a ship has been launched, it is sailed via the Eemskanaal Canal to open sea.

Industrie

Naast de suikerfabriek in Hoogkerk en de Veenkoloniale aardappelzetmeelfabrieken zijn er diverse industrieparken bij de grote provinciale kernen, zoals Veendam met een magnesiumfabriek en een enorme inland containerterminal.

Industry

Added to the sugar factory in Hoogkerk and the potato factories in the Peat Colonies, there are industrial parks at the large provincial nuclei, such as Veendam with a magnesium factory and a huge inland container terminal.

SUIKER

nfrastructuur

nelwegen verbinden Groningen net de Randstad, het midden van lederland en Noord-Duitsland. De poorwegen volgen dezelfde richngen, aangevuld met lijnen naar eeuwarden, Roodeschool, Delfzijl n Veendam. Het vliegverkeer gaat ia Groningen Airport.

nfrastructure

ighways connect Groningen vith Amsterdam, the middle of ne Netherlands and Northern ermany. The railways follow the ame directions, supplemented vith lines to Leeuwarden, oodeschool, Delfzijl and Veendam. here are also canals and roningen Airport.

Eemshaven

Naast overslag staat de Eemshaven ook bekend om haar energiecentrales. Duurzaamheid speelt daarbij een grote rol. De haven richt zich derhalve ook op offshore windparken in de Noordzee, waarvoor ze qua expertise, logistiek en ligging perfect geoutilleerd is.

Port of Eemshaven

The port of Eemshaven is also known for its power plants. Sustainability plays a major role in this. The port therefore also focuses on offshore wind farms in the North Sea, for which she is perfectly equipped in terms of expertise, logistics and location.

Kenniseconomie

Overal in de stad Groningen treft men onderwijsinstituten aan. Op de Zernike Campus aan de noordzijde bevindt zich een concentratie van de Rijksuniversiteit, de Hanzehogeschool en diverse hightech bedrijven.

Knowledge-based economy

Educational institutions are everywhere in the city of Groningen. The Zernike Campus on the north side is a concentration of the University, the Hanze University of applied sciences and various high-tech companies.

Ontspanning

Recreation

Ondanks de eeuwige strijd met het water, kan men er ook niet zonder.
Met mooi weer trekt men er naartoe om zich aan de waterkant te verpozen. Maar ook wanneer het vriest. Dan bindt men zich de scheuvels onder de voeten om een stukje te schaatsen over het diep, de brede maren en sloten.
Maar het water biedt vooral rust, zoals de vissers langs de Groninger kanalen goed weten. Stilletjes staren ze urenlang naar hun dobbers, terwijl het lome ritme van het water in hun ziel kruipt. Opgekikkerd keren ze huiswaarts, of ze iets gevangen hebben of niet.

Despite the eternal struggle with water, people can't do without it.
When the weather is nice, they pay a visit to the waterfront to repose. But also when it freezes. Then they go skating over the frozen rivers and ditches.
The water offers peace and quiet, as the fishermen along the Groninger canals well know. They stare silently for hours to their floats, while the languid rhythm of the water creeps in their soul. Refreshed they return home, with or without a catch.

Pieterburen

Bij wantij vertrekken wadlopers vanuit het kustdorp Pieterburen naar de noordelijk gelegen zandplaten in de Waddenzee. Zuidwaarts gaat het Pieterpad – een populaire wandelroute – dat het dorp over een afstand van 490 kilometer verbindt met de Sint Pietersberg in Zuid-Limburg. Pieterburen is ook bekend vanwege de zeehondencrèche, waar zieke of verdwaalde zeehonden kunnen herstellen, voordat ze weer in de Waddenzee worden vrijgelaten.

When the tide is right, one might walk from the coastal village of Pieterburen to the northerly sand flats through the shallow Wadden Sea. Southward, a popular walking route starts from the village to the utmost South of the Netherlands, covering a distance of 490 kilometres.
Pieterburen is also known for its seal sanctuary, where sick or stray seals can recover before they are released in the Wadden Sea.

Zoutkamp

Na de indijking van het Lauwersmeer vestigde de Zoutkamper garnalenvisserij zich in Lauwersoog. De voormalige vesting werd intussen gerenoveerd en is tegenwoordig een geliefde pleisterplaats voor waterrecreanten.

After the damming of the Lauwersmeer, the shrimp fishery of the town of Zoutkamp was re-established in Lauwersoog. Meanwhile the former fortress has been renovated and is now a popular stopping place for tourists.

Op zee

Zeezeilen doet men graag in de monding van de Eems of op de Dollard, een grote waterboezem aan de Groninger noordoostkust, ontstaan na diverse stormvloeden in de middeleeuwen, waarbij land weer zee werd.

At sea

Sea sailing is done in the mouth of the Eems River or on the Dollard, a large water bosom to the North-East Coast, created after various storm surges in the middle ages, when land became sea again.

DelfSail

Vanaf de dijk ziet men ze al aankomen: oogstrelende tallships uit alle windhoeken van de wereld, voor het periodiek georganiseerde evenement in de haven van Delfzijl.
In 2009 trok DelfSail maar liefst 900.000 bezoekers.

From the dike, one can see them arrive: beautiful tall ships from all over the world, for DelfSail, a periodically organized event in the port of Delfzijl.
In 2009 the event drew as many as 900,000 visitors.

;port

ı de provincie Groningen zijn er
o'n 1350 verenigingen die zich
ʋekelijks bezighouden met sport.
;uiten of indoor, op het water of
p de velden. Soms hoort men
et gejuich mijlenver als er net
escoord is, zoals bij een thuis-
ʋedstrijd van FC Groningen.

Sports

In the province of Groningen, there are about 1350 associations weekly dealing with sports. Outdoor or indoor, on the water or on the fields. Sometimes one hears the cheering miles away, as is the case with home games of FC Groningen.

De Toekomst

The future

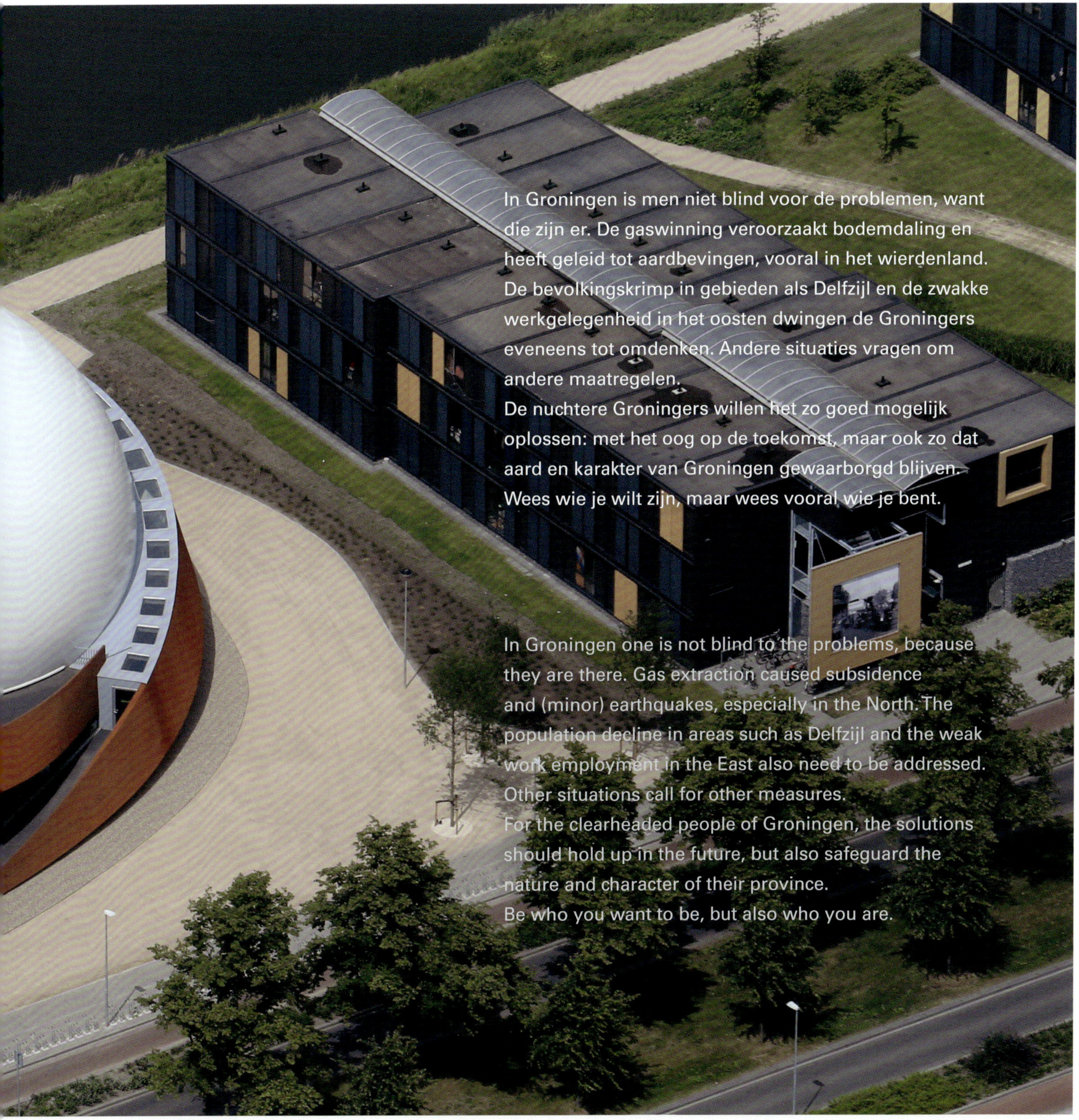

In Groningen is men niet blind voor de problemen, want die zijn er. De gaswinning veroorzaakt bodemdaling en heeft geleid tot aardbevingen, vooral in het wierdenland. De bevolkingskrimp in gebieden als Delfzijl en de zwakke werkgelegenheid in het oosten dwingen de Groningers eveneens tot omdenken. Andere situaties vragen om andere maatregelen.
De nuchtere Groningers willen het zo goed mogelijk oplossen: met het oog op de toekomst, maar ook zo dat aard en karakter van Groningen gewaarborgd blijven.
Wees wie je wilt zijn, maar wees vooral wie je bent.

In Groningen one is not blind to the problems, because they are there. Gas extraction caused subsidence and (minor) earthquakes, especially in the North. The population decline in areas such as Delfzijl and the weak work employment in the East also need to be addressed. Other situations call for other measures.
For the clearheaded people of Groningen, the solutions should hold up in the future, but also safeguard the nature and character of their province.
Be who you want to be, but also who you are.

Wonen aan water

Het creëren van woonomgevingen aan het water, zoals Blauwestad in het natuurgebied van het Oldambtmeer, schept – zeker in economisch zwakke regio's – extra werkgelegenheid qua bouw en voorzieningen, en het bevordert de (water)recreatie.

Living on the waterfront

Creating living environments on the waterfront, such as Blauwestad in the nature reserve of the Oldambt Lake, creates additional employment in terms of construction and facilities in an economically weak region. It also promotes (water) recreation.

Stedelijke ontwikkelingen

Aan de stadsrand van Groningen ontstaan in het vrije land nieuwe, hoogkwalitatieve woongebieden, terwijl voormalige bedrijfsterreinen in en om de stad voorlopig bestemd zijn voor verschillende manifestaties, zoals streekmarkten en muziekfestivals.

Urban developments

On the outskirts of the city of Groningen, new high-quality residential areas are formed in spacious land, while former industrial sites in and around the city temporarily serve for differen[t] manifestations, such as regional markets and music festivals.

Oplossingen

Het veranderende klimaat en de toenemende regenval kunnen problematisch worden. Vandaar dat er ondermeer in het zuiden van de stad Groningen een waterberging is gecreëerd. Waar mogelijk zijn er bij het zo ontstane natuurgebied ook huizen gebouwd.

Solutions

The changing climate and increasing rainfall can become problematic. Hence, among other things, in the South of the city of Groningen a water retention is created. Where possible, houses were also built near the resulting nature reserve.

Werken aan de toekomst

Ook in de toekomst blijft het goede behouden. Zoals deze voormalige strokartonfabriek, in 2009 gerestaureerd. Er worden nu voorstellingen gehouden, maa het is ook industrieel erfgoed: weet waar je vandaan komt, zoda je begrijpt waar je naartoe gaat.

Working on the future

The good will continue to be preserved. Like this former, in 2009 restored strawboard factory. Today exhibitions are held in it, but it is also industrial heritage: know where you're coming from, so that you understand where you are going.

Ambities

Van boven is Groningen vooral groen, net zoals haar ambities. Stimulering van duurzame landbouw en Energy Valley – het samen met onderwijsinstellingen en energieproducenten streven naar een verantwoorde energievoorziening – zijn daar voorbeelden van.

Ambitions

From above Groningen looks very green, just as its ambitions. Encouraging sustainable agriculture and Energy Valley, a provincial cooperation with educational institutions and energy producers that strives for a responsible energy supply, are examples.

De weg vooruit

Om vooruit te gaan moet je soms een stap terug doen. Daar is wijsheid voor nodig. En moed ook, want je weet niet of het een afkorting wordt of een omweg. Geen zorgen, want vanuit de lucht ziet zelfs de omweg er schitterend uit. 'Niet slecht.'

The road ahead

To move forward you sometimes have to step back. Wisdom is required. And courage too, because you don't know if it is an abbreviation or a detour. No worries, because from the sky even the detour looks great. 'Not bad.'

Plaatsen

Places